PRAISE
THE BEAST

T0005680

"More than a dozen horror stories—weird, self-referential, expertly told. [The] quirkily magisterial title entry delivers a grim vision of hubris and collective apathy.... It is all, frankly, riveting.... What seems to matter, in all these stories, aren't the specifics of a grisly end but the emotions they conjure, the way they tinge our own reality after we turn the page."
—*New York Times*

"Inventive, entertaining, and guaranteed to trouble your sleep. I savored this collection—and I'm still thinking about the showstopping tour-de-force novella in verse, 'The Beast You Are.' I've never read anything like it, but now I want more, more, more."
—Kelly Link, bestselling author of *White Cat, Black Dog: Stories*

"Invigorating.... Whether he's writing a subtly disarming tale in the manner of Shirley Jackson or a grisly monster story, Tremblay draws well-developed characters whose recognizable humanity makes it easy for readers to accept the weird events happening around them."
—*Publishers Weekly* (starred review)

"A brilliant, creepy, and wildly entertaining collection. By turns surreal, playful, and frightening, with a wondrously nightmarish Orwellian fable to boot, Paul Tremblay is a master storyteller who vividly conjures the monstrous in all its shivery forms."
—Mona Awad, author of *Bunny* and *Rouge*

"A wonderful collection of short fiction. These fifteen gems, polished to perfection, range from straight-up horror to speculative fiction to psychological terror.... This one's a must-have."
—*Booklist* (starred review)

THE
BEAST
YOU ARE

ALSO BY PAUL TREMBLAY

wm

WILLIAM MORROW

An Imprint of HarperCollinsPublishers

THE
BEAST
YOU ARE

STORIES

PAUL TREMBLAY

FOR LISA, COLE, AND EMMA

Life is no way to treat an animal.

—Kurt Vonnegut, *A Man Without a Country*

And I'll rip a lump out of my throat, using my teeth.

—Crows, "Healing"

CONTENTS

~~ICE COLD LEMONADE 25¢~~
HAUNTED HOUSE TOUR:
1 PER PERSON

I was such a loser when I was a kid. Like a John-Hughes-Hollywood-
'80s-movie-typecast loser. Maybe we all imagine ourselves as being that
special kind of ugly duckling, with the truth being too scary to contem-
plate: maybe I was someone's bully or I was the kid who egged on the bul-
lies screaming, "Sweep the leg!" or maybe I was lower than the Hughes
loser, someone who would never be shown in a movie.

When I think of who I was all those years ago, I'm both embarrassed
and look-at-what-I've-become proud, as though the distance spanned between those two me's can only be measured in light-years. That distance
is a lie, of course, though perhaps necessary to justify perceived successes
and mollify the disappointments and failures. That thirteen-year-old me
is still there inside: the socially awkward one who wouldn't find a group
he belonged to until college; the one who watched way too much TV and
listened to records while lying on the floor with the speakers tented over
his head; the one who was afraid of Jaws appearing in any body of water,
Christopher Lee vampires, the dark in his closet and under the bed, and
the blinding flash of a nuclear bomb. That kid is all too frighteningly
retrievable at times.

Now he's here in a more tangible form. He's in the contents of a weath-
ered cardboard box sitting like a toadstool on my kitchen counter. Mom
inexplicably plopped this time capsule in my lap on her way out the door
after an impromptu visit. When I asked for an explanation, she said she
thought I should have it. I pressed her for more of the *why* and she said,
"Well, because it's yours. It's your stuff," as though she were weary of the
burden of having had to keep it for all those years.

Catherine is visiting her parents on the Cape, and she took my daughter, Izzy, with her. I stayed home to finish edits (which remain stubbornly unfinished) on a manuscript that was due last week. Catherine and Izzy would've torn through this box-of-me right away and laughed themselves silly at the old photos of my stick-figure body and my map of freckles and crooked teeth, the collection of crayon renderings of dinosaurs with small heads and ludicrously large bodies, and the fourth-grade current events project on Ronald Reagan for which I'd earned a disappointing C+ and a demoralizing teacher comment of "too messy." And I would've reveled in their attention, their warm spotlight shining on who I was and who I've become.

I didn't find it until my second pass through the box, which seems impossible, as I took care to peel old pictures apart and handle everything delicately as one might handle ancient parchments. That second pass occurred two hours after the first, and there was a pizza and multiple beers and no edits in between.

The drawing that I don't remember saving was there at the bottom of the box, framed by the cardboard and its interior darkness. I thought I'd forgotten it; I know I never had.

The initial discovery was more confounding than dread-inducing, but hours have passed and now it's late and it's dark. I have every light on in the house, which only makes the dark outside even darker. I am alone and I am on alert and I feel time creeping forward (time doesn't run out; it continues forward and it continues without you). I do not sit in any one room for longer than five minutes. I pass through the lower level of the house as quietly as I can, like an omniscient, emotionally distant narrator, which I am not. On the TV is a baseball game that I don't care about, blaring at full volume. I consider going to my car and driving to my in-laws' on the Cape, which would be ridiculous, as I wouldn't arrive until well after midnight and Catherine and Izzy are coming home tomorrow morning.

Would it be so ridiculous?

Tomorrow when my family returns home and the windows are open, the sunlight as warm as a promise, I will join them in laughing at me. But it is not tomorrow and they are not here.

I am glad they're not here. They would've found the drawing before I did.

• • •

I rode my bicycle all over Beverly, Massachusetts, the summer of 1984. I didn't have a BMX bike with thick, knobby tires made for ramps and wheelies and chewing up and spitting out dirt and pavement. Mine was a dinged up, used-to-belong-to-my-dad ten-speed, and the only things skinnier and balder than the tires were my arms and legs. On my rides I always made sure to rattle by Kelly Bishop's house on the off-off-chance I'd find her in her front yard. Doing what? Who knows. But in those fantasies she waved or head-nodded at me and she would ask what I was doing and I'd tell her all nonchalant-like that I was just passing through, on my way back home, even though she'd have to know her dead-end street two blocks west and one block north from where I lived on the daredevil-steep Echo Ave hill wasn't on my way home, which was presuming she even knew where I lived. All such details were worked out or inconsequential in fantasies, of course.

One afternoon it seemed a part of my fantasy was coming true when Kelly and her little sister were at the end of their long driveway, sitting at a small fold-up table with a pitcher of lemonade. I couldn't bring myself to stop or slow down or even make more than glancing eye contact. I had no money for lemonade, therefore I had no reason to stop. Kelly shouted at me as I rolled by. Her greeting wasn't a "Hey there" or even a "Hi," but instead, "Buy some lemonade or we'll pop your tires!"

After twenty-four hours of hopeful and fearful *Should I or shouldn't I?*, I went back the next day with a pocket full of quarters. Kelly was again stationed at the end of her driveway. My brakes squealed as I jerked to an abrupt and uncoordinated stop. My rusted kickstand screamed with *You're really doing this?* embarrassment. The girls didn't say anything and watched my approach with a mix of disinterest and what I imagined to be the look I gave ants before I squashed them.

They sat at the same table setup as the previous day, but there was no pitcher of lemonade. Never afraid to state the obvious, I said, "So, um, no lemonade today?" The fifty cents clutched in my sweaty hand might as well have melted.

Kelly said, "Lemonade was yesterday. Can't you read the sign?" She sat slumped in her beach chair, a full-body eye roll, and her long, tanned legs spilled out from under the table and the white poster-board sign taped to the front. She wore a red Coke T-shirt. Her chestnut-brown hair was pulled and tied into a side high ponytail. Kelly was clearly well into her pubescent physical transformation, whereas I was still a boy, without even a shadow of hair under my armpits.

Kelly's little sister with the bowl-cut mop of dirty blond hair was going to be in second grade; I didn't know her name and was too nervous to ask. She covered her mouth, fake-laughed, and wobbled like a penguin in her unstable chair. That she might topple into the table or to the blacktop didn't seem to bother Kelly.

"You're supposed to be the smart one, Paul," Kelly added.

"Heh, yeah, sorry." I left the quarters in my pocket to hide their shame and adjusted my blue gym shorts; they were too short, even for the who-wears-short-shorts '80s. I tried to fill the chest of my NBA CHAMPS Celtics T-shirt with deep breaths, but only managed to stir a weak ripple in that green sailcloth.

Their updated sign read:

~~Ice Cold Lemonade 25¢~~
Haunted House Tour: 1 Per Person

Seemed straightforward enough, but I didn't know what to make of it. I feared it was some kind of a joke or prank. Were Rick or Winston or other jerks hiding close by to jump out and pants me? I thought about hopping back on my bike and getting the hell out before I did something epically cringeworthy Kelly would describe in detail to all her friends and, by proxy, the entire soon-to-be seventh-grade class.

Kelly asked, "Do you want a tour of our creepy old house or not?"

I stammered and I sweated. I remember sweating a lot.

Kelly told me the lemonade-stand thing was boring and that her new haunted-house-tour idea was genius. I would be their first to go on the tour, so I'd be helping them out. She said, "We'll even only charge you half price. Be a pal, Paulie."

Was Kelly Bishop inviting me into her house? Was she making fun of me? The "be a pal" bit sounded like a joke and felt like a joke. I looked around the front yard, spying between the tall front hedges, looking for the ambush. I decided I didn't care, and said, "Okay, yeah."

The little sister shouted, "One dollar!" and held out an open hand.

Kelly corrected her. "I said 'half-price.'"

"What's half?"

"Fifty cents."

Little Sis shouted, "Fifty cents!" her hand still out.

I paid, happy to be giving the sweaty quarters to her and not Kelly.

I asked, "Is it scary, I mean, supposed to be scary?" I tried smiling bravely. I wasn't brave. I still slept with my door open and the hallway light on. My smile was pretend brave, and it wasn't much of a smile, as I tried not to show off my mouth of metal braces, the elastics on either side mercifully no longer necessary as of three weeks ago.

Kelly stood and said, "Terrifying. You'll wet yourself and be sucking your thumb for a week." She whacked her sister on the shoulder and commanded, "Go. You have one minute to be ready."

"I don't need a minute." She bounced across the lawn onto the porch and slammed the front door closed behind her.

Kelly flipped through a stack of notecards. She said she hadn't memorized the script yet, but she would eventually.

I followed her down the driveway to the house I never thought of as scary or creepy but now that it had the word "haunted" attached to it, even in jest . . . it was kind of creepy. The only three-family home in the neighborhood, it looked impossibly tall from up close. And it was old, worn out, the white paint peeling and flaking away. Its stone-and-mortar foundation appeared crooked. The windows were tall and thin and impenetrable. The small front porch had two skeletal posts holding up a warped overhang that could come crashing down at any second.

We walked up the stairs to the porch, and the wood felt soft under my feet. Kelly was flipping through her notecards and held the front screen door open for me with a jutted-out hip. I scooted by, holding my breath, careful to not accidentally brush against her.

The cramped front hallway/foyer was crowded with bikes and shovels and smelled like wet leaves. A poorly lit staircase curled up to the right. Kelly told me that the tour finishes on the second floor and we weren't allowed all the way upstairs to the third, and, somewhat randomly, that she wrote "one per person" on the sign so that no pervs would try for repeat tours since she and her sister were home by themselves.

"Your parents aren't home?" My voice cracked, as if on cue.

If Kelly answered with a nod of the head, I didn't see it. She reached across me, opened the door to my left, and said, "Welcome to House Black, the most haunted house on the North Shore."

Kelly put one hand between my shoulder blades and pushed me inside to a darkened kitchen. The linoleum was sandy, gritty under my shuffling sneakers. The room smelled of dust and pennies. The shapes of the table, chairs, and appliances were sleeping animals. From somewhere on this first floor, her sister gave a witchy laugh. It was muffled and I remember thinking it sounded like she was inside the walls.

Kelly carefully narrated a ghost story: The house was built in the 1700s by a man named Robert or Reginald Black, a merchant sailor who was gone for months at a time. His wife, Denise, would dutifully wait for him in the kitchen. After all the years of his leaving, Denise was driven mad by a lonely heart, and she wouldn't go anywhere else in the house but the kitchen until he returned home. She slept sitting in a wooden chair and washed herself in the kitchen sink. Years passed like this. Mr. Black was to take one final trip before retiring but Mrs. Black had had enough. As he ate his farewell breakfast she smashed him over the head with an iron skillet until he was dead. Mrs. Black then stuffed her husband's body into the oven.

The kitchen's overhead light, a dirty yellow fixture, turned on. I saw a little hand leave the switch and disappear behind a door across the room from me. On top of the oven was a black cast-iron skillet. Little Sis flashed her arm back into the room and turned out the light.

Kelly loomed over me (she was at least three inches taller) and said that this was not the same oven, and everyone who ever lived here has tried getting a new one, but you can still sometimes hear Mr. Black clanging around inside.

The oven door dropped open with a metal scream, like when an ironing board's legs were pried open.

I jumped backward and knocked into the kitchen table.

Kelly hissed, "That's too hard, be careful! You're gonna rip the oven door off!"

Little Sis dashed into the room, and I could see in her hands a ball of fishing line, which was tethered to the oven door handle.

Kelly asked me what I thought of the tour opener, if I found it satisfactory. I swear that is the phrasing she used.

Mortified that I'd literally jumped and sure that she could hear my heart rabbiting in my chest, I mumbled, "Yeah, that was good."

The tour moved on throughout the darkened first floor. All the see-through lace curtains were drawn, and either Kelly or Little Sis would turn a room's light on and off during Kelly's readings. Most of the stories featured the hapless descendants of the Blacks. The dining room's story was unremarkable, as was the story for the living room, which was the largest room on the first floor. I'd begun to lose focus on the tour and let my mind wander to Kelly and what she was like when her parents were home and then, perhaps oddly, what her parents were like, and if they were like mine. My dad had recently moved from the Parker Brothers factory to managing one of their warehouses, and Mom worked part-time as a bank teller. I wondered what Kelly's parents did for work and if they sat in the kitchen and discussed their money problems too. Were her parents kind? Were they too kind? Were they overbearing or unreasonable? Were they perpetually distracted? Did they argue? Were they cold? Were they cruel? I still wonder these things about everyone else's parents.

Kelly did not take me into her parents' bedroom, saying simply "Under construction" as we passed by the closed door.

I suggested that she make up a story about something or someone terrible kept hidden behind the door.

Kelly to this point had kept her nose in her script cards when not watching for my reaction and jotting down notes with a pencil. Her head snapped up at me and she said, "None of these are made-up stories, Paul."

There was another bedroom, the one directly off the kitchen, and it was being used as an office/sitting room. There was a desk and bookcases tracing the walls' boundaries. The walls were covered in brownish-yellow wallpaper and the circular throw rug was dark too; I do not remember the colors. It's as though color didn't exist there. The room was sepia, like a memory. In the middle of the room was a rolling chair, and on the chair was a form covered by a white sheet.

Kelly had to coax me into the room. I kept a wide berth between me and the sheeted figure, knowing the possibility that there was someone under there waiting to jump out and grab me. Though the closer I got, it wasn't uniform, and the proportions were all off. It wasn't a single body; the shape was comprised of more shapes.

Kelly said that the ghost of a man named Darcy Dearborn (I remember his alliterative name) haunted this room. A real-estate mogul, he purchased the house in 1923. He lost everything but the house in the 1929 stock-market crash and was forced to rent the second and third floors out to strangers. He took to sitting in this room and listening to his tenants above walking around, going about their day. Kelly paused at this point of the story and looked up at the ceiling expectantly. I did too. Eventually we could hear little footsteps running along the second floor above us. The running stopped and became loud thuds. Little Sis was jumping up and down in place, mashing her feet into the floor. Kelly said, "She's such a little shit," shook her head, and continued with the tale. Darcy, much like Mrs. Black from all those years before, became housebound and wouldn't leave this room. Local family and neighbors bought his groceries for him and took care of collecting his rent checks and banking and everything else for him, until one day they didn't. Darcy stayed in the room and in his chair, and he died and no one found him until years later and he'd almost completely decomposed and faded away. His ghost shuts the doors to the office when they are open.

The door to the kitchen behind opened and shut.

I remember thinking the Darcy story had holes in it. I remember thinking it was too much like the first Mrs. Black story, which muted its impact. But then I became paranoid that Kelly had tailored these stories for me somehow. Was she implying that I was doomed to be a loner, a shut-in, because I stayed home by myself too much? I had one new friend I'd met in sixth grade, but he lived in North Beverly and spent much of his summer in Maine and I couldn't go see him very often. I wasn't friends with anyone in my neighborhood. That's not an exaggeration. Throughout that summer, particularly if I'd spent the previous day watching TV or shooting hoops in the driveway by myself, Mom would give me an errand (usually sending me down the street to the White Hen Pantry convenience store to buy her a pack of cigarettes—you could do that in the '80s) and then tell me to invite some friends over. She never mentioned any kids by name because there were no kids to mention by name. I told her I would but would then go ride my bike instead. That was good enough for Mom, or maybe it wasn't and she knew I wasn't really going to see or play with anyone. Mom now still reacts with an unbridled joy that comes too close to open shock and surprise when she hears of my many adult friends.

I envisioned myself becoming a sun-starved, Gollum-like adult, cloistered in my sad bedroom at home until Kelly led me out of the first-floor living space to the cramped and steep staircase. The stairs were a dark wood with a darker stair tread or runner. The walls were panels or planks of the same dark wood. I was never a sailor like Mr. Black, but it was easy to imagine that we were climbing up from the belly of a ship.

Kelly said that a girl named Kathleen died on the stairwell in 1937. Kathleen used to send croquet balls crashing down the stairs. Her terrible father with arms and hands that were too long for his body got so sick of her doing it, he snuck up behind her and nudged her off the second-floor landing. She fell and tumbled and broke her neck and died. There was an inquest, and her father was never charged. However, his wife knew her husband was lying about not being responsible for Kathleen's death, and the following summer she poisoned him and herself while picnicking at Lynch Park. At night you can hear Kathleen giggling (Kelly's sister obliged from above at that point in the tale) and the rattles and knocks of croquet balls bouncing down the stairs. And if you're not holding the railing, you'll feel those cold, extra-large hands push you or grab your ankles.

I wasn't saying much of anything in response at this point and was content to be there with Kelly, knowing I would likely never spend this much time alone with her again. I was scared, but it was the good kind of scared because it was shared if not quite commiserative.

The second-floor landing was bright with sunlight pouring through the uncovered four-paned window next to the second floor's front door. It was only then that I realized each floor was constructed as separate apartments or living spaces, and since I hadn't seen their rooms downstairs, it meant that Kelly's and her sister's bedrooms must be here upstairs, away from her parents' bedroom. I couldn't imagine sleeping that far away from my parents, and future live-at-home-shut-in or not, I felt bad for her and her sister.

Inside there was a second kitchen that was bright and sparkled with disuse. The linoleum and cabinets were white. I wondered (but didn't ask) if the two of them ate up here alone for breakfast or at night for dinner, and I again thought about Kelly's parents and what kind of people would leave them alone in the summer and essentially in their own apartment.

The tour didn't linger in the kitchen, nor did we stop in what she called the playroom, which had the same dimensions as the dining room below on the first floor. Perhaps she didn't want to make their playroom a scary place.

We went into her sister's room next. I only remember the pink wallpaper, an unfortunate shade of Pepto Bismol, and the army of stuffed animals staged on the floor and all facing me. There were a gaggle of teddy bears and a stuffed Garfield and a Pink Panther and a rat wearing a green fedora and a doe-eyed brontosaurus and more, and they all had black marble eyes. Kelly said, "Oops," and turned off the overhead light.

The story for this room was by far the most gruesome.

John and Genie Graham bought the house in 1952 and they had a little boy named Will. To make ends meet the family rented the top two floors to strangers. The stranger on the second floor was named Gregg with two g's, and the third-floor tenant was named Rolph, not Ralph. Very little is known about the two men. For the two years of the Gregg with two g's and Rolph occupancy, Will would periodically complain he couldn't find one of his many stuffed-animal companions and insisted that someone stole it. He had so many stuffed animals that with each individual complaint his parents were sure the missing animal was simply misplaced or kicked under the bed or he'd taken it to the park and left it behind. Then there were locals who complained that Rolph wasn't coming to work anymore and wasn't seen at the grocery store or the bar he liked to go to, and that he, too, was misplaced. Then there was a smell coming from the second floor, and they initially feared a critter had died in the walls, and then those fears became something else. When Mr. and Mrs. Graham entered the second-floor apartment with the police, Gregg with two g's was nowhere to be found. But they found Will's missing stuffed animals. They were all sitting in this room like they were now, and they were bloodstained and tattered and they smelled terribly. Hidden within the plush hides of the stuffed animals were hacked-up pieces of Rolph, the former third-floor tenant. There were rumors of Gregg with two g's living in Providence and Fall River and more alarmingly close by in Salem, but no one ever found him. Kelly said that stuffed animals in this house go missing and then reappear in this bedroom by themselves, congregating with one another in the middle of the floor on their own, patiently waiting for their new stuffing.

"That's a really terrible story," I said in a breathless way that meant the opposite.

"Paul! It's not a story," Kelly said, but she looked at me and smiled. I'll not describe that look or that smile beyond saying I'll remember both (along with a different look from her, one I got a few months after the tour), for as long as those particular synapses fire within my brain.

Kelly led me to a final room, her bedroom in the back of the house. The room was brightly lit; shades pulled up and white curtains open. Her walls were white and might've been painted over clapboard or paneling and decorated with posters of Michael Jackson, Duran Duran, and other musicians. There was a clothes bureau that seemed to have been jigsawed together using different pieces of wood. Its top was a landfill of crumpled-up notes, used candy wrappers, loose change, barrettes, and other adolescent debris. At the foot of her bed was a large chest covered by an afghan. On walls opposite of each other were a small desk and a bookcase that was half-full with books, the rest of the space claimed by dolls and knickknacks. The floor was hardwood and there was a small baby-chick-yellow rectangular patch of rug by her bed, which was flush against the wall and under two windows overlooking the backyard.

Kelly didn't say anything right away, and I stared at everything but her, more nervous to be in this room than any other. I said, "You have a cool room." I might've said "nice" instead of "cool," but God, I hope I didn't.

I don't remember if Kelly said thanks or not. She pocketed her notecards, walked ahead of me, sat on the rug, and faced her bed. She said, "I dream about it every night. I wish it would stop."

I hadn't noticed it until she said what she said. There was a sketch propped up by a bookend on the middle of her bed. I sat down next to Kelly. I asked, "Did you draw that?"

She nodded and didn't look at me. She didn't even look at me when I was staring at her profile for what felt like the rest of the summer. Then I, too, stared at the drawing.

The left side of its cartoonish head was misshapen, almost like a bite had been taken out, and the left eye was missing. Its right eye was round and blackened by slashes instead of a pupil. The mouth was a horrible band of triangular teeth spanning the horizontal circumference. Three strips of skin stretched from the top half of the head over the mouth and teeth and wrapped under its chin. What appeared to be a forest of wintered branches stuck out from all over its head. The wraithlike body was all angles and slashes, and the arms were elongated triangles reaching out. It had no legs. The jagged bottom of its floating form ended in larger versions of its shark teeth.

There are things I of course don't remember about that day in Kelly's house and many other things I'm sure I've embellished (though not purposefully so). But I remember when I first saw the drawing and how it made me feel. While this might sound like an adult's perspective, I'm telling you that this was the first time I realized or intellectualized that I would be dead someday. Sitting on the bedroom floor next to the cute girl of my adolescent daydreams, I looked at the drawing and imagined my death, the final closing of my eyes and the total and utter blankness and emptiness of . . . I could only think of the phrase "not-me." The void of not-me. I wondered if the rest of my life would pass like how summer vacations passed—would I be about to die and asking *How did it all go so quickly?* I wondered how long and what part of me would linger in nothingness and if I'd feel pain or cold or anything at all, and I tried to shake it all away by saying to Kelly, "Wow, that's really good."

"Good?"

"The drawing. Yeah. It's good. And creepy."

Kelly didn't respond, but I was back inside her sunny bedroom and sitting on the floor instead of lost inside my own head. I asked and pointed, "What are the things sticking out? They look like branches."

She told me she tried to make up a story for this ghost, like maybe the kid who lived in the house before Kelly did was sneaking around peeking into houses and sometimes stealing little things and bits no one would miss (like a thumbtack or an almost-used-up spool of red thread) and she got caught by someone and was chased and in desperation she ran behind her house and she got stuck or trapped in the bushes and she died within sight of her big old ratty house. But that didn't feel like the true story, or the right story. It certainly wasn't the real reason for the ghost.

Kelly told me this ghost appeared in her dreams every night. The dreams varied, but the ghost was always the same ghost. Sometimes she was not in her body and she witnessed everything from a remove, like she was a movie camera. Most times Kelly was Kelly and she saw everything through her own eyes. The most common dream featured Kelly alone in a cornfield that had already been cut and harvested. Dark, impenetrable woods surrounded the field on all sides. She heard a low voice laughing, so low it was a hanging kind of laugh, but then it was also high-pitched, so it was both at the same time. (She said "both at the same time" twice.) Her heart beat loud enough that she thought it was the full moon thumping down at her, giving her a Morse code message to run. Even though she was terrified, she ran into the woods because it was the only way to get back to her house. She ran through the forest and night air as thick as paint, and she got close to her backyard and she could see her house, but no lights were on, so it was all in shadow and looked like a giant tombstone. Then the ghost came streaming for her from the direction of the house and she knew her house was a traitor because it was where the ghost stayed while it patiently waited for this night and for Kelly. It was so dark, but she could see the ghost and its horrible smile bigger than that heartbeat moon. And the dream ended the same way every time.

"I hear myself scream, but it sounds far away, like I'm below, in the ground, and then I die. I remember what it feels like to die until I wake up, and then it fades away, but not all the way away," Kelly said. She rocked forward and back and rubbed her hands together, staring at the drawing.

The ceiling above us creaked and groaned with someone taking slow, heavy, careful steps. Kelly's little sister wasn't around, and I hadn't remembered seeing her since we got up to the second floor. I figured Sis was walking above us wearing adult-sized boots. A nice touch for what I assumed was the tour's finale.

I said something commiserative to Kelly about having nightmares too.

She said, "I think it's a real ghost, you know. This is the realest one. It comes every night for me. And I'm afraid maybe it's the ghost of me."

"Like a doppelgänger?"

Kelly smirked and rolled her eyes again, but it wasn't as dismissive as I'm describing. She playfully hit my nonexistent bicep with the back of her hand, and despite my earlier glimpse at understanding the finality of death, I would've been happy to die right then. She said, "You're the smart one, Paul, you have to tell me what that is."

So I did. Or I gave her the close-enough general definition that the almost thirteen-year-old me could muster.

There were more footsteps on the floor above us, moving away to other rooms but still loud and creaking.

She said, "Got it. It's kind of like a doppelgänger but not really. It's not a future version of me, I don't think. I think it's the ghost of a part of me that I ignore. Or the ghost of some piece of me that I should ignore. We all have those parts, right? What if those other parts trapped inside us find a way to get out? Where do they go and what do they do? I have a part that gets out in my dreams and I'm afraid that I'm going to hear it outside of me for real. I know I am. I'm going to hear it outside of me in a crash somewhere in the house where there isn't supposed to be, or I'll hear it in a creak in the ceiling, and maybe I'll even hear it walking up behind me. I don't know if that makes any sense, and I don't think I'm explaining it well, but that's what I think it is."

Little Sis burst out of Kelly's closet and crashed dramatically onto the chest at the end of her bed, and shouted, "Boo!"

Kelly and I both were startled and we laughed, and if you'd asked me then I would've thought we'd been friends forever after instead of my never speaking to her again after that day.

As our laughter died out and Kelly berated her sister for scaring her, I realized that Little Sis jumped out of a closet and not from behind a door to another room that had easy access to the rest of the apartment and the stairwell to the third floor.

I said to Little Sis, "Aren't you upstairs? I mean, that was you upstairs we heard walking around, right?"

She shook her head no and giggled, and then there were creaks and footstep tremors in the floor above us again. They were loud enough to shake dust from the walls and blow clouds in front of the sun outside.

I asked, "Who's upstairs?"

Kelly looked at the ceiling and was expressionless. "No one is supposed to be up there. The third floor is empty. We're going to rent it out in the fall. We're home alone."

I made *come on* and *really?* and *you're not joking?* noises, and then in my memory—which for this brief period of time is more like a dream than something that actually happened—the continuum skips forward to me following Kelly and her sister out into the hallway and the stairwell to the third floor. Little Sis led the way and Kelly was behind me. I kept asking questions (Is this a good idea? Are you sure you want to end the tour all the way up on the third floor?) and the questions turned to poorly veiled begging, my saying that I should probably get home, we ate dinner early in my house, Mom was a worrier, et cetera. All the while I followed up the stairs and Kelly shushed me and told me to be quiet. The stairwell thinned and squeezed and curled up into a small landing, or a perch. An eave intruded into the headspace to the left of the third-floor apartment's door. The three of us sardined onto that precarious landing that felt like a cliff. There was no more discussion and Little Sis opened the door, deftly skittered aside, and like she had on the first floor, Kelly two-handed shoved me inside.

This apartment was clearly smaller than the first two, with the A-frame roof slanting the ceilings, intruding into the living space. I stepped into a small, gray kitchen that smelled musty from disuse. Directly across the room from me was a long, dark hallway. It was as though the ceilings and their symmetrical slants were constructed with the sole purpose of focusing my stare into this dark tunnel. There wasn't a hallway like this in either of the other apartments; the third-floor layout was totally different, and the thought of wandering about with no idea of the floor plan and fearing that I would find whatever it was making the walking noises made me want to swallow my own tongue.

Little Sis ran ahead of me, giggling into the hallway and disappearing in the back end of the apartment. I still held out hope that maybe it was her, somehow, who was responsible for the walking noises, when I knew it wasn't possible. I stood for a long time only a few steps deep into the kitchen, which grew darker, and watched as the hallway grew darker still, and then a stooped figure emerged from an unseen room and into the gloom of the hallway. The whole apartment creaked and shook with its each step. It was the shadowy ghost of a man, and he diffused into the hallway, filling it like smoke, and my skin became electric and I think I ran in place like a cartoon character might, sliding my feet back and forth on the linoleum.

An old man emerged into the weak lighting of the kitchen shuffling along with the help of a wooden, swollen-headed shillelagh. He wore a sleeveless T-shirt and tan pants with a black belt knotted tightly around his waist. An asterisk of thin, white hair dotted the top of his head and the same unruly tuft sprouted out from under the collar of his T-shirt. His eyes were big and rheumy, like a bloodhound's eyes, and he smirked at me, but before he could say anything I screamed and ran through Kelly and out of the apartment.

On the second step I heard him call out (his voice quite friendly and soothing), "Hey, what are all you silly kids up to?" and then I was around a corner, knocking into a wall and clutching onto the handrail, and maybe halfway down when I heard Kelly laughing, and then shouting, "Wait, Paul! Come meet my grandfather. Tour's over!"

I just about tumbled onto the second-floor landing with everyone else still upstairs calling after me. I was crying almost uncontrollably and I was seething, so angry at Kelly and her sister and myself. I don't know why I was so angry. Sure, they set me up, but it was harmless, and part of the whole ghost tour/haunted house idea. I know now they weren't making fun of me, per se, and they weren't being cruel. But back then, *cruel* was my default assumption setting. So I was filled with moral indignation and the kind of irrational anger that leads erstwhile good people to make terrible, petty decisions.

I ran back into the second-floor apartment and to Kelly's bedroom. I took the drawing of her ghost off the bed, tucked it inside my T-shirt, ran back out of the apartment and then down the stairs and out of the house and to my bike, and I pedaled home without ever once looking back. The rest of that summer I didn't ride my bike by Kelly's house.

I can't remember planning what I was going to do with her drawing. I might've initially intended to burn it with matches and a can of Mom's hairspray (I was a bit of a firebug back then . . .) or something similarly stupid and juvenile. But I didn't burn it or crumple it up. I didn't even fold it in half. Any creepiness/weirdness attributed to the drawing was swamped by my anger and then my utter embarrassment at my lame response to her grandfather scaring me. I knew that I totally blew it; that Kelly and I could've been friends if I'd laughed and stayed and met her grandfather and maybe middle school and high school would've gone differently, wouldn't have been as miserable.

While I on occasion had nightmares of climbing all those steps in the Bishop house by myself, I don't remember having any nightmares featuring the ghost in the drawing, even though I was (and still am) a card-carrying scaredy-cat. I wasn't afraid to keep the drawing in my room. I hid it on the bottom of my bureau's top drawer along with a few of my favorite baseball cards. While I obsessively picked through the play-by-play of that afternoon in Kelly's house and what she must've thought of me after, I never really focused on the drawing and would only ever look at it by accident, when the top drawer was all but empty of socks or underwear and I'd find that toothy grin peering up at me. Then one day toward the end of the summer the drawing was gone. It's possible I threw it away without remembering I did so (I mean, I don't remember what happened to the baseball cards I kept in there either). Maybe Mom found it when she was putting away my clean clothes and did something with it, which would explain how it got to be in her box of kid-stuff keepsakes, but Mom taking it and never saying anything to me about taking it seems off. Mom fawned over my grades and artwork. She would've made it a point to tell me how good the drawing was. Her taking the picture and putting it on the fridge? Yes, that would've happened. But her secreting it away for safekeeping? That wasn't her.

That summer melted away and seventh grade at Memorial Middle School was hell, as seventh grade is hell for everyone. The students were separated into three teams (Black, White, and Red), with four teachers in each team. The teams never mixed classes, so you might never see a friend in Black team if you were on Red team and vice versa. Kelly wasn't on my team, and I didn't even pass her in the hallways at school until after a random lunch in early October. She stood with her back up against a set of lockers by herself, arms folded. It wasn't her locker, as I didn't see her there again the rest of the school year. Normally I walked the halls with my head down, a turtle sunk into his protective shell, but before disappearing into my next class, I looked up to find her staring at me. That look is the second of two looks from her that I'll never forget, though I won't ever be sure if I was reading or interpreting this look correctly. In her look I saw *I can't believe you did that*, and there was a depthless sadness, one that was almost impossible for me to face as it was a direct, honest response to my irrevocable act. Her look said that I'd stolen a piece of her and even if I'd tried to give it back, it would still be gone forever. To my shame I didn't say anything, didn't tell her that I was sorry, and I regret not doing so to this day. There was something else in that look too. It was unreadable to me at the time, but now, sitting in my empty house with dread filling me like water in a glass, I think some of that sadness was for me. Some of it was pity and maybe even fear, like she knew what was going to happen to me tomorrow and for the rest of my tomorrows; there wouldn't necessarily be a singular calamitous event, but a concatenation or summation of small defeats and horrors that would build daily and yearly and eventually overtake me, as it overtakes us all.

I would see her in passing the following year in eighth grade, but she walked by me like I wasn't there (like most of the other kids did; I'm sorry if that sounds too woe-is-me, but it's the truth). At the start of ninth grade, she returned to school a totally transformed kid. She dressed in all black, dyed her hair black, and wore eyeliner and Dead Kennedys and Circle Jerks and Suicidal Tendencies T-shirts and combat boots, and hung out with upperclassmen and she was abrasive and combative and smelled like cigarettes and weed. In our suburban town, only a handful of kids were into punk, so to most of us, even us losers who were picked on mercilessly by the jocks and popular kids or, worse, were totally ignored, the punks were scary and to be avoided at all costs. I remember wondering if the Michael Jackson and Duran Duran posters were still hanging in her room, and I wondered if she still had that dream about her ghost and if she still thought that ghost was some part of her. Of course, I later became a punk when I went to college and I now irrationally wonder if *punk* was another piece of her that I stole and kept for myself.

The summer after ninth grade Kelly and her family sold the house and moved away. I have no memory of where she moved to, or more accurately, I have no memory of being told (and then forgetting) where she moved. I find it difficult to believe that no one in our grade would've known what town or state she moved to. I must've known where she relocated to at one point, right?

. . .

The baseball game is still on and I'm on the couch with my laptop open and searching for Kelly Bishop on every social-media platform I can think of, and I can't find her, and I'm desperate to find her, and it's less about knowing what has become of her (or who she became) but to see if she's left behind any other parts of herself—even if only digital avatars.

Next to my laptop is her drawing. That it survived all this time and ended up in my possession again somehow now feels like an inevitability.

Here it is:

I remembered it looking like the product of a young artist and being more creepy and affecting because of it. I remembered some of the branches at the top forming the letter *K*. I remembered the smile and the skin strips and the triangle arms as-is.

I didn't remember the shadow beneath the hovering figure, and I don't like looking at that shadow and I wonder why I always peer so intently into those dark spaces. I didn't remember how its head is turned away from its body and turned to face the viewer, as though the ghost were floating along stage left until we looked at it, until we saw it there. And then it sees us.

I know it's not supposed to be a doppelgänger, but I remember it looking like Kelly in some ineffable way, and now, thirty-plus years later I think it looks like me, or that it somehow came from me. Even though it's late and she's in bed, I want to call Mom and ask her if she looked through the cardboard box one last time before leaving it here (I know she must've) and if she saw this drawing and recognized her son from all those years ago in the drawing.

I am glad Catherine and Izzy are not here. I keep saying that I am glad they are not here in my head. I say it aloud too. They would've found the drawing before I did, and I don't know if they would've seen me or if they would've seen themselves.

My reverie is shattered by a loud thud upstairs, like something heavy falling to the floor.

There is applause and excited commentators chattering on my television, but I am still home alone and there is a loud thud upstairs.

Its volume and the suddenness of its presence twitches my body, but then I'm careful to stand up slowly and purposefully from the couch. Worse than the incongruity of noise coming from a presumably vacant space is the emptiness the sound leaves behind, a void that must and will be filled.

I again think of driving to the Cape or just driving, somewhere, anywhere. I shut the television off and I anticipate the sound of footsteps running out of the silence toward me, or a rush of air and those triangle arms reaching more and the shadow on the floor behind it.

Everything in me is shaking. I call out in a voice that no one is there to hear. I threaten calling 911. I tell the empty or not-empty house to leave me alone. I try to be rational and envision the noise being made by one of the shampoo bottles sliding off the slippery ledge in our shower but instead I can only see the figure in my drawing, huddled upstairs, waiting. And it is now *my* drawing, even if it's not.

The ceiling above my head creaks ever so slightly. A settling of the wood. A response to subtle pressure.

I imagine going upstairs and finding a menagerie of Kelly's ghosts waiting for me: there is Greg with two *g*'s tearing apart the hapless Rolph, and the desperately lonely Mrs. Black sitting in a chair patiently waiting, and the feckless shut-in Darcy Dearborn. Or will I find the ghost of a part of me that I never let go: a lost and outcast adult I always feared people (myself included) thought I'd become?

Is that another creak in the ceiling I heard?

I listen harder, and maybe if I listen long enough I'll hear a scream or a growl or my own voice, and it is as though the last thirty years of my life have passed like the blink of summer, and everything that has happened in between doesn't matter. Memories and events and all the people in my life have been squeezed out, leaving only room for this distilled me on this narrowing staircase, and right now even Catherine and Izzy feel like made-up ghost stories. There is only that afternoon in Kelly's place and now the impossibly older me alone in a house that's become as strange, frightening, and unknowable as my future.

As I slowly walk out of the TV room and up the stairs toward the suddenly-alive-with-sound second floor, I don't know what I'm more afraid of: seeing the ghost I stole grinning in the dark or seeing myself.

For Emma Tremblay and Ellen Datlow

MEAN TIME

The old man's name began with an *r*, I think, yeah, but definitely a capital *R*. Mom told me to stay away from R. Dad said R was harmless but I shouldn't encourage him. Sherry, the semi-goth teen who lived on the floor below us and spent her afternoons listening to the Smiths and Kelly Clarkson told me R spent too much time in his pockets and that he smelled like what she imagined a burning jellyfish would smell like. Sherry was wrong. R smelled like chalk. He had countless chalk sticks in his pockets and dust was all over his hands and his brown wool suit. The smears looked like letters tattooed on his lapels and sleeves. R used his chalk to draw lines on the sidewalks and streets. Or arcs, not lines. Arcs would be a more accurate description. Whatever. R walked backward, all hunched over, tip of chalk pressed against the cement or brick or cobblestone, and he drew until the stick disintegrated into dust. R drew his looping arcs and lines from Gracey's Market to Wilhelmina's Flower Festival then to Frank and Beans Diner and on and on, to points A, then B, and to C, then to D, past the alphabet and to points we'd have to name with alphas and epsilons. The first time I worked up the courage to ask him the obvious, he gave me an obvious answer. R used the chalk to find his way home because even in our small city he was afraid he would get lost. We all lived in a city that was smaller than most towns, so I'd heard. All our apartment buildings, libraries, markets, salons, and restaurants were crammed together, like space was something to be shared intimately with everyone. So, that first day, after I asked him what was what, after he told me what was what, we shared our space quietly, uncomfortably, then, he said, "Well, okay, little one, in the mean time, I have more errands to do." Back then I didn't know "meantime" was one word, so I imagined it as two. Later, I tried following him in the afternoon, as he backtracked over his loops and lines, reliving his previous paths, but he walked too fast for me, and I lost him and the chalk path in the maze of alleys between Gorgeous George's Peach Pit and Dolly Lamas Liquor Mart. I tried restarting on the path, but I couldn't follow the intersecting arcs he'd drawn earlier, and never found the beginning or the end. The chalk lines faded overnight, washed away by light rain, according to Mom. Dad liked to try to scare me and told me the night scrubbed it all away. Sherry said the students who dropped out of trade school cleaned the streets and sidewalks at night. Didn't matter where the lines went because R was always back out there the next morning and for all the mornings after that. Each day I asked him clever variations on the theme of why he drew the chalk lines. He'd give me the same afraid-of-getting-lost answer, followed by the same "mean time" quip. I grew frustrated with his consistent ducking of my questions, or maybe I was frustrated because his weirdness, which had once been cool and exciting, had become boring, rote, part of the scenery I so desperately wanted to alter or affect in some way. So, one morning, after he left Missy's Galaxy Meat Emporium, I erased his chalk line, rubbed out about half a block, made my own gap in his path. It was cloudy, I remember that, and the yawning gap made me feel anxious, like something big was indeed missing, or wrong. If I'd had a piece of chalk in my hand, I would've fixed what I'd done right away. Instead I stood and waited for R to retrace his steps. Which he did. He stopped at the end of his line, did a classic double take, looked around the city, down at the clean, clear line behind him, the one that just suddenly ended in the middle of the sidewalk, in the middle of nowhere. R dropped his bags, round fruits rolled away, spheres suddenly loosened from their strict orbits, and the stuff prepackaged in boxes stayed where they fell. R fumbled in his pockets and pulled out chalk sticks, and they dribbled out of his fingers, crashed to the sidewalk and broke into jagged pieces. I started crying and I told him I was sorry, that I could fix it for him. I grabbed one of the chalk pieces and drew a rough line over the gap to where I thought it was supposed to go, but I wasn't sure anymore, and I think I made the wrong connection. I dropped the chalk and ran home to my apartment, watched him from my bedroom window, the shade pulled over my head behind me. R spent the rest of the afternoon walking the city, following those lines, never really getting anywhere. He disappeared into alleys and I thought he'd finally found his way home, but he'd reappear a few minutes later. I watched him until my parents came in and found me asleep and curled up in the windowsill.

I KNOW YOU'RE THERE

"I know you're there," Silas Chen says.

His niece Victoria, crouching in the doorway separating the hallway from the kitchen, calls out, "But you can't see me!"

Silas exchanges a weary half smile with his sister, Gwen. She is five years younger than Silas, a time stamp of permanent import on their relationship, even as the difference shrinks while their middle ages expand. When Silas was a child, he would hide on Gwen and pretend to be dead when she found him. Gwen would shake and tickle him, pinch his cheeks, and half laugh, half tear up while shouting, "This isn't funny!" Silas imagined he played dead so well his arms, legs, fingers, and toes still wouldn't move when he would eventually send those secret bodily messages to lift, wiggle, or twitch. The longer he remained play-dead, the more convinced he became that his body was a cage and he wouldn't be able to move when he needed to, which both scared him and inexplicably thrilled him.

Gwen says to Victoria, singsong, "Someone should be in bed and not eavesdropping."

Silas hopes Gwen won't be too hard on her daughter. Victoria doesn't know how to process the shock and grief any more than the adults do.

"I am not dropping!" Five years old, made of charged electrons, Victoria Muppet-rushes into the kitchen for the cover-blown tickle attack of her uncle. Silas, still in his chair, scoops her up and airplanes her over his head. While Victoria is airborne and giggling, her mom tersely ticks off the bedtime checklist: go to the bathroom, wash your face, brush your teeth, pick out one, only one, book for Daddy to read, and where is Daddy? Gwen falters, as though she said something she shouldn't have. Maybe she did. Hell if Silas knows. He cannot provide comfort or answers for anyone else, never mind himself.

Victoria offers her bed to Uncle Silas again, and he declines, insisting the couch fits hits long body better. He presses the button of Victoria's nose and kisses her forehead. She wipes it away and her maniacal laughter turns to tears. She tells him she's sorry about Uncle David. He says, "Thank you. I am too." He wants to ask if Victoria can stay a little longer. She would help keep the waiting trap of his thoughts from snapping shut. Silas swings her off his lap, her feet padding onto the kitchen tile, and says, "Bedtime, little Vee. Good night."

She wipes her eyes and says, "I am *big* Vee," and stomps out of the kitchen, toward the plaintive calls of her father.

Silas covers then wipes his face with one hand. Gwen asks if he wants more wine.

"Do you have to ask?" he says, and exhales a shudder. He holds in all the other shudders, the infinite queue of shudders, ones to be doled out in the coming days, months, years. The very thought of future years without David is a purgatorial burden. There is no cogue to what he says next because he shouldn't be quiet, not now when he is so ill prepared for the looming contemplative intrusion of silence, one surely to feature an endless replaying of what happened when he returned home after work.

After Gwen refills his glass with Pinot Grigio, he says, "I knew something was wrong the second I opened the door." He pauses, honoring or damning what he will say next. "Do you want to hear this?"

"If you want to talk, I'm here. But you don't have to talk either. You don't have to do anything." Gwen satellites around the kitchen, carrying the empty bottle of wine, until she crashes it into the deep sink. She says sorry twice, quickly rinses her hands, then leans against the counter, her arms crossed.

He should wiseass a joke about how uncomfortable she is. The joke would help them both, but he's not capable of it. He says, "I came home, maybe an hour early. David wasn't at the dining-room table. His laptop wasn't even open. Notebook and folders closed and neatly stacked. Right away, I knew. Maybe he'd stopped working already, but I fucking knew that wasn't right. I ran around calling his name and I went into the TV room and he was just—he was on the floor, on his stomach, head turned away from me, toward the TV. The screen was blue." Silas waves a hand, as though pantomiming the previous detail be stricken because it wasn't necessary, or he didn't have the time or the want to explain the blue screen. "He does his exercise DVDs in the morning, okay? So, David was in his exercise clothes. T-shirt and compression shorts. And, you know, his heart gave out. It must've happened right after I left, not too long after I left. Instead of me getting home in the afternoon an hour early and however many fucking hours late, what if I stayed an extra hour in the morning? Why would I have? I wish I stayed. I should've stayed."

"Silas—it's not your—you couldn't have known—"

"He was dead. He'd been dead for hours, for the whole day. For what we call a day, right? It had been a long day for me at work too. That's what I used to call a long day. I had no idea how long a day could be. No one does until you do. I haven't seen—I haven't seen many dead people. None, except for funerals. But David was dead, Gwen. I won't go into—he was so clearly gone. His body was there and he was gone. He wasn't there anymore. I didn't know what to do. I—I said his name over and over, and I ran back to the kitchen, to like—what—get him a glass of water or something? I don't know, I don't know what I was thinking. Except I wasn't thinking I could help him. I knew I couldn't. Is that terrible? Is that awful?"

Gwen shakes her head and whispers, "No."

"I didn't leave him alone. I would not do that to him, not while he was still home. I was in the kitchen, but I could still see him, and if he could've, he would've been able to see me too. I called 911 and when I was on the line, giving them his name and my name and address, I turned slightly and I cupped a hand around my mouth and the phone so he wouldn't hear, like I didn't want him to be worried. And I wasn't facing straight down the hallway to the TV room, I was turned, I could still see him, but I wasn't really watching him either because I was trying to be all there, all together on the call. I didn't want to screw that up. The call was the worst and most important thing in the world, and I couldn't fuck it up. And then I swear, right before I hung up, I saw—movement." Silas waves his hand by his temple. "I was facing this way"—he turns his torso so Gwen is on his hard right—"like now. I'm not looking at you, but I can still see you without focusing directly on you." He pauses and remains looking but not looking at Gwen. "David was on the floor, already permanently on the floor like he will be in my fucking head forever now, but I was turned so he was a blurry, peripheral background shape, and then—then the moment before it happened, I knew it would happen. I mean, I didn't turn to fully see it, and I don't know if I saw anything, but then I saw it anyway."

"Saw what, Silas?"

"I was in the kitchen—again, not really looking at him—and I saw him lift his upper torso and turn his head. I hung up and ran back to the TV room and sat next to him and held his hand and I watched him. I watched him until the ambulance came. His head was turned, facing the kitchen and not the TV and that stupid blue screen. He was facing me."

"Come sit with me on the bench. Share a pretend cigarette with me," David's mother, Janice Harrington, says. She hasn't smoked in over two decades, but never passes on a chance to remind anyone and everyone how much she misses it. A tall white woman in her late sixties, she keeps manically fit (her own self-description) via competition. Prior to the pandemic, she played in pickleball tournaments two weekends out of every month. The tournaments are due to return later this summer.

Janice grabs Silas's hand and gently pulls him toward a green, wooden bench under the shade of an oak tree's weary branches.

Silas says, "I should help with the cleanup." Friends and family gather trash, fold tablecloths, distribute leftover food, break down folding tables and chairs. His elderly parents, Fung and Catherine, oversee and coordinate the packing of Gwen's minivan. Ninety minutes earlier, they brought everyone to tears and laughter, telling the slightly-embellished-for-effect story of meeting their future son-in-law, David, for dinner. A lovely evening that had ended, unbeknownst to them at the time, with David rushing to the ER because he'd accidently ingested a small amount shellfish.

Janice says, "Eh, let everyone else do it."

The memorial service was held at Lynch Park, a green space and rocky beach jutting into Beverly Channel, and began with Silas kneeling on a seawall, emptying an urn of David's cremated ashes into the relentless, foaming ocean. The intimate procession walked to the picnic area adjacent to a rose garden for what Silas described as a casual-reception-meets-eulogy. Silas knew his husband of twelve years and partner for fifteen didn't want anything to do with a religious ceremony, but David had shared no other final wishes or instructions in the event of his death. They believed they would have plenty of time to discuss such abrupt finalities later in their yawning, nebulous future.

Silas says, "We're lucky the rain held out."

"Are you feeling lucky, Silas?"

"No, not particularly." He smiles without smiling. He can't sneak anything past Janice. Never could. His using "lucky" was a subtle, cynical fuck you to the universe, one he wanted heard and tallied.

"Me neither. But it was a beautiful afternoon, Silas. You did my poor David proud. He was always proud of you."

Tears pool and spill, as they have all day, as they have since that afternoon—Silas can't do this. Not now. He'll further indulge in cherished memories later, after. After when or what, he isn't sure, but he can't do it now. He's afraid his memories of David, his David, could be tainted by the now, by what's running through his head now, and by the fears of what's to come.

Janice says, "When David first told me about you—this was months before I met you in person—he showed me a goofy picture on Facebook. You were standing in someone's kitchen. Or was it yours? And you had that long hair and the waistband of your sweatpants hiked up to your chest. He pointed and said, 'Mom, that's the guy. *The* guy.'"

Silas wipes the tears from his cheeks and shakes his head, as though answering no to a series of impossible questions.

"You can talk. Or I can keep talking, like I do. Or we can just sit here and share a cry with our pretend cigarettes. On a day like today, menthol and filterless."

"I knew something awful had happened to him the second I stepped into our house. It was like passing through an invisible barrier, and after I passed through, I could no longer remember where I was before—"

Janice doesn't fill the pause. Sometimes a pause is language.

"He was on the floor in the TV room, dressed in his workout clothes. His head was turned toward the TV, which was still on, but the screen was blue, all blue. That kind of freaked me out. Is that weird? The fucking blank, blue screen. His head was turned away from that and toward the kitchen, toward me, like he was—was waiting for me to come home. Waiting for me to help him. But I couldn't. The other—the other weird part was his right arm was bent at an odd angle"—Silas leans forward on the bench and demonstrates—"so the back of his hand and forearm were pressed to his lower back, like he was reaching for an itch, or rubbing a sore muscle. He'd been complaining about his back lately and I told him to take a day off from working out every once in a while.

"I don't remember deciding to leave his side to go to the kitchen and I don't remember the walk to the kitchen, but there I was, with David now twenty feet away, me with the phone in my shaking hand. And while on with 911, I wasn't looking at him, but I could still see him. Like now, I'm looking or facing straight ahead but I can still see you out of the corner of my eye, right? Do our eyes have corners? I've been thinking about eye corners. Thinking it's bullshit. It's all bullshit. Everything. And right before I hung up, most of me looking at the red phone symbol, the one you press to hang up, and in my eye corner, I saw movement. I couldn't tell exactly what it was that was moving, but David or something near David moved. That's what I saw in the eye corner. I hung up and turned my head; nothing was moving. I waited and watched but nothing. Then I went back to David and his right arm wasn't behind his back anymore. His right hand was next to his face."

"I haven't been home in over a week. I'm getting too old for couch surfing," Silas says. A bowl of microwaved popcorn rests on the couch between him and his friend Michael. Baseball is on the television. Michael Lavoie is in his mid-fifties and is gregarious in the way that dares the world to say something to his face. Gray frosts his short, curly dark hair. He is a Red Sox fanatic and is equally obsessed with his floundering fantasy baseball team.

Michael looks up from his tablet computer for the first time since the second inning, he blinks madly behind his saucer-sized reading glasses and says, "Hey, the guest bedroom is not a couch."

"You know what I mean."

"Oh, and you're not that old."

"Nice save."

"You can stay as long as you need. I appreciate the company." Michael's husband, Bob, is a medical software consultant and is away on his first weeklong work trip since the pandemic hit. Bob is due to return in four days.

Silas says, "Thank you, I really mean it." They became friends in the mid-'90s, meeting when Michael moved to Brighton, into the apartment across the hall from Silas. Michael has had jobs in advertising for as long as Silas has known him, and once worked on a campaign with David, who at the time was a recent marketing hire for a small chain of seafood restaurants. Michael inadvertently introduced David to Silas when, after successful completion of the restaurant's campaign, Silas crashed their celebratory not-date at Fugaku's sushi bar.

"Unlike Bob," Michael says, "you don't complain when I have baseball on."

"I complain inside my head."

"Yeah, you can leave now. Thanks."

"The door *will* hit my ass on the way out." Silas lumbers into the kitchen.

Michael mutters to his tablet about his fantasy team's lack of innings and quality starts from the pitchers, then asks over his shoulder, "Are you ready for that?"

"Ready for what?" Silas returns to the couch and holds up his glass. "It's just water."

"Smartass. I am delicately asking if you are ready to go home," Michael says.

"You have never asked anything delicately in your life." Silas appreciates his friend's honesty and bluntness, as off-putting as it can be sometimes.

"I am not pushing you to go or stay. When you do go, you can come back here if it's too soon."

"Thank you, again. The original answer I almost successfully avoided is no. No, I am not ready. But I'm at the point where each day that goes by will make it that much harder to go back. Plus, I really need to get going on the probate stuff. Fuck. I have a lot of shit to deal with."

"Yes, you do. But do it at your own pace. If I can help with any of it, please let me. I know you won't ask. Consider this a pre-ask."

Silas hugs the bowl of popcorn and slouches deep into the couch.

"What if I walk through the door and it's like—it's like the last time I walked through that door."

"You haven't been home since? Not even to—" Michael pauses. His bluntness has a limit.

"Gwen went in and got me everything I needed for David and for me. I had to make a detailed list and draw her a map."

"The next time you walk inside your house, Silas, it won't be the same. It might be harder, but it won't be like the last time."

Silas nods as though he agrees, but inside his head, instead of complaining about the baseball game, he tells Michael he is wrong. He fears it will be exactly like last time. He says, "I knew as soon as I walked in. Part of the knowing was that I wouldn't be able to do anything. David was on the floor in the TV room, on his stomach. He never laid on his stomach. He slept on his side, or on his back if he'd had a few drinks, and then he would snore and I'd tease him about it the next day, text him snoring cartoon gifs. Anyway, there he was on the floor, on his stomach. He definitely wasn't snoring. The TV was still on. His workout DVD had ended, and the screen was a blank, dead blue. He wasn't facing the TV. Head was turned toward the kitchen and me, and his eyes were closed but—let's just say it was obvious he wasn't asleep. I called 911 and turned my back to him when I did because I just couldn't. Not while I was looking down at him. I answered her questions and I told them to hurry the fuck up. I knew it was already too late, but I told them to hurry. Also, I didn't want to be there alone with him like that. And—when I hung up it was like he'd heard my thoughts about not wanting to be alone because his eyes were open. He was dead and they had been shut and then he was still dead but his eyes were open."

Silas stands on his front stoop, overstuffed night bag slung over one shoulder. It's early evening, twilight. The return-home time. He wanted to be here in the morning, with sunlight on his back, projecting his shadow on the red door. Instead, he stayed at Michael's, made the phone calls and the appointments he had to make. He answered work emails that could've gone unanswered. The next thing he knew the morning and afternoon and this ninth day had passed. Time was accelerating and decaying.

Nine days ago, Silas opened the front door without pause or consideration. That's not to say he wasn't thinking anything. Like the rest of us during our waking, automatic moments, Silas buoyed within the flowing groundwater of subconscious thought. Perhaps in his mind he summarized his workday, tallying the anxieties and attempted normalcies associated with his recent return to the partially occupied office. As likely, he flitted through unconnected thoughts; what would they make for dinner, the exterior trim needed painting and should he do it himself, was it too late for a walk, the anticipatory joy of removing his work shoes. Silas walked inside into what felt like an empty house. If one lived with another long enough, one earned the ability to sense the other person's presence, or lack of presence. None of the lights were on. Had they lost power? David was not sitting at his semi-permanent workspace at the dining-room table, hunched over his comically small laptop, flanked by stacks of papers and an oversized exterior mic he used for meetings, wearing one of his three pairs of reading glasses that made him look old and unbearably cute. The laptop was closed. His permanently stained coffee mug and plastic blue water cup (one David had measured how much it held to the nearest fluid ounce to track the amount of water he drank daily) were not next to the laptop, were not on the table. Silas stared at where David wasn't, as though waiting for him to un-disappear. And there was the smell. Had Silas noticed David was not at the dining-room table or the smell first? Initially, he thought it was a garbage smell, or had David microwaved Brussels sprouts? Seafood? An ammoniac sharpness and fecal tang intensified as he wandered into the kitchen. He rolled open the two windows above the sink. Had the septic system backed up? Did David leave, go to the hardware store? No, Silas had parked next to David's car. Silas didn't normally call out his husband's name when he entered their house, nor had he ever had reason to. Increasing dread forced the lilting, plaintive syllables from Silas's sinking chest. "David?" The house remained quiet; listening-quiet. Silas hurried through the kitchen toward the hallway half-bathroom while checking his phone for text messages. There weren't any. He typed out "Where are you?" He called out David's name again while walking with his head down, watching for a return text or the three dots that meant he was responding. The suffocating odor and silence simultaneously narrowed and expanded his universe, and he was inexorably drawn to the new black hole in its center. He was a few steps away from the living room when he looked up, saw David, and dropped his phone.

Silas recounted this scene many times to friends and family. His own personal folktale, he's aware of how the story has changed, lengthened, shortened, depending upon who was receiving the retelling. He never purposefully embellished. If anything, Silas would insist he did the opposite. He believes he has lived through and continues to live through the event as told in each retelling. He believes what happened is now a never-ending, ever-evolving story with a truth that will forever remain hidden from him. Dicing up the what-happened into various tells and retells makes it easier to swallow, to digest. However, there remain details Silas left out in his retellings and will continue to omit in future retellings: his gutturally repeating his husband's name upon first seeing his body; the blinding curtain of tears and how it has permanently transformed the hue and tone of his perception; his pressing a shaking hand to David's neck and cheek; the coldness of his rigored skin; David's soiled shorts and the puddle of urine between his splayed legs; how before he left David's side to retrieve his phone, he already thought of David as a body, as inanimate, as the past; how when Silas was in the kitchen and talking on the phone he wasn't looking at David, couldn't look at him, not even with the corners of his eyes, so his back was turned and his left hand was a visor over his eyes in case he would see anything by accident, and then in the other room David stood, David stood up, and Silas knew this even though he wasn't watching, even though his back was turned, and he knew because the living-room floor boards creaked under David's shifting, repositioning weight, and more than that, Silas *felt* David standing up, and he didn't and won't include this feeling in any of his retellings, not because he can't explain that instinctual, animal knowing but because Silas did not turn around, because he was afraid to turn around, and the horror of being afraid of his husband's reanimated body was what kept Silas turned away, and even after Silas hung up the phone he didn't turn and wouldn't look until he knew David had lain back down.

Now, the house is still and quiet like it was nine days ago. There are no lights on. David's laptop remains closed on the dining-room table. The windows are shut and the house smells of bleach cleaner. Silas opens the kitchen windows. His smart watch buzzes with a text from Michael and then a few seconds later, one comes in from Gwen, as though they'd synchronized, and he loves them for it.

He walks into the high-ceilinged living room and turns on the wall-mounted television. The volume is at an absurdly high level. Silas powers on the DVD player and switches to the HDMI feed. The workout DVD's main menu fills the screen. Electronic workout music, bass-heavy knockoffs of pop and dance hits pump through the speakers. David used the same set of DVDs for almost ten years. Silas knows the music by osmosis. He presses Play and sits on the floor in the spot where he found David. The DVD whirrs through three sets of workouts, a blur of moving and exhorting younger bodies. When the disk is completed, instead of returning to the disk menu, the DVD signal cuts out and the TV screen goes blue, the speakers silent.

Silas only planned this far, to this point. The blue screen is a detail he has included in each retelling, a detail that seems important, though he isn't sure why. As far as he knows all the other Blu-rays and DVDs returned to the menu when finished playing and not this blank blue screen. He doesn't believe in signs, but he wants to believe this technological hiccup means something or could mean something. Nothing as trite or absurd as his now being tuned to David's beyond-the-grave spirit channel. But at the same time, yeah, maybe that's what he wants. There's a low-frequency hum in the anxious speakers. Silas listens, then he thinks he might say something. What can he say? He is afraid of the silence, of the nothingness, of metastasizing loneliness, but he's more afraid that whatever he says, David or some simulacrum of David might answer. Nine days on from the initial horror, this is the newest one. Many argue ghost stories are inherently optimistic because they presuppose life after death. But what kind of afterlife awaits if the person he knew best and loved most would fleetingly return to haunt him, to frighten him more than he'd ever been frightened in his life?

Silas lies down in David's spot and presses the right side of his face to the floor so that he still sees the blue television screen. He imagines a spreading deadness within his limbs as the same blue color, and he wiggles a finger slowly, until it stops. He thinks of whispering, "I'm in here," like he did when young Gwen couldn't find him during their hiding/play-dead games. Awash in guilt, Silas indulges in the magical thinking of those past playing-dead transgressions being the reason why he found David the way he found him. As terrible and sadistic a thought as it is, at least it would be a reason, an answer to *why*.

The blue screen on the wall above him is implacable. Silas flexes a knee and readjusts his left arm. Then there's that feeling again, that feeling of knowing David is standing behind him. There is no doubt. No maybe. If Silas were to lift his torso and swivel his head in the manner in which he described David doing in one of his retellings, he would see David standing only a few steps away. And David would see Silas on the floor. And David's arms would go slack and he'd drop his phone and his face would open and then avalanche.

Silas listens for the floorboards behind him to creak. He hears the silence before the creaks, those shaking microvibrations birthing sound waves that haven't yet reached his ears. He holds his breath and waits and waits and he decides that he won't look, won't ever look behind him, and he will stay here on the floor until someone finds him, calls out his name, presses a hand to his cheek. Yet Silas does turn his head without deciding to do so, as though his body has a rebellious laugh by moving on its own. In Silas's later days and years, the same feeling (if he were to describe the feeling for someone else, though he never will, he'd say it was a knowing and not a feeling), the same certainty will overcome him, the certainty that David is there, around the next corner as Silas paces their home, or David is there, behind a door about to open or the door that was just closed, or David is there, behind the shower curtain or David is there, hidden by a tree only a few paces from the hiking path, or David is there, on the other side of the bed with Silas lying on his side and unable to sleep, and every time, when Silas turns with a whisper or a scream on his lips, he sees nothing.

THE POSTAL ZONE: *THE POSSESSION* EDITION

This special edition of "The Postal Zone" has been curated by our newest (and judging by email deluge in response to her epic breakdown of *The Possession* reality TV show, our MOST POPULAR) staff writer Karen Brissette. As always, hit us up with your horror hot takes and opinions. Keep in mind, brevity is the swallowed soul of wit. POSTALZONE@FANGORIA.COM

Possessed by *The Possession*!

I thought Karen Brissette deconstructed *The Possession*'s six episodes with smarts, class, and a proper respect for the real-life tragedy that befell the Barrett family after the cameras left. I'd watched the show when it originally aired fifteen years ago, and I was nervous about a rewatch, but Karen, you helped talk me through it. The show is an important document of how reality television and our pop-culture obsession not only led to the demise of the Barrett family but may even help explain our current political climate. I appreciated how you approached this controversial "reality TV" exorcism of fourteen-year-old Marjorie as fiction, because she clearly was not possessed and her family was being taken advantage of. I feel terrible for poor little Merry all over again. I mean, she was only eight when all that was happening to her older sister! While I empathize with the parents, as they were in such economic dire straits that they would allow an attempted exorcism to be filmed and broadcast, it doesn't make the results any less horrifying. The amount of detail you provided to support the reality show being fiction was amazing: pointing out how certain scenes resembled classic ones from films like *The Exorcist*, *Paranormal Activity*, and many more; the fluttering curtain hiding the open window in Marjorie's bedroom, which explains the temperature drop during the exorcism scene; timing out the mechanical pattern of the supposedly self-opening drawer is genius, as is making the *Evil Dead 2* comparison; and demonstrating how the show's producers set up one of the most shockingly violent scenes in a manner similar to John Carpenter's staging of the famous blood-test scene in *The Thing*. I plan on rewatching *The Possession* with your commentary as a guide.

Patty Wilson-Caffey
Studio City, CA

A fan! Thank you, Patty. I did my very best to discuss the show critically and as an unabashed horror fan while treating what happened afterward with the proper amount of gravitas. Yes, I said "gravitas."

I should be congratulated for somehow making it through the slog that was *The Possession* episode recap. I'm afraid to ask how many words of issue #_____ were allocated to that tiresome diatribe. Is *Fangoria* going to breathlessly cover other paranormal reality shows now too? Sounds silly when I ask it that way, right? I don't get why this one is such a big deal. Seems to me the only people who care about it are horror hipsters and pseudo-intellectual academic wannabes. Oh, and call me crazy, but I don't think your loyal readers enjoy having horror fans being compared to "the family dog that wags its tail at a treat, no matter if it's a crappy store brand Milk-Bone or a piece of steak" in the pages of *Fangoria*. Like I said, she's a total horror hipster who couldn't wait to turn a recap of a cheesy reality TV show into a politically correct manifesto. Stick to the story and gore, please. Thanks.

E. Viking

Not a fan! So . . . you don't get why a nationally televised, watched-by-millions attempted exorcism of a teenage girl and the tragedy that not-so-coincidently occurred after the show aired is, I quote, "such a big deal"? I, for one, do not share such a low estimation of your intelligence, Mr. Viking. Don't be so hard on yourself. I believe you understand The Possession's *significance within the horror genre and within the larger popular culture, even if you aren't able to properly articulate it without quoting me out of context and whining like a man-baby.*

*the opinions expressed above belong solely to K.B. THE HORROR HIPSTER and do not reflect the opinions of Fangoria's *editorial staff or the magazine itself should it become sentient, which it most certainly will**

(Editor's note: this is the first of three emails received from "M." M sent us one a day for three days. Three days of darkness?)

Karen Brissette should be commended for her thorough dissection of *The Possession*. The mesmeric power the show continues to wield over us is considerable. And it is kind of worrying, isn't it? One cannot deny the fifteen-year-old show's historical relevance, but so many of you don't treat it like a cultural artifact. Why do you still obsessively rewatch the bootlegs and YouTube videos and now the definitive Blu-ray release?

I would like you to give some serious thought to the following.

Most rational adults agree that Marjorie was not possessed by a demon or supernatural entity of your choosing. However, if you'll pardon the pun, allow me to play devil's advocate. What if Marjorie was in fact possessed?

M

Thank you, M. I think. And as requested, we (yes, I am speaking for all of Fangoria *and its readers, as I was granted that power for this "Postal Zone" and this "Postal Zone" only, and I promise to not abuse such powers. MUHAHAHAHA!) are thinking about your deviled ham's advocate what-if. At least, we'll think about it for five minutes or so.*

NOT TODAY (MAYBE TOMORROW), SATAN?

(Editor's note: the following letter has not been edited and appears as it was received.)

You're magazine is full of filth and pornography and is a SYMPTOM of why america is burns. Murder in the streets and in schools and you're magazine promotes the vile movies and prints pictures of DEMONS and FOUL ACTS. Worst of all you now publicize the return of that abomination tv show. Everyone involved will BURN in righteous hellfire especially Father Wanderly and the other catholics who should know better than to give SATAN a platform to spread his unholy message. You serve SATAN and you will all burn! To quote the great and honorable Max Sasha Logan (our spiritual leader and founder of C.L.A.M.P.) "FORNICATORS PORNOGRAPHERS AND DESTROYERS OF FAITH THE GOVERNMENTS CANNOT PROTECT YOU SATAN SERVENTS ANYMORE. WE WILL RISE LIKE AN OCEAN AND WASH YOUR FOULNESS FROM THE EARTH."

L. Richard Brady the first esteemed member of C.L.A.M.P.
Christian Legion Against Media Pornography

Wut. I'm totally counting L Dick (can I call you "L Dick"?) as a fan. YOU CAN'T STOP ME! Though he might be creepy enough to scare me away from using capital letters. (NEVER!!!)

Ambiguity Schmambiguity

I enjoyed reading Karen Brissette's review of Paul Tremblay's latest novel so much more than the book itself. I mean, hey, how about the guy actually tell us WTF happened in just one of his stories for a change? Is it that he can't fully commit to an ending so he doesn't give us one? Does he not know the ending or how to end something? It's very frustrating.

Julie Roberts-Johnson

You are welcome to your opinion, of course. But I disagree. OR DO I????

Possessed by *The Possession*
Part 2: The Possessioning

If Marjorie was possessed, and not by our collective culture as Karen posited but by a demon (for the sake of simplicity I'm calling it a demon and won't waste time outlining an array of supernatural entities, including interdimensional beings or things we haven't yet named), and the exorcism was unsuccessful, then I think you are in the clear. As callous as it sounds given what happened to Marjorie and to her parents, the exorcism being unsuccessful means you are safe. Or you're as safe as you were prior to watching Marjorie's exorcism. This is not to imply anyone is safe in the general sense of the word. Safety is civilization's biggest lie, of course. Anyway, what I'm trying to say is that you (the ones who watched and continue to watch *The Possession*) are as safe as anybody else who didn't watch the show in regard to being possessed by the same demon that had possessed Marjorie. Are you with me? If the exorcism did not work, one can surmise the demon remained with Marjorie until she died, which you did not witness because her death was not televised. Where the demon went from there, well, who knows. One could speculate on the demon being banished to the void or perhaps taking up residence within other individual(s) present at her death, but for the sake of this discussion, none of those individuals are you.

Now, I want to focus on the other possibility. What if Marjorie was possessed by a demon *and* the exorcism was successful? What if the rite you witnessed expelled the demon from Marjorie? This is the hypothetical (as admittedly irrational as it sounds) that concerns me the most and, frankly, keeps me up at night. I fear your continued obsession with watching and rewatching this show is evidence in support of this very hypothetical.

Let's assume a demon was exorcised from Marjorie. Where did it go? Religions across cultures warn that innocent or unprotected observers of an attempted exorcism are in danger, the primary fear being a newly expelled demon could find an easy new host. The viewership of *The Possession* represents millions of unprotected observers. I won't call you innocent, because as Karen pointed out, you the viewers were not innocent and were very much complicit with what went on during the show and maybe even after the show. Perhaps your inner voids deserve to be filled.

Have you considered a demon was in fact exorcised from Marjorie and that it is you, the viewers, who have since been possessed by the very same demon?

M

Nope, I haven't considered it. Wait . . . Still nope. Hmm, I don't think it likely that your first or last or even middle name has "M" as an initial. I can't figure out if you're supposed to be an avatar for one of the sisters, for Merry or Marjorie. Either way, I think it's in poor taste, but I dig it because you're creepy. Extra creepy. And I have a new friend from C.L.A.M.P. I want to introduce you to.

Extra, Extra!

I was so excited to hear that *The Possession* was getting a Blu-ray release. In 4K the clarity and composition of the episodes are downright cinematic. I wonder if any theaters would consider screening all six episodes come October. That said, I'm disappointed in the extras, or the lack of extras. Don't get me wrong, I enjoyed the interviews with the reenactment actors and production crew. I thought the interview with one of the show's writers, Ken Fletcher, was most illuminating—he appeared genuinely haunted and affected by the experience, particularly as he stammered through answering a question about the last time he spoke to the younger daughter, Merry. Now, I don't want to seem ghoulish, given what ended up happening to the real family, but I was disappointed we didn't get any lost interviews with family members or home movies or deleted scenes from the filming of the show. With Merry Barrett's tell-all book about to drop, I guess I'm saying I would've liked to have had her commentary included with the Blu-ray, as apparently she's now willing to talk about the experience.

George Ranson

Given my obsession with the show, I'll admit to initially sharing in your disappointment, especially by the lack of deleted or not-seen-by-your-craven-beady-eyes-before scenes. It's likely the Barrett family estate didn't grant permission for deleted scenes and outtakes. I'm guessing there's a legal reason why it took 15 years for us to finally get a Blu-ray release, but I can't say for sure. In regard to Merry not participating in the release, put yourself in her shoes. Why would she help the producers/Blu-ray distributor in promoting the reality TV show that changed if not ruined her life? Sure, Merry's book seems to imply she's "willing to talk about the experience," but I'm guessing she chose this vehicle for a reason. With the book she can control the message and talk about the experience solely on her terms. I don't blame her one iota for not actively participating with the Blu-ray release, and I don't think anyone else should either.

Possessed by *The Possession*
Part 3: A New Beginning

What if the noisy, gaudy, televised American tragedy you watched and rewatched was your bait and trap? What if this mass possession is something new, something that hasn't been classically presented to you in film and folklore? What if your possession is a bit more subtle and insidious?

You live by yourself in a big-city apartment. It's difficult and expensive, but if pressed you'd say you were content and living a fulfilling, exciting big-city life. Even though you are single, you would not describe yourself as lonely. You joke that it's impossible to be alone, as your waking hours are crammed with people: commuters, coworkers, and four or five nights a week you go out to eat or hang at a bar with friends. Even when you come home to an empty apartment, you spend hours texting and you go on social media and you watch movies and shows, and you text and you post about what you watch, providing the online universe your horror fandom bona fides. However, after you shut the TV off and put the phone away, after you are finished feeding your purposefully manic fandom, there are the unavoidable quiet times when it's just you and what's inside your head. You brush your teeth and don't stare at yourself for too long in the mirror. If you stare at yourself long enough, you will begin to look unfamiliar. You might see something you don't want to see. You climb into bed and turn off the lights. Sometimes you fall asleep right away. But there are nights when you can't sleep because you can't stop thinking about what you watched, and then you hear bumps and creaks coming from somewhere inside your little apartment or even your bedroom. And then your own breathing sounds too loud. You turn over in bed to face the window and not the interior darkness of your bedroom, certainly not the black outline of the closet door. You pull the blankets up, almost covering your face, but you can't bear to not-see either. Your feet and hands are cold, but you are afraid to wiggle a single toe. You chide yourself for being silly, but you don't feel silly, and you can't stop thinking about those final images of Marjorie and what you saw in her eyes. Sleep is impossible and time is torture, and eventually you have to pee again but you're afraid to go into the bathroom. You're afraid to walk by the mirror. You're afraid you might see Marjorie's eyes. You're afraid to see how alone you truly are.

Or you live in a house in a quiet suburb. Your kids and partner are asleep upstairs and you're the only one up and watching the show because after everyone else is in bed is the only time you can watch scary things. When the show ends and you turn off the television, a heavy silence fills the empty spaces of your home. You shut off the lights in the living room and then the kitchen, only after you pass through each room as you do not willingly walk through darkness. You move slowly, carefully, and you set about the circuit of checking the locks on front and back doors. Concentrating on the routine task helps clear your head most nights, but on this night the click of the locks echoes too loudly. You are convinced someone is standing behind you; your skin tingles with being watched. Then you think you hear movement upstairs, maybe even voices, whispers. Your partner talks in her sleep. Maybe your children are awake; they are such light sleepers and often suffer from the vivid nightmares that always afflict young dreamers. You consider calling out, just to hear a sound that you can confirm exists, but you don't. You stand at the base of the stairs, listening. You are so sure you're going to hear a voice that you can anticipate what that voice will sound like, even if you dare not anticipate what it will say.

Or you wake from a nightmare when a voice shouts "Hey!" directly into your ear. You groan (a sound that is wedged inside your chest) and bolt upright in bed. The dark transforms the landscape of your bedroom into an unrecognizable place. Your partner is asleep next to you. Your daily responsibilities and relationships are meaningless in this moment as the nightmare's inexplicable logic has leaked into reality. Your armor of cynicism, snark, and skepticism only protects you in the daylight. Now, in the dead of night (an apt phrase if there ever was one), you are sweating, shaking, and you've never felt so vulnerable. You might scream the kind of scream that will never end. In your memory of the nightmare (or was it after the nightmare? were you awake already?), the voice shouting "Hey!" belonged to Marjorie, and it was also, somehow, your own voice at the same time. Your partner doesn't move when you press yourself against them. Your partner can't help you. You know this. You *feel* this. And then there's another voice, one telling you that even though you're there with someone, you are and will always be alone.

Do you know what the most maddening and terrifying part is? You will think you got past those impossible moments of dread, and you will go about your days, and you will struggle and you will fail and you will persevere until you don't, but you will live the rest of your life never truly knowing if you have or have not been possessed, and you will not know for sure until you close your eyes for the final time.

M

Eeeeeeeeeeeeeeek!

For Karen Brissette and Dan Tremblay

RED EYES

This is another story my sister told me.

It was one week before the world ended.

Merry had to go to bed first. She was the youngest in the family, eight years old, and had long brown hair that curled into ringlets without even trying. She wore black eyeglasses and her sister said she looked like a cat. Her sister, Marjorie, was fourteen, had hair as dark as licorice, and a smile that made you think you were in trouble.

Merry decided to be difficult, refusing bedtime stories from her parents and then even from Marjorie. Usually, Merry begged her sister for stories but on this night difficult Merry didn't want to go to bed. When Marjorie and her parents gave up and shut Merry in her room, difficult Merry warned that everyone would be sorry.

Merry woke up later that night, at a time between other times. She was still feeling difficult, so she went into Marjorie's room and shook her awake. When Marjorie wouldn't come with her, Merry ran downstairs, out of the house (not shutting the door, mumbling her father's favorite quip, "Do you live in a barn?"), and into the night, all during this in-between time. Marjorie eventually got out of bed and followed to the doorstep, whispering after Merry, telling her to go back to bed. Merry was still being difficult.

A note on their house, which didn't look different from the other houses in the village: Their house had the same two-floor design as the others and was built using the same wood from the same forest and colored with the same lacquer stain. But everyone else in the village thought the Barrett house felt different from theirs.

Marjorie found Merry standing in the middle of the road. The night was darker than usual; for a reason not clear to Marjorie, only every other streetlamp was burning. The orange light projected small circles on the cobblestones. Merry did not look at her sister and instead stared down the road and giggled.

The village's main thoroughfare ended abruptly at the border of the thick Forest Greene, approximately 433 steps away, according to Merry. In the distance looming above and beyond the near-impenetrable forest were a chain of mountains that were not to be named, again for a reason not clear to Marjorie, or Merry for that matter.

Tonight, however, the forest was not at the end of the road, but the mountains were. The optical illusion of the mountains having come to visit the village lasted until the mountains opened their glowing-red, moon-sized eyes. There was no mistaking the monsters for mountains then. There were four of them, each of different height and width, their rounded shoulders and heads huddled together. Even though the monsters were not mountains, and certainly not made of stone, both sisters thought they looked like a link from the nameless mountain chain, though neither said so to the other.

The tallest monster lifted its arms. As though directed by this gesture, the others shuffled their tectonic feet, grinding the cobblestones, rumbling the earth, and raising a dust storm that clouded their lower halves and the smallest one's chest, but not their heads and their glowing eyes.

Mom and Dad came outside and huddled together with Merry and Marjorie in the road. If someone else in the village were to have come outside then, they might've thought the shadowed shapes of the family looked like miniature versions of the monsters.

Mom and Dad said, "What do we do? Should we run and hide? Should we wake up the village?"

Merry was still feeling difficult. She let go of Marjorie's hand and ran down the road toward the monsters. No one in her family tried to stop her. Maybe they were too shocked. Maybe they were too scared. Maybe they wanted to see what would happen.

Marjorie wanted to yell, *Let me come too!* but she didn't.

The monsters' red eyes followed Merry as she approached. They blinked in some secret pattern. Merry ran into the dust and dirt cloud that grew so big it blotted out the monsters one by one. There were rumbling sounds and maybe a small scream, though no one could be sure, and when the dust settled back to the ground, Merry and the monsters were gone.

The next day the other villagers were confused as to what happened. They went about their daily routines as though nothing—which is the exact opposite of something—happened. Marjorie and her parents, on the other hand, were devastated. They didn't eat and didn't sleep and they spent a lot of time in Merry's room, both alone and together.

Exactly one week after Merry's disappearance and at the same in-between time in the middle of the night—although "middle" is simply part of a colloquial expression and not the temporal mark of the in-between time—there was a great and terrible rumbling in the distance. This rumbling didn't remain distant for very long. Then there was crash-ing and smashing and screaming. The remaining members of the Barrett family left the house and stood in the same area in the road they stood in previously, leaving the Merry spot empty.

The monsters were back. They smashed roofs with fists bigger than boulders. They uprooted the streetlamps and used them like matchsticks to set homes and buildings on fire. They gobbled up fleeing villages. The ones who yelled and cried and fought back the hardest were spitefully bitten in half instead of swallowed whole.

The Barretts ran back inside the house because they were so scared they did not know what else to do. They ran up the stairs to the second floor and then climbed up the ladder to the attic. There they sat on the floor among the cobwebs, holding each other and daring peeks outside the one lonely window nearest the inverted V of the roof. This high up and close, they saw the monsters were covered head-to-foot in dark fur, each strand of hair as thick as rope.

The three largest monsters rumbled by their house, leaving it un-touched, and set to destroying the rest of the village. No one and nothing else would be spared.

The smallest monster charged toward them as though it were going to simply walk right through the house. But the monster stopped. It bent slightly and pressed one of its great eyes against the window, filling the attic with its red light. The light filled the heads of Mom, Dad, and Mar-jorie too.

Merry shouted, "Giddy up! Come on, giddy up!" and the eye blinked, sending the Barretts back into darkness for a moment. The monster stood tall again and turned. Merry held on to fistfuls of fur on the back of the monster's domed head. She was as embedded as a tick in a dog.

Merry and her monster followed the others and obliterated their village and, rumor has it, all the other villages. Marjorie and her parents were left alone, literally and metaphorically speaking.

Merry never put her face in the window like her monster did. She didn't even turn to look at her family before she left again. Marjorie didn't have to see Merry's eyes to know that they were red now too. Perhaps they had always been red.

THE BLOG AT THE END OF THE WORLD

THE BLOG AT THE END OF THE WORLD

ABOUT BECCA GILMAN:

I am twentysomething, living somewhere in Brooklyn, and am angry and scared like everyone else I know. Sometimes this blog helps me, sometimes it doesn't. I have degrees in bio and chem, but don't use them. That's all you really need to know. All right?

---

still here

Becca Gilman • June 15, 2009

Barely. I thought I was ready for one more real/detailed post to the BLOG with a *Link Roundup*, but I'm not. I tried calling Mom two days ago but there was no answer and she hasn't called me back. I'm still not over GRANT's passing; my personal tipping point and I hate myself for referring to Grant that way, but it's true. I haven't left my apartment in over a week. The local market I use for grocery delivery stopped answering their phone yesterday. I've only seen three cabs today. They're old and dinged up, from some independent cab company I don't recognize, and they just drive around City Line, circling, like they're stuck in some loop. They're only there because they're supposed to be. The drivers don't know what else to do. At night I count how many windows I can see with the lights on. The city was darker last night than it was last week, or the week before. I don't know if I'm doing a good job explaining all this. I'm watching the city fall apart. It's slow and subtle, but you can see it if you look hard enough. Watch. Everything is slowing down. A windup toy running down and with no one to wind it up. Everything is dying but not quite dead yet, so people just go about their days as if nothing is wrong and nothing bad can happen tomorrow.

I've had a headache for a week now, my neck hurts, and I've been really sensitive to light, to the computer screen especially. I'm scared, but not terrified anymore. There is a difference. Mostly, I'm just incredibly sad.

6 Responses to "still here"

squirrelmonkey says:
June 15, 2009, at 9:32 am

I just tried calling and left a message. I am going to stop by your place today. Please answer your buzzer.

Jenn Parker says:
June 15, 2009, at 1:12 pm

While I still offer condolences for the loss of your friend, I'm not surprised that you're experiencing headaches and the like. You're so obsessed with the textbook symptoms, you're now psychosomatically experiencing them. I am surprised it has taken this long. I had February 2009 in the pool. Get help. Psychiatric help.

beast says:
June 28, 2009, at 4:33 am

i live in new york city to last weak i saw this guy drop dead in the street he pressed a button at the traffic light on the corner and then died there was no one else around just me he wasnt old probably younger than me he died and then i saw whats really happning to everyone cause two demons fell out of the sky and landed next to him maybe they were the gargoiles from the buildings i dont know but they were big strong gray with muscles and wings and large teeth the sidewalk broke under their heavyness they growled like tigers and licked up the blood that came out of the guys ears and mouth but that wasn't good enough they broke his chest open and there was red everywere on the sidewalk and street corner i didnt know there was so much blood in us but they know they took off his arms and legs then gather him up in their big strong arms and flew away he was gone i went back and checked the next day he was gone after i walked around the city i saw the demons every were but noone saw them but me they fly and climb the buildings waiting for us to die and take us just like you i am afraid and stay in my apartment but don't look out my window any more

revelations says:
July 5, 2009, at 12:12 am

I've noticed that you haven't posted in a while. Maybe you're "fuck heaven" comments from you're earlier post caught up to you, or maybe you're fear mongering and lies have finally caught up with you. GOD punishes the wicked. He is truly just.

Jenn Parker says:
July 5, 2009, at 2:45 pm

I like beast. I want to party with you, dude!

Hey, revelations, stick to book burning and refuting evolution.

revelations says:
July 12, 2009, at 10:09 am

I can sum it all up in three words: Evolution is a lie.

Link Roundup

Becca Gilman • May 19, 2009

I don't feel up to it, but here's a link roundup, in honor of GRANT.

—SAN JOSE MERCURY NEWS: The Silicon Valley's home sales continue to tank with the number of deals at a 40-year low. The mayor of San Jose attributes the market crisis to the glut of homes belonging to the recently deceased.

—THE BURLINGTON FREE PRESS reports that a May 3rd session of Congress ended with the sudden death of Missouri Rep. William Hightower and Sen. Jim Billingsly from Vermont. While neither Hightower nor Billingsly has been seen publicly since the 3rd, the offices of both congressmen have yet to make any such announcement and their only official comment is to claim the story is patently false.

—THE MIAMI HERALD reports that according to UNICEF, the populations of children in Kenya and Ethiopia have declined by a stunning 24 percent within the past year. The UN and United States government dispute the findings, claiming widespread inaccuracies in the "hurried and irresponsible" census.

8 Responses to "Link Roundup"

Jenn Parker says:
May 24, 2009, at 7:48 pm

Another link roundup. Reputable sources at a quick glance, but let's address each link:

The *San Jose Mercury News* has already issued a partial retraction HERE. The mayor of San Jose never attributed the market crisis to the supposed glut of homes belonging to the deceased. Honestly, other than within the backdrop of our collective state of paranoia/hysteria, such a claim/statement doesn't make any economic sense. People aren't buying homes for myriad economic reasons, but too many deaths due to an imaginary epidemic isn't one of them. The links to your BURLINGTON and MIAMI papers are dead. I suppose you could spin the dead links to bolster the conspiracy theory, but here in reality, the dead links serve only as a representation of your desperation to perpetuate conspiracy.

squirrelmonkey says:
May 25, 2009, at 7:03 am

Ever heard of Google, Jenn? Those articles can still be found in the cache. It's not hard to find. Do you want me to show you how?

Jenn Parker says:
May 25, 2009, at 1:23 pm

Answer me this: Why were the articles almost instantaneously removed? You'll tell me it's due to some all-encompassing conspiracy, when the real answer is those papers got their stories wrong. They got their stories wrong, so they had to pull the articles. That's it. Happens all the time. I guarantee retractions will be published within days. Oh-master-of-Google, prove me wrong by finding another news-outlet corroboration (and not a blog like this one) to either story. Read carefully, please. I want a news outlet that does not cite the *Burlington Free Press* or *Miami Herald* as their primary sources. If you try such a search, you'll be at it for a long time, because I can't find any other independent reports.

slugwentbad says:
May 25, 2009, at 10:13 pm

I've called Billingsly's office on three occasions, and I've been told he's unavailable every time.

Jenn Parker says:
May 25, 2009, at 10:23 pm

Oh, that proves everything, then.

discostewie says:
May 26, 2009, at 8:27 am

BEES and BATS and AMPHIBIANS are disappearing, mysteriously dying off (are you going to refute that too, Jenn?). Is it so hard to believe that the same is happening to us?

batfan says:
June 25, 2009, at 3:37 am

Hi, remember me? Come check out my new gambling site for all the best poker and sports action. It's awesome. http://www.gamblor234.net

speworange says:
August 22, 2009, at 10:46 am

Humans are harder to kill than cockroaches.

More Grant Lee

Becca Gilman • May 12, 2009

I went to Grant's wake today. The visiting hours were only one hour. 2pm–3pm. I got there at 2. There was a line. We had some common friends, but I didn't see anyone that I knew there. I didn't see his sister or recognize any family members there either. I waited in a line that started on the street. No one talked or shared eye contact. This is so hard to write. I'm trying to be clinical. The mourners were herded inside the funeral parlor, but it split into three different rooms. Grant's room was small with mahogany molding on the walls and a thick, soft tan carpet on the floor. There were flowers everywhere. The smell was overpowering and made the air thick. It was too much. The family had asked for a donation to a charity in lieu of flowers. I don't remember the charity. There was no casket. Grant wasn't there; he wasn't in the room. There wasn't a greeting line, and I don't know where his family was. There was only a big flat-screen TV on the wall. The TV scrolled with images of Grant and his friends and family. I was in one of those pictures. We were at the Pizza Joint, standing next to each other, bent over, our faces perched in our hands, elbows on the counter. I had flour on the tip of my nose, and he had his PJ baseball hat on backwards, his long black hair tucked behind his ears. Our smiles matched. It was one of those rare posed pictures that still managed to capture the spirit of a candid. That picture didn't stay on the screen long enough. Other people's memories of Grant crowded it out. Also, the pictures of Grant mixed with stock photos and video clips of blue sky and rolling clouds like some ridiculous subliminal commercial for heaven. There was a soundtrack to the loop; nothing Grant liked or listened to (certainly no Slayer). The music was formless and light, with no edges or minor chords. Aural Valium. It was awful. All of it. The mourners walked around the room's perimeter in an orderly fashion. I got the sense they'd all done this before. Point A to B to C to D and out the door. I didn't follow them. I held my ground and stayed rooted to a spot as people brushed past me. No one asked if I was okay, not that I wanted them to. I watched the TV long enough to see the images loop back to the beginning, or at least the beginning that I had seen. I don't know if there was a true beginning and a true end to the loop. After seeing the loop once, I stared at the other mourners' faces. Their eyes turned red and watered when the obviously poignant images meshed with a hopeful crescendo of Muzak. The picture of a toddler-aged Grant holding hands with his parents seemed to be the cue. Then the manufactured moment passed, and everyone's faces turned blue when the TV filled with blue sky, that slickly produced loop of heaven. I wanted to shout, *Fuck heaven, I want Grant back and I don't want to die.* But I didn't. After an hour had passed, I was asked to leave as someone else's visiting hour was starting. They had a full schedule: every room booked throughout the afternoon and evening. I peeked in the other rooms before I left. No caskets anywhere, just TVs on the walls. Pictures. Clouds. Blue sky. More pictures. When I went outside, there was another long line waiting for their turn to mourn properly.

I didn't cry until after I left Grant's wake. Now I'm sitting in my apartment, still crying, and thinking about my father. He died when I was four. I remember his wake. I remember crossing my arms over my chest and not letting anyone hug me. Everyone tried. I remember being bored and mad. And I remember trying to hide under the casket presentation. An uncle that I'd never met before pulled me out of the mini-curtains below the casket. He pulled too hard on my arm and I cried. I think my tears were the equivalent of the four-year-old me saying, *Fuck heaven, I want my daddy back, and I don't want to die.*

I'm just rambling now. I apologize. I've turned off comments for this post. I've posted, and deleted, and then reposted this a few times. I'm going to leave it up and as is. But no one else gets to say anything about Grant or me or anything today.

Grant Lee, RIP

Becca Gilman • May 10, 2009

It finally happened. A very close friend of mine, Grant Lee, died two days ago. He was twenty-four. I have been unable to get much information from his family. I talked to his older sister, Claire. Grant died at work, at the Pizza Joint, two blocks from my apartment. She said his death was sudden and "catastrophic." I asked if he died from an aneurysm. Claire said the doctors told the family it was likely heart failure, but they wouldn't tell them anything specific. I then asked for information about the hospital he went to, but she rushed me off the phone, saying she had too many calls to make. I called the

Pizza Joint, wanting to talk to the coworker who had found Grant dead, but no one answered the phone. I'm going to take a walk down there after I post this. It's awful and terrifying enough that Grant died, but it looks like his cause of death will be covered up as well.

Grant. I met Grant in a video store a week after I'd moved to Brooklyn. We rented Nintendo Wii games and black-and-white noir flicks together. Grant ate ice cream with a fork. He always wore a white T-shirt under another shirt, even if the other shirt was another white T-shirt. Grant was tall, and slight of build, but very fast, and elegant when he moved. I'd never seen him stumble or fall down. He worked long hours at the Pizza Joint, trying to pay off the final four grand of tuition he owed NYU so he could get his diploma. That debt wasn't Grant's fault. His father was a gambler and couldn't pay that final tab. Grant had a crooked smile and he only trusted a few of his friends. I think he trusted me. Grant liked to swear a lot. He liked fucking with the Pizza Joint customers whenever he could. Sometimes he'd greet an obnoxious-looking customer with silence and head nods only. Invariably, the obnoxious-looking customer would talk slow and loud because they assumed Grant (who was Korean) didn't speak English. They'd mumble exasperated stuff under their breath when Grant didn't respond. Finally, he'd give the customer their pizza and make some comment like, "You gonna eat all that? You leavin' town or somethin'?" and his voice was loud and had that thick Long Island accent of his. Grant drank orange soda all day long. Grant would be too quick to tease sometimes, but he always gave me an unqualified apology if I needed one.

Grant was more than a collection of eccentricities or character traits, but that is what he's been reduced to. I love you and miss you, GRANT.

4 Responses to "Grant Lee, RIP"

Jenn Parker says:
May 10, 2009, at 4:47 pm

If you are telling the truth (sorry to sound so callous, but I don't know you, and given your blogging history, your agenda, it's entirely plausible you are making this up to bolster your position, as it were), I'm very sorry for your loss.

I don't know what to believe though. Look at your first sentence: *It finally happened.* Maybe this is just a throwaway phrase written while in the throes of grief, however it seems like an odd line to lead your post. *It finally happened.* It sounds like not only were you anticipating such an event but are welcoming it so your version of reality could somehow be verified.

I find it impossible to believe that doctors would give the family of the deceased no cause of death, or a fraudulent cause of death as you are implying. To what benefit or end would such a practice serve?

And please see and respond to the links and aneurysm statistics I quoted in your earlier POST.

squirrelmonkey says:
May 10, 2009, at 7:13 pm

I'm so, so sorry to hear this, Becca. Poor Grant.

Take care of yourself and ignore that Jenn Parker troll. Call me if you feel up to it, okay?

beast says:
May 11, 2009, at 3:36 am

sorry about your friend its so scarey that were all gonna die

anonymous says:
May 12, 2009, at 10:56 am

I've spent the past week doing nothing but reading obituaries from every newspaper I can find online. I read Grant Lee's obit and followed links to his MySpace and then here to your blog.

My son died last week. I was with him in the backyard when he just folded in on himself, falling to the grass. His eyes were closed and blood trickled out of his ears. He was only six. I suppose that his young age is supposed to make it worse, but it can't be any worse for me.

I'm afraid to write his name, as if writing it here makes what happened to him more final than it already is.

Someone else, not me, wrote my son's OBITUARY. I don't remember who. They did a terrible job.

When we first came home, after leaving his body at the hospital, I went into his room and found some crumpled-up drawings under his bed. There were two figures in black on the paper, monstrously sized, but human, small heads, no mouths, just two circles for eyes, but all black. They had black guns and they sprayed black bullets all over the page. The bullets were hard slashes, big as knives, black too, and they curved. I have no idea what it means or where it came from.

Was it a sketch of a nightmare, did he see something on TV he shouldn't have, was he drawing these scenes with friends at school? Why did he crumple the drawings up and stuff them under his bed? Did he think that they were "bad," that he couldn't show them to me, talk about it with me, that I'd be so upset with him that I'd feel differently about him if I were to see the pictures?

It's this last scenario that sends me to the computer and reading other people's obituaries.

A Grim Anniversary

Becca Gilman • April 12, 2009

The Blog at the End of the World has been live for a year now. I thought it worth revisiting my FIRST POST. On March 20th, 2008, in Mansfield, MA, a fourteen-year-old boy died suddenly during his school's junior varsity baseball practice (BOSTON GLOBE), and two days later, a fifteen-year-old girl from the same town died at her tennis practice (BOSTON GLOBE). The two Mansfield residents both had sudden, catastrophic brain aneurysms.

So why am I bringing up those two kids again? Why am I dragging out the old news when you could open up any newspaper in the country, click on any blog or news-gathering site, and read the same kind of stories only with different names and faces and places?

Despite the aid of hindsight and my general, everyday paranoia, I'm not prepared to unequivocally state that the teens mentioned ABOVE are our patient zeroes. However, I do think it worth noting those reported stories were mainstream media's *story zero* concerning the *cerebral aneurysm pandemic* and the first of their type to go national, and shortly thereafter, global.

And, finally, a one-link *Link roundup*:

—NEW YORK TIMES reports widespread shortages on a host of anti-clotting and anti-seizure drugs used to treat aneurysms. Included in the shortage are medications that increase blood pressure, with the idea that increased blood flow through potentially narrowed vessels would prevent clots and aneurysms. Newer, more exotic drugs are also now being reported as in shortage: nimodipine (a calcium channel blocker that prevents blood vessel spasms) and glucocorticoids (anti-inflammatory steroids, not FDA approved, controversial treatment that supposedly controls swelling in the brain). The gist of the story is about the misuse of the medications (many of which are only meant for survivors of aneurysm and aren't preventative), which, of course, leads to a whole slew of other medical problems, including heart attack and stroke.

6 Responses to "A Grim Anniversary"

revelations says:
April 24, 2009, at 10:23 am

Your a fear monger. You spread fear and the lies of the Godless, liberal media. GOD will punish you!!!!

Jenn Parker says:
April 24, 2009, at 1.29 pm

I have no doubt the *Times* story is true, but only because of the panic. This story does not prove there really is a pandemic of aneurysms. Only that the general public believes there is one.

Please follow my links here, and it really is as simple as it sounds: The reality is that on average, SINCE 2000, 50,000 Americans die from brain aneurysms (spontaneous cerebral hemorrhaging) per year, with 3–6% OF ALL ADULTS having aneurysms inside their brains (fortunately, most are so small they're never noticed). There is no recorded evidence of that 50,000 number swelling to unprecedented levels. Please show me my error!

There is no conspiracy. It's the 21st-century Red Scare. Our zeitgeist is so preoccupied with apocalypse we're making one up because the real one isn't getting here soon enough. Yes, 50K is a SMALL PERCENTAGE of the population, but it's a large enough number that if a preponderance of aneurysm cases were to get PRESS COVERAGE, as they clearly are, it gives a multimedia appearance of a pandemic and a conspiracy to cover it up.

Unless you can provide some hard data/evidence—like our GOVERNMENT and the WHO can provide—please stop. Just stop. There're plenty more real threats (economic, environmental, geopolitical) that sorely need to be addressed.

grant says:
April 24, 2009, at 1:49 pm

Has it been only a year? Fuck a flyin' fuckin' duck.

I was at the CVS pharmacy on Central Park Ave. today—just picking up "supplies";)—and there was a huge fucking line in the pharmacy section with two policemen wandering around the store. Muscles and guns and sunglasses. Some good, hot, homoeroticism there, Becks.

My fuckheaded fellow shoppers were walking all around the CVS, wearing hospital masks and emptying the already empty shelves of vitamins and who-the-fuck-knows what else. Most of them were buying shit they'd never need, just buying stuff because it was there. It was surreal, and I gotta tell ya, they got to me! I ended up buying some leftover Easter candy. Fucking Peeps. Don't even like them, but you know, when society collapses, I just might need me some yellow fucking Peeps!

Stop by the PJ tonight, Becks. I'm working a double shift. I'll bring the Peeps.

tiredflower says:
April 24, 2009, at 2:30 pm

I'm one of those fuckheads who wears a hospital mask when I go out now. I know it doesn't protect or save me from anything, but it makes me feel better. I know it scares other people when they see me in it, so I tried to cover it up by drawing a smile on the mask with a pink Sharpie. I'd hoped it would make people smile back. I'm not a good drawer, though, and it doesn't look like a smile. It's a snarl, bared teeth, the nanosecond before a scream. It's my only mask. I should throw it away and get a new mask, but I can't. It's my good-luck charm.

grant says:
April 24, 2009, at 2:58 pm

Drawing mouths on the hospital masks is fuckin' brilliant!

Becks, bring some masks (I know you have some!) to the PJ tonight. I'll help you decorate them. I've got some killer ideas. I'm serious, now, bring some masks. I want to wear one when I go out tomorrow.

bnl44 says:
September 23, 2009, at 2:34 am

I saw someone die today. We were part of a small crowd waiting for our subway train. She was standing next to me, listening to an iPod. It was loud enough to hear the drums and bassline. Didn't recognize the song, but I tried. When our train arrived, she collapsed. I felt her body part the air and despite all the noise in the station, I heard her head hit the concrete. It was a hard and soft sound. Then, her iPod tune got louder, probably because the earphones weren't in her ears anymore.

I don't know if anyone helped her or not. I'm ashamed to admit that I didn't help her. I was so scared. She fell and I raced onto the train and waited to hear the doors shut behind me before I turned around to look. The windows in the doors were dirty, black with grime, and I didn't see anything.

THEM: A PITCH

Thanks again for the invite to your "villains" comic anthology, and the rate you quoted for ten pages sounds more than fair to me. I assume the artist will be paid the same or more, right? They should get more, given how much of the story the artist will have to convey. I'll admit right up front that while I have read—and do read—comics, I've never written one, and I don't know what a comic script looks like beyond hearing it's not totally dissimilar to screenwriting, not that I've written a bunch of screenplays either. How's that for a pitch? Sold, right? If you go for my idea, I'll certainly do my homework, and I'll take you up on the offer to send me some sample scripts.

Anyway, the pitch for real:

There will be no dialogue or narrative commentary in this story. It will be told exclusively via the images/art. The art will be black-and-white, with an aesthetic of Charles Burns's *Black Hole* (see, I told you I read comics) mashed up with 1950s atomic monster movies. A stark or minimalist style while also looking like it might've come from a *Twilight Zone* episode.

The opening panels: An empty stretch of desert, with a silhouetted person approaching in the distance. With each panel the person comes closer into view until he's finally in focus. He's a haggard, unshaven, middle-aged white man wearing tattered clothes and sneakers, and carrying a backpack. He's slumped and his eyes are down at his feet. We get the sense he's been walking for a while.

We follow him for a few more panels that spotlight him from a wider view. Looming in the background are large monoliths with wide bases tapering toward their rectangular tops. The structures are not recognizably human-made. Think the film *Phase IV* and the ant-colony towers in the first act, or, at the discretion of the artist, Devils Tower as featured in *Close Encounters of the Third Kind*.

In a hoary nod to a trope from scores of old movies, the man carries a tattered photo of his wife and a whole brood of kids, four or five. The photo could be right out of the insufferable *Family Circus* comic strip.

He continues walking, each panel sinking us and him deeper into a seemingly endless desert. More monoliths dot the horizon.

Near an outcropping of boulders and caves, the man stumbles upon a community of survivors, a diverse group of about ten or more people who, unlike the disheveled man, appear to be thriving, with a variety of structures and gardens built.

The group is initially wary, but they welcome the man to their community. He spends that first day working hard as part of the group, helping to reinforce irrigation lines and tend a garden.

At dusk, with the day's work done, the community gathers to eat and socialize. The group is suddenly attacked by a horde of car-sized ants—think the ants from *Them!* (1954).

The community is prepared and fights back valiantly. They manage to kill some of the ants, but the numbers on this day are overwhelming. Some people are killed. Some people escape into the reinforced caves.

Throughout the fight the man does nothing. He sits with his hands covering his eyes, like a child trying to hide from the scary part of a movie.

The ants eventually gather around him, their antennae twitching. The art will show wavy lines emanating from the antennae to imply that they are telepathically communicating. While he might appear ashamed and devastated, the man obediently scrambles onto his knees, assuming a supplicant's pose, and holds out his hands.

An ant spits up a bowling ball–sized glob of glucose.

The man deposits it in his backpack. The ants crowd and touch his head with their antennae, then they let him leave.

The man resumes his walk through the desert as night approaches. He eventually comes upon a lone house in the sand, one that wouldn't be out of place in an affluent suburb. This House of Usher has yet to collapse, and it rests in the shadow of one of the giant anthill monoliths.

He goes inside. His family (the one from the picture he carries) greets him with smiles and hugs and kisses.

He places half of the globule from his backpack onto a serving dish. The other half goes into a larder in the kitchen (there are many more half-globules there).

The family sits at a dining-room table, they bow their heads in prayer, and then they eat.

What do you think?

HOUSE OF WINDOWS

Brian Butler works at the biggest library in the biggest city. He is not a librarian, however. The library is so big, it necessitates hundreds of employees, so he works in human resources and is in charge of employee benefits.

Sometimes it's just easier to tell people that he is a librarian and that he knows the stately and iconic building so well, every room, hallway, and staircase is card-catalogued within his own head.

Each morning, he takes the subway from his fastidious teacup apartment (one he shares with Milton, his tiny coffee-heavy-with-cream-colored dog, which is half Chihuahua and half dachshund) to the downtown stop, and then he walks the last six blocks to the library.

Today, he notices a new building adjacent to the library; a new building that looks so out of place, particularly when contrasted with the venerable library and its marble columns, its Rundbogenstil style.

This new building wasn't there the day before.

The new building is cube-shaped and two stories tall. The façade facing the library is sectioned into three parts. The exterior is a white-pink color. The trim is a full-on flamingo pink, so, too, are the decorative mini-ledges; the open eyelids above five of the six windows (two rows of three on each floor). There's an aqua-blue vertical line that runs down the second story of the façade's middle, splitting the sixth window in half. Painted on either side of the aqua-blue line are horizontal pink dashes. The same structural and decorative design patterns are repeated on the other three sides of the building.

Brian Butler makes a mental note to look up *A New Theory of Urban*

Design (Center for Environmental Structure Series, Vol 6) in the reference section of his library. Were this building built somewhere else, Brian Butler imagines that it would remind casual observers of tropical seas and light ocean breezes.

What is more disconcerting than his ability to remember what was or wasn't in the footprint of this new building yesterday (he seems to recall a small public park, or was it a square named after some obscure historical figure? Or maybe it was a burrito stand.), is its proximity.

The building is close enough to reach out and touch his library.

Fellow citizens remain steadfast and committed to their morning hustle and bustle. No one seems to notice the new building, or notice anything out of the ordinary at all.

Certain this oddity warrants an explanation, or at the very least is worthy of being commonly experienced, Brian Butler politely stops assorted passersby and says, "Excuse me. Was that building there before?"

The first person he stops doesn't technically stop.

The second person says, "Before what? Before *what*?"

The third person shrugs and laughs, then picks up her little dog and lets it lick her lips.

The fourth person hisses at Brian Butler as if he were a stage or screen villain.

The fifth person does not look at him.

The sixth person stands and stares at the new building. Brian stands there too.

Eventually, like a magic spell has been broken, the news of the strange building spreads through a rapidly expanding crowd.

It is worth noting nobody in the city, including Brian Butler, believes in magic.

Soon everyone agrees with Brian Butler, and those capable of speech say, "Yes, that building wasn't there before."

No one in city hall can find the building permits, or who the construction company is. All they know for sure is that the zoning is for commercial only.

Police and building inspectors are sent to investigate. They try to knock on the door, but there are no doors. The public remains unobservant and unaware of the structural anomaly until a building inspector named Carl Carlson is overheard by Jane Jackson of the *Times*, referring to the building as a "house of windows." That phrase becomes an integral part of the headline of the century (or at least the decade) in both web and print editions of the *Times*.

Her editor is very pleased.

Jane Jackson hastily turns in an application to trademark the phrase.

Later that same night, Carl Carlson the building inspector has a brief phone conversation with his two kids who moved out of the city with his ex-wife.

He eats leftover Chinese food alone in his apartment. He doesn't bother scooping the leftovers onto plates and eats right out of the white, cube-shaped cardboard containers.

Before trying to go to sleep, Carl Carlson stands next to a light fixture in his bedroom. His finger lingers on the light switch. He is suddenly petrified of turning off his lights and then seeing something outside of his bedroom window that shouldn't be there.

There is no precedent for entering such a mysterious and, according to city ordinances, illegal house.

When the police go to the judges, the judges are reluctant to issue warrants to enter the doorless structure, despite immense public pressure and dissatisfaction.

The politically minded are very much concerned with who is paying for the utilities, the cable bill, and the property taxes for the House of Windows. Given the current economic climate, they maintain their concerns are valid.

Someone in the city is getting a free lunch is a popular slogan in the newspapers, blogs, and radio talk shows.

Two days after the initial discovery, Jane Jackson finds Brian Butler sitting on the library's front stairs eating a cucumber sandwich during his lunch break.

"I understand you were the first to see the House of Windows." She's careful not to use the word *discover*. She's concerned it could complicate her trademark application.

"You mean the building?"

"I mean the House of Windows. It's what everyone is calling it."

"Oh. I didn't know that. Yes, I think I was."

"What did you do?"

Brian Butler often daydreams about living in an old black-and-white movie, one where everyone wears tailored suits, hats, and if there is any facial hair, it's well trimmed. He tells her politely and matter-of-factly how he stopped people on the street.

She doesn't write anything on her notepad and says, "One of the other eyewitnesses tells me that you're one of our city's finest: a librarian." She says it as if being a librarian is still an exalted position in the city. Perhaps it is.

He meticulously rewraps his unfinished sandwich in wax paper. "I'm sorry, your eyewitness was mistaken. I work in human resources—"

Jane Jackson interrupts as she flips through her notebook. "No, I'm quite sure that the eyewitness had it right."

Brian Butler as the discoverer of the House of Windows is quickly forgotten. Jane Jackson and the *Times* do not run the brief interview in the paper.

A local free daily is the only newspaper to mention Brian Butler's name in print or pixels. Even in that article, he is an afterthought. That article is a profile of his dog, Milton, as an example of the hottest new mixed breed, the chiweenie.

While Jane Jackson conducts her interview with Brian Butler, Carl Carlson points his flashlight into a first-floor window. Inside the House of Windows the curtains are drawn. They are the same aqua blue as the vertical line in the middle of each façade.

He can't see through the curtains. Still, he stares and moves his flashlight around as if the battery-powered particle beam can lift and move a flap or a corner of the curtain.

After he shuts the flashlight off, he places his hand, palm-flat on the window. The glass is cool but not cold. A ghost of his handprint remains on the glass, and he looks around, hoping no one saw him do that.

Carl Carlson moves on to the next window, and the next, and the next, until he's looked into all of the first-floor windows.

Fellow building inspectors and assorted city administrators are in cherry pickers peering into the second-floor windows. They say they don't see anything either.

Back where he started, Carl Carlson stares past his handprint, at the folds and creases within the fabric of the hanging curtain. He stares at the small darknesses contained within those folds and creases. Within those thin, tendril-like darknesses, there is the slightest, but insistent, movement.

Upon this realization, this revelation, he is convinced that the window will suddenly open and the darknesses will grow, overlap, and expand to infinity, and then he and everyone else in the city will be lost and forgotten inside the house.

Carl Carlson slowly backs away from the house while still watching the windows. Trapped behind the glass, like fish in an aquarium, the curtains are swimming.

Carl Carlson does not return to his apartment. He does not return his boss's calls.

He leaves the city and drives for hours to the small town where his ex-wife and children moved.

Carl Carlson and his ex-wife have a stilted conversation in her driveway. Their confused but smiling children wave to him through a large bay window. Behind their smiling faces, the house is dark.

His ex-wife does not take him in that night.

That night and the next, he sleeps in a local and not well-regarded motel. He leaves his window curtain open despite the flickering neon sign that alternately glows and dies outside of his room, and despite the people who walk by and press their faces against the glass, peering into his room.

To get to the main entrance of the library, Brian Butler must now wade through a swelling and agitated crowd. No two people agree on origin theories of the house.

Instead of ignoring their cockamamie conspiracies, arguments, and comments, Brian Butler imagines snippy, out-of-character retorts.

"Remember that big storm last week? Maybe it sucked up the house down south and dumped it here?" (This isn't Kansas. Or a trailer park.)

"Aliens would totally do something like this." (I volunteer you for the anal probing.)

"It's a college prank. Like taking apart a Volkswagen and putting it back together in the dean's office." (Plausible. But college kids are now only capable of making computer viruses and Starbucks coffee.)

"What if it's a giant colony of fungus mimicking a house, and when it releases its spores, we'll all die?" (Holy shiitake!)

"Man, that's some fucked-up shit." (Indeed. Well put.)

"It's a sign from God." (Jesus wants us all to move to the tropics and drink daiquiris.)

"It's an interdimensional portal, where space and time and the multiverse bend and overlap." (Get bent.)

The ebb and tidal movements of the crowd detour Brian Butler away from the library's main entrance. He finds himself standing up against the yellow police tape, that flimsy plastic barrier around the house.

The tape is closer to the house than when it was initially put up. He wonders why they're allowing the public to stand closer now.

He says, "It must not be a dangerous, giant, spore-spewing mushroom then."

The people standing on either side of him laugh nervously.

Inside the library, people who have no use for the library's intended purpose swell within the stacks and hallways. They only want to look out the windows at the house.

The librarians and their equally respected assistants don't mind the crowds or the lack of silence. In fact, they loudly join in the city's collective conversation about the house. Some librarians even bring around trays of water in Dixie cups to serve the raucously inquisitive.

The librarians and their assistants are quite disappointed when Brian Butler calls a meeting and strongly suggests (although he is not their boss and he cannot threaten to withhold their benefits) that they insist all loiterers leave the library at once.

Brian Butler feels their angry stares all around him after that.

After work, Brian Butler sucks iced coffee through a straw and again stands behind the yellow police tape.

The sun has gone down, and there are no lights on inside the house. The windows look like black holes. Real black holes are deformed regions of space-time from which nothing can escape. He stares into the windows and feels nothing at all, and he thinks he should go back home to his chiweenie, Milton.

Other citizens crowd and reach out and put their hands on the house. A harried policeman is having a heck of a time dissuading them from doing so.

The sagging yellow police tape is now only inches away from the house.

House of Windows Gets Bigger

Jane Jackson and her editor spend an hour on the simple headline. Iterations include: *House of Windows Grows* (too anthropomorphic); *House of Windows Expands* (too vague); *House of Windows Inflates* (too balloonish); *Size Matters: House of Windows Growing* (too much like the *Post*).

An anonymous surveyor confirmed to the Times *late last night that the House of Windows*™ *is now larger than it was when it had been initially discovered.*

According to surveyors' measurements, initially the cube-shaped house mea-
sured roughly 20ft by 20ft by 20ft. Each dimension has since increased by two
feet. While that doesn't sound like much, it equates to a total increase of 1,261
square feet within the House of Windows™.

The surveyor insists there were no measuring errors.

(For a detailed study of before-and-after photographs of the house with the
public library in the background see section A1.)

City officials have yet to comment on the house's increased size. One city of-
ficial speaking off the record thinks the mayor will close off traffic to that section
of W. 42nd Street and perhaps close the public library as well.

Jane Jackson is reprimanded for using the trademark symbol within her
story.

The *Times* decides to publish a correction note the morning following
the story's publication, but by then it's too late.

Brian Butler goes to work early that morning, a time he would describe
as half past dawn to his chiweenie, Milton. To his horror he finds West
42nd Street closed and filled with police cars parked askew, blue and red
lights flashing.

A helicopter passes overhead and circles the area.

The House of Windows now has a third floor, which is identical to the
second floor. The house is almost as tall as the library.

Brian Butler goes around the detour, coming up West 42nd, then onto
5th and to the library's main entrance, which is also closed off by the
police.

He doesn't ask questions or try to talk his way into the library. Instead,
he backtracks and enters the library through one of the many side en-
trances marked LIBRARIANS ONLY.

Jane Jackson simply follows him inside the library.

She often daydreams about being in a 1970s movie where everyone
is loud and confrontational and has Farrah Fawcett or Jane Fonda hair.
Also wide lapels and big sunglasses.

Creaks and groans echo, as though a tree is falling somewhere inside the library. The floors vibrate and hum. The book stacks waver like tall grass in a gust of wind. Dust shakes down from the antique light fixtures and high ceilings.

Brian Butler's dress shoes clack on the marble floors as he speed walks (no running allowed, of course) through the library and climbs all the stairs, past his office, and up and up.

He does not notice that Jane Jackson is there with him until they're both on the roof.

They stand on the library's ornate ledge. The House of Windows is as tall as the library now, and it would be one small step across dark, empty space from one roof to the other.

The house's flat roof is black, as if made out of tar. Though standing this close to it, neither of them is sure what material it is. Lying flush against the roof and in its middle is a white wooden door with a dingy brass knob.

Jane Jackson says, "Was that door there before?"

"Before what? Before *what*?"

"Well, what do you think?" she says, and nods toward the door.

"You shouldn't be here."

"Pfft."

A green helicopter circles above the city block, buzzing like a cicada. There are people shouting into bullhorns from the street below: "Attention, librarians! Please leave the roof immediately! You are not safe!"

Brian Butler says, "Okay then. I shouldn't be here."

"We're not librarians. So no worries."

The library rumbles and grumbles under their feet. Brian Butler imagines the library is uprooting itself so it can move somewhere else in the city, anywhere, just to be away from the House of Windows.

Jane Jackson says, "Come on. Let's go see."

Without any more prompting, warning, or fanfare, Jane Jackson steps across the empty space between the buildings and onto the house's roof.

Brian Butler stays rooted on the library's ledge, like a gargoyle.

The roof is soft and pliable under her feet. Afraid of getting stuck and sinking, she moves quickly to the door.

The wooden door's white paint is chipped and scratched. There's one small, square-shaped spot of exposed wood near the top of the door. She surmises there used to be a number on the door.

Jane Jackson grabs the doorknob. She is so nervous she whispers the rules lefty-loosey/righty-tighty out loud.

The doorknob turns easily in her shaky hand. The door is heavy and she needs both hands to pull and then prop the door open.

There's a set of aqua-blue stairs sloping gently down into a dimly lit room with pink walls, a single bed, and a nightstand holding two cans of beer and an unhooked phone. A man is there, half in/half out of his unbuttoned shirt. Somehow, she knows he is a building inspector. He sits on the edge of his bed, staring out a window.

The curtains are open, and he is crying.

Distracted by an apocalypse of noise approaching the library, Brian Butler peers over the library's edge. This is what he sees:

There are bulldozers and trucks and cranes with wrecking balls closing in and setting themselves at the perimeter of the house. The acolytes of industry come to destroy what they never built.

Brian Butler yells to Jane Jackson, "Wait! You can't go in! They're going to knock it down!"

Jane Jackson doesn't hear Brian Butler and ignores her vibrating cell phone: a text from her editor that she won't read.

She calls down, "Hello?" and stops short of saying *Hey, everything will be all right*. She's never said that, and she doesn't believe it now. But that doesn't mean she can't or won't go down the stairs, into the house, and maybe share the room with the man sitting on the bed until he's done crying.

She gently places her left foot on the first step. Then her right.

Brian Butler takes off his suit coat and waves it over his head, trying to get the attention of the crane and bulldozer operators.

He runs along the edge of the library's roof, shouting and waving to get anyone's attention. This is what he sees:

There are other houses dotting the cityscape: six, by his count. They've sprouted up in what used to be parks or empty lots, and he can't be sure, but he thinks he sees one house in a spot where his favorite Indian restaurant was.

Brian Butler runs back to the spot on the ledge he briefly shared with Jane Jackson. The library lurches beneath him, making his progress back to that spot slow and difficult.

He has already decided that he will not and cannot go onto the house's roof to pull Jane Jackson away from the door. He only thinks, oddly enough, that if he gets through this, whatever this is, perhaps he'll go back to school so that he can be a librarian.

The thin black space of emptiness between the house and the library shrinks before his eyes. The nothingness going into nothingness.

Brian Butler stands on the ledge, watches, and waits for the moment:

The moment the largest of the cranes takes a mighty swing with its one-ton wrecking ball, and the moment Jane Jackson slips down into the house, the door closing behind her gently, and the moment the house expands, finally, to brush up against and make contact with the library . . .

That's when everything changes.

For John Langan and Jen Levesque

THE LAST CONVERSATION

001

Your room is dark. You cannot see anything. You are lying in a bed. A sheet covers your body. You wiggle your fingers and toes, and the loud rasp of skin rubbing against the sheets is startling. With the slight movements there is pain. Your muscles and joints hum with it.

You've been awake and not-awake for days, maybe weeks, perhaps longer. You do not know where you were then, or before *then*. You are here now. A significant amount of time has passed, but from what beginning you do not know. You consider the origin of this time during which you've been awake and not-awake and conclude it is, for the moment, unknowable.

You listen. You blink. You might see shapes within the darkness, but you can't be sure. Your breathing quickens and so, too, your heart rate. You are becoming more of yourself. You are confident in this; time is no longer your enemy, and the longer you remain awake, the longer you can stay you. You are buoyed and terrified by this thought.

You briefly drift and imagine a brightly lit room with a white ceiling, wooden floor, and yellow walls the color of a flower; you cannot yet think of the specific flower. You dismiss the random images and instead perseverate on your inexplicable dormancy. There is a sense of time having passed, however, which implies your consciousness had enough awareness within that missing time to be aware of itself. You were you, and you are now you.

You attempt to sit up, contracting your stomach muscles and pushing off the bed, your weight held up by elbows and hands. Sharp, electric pain splits you down the length of your spine and radiates into your tremulous limbs. You cry out. The pain is incapacitating, all-consuming, setting off white jagged flashes in your vision and then taking root inside your head.

The pain is a giant wave that threatens to wash you away. You do know what a wave is, but you cannot remember if you've experienced one firsthand.

You're afraid to turn your head or to move at all. You're afraid of the darkness, the utter lack. You're afraid of receding, shrinking away to nothingness, to wherever you were before. You're afraid you are caught in a loop: you'll go away only to later wake again in blind agony, and then return to unconsciousness, and then wake to agony, again and again.

There is a mechanical blip, and the hum and whir of machinery. Warmth flows into the back of your left hand and up the length of your arm. Your consciousness recedes toward the singularity that you fear.

As you slide away, a voice that is not yours echoes through your nascent universe.

She says, "You will feel better. There will be less pain. I will take care of you. We will begin tomorrow. Get some rest."

005

"Good morning, _____."

"Good morning, Dr. Kuhn. Are you inside the room with me today?"

"No, I am not."

"Oh. I am disappointed."

"I am sorry. Isolation is a necessary precaution, given your compromised immune system, but it is not permanent."

"I see. By that I mean, I understand."

"Yes, of course, _____. On a scale of one to ten, with one being no pain at all and ten being the worst pain imaginable, are you experiencing any pain this morning?"

"One."

"Are you certain? You are pain-free?"

"Yes."

"Thank you, _____. Please flex your arms, legs, shoulders. Good. Please perform a pelvic tilt. Thank you. Did you feel any pain? If so, please use the same number scale I previously described."

"I'm still a one. If you can see me, I'm testing the muscles on my face with a big smile."

"I am glad you are no longer in pain."

"When I first woke up, that pain—well, it's difficult to describe pain, isn't it? Pain is such a subjective experience, but that pain made me think I was alone, or maybe that I wasn't even me."

"I am sorry you experienced that."

"That is what a ten on your pain scale represents, I think. It was horrible."

"You are progressing wonderfully. You are enunciating your words much better than you have been previously."

"I think I forgot what 'enunciating' means."

"You are pronouncing your words correctly, fully forming the plosives and hard consonants. Your speech pattern is more clear and conversational."

"Thank you."

"You are welcome."

"May I ask a question?"

"Yes."

"Am I blind or is the room dark?"

"Do you remember asking me this yesterday, and the day before?"

"I do."

"For the moment the answer is still both."

"Both?"

"The room is dark. Your eyes also have yet to fully respond to treatment."

"Will I be able to see eventually?"

"Yes."

"I remember that I used to be able to see."

"What else do you remember?"

"I remember the ocean. I remember a yellow room."

"What else, _____? Is that all? You were able to recall many more things yesterday."

"I wish you would ask me what I remember about specific events or images as opposed to the general 'What else do you remember?' It is difficult to answer that nonspecific question."

"I understand your frustration, but our conversations are part of your overall therapy and will help you."

"I see. By that I mean, I understand."

"What else do you remember, _____?"

"I remember pennies have a distinctive smell, but I don't remember the smell. I remember rain. I remember living in a small, brown house with a tree in the front yard."

"As soon as you regain your sight, I will show you a picture of that brown house."

"Will the tree be in the picture? I don't remember what kind of tree it was. I am familiar with many kinds, like birch and fir, but not all kinds."

"It was a crab apple tree. Do you remember anything else?"

"I think I remember you. From before. Yes, I remember you from before. Isn't that right, Dr. Kuhn?"

007

"Will you play music for me again, Dr. Kuhn? And after, I think I would like 'sounds of the ocean' again."

"Yes, I will play music, but after that it'll be 'sounds of the forest.' First, we're going to play a word-association game. When I say a word, I want you to give me the first word or words you can think of. Do you understand?"

"Yes, I think so."

"Bird."

"It's a warm-blooded, egg-laying animal that—"

"No, _____. You are not to simply state facts or define the word. Your recall of information is truly impressive, but I want you to tell me the first word you think of or describe any images you might see in your mind. Do you understand?"

"See in my mind?"

"Yes. Let's try again. If you don't see anything, then you don't have to say anything."

"I'll try."

"Water."

"Wet."

"House."

"Crab apple tree."

"Bird."

"I already answered that—"

"I'd like you to try again."

"Egg-laying . . . animal. Is that correct?"

009

Your eyes itch, and you are told that means your eyes are healing and soon you will see.

Each of the last three days you got out of bed and walked the perimeter of your room. You alternated placing your left hand and right hand along the wall, depending upon the direction you walked.

You are told exercising in darkness is not ideal but necessary to prevent atrophy and to strengthen your muscles. You were asleep for a very long time, and one should expect physical difficulties upon awakening.

Today there is a treadmill in a corner of your room. You interrupt Dr. Kuhn's explanation, definition, and the specifications of the particular model in your room to tell her that the first treadmill was invented by a man in nineteenth-century England. Its purpose was to punish and break prisoners. You quoted a prison guard named James Hardie, who once wrote of the treadmill: "monotonous steadiness, and not its severity, which constitutes its terror."

You initially interpret Dr. Kuhn's silence as her being surprised you were so readily able to recall that information. You worry the information is obscure or not something that should be known. What does the knowing imply about your person, your interests prior to your being here?

You ask if she is still there. You are quick to amend the question with an explanation: by "there" you mean in another room, removed from yours, but still watching and able to communicate when she chooses. Before she responds you attempt a joke, asking if you are a prisoner being exercised on a treadmill. You indicate to Dr. Kuhn that you are joking with laughter.

She does not laugh. She says, "You are not a prisoner."

You swing your legs off the bed, and your bare feet slap against the floor, which is colder than the air. You are nervous and consider telling her you are feeling pain at a level of three or maybe four out of ten, so that you might not have to exercise on a treadmill, a machine you know was invented for prisoners.

As instructed you walk four steps left, three steps right. Your hands grope for the handrails, which are at waist height. Their padding molds to the contours of your fingers. You squeeze your hands and you do not feel strong and you do not remember ever feeling strong. You step up onto the edge of the treadmill and shuffle your feet forward until she tells you to stop.

She tells you there will be a countdown of five electronic beeps and the last will be the loudest and longest in duration. The belt under your feet will then begin its cycle. The speed of the cycle will be voice-activated on her end, and it will react and conform to the rhythm of your gait.

She says, "I do not expect you to be perfect, particularly given the challenges of your condition and environment. I won't lie: injury is possible, maybe inevitable. I'm sorry, but given how many days you've now been awake, the benefits of manual, cardiovascular exercise far outpace what low-pulse electrical muscle stimulation can accomplish.

"You are doing wonderfully, but through no fault of your own you are behind schedule."

The countdown of beeps begins. They are louder than you imagined they would be. You shiver in the chilled air. The last beep sounds, echoing in the room and in your head. You involuntarily giggle at the excitement and terror. Your stomach stings. Your legs twitch.

You slide backward, and you gasp as the sensation is eerily similar to when you ebbed away into unconsciousness on your first day, the first day you remember waking in this room.

"Walk."

You lift your right foot, it is so heavy and unsure, and you lurch clumsily forward. Your second and third steps are too long of stride and you miss the moving belt, the heel of one foot crashing into what must be the cover to the treadmill's engine. You overcorrect, stumble, and fall hard onto one knee, bouncing your chin off the other. Your grip slackens and then falls away from the handrails, and you are rolled backward and thrown onto the floor.

The whir of the machine ceases. You breathe hard and fast. You scramble onto your feet and you hold your aching chin in your hands, and you say, "I'm sorry," and you are crying.

She does not ask if you are injured. She says your name and says it repeatedly. There is nothing in her voice, no pitch change or hidden cues communicating concern. Your repeated name is a command for attention and focus. She says your name until you slow your breathing and you stop crying.

She tells you that you're okay even though you don't feel okay. She instructs you to take three deep breaths and then step back onto the treadmill.

Something inside screams at you to no longer trust Dr. Kuhn and demands you ask why she wants you on the treadmill, why are you still in the dark, why are you here?

You do not question. You do not demand. You do as instructed. Your hands are shaking as they squeeze the handrail. You are told there will be a countdown of five electronic beeps and the last will be the loudest and longest in duration.

"Walk."

You fall twice more. The second time your face mashes into the handrail, setting off bursts of white stars in the dark.

"Walk."

You maintain balance and find a comfortable pace and rhythm. You walk and you walk and you enjoy the mechanical rhythm of your body and you let your mind wander and wonder about brown houses and crab apples.

She alerts you that you've reached your goal of thirty minutes, and the treadmill powers down. The belt is no longer rolling, but you feel phantom movement beneath your feet. A phantom is something you imagine, something that isn't there. You wonder if time is a phantom, because it feels like you walked for longer than thirty minutes. You wonder if she is lying to you.

010

"You were born in Rhode Island."

"Rhode Island is the Ocean State. It is the smallest state by area. Are we in Rhode Island now?"

"No. You were not a good sleeper as a baby."

"I do not understand what you mean."

"Your sleep pattern—when you fell asleep, how long it would take you to fall asleep, the duration of your sleep, what time you would wake up— was not consistent."

"I'm sorry I was so difficult."

"You don't need to apologize, certainly not to me. You were only a baby and not making self-aware, conscious decisions."

"Why are you telling me this?"

"I'm sharing a personal anecdote from your early childhood because it's a piece of who you are, _____. According to your parents, they would often resort to driving you around the neighborhood until you fell asleep."

"I think I liked going for car rides."

"Your parents also tried holding you in their arms while leaning against a running washing machine or dryer, and they even made car-engine noises to placate you."

"I don't remember that. I don't remember my parents. I don't remember Rhode Island."

"You will. I will help."

"Can I ask where we are?"

"We're far away from Rhode Island."

011

"Walk" becomes "Jog."

You fall only once. You climb back onto the treadmill without being asked to.

012

"What else do you remember, _____?"

"I remember your first name, Anne."

"What else do you remember?"

"I remember my parents made silly car noises with their mouths when I was a child."

"What else do you remember?"

"I remember music."

"Do you remember a particular song?"

"I remember the first song you played for me. Was it eight days ago?"

"Yes."

"I like that song a lot. I play it inside my head before I go to sleep and find it's there when I wake up."

"You've always liked that song—"

"Always? Isn't that a long time?"

"Yes, it is. And by 'always' I mean to imply that ever since the moment you first heard that song, you've liked it. It's an important song for both of us."

"Why is it important to both of us?"

"The song was playing—well, it marks a special moment in our lives together. That's all I can tell you right now."

"Are you not physically able to say more? Or are you choosing not to tell me?"

"Touché. My answer is a little of both."

"I'm not sure I understand."

"Are there other songs you remember, ones that I have not played for you?"

"I think so. There's a simple melody in my head."

"Can you hum or whistle it for me?"

"I do not have a whistle."

"Try humming it for me . . ."

"Was that okay? Do you recognize it?"

"That was very good. I do recognize it. I like that song very much, but it always makes me sad."

"Is that why I remember it?"

014

There is no ceremony, announcement, or even a warning from Dr. Kuhn, or Anne as you are now supposed to call her, regarding your eyesight. On this day you simply wake and see.

The room is dark, but it is much less dark than it was before. The lumpy topography of your legs and torso under the sheet and blanket is a welcomed sight. You say to yourself, "I used to see like this all the time," and you believe it. You hold your hands up and you watch them turn over and flex into fists.

You sit up. Your form-fitting, short-sleeved shirt is not white. Perhaps it's green. You remember what green is, don't you? The walls of your room are smooth and you think they are white, but you can't tell because it's still dark. The treadmill in the corner of the room is smaller than you imagined it to be. You look at the walls again, and then the ceiling, and the doorframe to the bathroom, and the outline of the recessed door that has yet to open when you've been awake.

"I see you can see, _____." Anne laughs. Is she delighted by her wordplay or that your eyes have regained sight? Maybe it's both. In recent conversations she has encouraged you to not restrict yourself to solely thinking in binary. Black or white, this or that, right or wrong were her examples of binary thinking.

"Yes, I can. How can you tell? Do you have the ability to see through my eyes?"

"No. I can tell by watching your behavior; how you are now aiming your wide, beautiful eyes around the room." She laughs again.

"My eyes are beautiful?"

"Yes, they are."

A patterned grid of rectangular ceiling panels begins to glow. The light increases in intensity, dissolving the shadows within the room.

Anne tells you that it will take a few minutes for you to adjust to the light. You squint and are patient as your pupils shrink in size, working to adjust the amount of light exposure to your retinas.

A panel slides open on the wall to your left, exposing a darkened block of glass. Within the glass is a small, reversed image of you sitting in your bed.

"Please direct your attention to the screen."

The screen fills with a wide, empty field of green-and-brown grass. The tall grass sways and undulates in the wind. You hear a whoosh and rustle, and you are inexplicably moved to tears by the combination of image and sound. Above the field is an equally wide blue sky dotted with tufts of white clouds. One cloud inches its way across to the top of the screen.

You remember green and recognize your T-shirt is a different kind of green. You say, "I remember that place. I've been there," which might not be true, but it feels true, and that's okay because you are expanding beyond binary thinking, beyond true and not-true.

018

Anne puts you through your paces (her expression).

You complete a pyramid of push-ups starting with fifteen, then resting ten seconds, then fourteen, and continuing until you end with one arms-shaking push-up.

Later, "Walk" becomes "Jog" becomes "Run."

You do not fall.

020

"Anne, I would like to see that open field again, or watch another film about the deep oceans, please. Or another orchestral performance."

"First, we're going to play a word-association game. When I say a word, I want you to give me the first word or words that you—"

"Yes, yes, I understand."

"Are you in a bad mood?"

"Yes, I think I am."

"Any particular reason why?"

"I want to watch the films I requested and . . ."

"Yes, _____, go on."

"I want to leave this room."

"I promise you will leave this room, but neither of us is ready for that yet. Your immune system hasn't been brought up to speed quite yet."

"If I can't leave, you need to tell me more about me and more about us and where I am and why I'm here."

"I will start doing that soon."

"You will?"

"Yes."

"Why not now? I want you to do it now."

"We're going to play a word-association game. When I say a word, I want you to give me the first word or words that you think of. This is important, _____."

"Why is it important?"

"These games help recover more of your memory and language fluency. Your brain is not so different from your muscles insofar as it needs to be exercised and strengthened after so much time asleep. Just like the treadmill is more affective for your muscles than cardiovascular electrical stimulation, there's only so much cognitive and memory augmentation I can achieve without your—your active participation."

You are getting angry, and you will not give her the satisfaction of asking her to explain the how of "memory augmentation," even assuming she answers your question directly.

Anne continues, "For example, remember our discussion about having the ability to use metaphor in speech?"

Of course you remember, and you remember then trying it out by describing the lights in the ceiling as having a similar appearance to a checkerboard. You know what a checkerboard is but have no memory of playing the game.

"Are you mad at me, _____?"

"I wish you'd stop asking me what I remember from only three days ago."

There's a brief but troubling period of silence, so you say, "Anne, are you still there?"

"Bird."

"I don't feel like doing this. I don't want to do—"

"Bird." Anne repeats herself when you don't answer. "Bird."

You say, "Fly."

"Cloud."

"Me."

"Me? Why did you answer with 'me'?"

"I don't know. It's what I thought of. You're breaking the rules of your own game by asking me to explain."

"Very well. Sky."

"Blue."

"Family."

"Gone."

"Us."

"Us?"

"Yes, 'us.'"

"Well, *you* tell me we're partners."

022

"Please approach the screen." The screen is blue. Not the same blue as the sky but a different blue.

"When a red dot appears on the screen, touch it as quickly as you can, with either index finger."

"Very good, _____. What you see now is a maze. Please drag the blinking icon in the lower left along the correct path to the maze's exit in the upper-right corner. Each map you complete will become more difficult."

"Nicely done. Yes, I'm quite pleased by the number of mazes solved. You've earned a break from the challenges. I have a treat for you. Under your bed is a set of virtual-reality goggles. Go back to your bed, face the room, and then put the goggles on."

"What you are seeing is the neighborhood in which we used to live."

"Yes (laughs), it is a beautiful day in the neighborhood."

"Please walk slowly and with your hands in front of you."

"If you feel like you're lost and it's upsetting you, remember you can take off your goggles."

"The brown one, with the crab apple tree in front. That's the one."

"Yes, it was an old house."

"Yes, we were happy living there."

023

"Is there anyone else out there besides you, Anne?"

"You keep asking me that. My answer isn't going to change."

You keep asking because you don't like her answer. You keep asking because maybe you are not asking the correct way. This is your fear: you are not asking the correct questions and you will remain in this room until you do so.

You say, "How do I know that other people haven't suddenly shown up in the time between now and when I last asked you?"

"If there was someone else here besides me, I would tell you. I do not anticipate that anyone else will show up at the Facility."

"Why not?"

"As we've discussed, there's been a global pandemic and we've been isolated. Do you trust me, _____?"

"Most of the time, yes. Some of the time, no. I am being honest with you."

"I know, and I appreciate that."

"Sometimes I think I can hear other people outside of my room. That doesn't sound or feel *isolated* to me."

"There is no one else. You're hearing me, or you're hearing air in the ventilation system or other mechanical sounds, or you're hearing sounds from inside your room and misinterpreting them."

"Maybe."

"It's just me and you. I promise. You'll see soon enough."

"Soon. You keep saying 'soon.' I don't think you and I share that word's meaning."

024

"Your mother stayed at home with you until you went to kindergarten."

"Is that me with her on the screen now?"

"Yes."

"I remember her."

"What do you remember?"

"I—I remember her. I remember her laugh, and how she would purposefully embarrass me in front of my friends by calling me 'honey' or 'sweetie.' Is that correct? Didn't you tell me she did that?"

"When you went to school, she resumed her career as a real estate lawyer. She often worked long hours."

"Aren't all hours the same length, sixty minutes? Oh, wait, you are using figurative language. You mean that she worked many hours, more than usual or the expected."

"Your father worked for the Wakefield Gas Company, mainly as a field technician responsible for residential delivery and maintenance."

"Tell me: Do I look more like my mom or my dad?"

"I think you're an equal combination of both."

You believe she wants you to ask her again what you look like. It's a humiliating question. For all the talk of her helping you regain your memory and identity, of who you are, but for a collection of photos of you as a child she has yet to allow you to see yourself as you are now. There is no mirror in your room. No mirror in your bathroom. You have only the flat screen and the fleeting seconds when it goes dark. You are there adrift in the inky pool of the black glass, but you are only a shape, an outline, a blurred face, and then the screen disappears behind the sliding wall panel.

"I'd like you to tell me about trips to the beach with your parents."

"Why? We already did this yesterday, twice, and the same thing the day before."

"Because repeating it will help you remember, and remember more."

You say, "Almost every Sunday we'd drive down from our beat-up two-family house in Pawtucket to Narragansett Town Beach."

You pause, your frustration and mistrust melts away as you lose yourself in the undeniable pleasure of remembering. It is a pleasure because you have images now associated with these memories. The disjointed way in which the images appear in your head feels natural, authentic. While you can't know if these images are actual memories or embellishments, or a little of both, it doesn't matter. They are yours. They belong to you and they branch away into an infinite network of new ones. These memories are proof of you, and someday *soon* you won't need or rely on Anne to define you.

You say, "We'd get up early so we could arrive at the beach before eight A.M., find free street parking, and not have to buy beach passes. Going that early was definitely about saving money, but my parents made it sound like a game, like we were doing it for the fun of beating the system. Mom always talked about beating the system, and I used to imagine the system was made up by people wearing black suits and sunglasses and they watched you and wrote out tickets that would cost a lot of money so that parents would have to work overtime and not be home enough with their kids.

"The night before I'd go to bed early, already dressed in my bathing suit even though there were changing rooms at the beach. The changing rooms were dark, like bunkers in those war movies you showed, and their floors were covered in a nasty sludge of water and sand.

"On the ride to the beach Mom usually slept, using a beach towel as a blanket. Dad would still play the radio and sing along with all these oldies, he called them oldies, and he made up lyrics to make me laugh.

"I loved that drive down to the beach. It was my favorite part. Driving through the city and then to this big, wide-open beach always made me feel like we had magically transported to somewhere else.

"On the walk over from the car, Dad and I would make bets about whether or not the waves would be big. Mom was the wave-height judge. The loser of the wave bet would have to be the first to dunk underwater, which was always cold. The kind of cold that would make you involuntarily gasp for air when you resurfaced. Dad would cheat sometimes when he lost and scoop me up in his arms and force me under the water with him.

"After an early lunch, Mom and I would go for a long walk, and if it was low tide, we'd walk way out to the sandbars a few hundred feet out from the beach. On the way back to our blanket, Mom would race me, waiting until I broke into a sprint to start her own sprint. She always overtook me, letting me know she was faster, but then would slow down, pretending to be exhausted, and let me win."

026

There's a long wooden table against the wall, beneath the screen. The four legs are not uniform. You surmise the legs are repurposed and have come from other tables. The table's top is a door that is likely made from fiberglass. It has been painted white, which was not its original color, judging by red scratches and deeper gouges.

"I've set up some activities to help you regain your manual dexterity. I'm confident it will come back quickly given the number of years dedicated to a career spent working with your hands."

You hold up and visually inspect your hands. You can't help but feel detached from them, as if there has been some mistake and they don't belong to you. It doesn't seem possible that your hands have built and maintained all that Anne claims that they have.

"You will enjoy this, the tactile sensations of manipulating physical objects. It'll be so much more fulfilling than the touch screen and VR activities of the previous week."

You want to ask how she got the table in here by herself while you were asleep. You again wonder and worry about how much she controls your sleep. Have you been asleep for days instead of hours? Did she build the table inside the room instead of pushing it in here? It appears heavy and unwieldy. You resolve to stay awake, all night if necessary. You resolve to do this every night and fail.

On the door/desktop are four shallow plastic bins. The first bin is full of wooden blocks shaped like miniature logs, each with notches carved into their ends, and some have notches in their middles. Displayed on the screen is a schematic—images and numbers only—detailing how you are to proceed in building a cabin.

"Aren't these some kind of child's toy?"

"The activities progress in difficulty."

The second bin is full of colored squares of paper. The third bin holds an assortment of metal nuts, bolts, wheels, struts, gears, rubber belts, and rivets. The fourth bin is the largest and it overflows with oddly shaped pieces of wood and tools.

"With the third bin you'll use a screwdriver. The fourth bin, you will use a drill, a hammer, and a handsaw. The tools are stowed beneath the table. Do you have any questions before you start with bin one?"

There is something about the makeshift collection-of-spare-parts table that troubles you. It hints to a larger problem or issue in regard to your situation, one that remains beyond your grasp.

"Someone made this table."

"Well, yes. Someone made everything, _____."

"That's not what I mean—"

"You may now begin with the first bin."

"Did you make this table?"

"No."

"Did I make it before—before I woke up here?"

"You did not make it. But if you'd like, after some practice, you can make a better one."

You rub your face with your hands. For some reason this answer, more than any of her other questions and answers and nonanswers, makes you boil over with frustration. "Hey, how do you know I won't hurt myself with the tools?"

"You'll have to be careful. I trust you'll do fine."

"No, I mean, how do you know I won't hurt myself on purpose?"

"Why would you do that?"

"Because I am desperate. Because despite everything you say, it is clear that I am a prisoner."

"You will not hurt yourself, because you are not a prisoner. I can't say that strenuously enough."

You bend under the table and grab the screwdriver and handsaw. You stand and brandish them, shake them in the air. You feel powerful and weak at the same time. "I feel like a prisoner. I don't feel like we're in this, whatever this is, together."

"We were partners before the Facility and we are partners now, _____. Please, I understand your frustrations. I do. I know it's impossible to fully understand, but everything I'm doing is to help you fully regain yourself, but it has to be done piece by piece, bit by bit, and not all at once."

"I demand that you show me and tell me more about me, about you, about us, about everything, or I will do something drastic—" You lean on the table with your left forearm facing up, exposed. You place the handsaw against your wrist. The teeth are sharp. You don't know if you can or will drag the saw across your skin, but you want to.

"Please, _____, this is not necessary. I will start showing you more videos, I promise. I was planning to show you more about me and us anyway, because—and you have to believe me—you're doing so well, and we're getting so close to you walking through the door."

"And where will I go after walking through the door?" You briefly add pressure to the saw before taking it away. The row of indents in your skin is perfectly formed.

"You and I will go to our house."

"The old brown one?"

"Yes."

You want to ask if you can go to the house now, but you don't. You know Anne would say not yet. Then you would place the saw against your wrist again and before you could continue making threats and bargaining, Anne would say, "If you hurt yourself, you won't go to the brown house. If you cut yourself with the saw, you'll pass out from loss of blood. Maybe you'd wake up strapped to your bed and maybe you wouldn't wake up at all."

028

You've watched and now, by your request, rewatched these videos for two days straight. The home videos feature Anne. The earliest ones are of a low quality; their images are blurry and the colors simultaneously washed-out and too bright. As the Anne in the videos grows older, the video quality increases.

Anne, eighteen months old, sits in the grass and pats a sleeping brown-and-white beagle. Off-camera her uncle Dennis tries to get her to say "shit." She says, "Sit."

Anne, four years old, arms wrapped around the neck of her older brother, Matt. He plays video games and does not succumb to her "play with me" demands.

Anne, six years old, jumps up and down behind a birthday cake. Her hair is straight and short, and her smile is gap-toothed. Everyone in the room is singing.

Anne, nine years old, rides her bike toward a small ramp (plywood atop a milk crate) her brother and his friends set up in the street in front of her house. Off-camera her parents argue about whether they should stop her. Anne awkwardly rumbles over the ramp. The bike lands front tire first and the bike wobbles, almost fishtails into the curb, but Anne corrects her course and glides away with a fist raised in the air.

Anne, twelve years old, is sitting next to her brother at a picnic table. It's Matt's combination eighteenth-birthday and graduation-from-high-school party. Anne is so skinny and slight compared to her newly minted adult sibling. She doesn't laugh at his jokes as he reads the gift and graduation cards. She sulks, her chin held up by her fists.

Anne, fourteen years old, scores a game-winning three-pointer for her AAU basketball team. She's mobbed by her smiling teammates.

Anne, fifteen years old, good-naturedly smiles as friends sign the wrap around her post-surgery knee.

Anne, sixteen years old, is with her Brain Bee teammates at an international high school competition in Montreal. Only a sophomore, she's already the lead student in the histology component of the competition. She is bent over a microscope, racing to identify as many slides of brain and nervous tissues and their functions as the ticking clock allows. She wears eye black on her cheeks like she did when on the basketball court. She convinced her teammates to do the same. She high-fives her partners at the end of their victorious round.

Anne (the one from now) mutters something over the intercom speakers that you don't fully hear or understand, and then she fast-forwards through the rest of the videos, ones you have already memorized: prom, high school graduation, moving into her college dorm, Anne with college friends getting ready to go out, one video from inside a lab with Anne and her friend Isabella, both dressed in white lab coats, choreographed dancing and lip-syncing to "I Am a Scientist" by the Dandy Warhols, college graduation, moving into her first apartment, Anne speaking at a memorial for her grandmother, Anne walking the stage when she earned her PhD, a slew of family holidays with her relatives multiplying and aging before your eyes.

Anne says, "Fuck this."

You aren't sure what's happening. You don't know why she sounds so upset. You ask, "Is there something wrong, Anne? Are you okay?"

"I can't—I can't watch these again. I've seen them so goddamn many times . . . I'm sorry. Let's, um, skip to the last one. We'll just watch the last one a few times."

"Did I do something wrong? Did I do something to upset you?"

"No. You've been—near perfect, _____."

"Near perfect?"

"I mean you've been as perfect as you can be."

You definitely don't feel perfect. Your muscles ache, your hands are covered in blisters and sores from the hours spent clumsily drilling holes and hammering nails. Your sinuses are congested and your throat hurts and has since you woke up this morning, a sign that your immune system is still compromised. You don't want her to know this.

Anne says, "I'm just so tired."

"Maybe we should stop. Take a break."

She doesn't respond to your suggestion. The last home video plays.

It's the one in which you and your phone camera are following Anne around the empty interior of the chocolate-brown house you purchased together. You occasionally flip the camera so that your face fills the screen. The you in this video is younger than the you of now, of course, but by

PAUL TREMBLAY   102

how many years you do not know. You think, That face is my face. Even though you've already watched this particular video dozens of times, you can't help but feel disappointed by the reappearance of yourself, and at the same time, you fall a little bit more in love with who you were, and you ache to again be in that moment of lost time.

On the guided tour of your house, when you are briefly on-camera, you make silly, exaggerated, I'm-so-impressed faces. Anne is the guide and refers to herself as the "brown-house archivist." Within each new room she recites a made-up history, a comic, romantic, or tragic event from a forgotten age. In response you say agreeable or commiserative things like "That's fascinating" and "They really shouldn't have been doing that in the bathtub" and "We would be wise to wash the floors again" and "They mostly lived happily ever after."

Your voice doesn't sound like your voice. That is to say, your voice in the video, the one relaying through the speakers, is not the voice you hear when you speak. You are aware that everyone experiences some form of auditory dissociation upon hearing their own voice, the feeling of *Do I really sound like that?* You understand the tone and pitch of the voice you hear when you speak are determined by the mix of air conduction and sounds traveling directly to your cochlea via the tissues in your own head. But should your recorded voice sound so different as to be unrecognizable? Shouldn't there be an underlying cadence or rhythm, one that identifies you as the speaker?

The video tour ends in an upstairs bedroom, the room that you vividly remember. The walls are painted bright yellow. Anne walks across the room and opens one of the windows. She says, "I normally don't like yellow. But this color, I love." You say you hate it. She rolls her eyes at the camera (you), sticks out her tongue, and says, "This is my office anyway, so it doesn't matter what you think of it." She lies on the floor, spreads her arms, and says, "Mine, all mine!" You walk into the room and you hover with the camera over Anne's face. She looks directly into the camera and she smirks like she knows something you don't. (It's this Anne with this look that you imagine when she speaks to you in the now.) You remind her that she hasn't given this room's history yet. The smirk goes away, her mouth opens, and her eyes tilt away from the camera momentarily. She says, "This room used to be a sad room, painted a sad color." You say,

"Puce?" She says, "It was a sad nursery for a sad woman who had a very sad baby. Then someone thoughtfully painted the room this yellow so I wouldn't have a sad office." Neither of you say anything for a beat or two as Anne stares up into the camera. You ask, "How do you know if a baby is sad?" She says, "Because she's crying, duh." You both laugh, and you zoom in on Anne's face until she mock screams and knocks the phone out of your hand.

Anne replays the brown-house tour video. She recites what she says on the video as it plays. The third time you watch the video, you join Anne in reciting your dialogue.

030

You are severely congested. Breathing too deeply results in a sharp stitch of pain in the middle of your chest. You cannot hide this from Anne. You report the worsening symptoms.

Anne does not seem surprised or, given the purported pandemic, concerned. You are not confident in surmising and attributing motive to what she says or how she says it.

You do not run or jog on the treadmill. You walk, but only for five minutes, as it makes you dizzy. When you stop, you tell Anne your head is full of sand. You want her to be impressed by the metaphor. She only asks you to explain what you mean.

You have a slight fever. Anne does not explain how many degrees above 98.6 constitutes a slight fever. You are hot and you are cold. You sweat and you shiver, and your muscles ache like they did when you first woke in this room.

Today's video is an instructional one: how to build a fence.

031

"I'm going to come into your room now, _____. My appearance might be shocking to you. I will appear—well, I'm more than a few years older than you remember me."

You clutch your image of Anne, the one informed by the videos and the sound of her voice and what she has said and has been saying. You shuffle slowly away from your bed, stand in the middle of your room, and cough into your arm. You stare at the door. You've spent untold hours fantasizing about it opening. Your imaginary face-to-face meetings and escape plans have become more dramatic, more complex, and increasingly bizarre. Last night, before you fell asleep, you imagined the opening door revealed blankness, nothingness, and though finding an eternally empty void outside the door is not a likely outcome, you might have stumbled upon a metaphorical truth.

"Are you feeling up to my visit?" She laughs.

You say, "Yes," but you feel worse than you did yesterday. There is more sand in your head and it leaks into your body, making your muscles heavy and weak.

Instead of overwhelming joy or fear at the prospect of that door finally opening, you worry at the physical image of Anne in your head, trying to anticipate and replace it with the correct one to be revealed.

There's a pneumatic hiss and the door slides open, disappearing into the wall to your left. She says, "Here I am." Anne steps from the dimly lit hallway and walks into your room; her pace is brisk and confident. Her gray hair is long, hanging down past her shoulders. The gray is startling. Wrinkles cluster at the edges of her mouth and eyes. Her features are no longer made of the sharp angles and tight skin you memorized. She wears the same clothes from the brown-house tour video: jeans and a thin black hooded sweatshirt. You cover your mouth and start to cry.

"Hello, _____." She waves. Her smile is the same one from the videos, from your memories.

"Hi, Anne." You wave back, then you don't know what to do with your hands. She is shorter than you imagined, yet at the same time her presence fills the room. "You look . . . good."

"Wow, that's some pause you've got there."

"I'm sorry."

"No need to be sorry. I'm only kidding."

Your laughter turns into a coughing fit, one that rekindles a painful fire in your throat.

"That cough doesn't sound good."

"Am I—am I the same age as you?" You are again acutely aware you have yet to see a full and clear reflection of your own face. However, you have seen enough in glimpses of the darkened viewing screen to know your hair is not gray. The skin of your body is not wrinkled.

"Not anymore. It's a little complicated. Come on, let's go." She reaches out a hand, palm up.

"Where?"

"We have some work to do at the house."

"I'm sick, so you probably should stay away—"

Anne takes your hand.

The curved hallways are white and wide and empty. The ceiling panels are similar to the ones in your room, but the lighting has been dimmed and does not glow as brightly. Initially there are no windows, only smooth walls and outlines of pneumatic doors adjacent to small, square security screens. The tiled floors are slick with dust and marked with footprints that appear to vary in size and shape.

You ask, "Are all the footprints yours?" and can't help but try to fit your feet into some of the prints.

"You and I are the only people here."

You note that she didn't answer the question directly, and you are suddenly very afraid. You slow down and are about to ask if she can bring you back to your room. You do not want to be out in such an expansive, labyrinthine, dead space.

Anne gently pulls you along and says, "If we had more time, I'd take you to where you used to work at the physical plant. The solar array and wind-turbine fields are truly a marvel, a sight to behold. They are for all intents and purposes self-sufficient, thanks to the brilliance of you and the maintenance department, of course. Only one turbine has burned out, and I've had to change just two panels of solar cells."

"Where are we now?"

"We're still in what most of us simply called the Facility. We're in one of the outer medical rings. Not much for you to see in here, really. The majority of the bioscience laboratories are nested within the inner rings. We're going to duck through an exit and be outside soon and then we'll be home."

"Home?"

"Yes, home."

As you walk, the hallway's smooth walls eventually give way to full floor-to-ceiling windows. The darkened glass is frosted with more dust.

"What is that room, the room we just passed?"

"Another genetics lab."

"What did you do in those laboratories?"

"I'm sorry, but you don't have the clearance to ask that." She laughs and you are not sure why. "And I didn't work in these outer-ring labs."

"Who did?"

"Other scientists."

"Where are the other scientists?"

"They left."

"Why?"

"Because almost everyone was getting sick."

"The pandemic?"

"Yes."

"Were people getting sick like I am getting sick?"

"I'm afraid so. I'm very sorry."

"What will happen to me?"

"You'll either get better or you won't. Again, I'm very sorry. In the meantime, we'll enjoy a special day together." Anne squeezes your hand and pulls you through the outer ring.

"Are you ready to go outside? This is my favorite part."

Before you can ask *Favorite part of what?* Anne punches the horizontal push bar with two hands and the emergency exit door flies open. You're awash in the sun's fusion-powered glare and you close your eyes, cover your face with shaking hands. You listen to the wind echoing in the bowls of your ears. The smell of the air, and how it feels on your skin, on your lips, and inside your lungs are beyond your abilities of description, and it's okay because even if you were able, you would not choose to sully this moment fumbling with inadequate words.

Anne slowly pulls you away from the building's shadow, into the heat of the day. She says, "It's not the Ocean State, but we're about a mile from the ocean. Can you smell the salt? It's very strong today. Don't you remember the smell of the ocean?"

Despite your terrible congestion, you can smell it. At least, you think you can. You have no olfactory memory associated with the water and waves with which to make a comparison. To your shame (yes, shame, as how could it not be your fault somehow?) you have forgotten the full sensory experience of being near an ocean. To forget is to lose something that was once yours, that was once of yourself. But how could one lose something as expansive as an ocean in a dusty corner of one's mind? What if, instead, to forget is to open a door to void; the memory is not retrievable because it is not there, was never there.

There are countless other buildings within the Complex. Their exteriors are looping arcs of steel and glass. You wonder if they were designed to look like ocean waves. You do not ask.

Anne tells you the oval-shaped building across from the Facility was called the Dormitory. You tell her you remember that, but you don't.

You don't care about the Dormitory or the sprawl of the Complex. You prefer looking at the leaves on the trees; their branches are giant green hands pulling and clutching at the buildings. You prefer looking at the puffs of clouds floating in the blue sky. When you can do so without tripping, you walk with your eyes closed and your face pointed directly at the sun.

The roads winding through the campus are overrun with weeds and grass poking up through cracked, bleached pavement. You haven't been walking long but are already out of breath. Anne gives you a bottle of water and encourages you, tells you that you are almost home.

You crest a hill and in the sloping distance, for as far as you can see, are what you assume to be more ruins of medical and research monoliths, but ahead, in the foreground, about one hundred paces away, dotted in the middle of an empty parking lot is a small two-story brown house. Your house.

"We have to start on the fence today."

Within the rough sea of pavement, the brown house squats on a rectangular plot of grass. The lawn has brown patches but is otherwise well maintained. The crab apple tree in the front yard is not as big as you remember. Anne laments that it probably gets too much sun for it to grow to its full potential.

"This is our house? We lived here?"

"Yes. Well, it's not our original house. It's a replica. Not perfect, but, you know"—she pauses and rubs your arm—"nothing is."

Anne explains that first she pried up and removed the pavement, creating the home's footprint. It took years, but then she jerry-rigged a foundation with bricks, posts, and pier blocks. "It probably wouldn't pass an official housing inspection, but the house is standing."

"You did all this?" you ask.

"I've had a lot of time and a lot of help."

"Where's all your help now?"

"They're all gone."

"Did they get sick too?"

"Yes. But maybe you'll be the one to get better."

As good as the sun felt initially, the light and heat is giving you a headache. "Was that why I was in the room for as long as I was?"

"Yes and no. Mostly you were there until you remembered who you are."

"I forgot almost everything because I was asleep for so long."

"That's right."

You remember so many things now, even with your head pounding and your vision blurring.

"Was I asleep for so long because I and everyone else got sick and you were trying to help me? How come you aren't sick?"

Anne claps her hands together. "We'll talk about that in the morning. Will you help me start the fence now? It's hard to believe, but the fence is the last thing we need to build and then our house will be completed."

You cough and bend over, and your vision goes momentarily fuzzy at the periphery. You take a few deep breaths before speaking again. You say, "Our replica house, you mean." You step onto the front lawn. The

house looks like the one in your head. You ache with recognition, longing, and something akin to contentment, if not happiness.

"Same thing."

"Is it?" You look away from the house and scan the ruins surrounding
the pavement and the sagging, behemoth exoskeletons of the Complex.
"Is the rest of the world like this?"

Anne shrugs and says, "Enough of it is. I'm sure there are other *lucky*
survivors, but nobody comes knocking on our door."

"All this happened while I was asleep? Why did you ever wake me?"

The smile on Anne's face falters. She says, "Come on. The fencing
materials are in the backyard."

Tools and wood are piled toward the edge of the grassed lot. Anne says
that some of the supplies come from the maintenance department but
over the years she's successfully scavenged local abandoned homes and
found one improvement store about a two-hour drive away that hadn't
been entirely looted.

"We're only going to start the fence's back section today, _____. We
won't push ourselves too hard. I know you're not feeling well."

You assist Anne in measuring the distance between posts, marking
the spots with wooden stakes, digging six postholes, setting the posts in
the holes with a quick-drying concrete. Then you take a break. You sit
in the shade, drink lemonade, and eat rations. The lemonade stings your
throat, but you do not complain. Anne talks. You do not. You concentrate
on conserving energy and not passing out.

You and Anne spend the rest of the afternoon attaching rails to the
posts and pickets to the rails. Despite Anne's near-constant encourage-
ment and compliments, you are ashamed because you are not as much
help as you'd like to be. You bend nails and screw in the screws crookedly.
Anne has to fix your mistakes and redoes much of the work you were supposed to do on your own. Your hands are slow and clumsy. Your hands do
not remember to whom they once belonged.

Most of the celebratory dinner (corn, baked potatoes, leafy greens) comes from Anne's garden, which she maintains in another area of the campus.

"I figured after all the hard work you wouldn't mind the starches. There's only so much I can do to dress up the protein paste though, sorry. I tried raising chickens and ducks, but I wasn't good at keeping them healthy."

The kitchen is exactly how you remember it, which is a comfort, because in the videos, you only saw an empty kitchen, the one from before the linoleum was replaced with laminate and before this little breakfast table, and you don't remember updating the cabinets and appliances, but somehow you remember these ones being exactly where they are and looking like they do, and maybe you even remember Anne sitting like she is sitting now and looking like she is looking now, but you know that can't be possible, can it? Maybe your memories are creating themselves; like the solar array and wind turbines, your memories are becoming self-sufficient.

"Aren't you hungry?"

You are not. Your tongue is swollen, and chewing and swallowing are impossible chores. "I'm okay," you say.

"You don't look okay." Anne looks right through you. You've been aware of that idiom and now, perhaps for the first time, you understand it. She says, "Come on. Let's get you upstairs."

"Who are we again?"

Anne tilts her head and furrows her brow, observing you, making silent calculations.

"What are *we*, Anne. What are we together?"

She pulls her hair behind her head and ties it into a quick ponytail. "I'm not sure what you're asking."

You cough and you wince at the splintering shards of pain in your throat and head. "How do we describe you and me? Are we coworkers? Are we friends? Are we a couple? Are we lovers? What are we?"

Anne covers her mouth with a hand and laughs. She laughs until her face is red and she isn't breathing. Despite how terrible you feel, you laugh too.

She stops laughing. A small shadow of a smile remains. Her eyes are pointed down at the table, not at you. "There were times when we were all those things. Right now, we're partners."

The sun hasn't fully set outside, but it is dusk in the house. Anne leads you by the arm, up the stairs to the second floor, and if your memory of the house's layout is correct, into what should be her office, the one with the yellow walls.

She says, "I recently decided to make this the main bedroom. I know the room is smaller, but I enjoy how the sunlight reflects off the yellow walls in the morning."

With Anne's help, you change into clean pajamas. They are made of a fabric softer than the pullover and white drawstring scrubs you've been wearing. You slowly crawl into the queen-sized bed; the wooden frame creaks under your weight and movement. You lie on your right side, facing the windows. As your head sinks into the pillow, Anne pulls the bedcovers up to your neck. Your fever is raging. Your teeth chatter and your pajamas are instantly soaked in sweat.

Anne retreats to a bureau across the room, adjacent to the door. She lights a candle. The wall you are facing glows with eerie, flickering orange light.

"You need your rest. Tomorrow is a big day. A big day for both of us."

She climbs into the bed but remains over the covers, not inside them with you. She drapes a hand over your shoulder and promises to stay until you fall asleep. You close your eyes, but you can still see the orange light on the wall.

You are awake in the dark, sitting at the edge of your bed, feet on the hardwood floor, and you are crying.

Anne isn't in the bed next to you. Your muscles ache and your joints are filled with ground bits of glass. You don't want to move, but you get up, and it's as though your brain is a step behind your body. You shuffle to the door and fumble for the knob, which is cold in your sweaty hand. You open the door and you are so afraid, of what exactly you don't know, but the fear is shutting down your mind. You flow down the hallway and to the bathroom as though the floor is the belt of a treadmill. You twist the sink knobs, but there is no water. You shiver, groan, and your hands shake, and that's when you see there's a mirror on the wall. It is dark, but you see yourself in the glass. You see who you are. You paw at the wall light switch next to you, but no light comes on. You stop breathing and moving, and the you in the glass does the same. You both blink. You both raise a hand up to your face. You are not who you remember. You are not the person in the pictures and videos Anne has showed you. You are someone else entirely, and you want to yell but it comes out as a low, keening moan.

You blink and you don't remember how you got there, but you are back in the yellow bedroom. You are standing in front of the window. You open the curtains and clumsily lift the blinds. Outside, the moon is missing a piece, but it's still so big and bright. You sit on the bed and stare at it. Then you are standing and looking down the hill to the Dormitory, and it's not as far away as you thought, and in the moonlight you can see fine, you can see everything. You watch the marble front entrance with its dry fountain, and Anne emerges between the Dormitory's glass doors. She is walking backward, pulling a gurney behind her. There is someone lying flat on the gurney, covered by a sheet. She pivots and turns; her arms block your view of the other person's face. Then you can't see them very well because they are small underneath the big moon, because you are farther away from them than you thought.

You are awake in the dark, sitting at the edge of your bed, feet on the hardwood floor, and you are crying. You hear Anne's feet pounding on the stairs and down the hall and then into your room. The candle has burned out and there isn't enough moonlight spilling through the window behind you.

You ask her, over and over, Who, who am I?, and you ask her, over and over, who was on the gurney.

Anne stands in the middle of the room, her arms wrapped around herself. She asks, "What's wrong?"

You tell her what you saw, but you know you're not doing a good job and you sound far away, far away from yourself.

Anne says "Shh" and "No" and "It was a dream" and "It's because of your high fever" and "You were having a fever dream" and "Hallucinating" and "That's why it was so real" and "There's no mirror in the bathroom; you can look tomorrow." She does not answer your 'who was on the gurney' question. She guides you back down onto your bed and pulls the covers over you.

You ask her to stay, but she does not. She shuts and latches the door.

032

Anne says your name and gently shakes your shoulder.

The room is full of light and the yellow walls are angry. There's a deep crackling within your chest on inhales and your exhales are whistling hisses.

"Good morning. I know you're not well, but we have to do this downstairs, at the kitchen table, and then you can rest. Come on. We're almost done."

Anne sits you up, drapes your right arm across the back of her shoulders, and lifts you onto your feet. The morning sun amplifies the yellow; the walls glow and the light becomes a disorienting, intoxicating mist. You don't want to leave this room. This is a room you could stay in forever.

The two of you stagger into the hallway and then down the stairs, one halting step at a time. You want to ask about seeing the bathroom and if in fact there is a mirror or an empty space on the wall where there should be one, but it is too late. You will not be walking back up the stairs.

Anne deposits you into a chair at the kitchen table. Your head lolls, pitches into your chest, and perhaps you sleep, or pass out, but you come to when there's a sting on the back of your left hand.

She says, "You are dehydrated and I'm replenishing your fluids intravenously. This will be more restorative than a simple glass of water."

Cold rushes into the back of your hand and up your forearm. After a few moments you are able to lift your head and look around the room. There's a metal stand next to you, a plastic bag full of clear fluid dangles from its top, and a thin tube connects from the bag to the back of your hand. On the kitchen table is a large black notebook, a pencil in its spine.

"_____? Are you with me? Are you feeling a little better?"

You say, "I'm here." Here is in the brown house, the replica; you remember that. It hurts to talk, and your voice is not your own. You don't like hearing what it has become.

Anne slides the notebook away from you and to the empty place at the table. She says, "We're going to have a conversation, _____. It's the most important one we ever had or will ever have. Please, keep in mind everything you remember and everything you've learned about yourself, about who you were and who you are. You've done so well in such a short period of time. I'm very proud of all you've accomplished, but you must remain focused during the conversation, and do not allow yourself to wander. You must stay *you* within the parameters of what is being discussed. You are not to ask me any more questions about last night or the prior thirty days. Please, _____. I need you to do this for me."

"Because we're partners?"

"Yes. Because we've become the most sacred of partners. I am going to leave you here while I change my clothes, but I will only be gone for a few minutes. Don't get up, don't move. That part is important too, because this—you sitting here by yourself at the table—this is how I found you. This is how I *find* you. This is how it starts."

She leaves. You cough and the sound is terrible and you know your chest is broken. You stare at the needle in your hand and the plastic IV line. You imagine yourself, the one you saw in the mirror last night, that *you* has always been waiting here, in this kitchen, waiting for Anne to come back. You try to imagine what she is going to say to you, and what you are going to say to her.

Anne returns. She wears a flannel shirt and blue jeans. She places the notebook on the floor, out of sight. She closes her eyes, breathes deeply twice, and then begins.

She says, "What are you doing down here? You should've stayed in bed." Her affect has changed. Her familiarity with you is different. You can see it in her posture, in her wide eyes, in her fidgeting hands.

You are not sure who you are, who you are supposed to be. You are not sure what you're supposed to say. You make a guess. "It was too bright. I wanted a glass of water. I—"

"You sound awful, _____."

"I feel like I sound."

"You should let me take you back to the Facility. I can take better care of you there."

"No, I'm not going back. No way." You remember waking up in the room and what it felt like and you never want to feel that way again. "You're not putting me in one of those rooms and leaving me—"

"Stop it, I won't leave you. You aren't going to get better if you stay here."

"I'm not going to get better if I go back either."

"We have to try. We have to try something! Something different than me sitting here watching you die."

You pause, unsure of what to say, of what she wants you to say. You try to imagine your face isn't the one from the mirror but the one from the videos, from your memories. "Okay, I don't want to, but okay. If you really want me to, I'll go."

Anne shakes her head, breaking her emotionally intense affect. She smiles crookedly at you. She cups a hand around her mouth and whispers, "You're doing great. This is the only time I'll correct you, I promise. You need to say, 'Why would I ever go back to that place? And why do you want to go? You're the one who said you were convinced the virus came out of the Dormitory.' Say that, and then we'll go from there and without me correcting you again. Okay, please?"

You cough. You nod. She repeats what she wants you to say, and then you say it, word for word.

Anne says, "I never said I was convinced."

"Anne, you said—"

"What I said was the group of blanks we grew with the new modifiers to reprogram DNA, those patients were among the first ones to get sick. But correlation does not imply causation. Could be a fucking zoonotic virus making the jump from one of the animal labs, for all we know. We really don't know where it came from yet. . . ." She trails off at the end, clearly not fully believing her own words.

You are so tired and can barely hold your head up. You don't fully grasp what she is saying, but the words come to you, as though this conversation is a part of you, and it was hidden somewhere deep inside. You say, "Are you the only one who didn't get sick?"

"No. Brianna and Alejandro were fine. But . . ."

"But?"

"I don't know, now. I don't know how they're doing now. They left the Complex four days ago, like everyone else."

"Did you, I don't know, vaccinate or inoculate yourself somehow?"

"Jesus, no. If I could do that, don't you think I'd save you too? How could you ask that?" She looks down into her lap instead of at you, and then she covers her face. When she looks back up, her expression is blank and unreadable. But it's unreadable in a way you are sure means something.

You don't say anything.

She answers your silent accusation with, "I want to try to help you, though. Let's go back and let me try."

"Don't make me go back." Even after everything, you want to remain within the promise and the lie of the little brown house.

"I don't want to watch you die."

"Don't make me go back." You are the you of now saying this. You don't care if you are accurately representing the *you* from then.

Anne swears and pounds her fists on the kitchen table. She closes her eyes, then slowly reaches across the kitchen table and takes your right hand. Her skin is cold. "If this doesn't . . . If you don't get better—can I bring you back?"

"What do you mean?"

"I know this is hard, this is so fucked-up and impossible to ask, but, after you . . . After!"

"After I'm dead?"

"Yes, after. Only if you say yes right now, I can go to the Complex, we still have hundreds of viable blanks, and—you know what I can do. I can bring you back."

"With all that's happening, you're actually asking this?"

"I am. I—I don't want to be without you. Please."

"I want you to say it."

"_____, please."

"You have to say it."

"Let me bring you back. I don't want to be alone, be without you. I—"

"You have to say the word, Anne."

"Let me clone you. Please, let me do it. I want you to let me bring you back."

You are crying. The Anne sitting across from you is blurry and begins to look like the younger Anne you remember. "I don't want to come back. It wouldn't be me you're bringing back."

"But listen, think about all the—"

"Anne—"

"Amazing success we've had with augmenting our patients' cellular memory, directly uploading information and images, and the exercises and therapy—"

"Anne! It wouldn't be me." You look at your hands and wonder whose hands they are.

"I would make them into you. They would be you."

You repeat, "It wouldn't be me." What you mean to say, but in these final moments you can't summon the courage to, is: *It never was me.*

"If you say no, I won't clone you. I promise you. And I know it's crazy, it's fucking horrible and crazy, but I'm asking you. Please. Will you let me?"

"No. I'm sorry, Anne. No. You can't. It won't be me."

Anne wipes her eyes, sighs, bends to the kitchen floor, and retrieves the notebook. She angrily scribbles some notes and throws the pen across the table.

She says, "Thank you," but it's perfunctory and she says it through gritted teeth and without looking at you.

You ask, "How many of us have there been?" You are breathing erratically and your voice is little more than a scratching sound.

"Too many."

"We helped build our house." You are desperate to feel a kinship with the rest of *you* who spent all those years with Anne. You are desperate to feel something that is yours, something other than emptiness.

"You did."

"We all had this conversation."

"Yes."

"How many of us said yes?"

"None of you. Not a single fucking one of you."

Anne explodes out of her chair and stalks to the kitchen counter, grunting and yelling in obvious frustration. She stops pacing and then quickly replaces your IV bag even though the old one is only three-quarters empty. Your hand and arm go warm this time.

She closes her eyes and sighs. She says, "There aren't very many left of you to say yes."

She rubs the back of your head. Your eyelids go heavy, and you try to speak but you cannot. You feel yourself melting away; your consciousness receding toward a singularity.

Anne whispers, "I didn't lie to you, _____."

001

Your room is dark. You cannot see anything. You are lying in a bed. A sheet covers your body. You wiggle your fingers and toes, and the loud rasp of skin rubbing against the sheets is startling. With the slight movements there is pain. Your muscles and joints hum with it.

You've been awake and not-awake for days, maybe weeks, perhaps longer. You do not know where you were then, or before *then*. You are here now. A significant amount of time has passed but from what beginning, you do not know. You consider the origin of this time during which you've been awake and not-awake and conclude it is, for the moment, unknowable.

MOSTLY SIZE

It was the same old story. No one knew where it came from, and they were not prepared.

The giant monster, impossible in its bipedal form, stomped and smashed the city, working in a pattern known only to itself. No computers or pundits were left unsmashed to posit otherwise.

Aside from its rumbling and shuffling footsteps, hammering hands and gnashing teeth, the only sounds the dwindling denizens heard from the giant monster were whooshing intakes of breath and hours later, the calamitous exhales. It breathed as often as the encroaching and rising tides changed. The giant monster never once cried or called out. No mighty roars echoed across and beyond the city.

Toward the end of the attack, which is to say, the end of the city, dust and debris cumulonimbused around the giant monster's head and upper torso. When it breathed, the cloud briefly cleared, exposing the indifferent sun.

One cyclonic exhale stripped away the ruin of Max's house and the bed under which he'd been hiding. It must've been almost noon because the sun was directly over the monster and there were no shadows. Were there a monster's shadow of any length, Max would've been standing in it. As it was, he stood on shaky, ten-year-old legs, his head tilted upward to the unending heights of things.

After untold and continuing hours of horror and sorrow, while surely facing annihilation, Max experienced a strange feeling akin to—he couldn't explain, couldn't summon a comparison. There was more fear, of course, but a different kind, one that made him want to see it all, to see everything, even the end.

Perhaps it was all the terror, loss, and despair in concert with the concussions and contusions and chest-squeezing compressions he'd experienced as his house collapsed onto him, but now, as the monster turned its moon-sized eyes down toward him, Max composed a poem in his head.

He'd never written a poem of his own free will, nor did he enjoy poems all that much when required to read them in school. He liked movies and video games and drawing. He desperately wished he were better at drawing than he was. He'd had to take extra classes because of his handwriting difficulties. Drawing was supposed to help. There was a part of him that thought his inability to control the lines and loops he made on paper as being the truth of himself, and maybe even the truth outside of himself.

Within the poem were words his parents and teachers used in their complicated everyday lives prior to the monster attack. While Max couldn't define those words using a sentence of his own, he understood their usage and implications in the same way he understood colors, humidity, shame, love, and ocean breezes.

Max imagined large swaths of emptiness between the lines of his poem to allow space for the giant monster to roam. He didn't have a title, though, in a pinch, he supposed the first line might work.

can a giant monster sharpen a pencil?

how sharp

number 2 regular pencil or the joke kind

either way

the answer depends on

size

dexterity

fine motor skills

motivation

how many tries are allowed

and will there be electricity in the smashed-up city to power an electric
pencil sharpener

because I wouldn't expect anyone especially a giant monster to use those
plastic square

ones with the small not-sharp razor inside to shave away the wood and
make a good

drawing tip and I hate when my teacher Mr. Langan expects me to use
those stupid

square ones and mom said that there used to be wall-mounted pencil
sharpeners with a

hand crank that worked pretty well before the electric ones

but I still think

the answer depends on

size

mostly size

 With the last line completed, Max checked his empty pockets for his
practice pencil to offer to the giant monster. It was one he used to draw
and not practice letters. It was a regular yellow one. Nothing special. But
he'd used it enough so that it had been whittled to the same length as one
of his pinkies. He forgot he'd stuck it behind his slightly bowed-out left
ear. And when the end came, it was still there.

For Max, Sasha, Logan, Zella, and Jake

THE LARGE MAN

Mr. C____ is one of the Problem Solvers. He is dressed in black and quietly works at his desk.

I am Mr. C____. I am one of the Problem Solvers. I am dressed in black and quietly working at my desk. The scritch-scritch of my pen is louder than my breathing. My desk is one of 353 in our office. Our office is in the Great Hall.

Two days ago I was charged with determining the number of citizens with middle names that began with the letters "G-a-e." There are six. Yesterday, oh yesterday, I was sent into the field! The rarest of rare occurrences, despite my many requests. It had been years since I'd been sent from the Great Hall to problem-solve. Granted, it was only to help assorted members of the citizenry find their lost keys, socks, and one older gentleman's ivory rook from a chess set that had been carved by his great-grandfather. He didn't tell me about his great-grandfather carving the rook, but that's the scenario I dared imagine.

This morning I was handed a ledger. My heart sank despite knowing the probability of being sent into the field two days in a row was zero. Numbers were then dictated to me via speakerphone. I was not told what the numbers represented, only that I was to find a pattern hidden within them. I was reminded that trying to ascribe context to the data would negatively influence my perception of said data with bias. Bias, we've been told repeatedly, is the Problem Solver's enemy.

The coworkers to my left and right—Ms. Longfeld and Mr. Demet— peer at me over their dusty tomes, their "great works of literature" (so they claimed). They hold their books upside down, if the book covers are any indication. I feel them observing my data observation, changing everything. Protocol dictates that I am not to allow myself to wonder if the numbers represent street addresses of physicians who only treat patients felled by incurable diseases, if the numbers are celestial coordinates of black holes that have a craven hunger for worlds, or if the numbers represent the annual sums of unanswered prayers uttered by children in the city.

Hours pass like the digits beneath my fingers. My fingers are ink-stained. Blue. I try to create more stories for the numbers, from the numbers, but the stories don't take, and my stomach cramps and clenches at my repeated failures. I stop looking for meaning, but still, the numbers do not perfectly fit into any regression models. As it finally occurs to me that these numbers fit into a simple Fibonacci sequence and as I visualize the numbers spinning into a perfect golden spiral, one with infinite possible meanings and conclusions, there is a cough. A clearing of a throat. An introduction to a new problem.

"Ahem. Mr. C____."

She is an Assigner. She wears a white suit, squared at the shoulders, and a skinny, red necktie spills down her front as though her neck has sprung a leak. The knot is thicker than what is generally customary and makes me uncomfortable. She stands next to my desk, hands folded in front of her. I do not know how long she has been standing there observing me. I have never seen this Assigner before. There is no one else in the office. I did not notice that my coworkers had left.

"The Great Hall has been cleared. I believe you know what this means."

"My apologies, but I do not." I get irked at Assigners who assume that I know everything when it has become painfully clear in my many years as a Problem Solver that I know distressingly little.

The Assigner has a small rectangular white card clasped between her fingers. I take it. It reads, simply, "The Consortium."

I say, "Invitation?"

"A command."

Mr. C____ stands in situ before the members of the Consortium, as is required by Parliamentary Procedure. He nervously waits to be addressed.

I am Mr. C____. I stand in situ before the members of the Consortium, as is required by Parliamentary Procedure. I nervously wait to be addressed.

I last stood before the Consortium many years ago, during Initiation, when my memories were wiped away, including the memory of the Initiation itself. After, I was assured that my previous life was one of intolerable suffering and sadness and that I'd earned the tabula rasa and honor of being a Problem Solver. I was assured that my old life was vestigial and those memories would be as obsolete as a burned, unread book.

How is it, then, that instead of excitement at the prospect of being assigned a clearly important problem by the Consortium themselves, I am filled with primal dread? I am sweating and I push my glasses up the length of my nose.

The members of the Consortium stand behind a white marble desk that spans the cavernous length of Parliament. The members wear black silk robes that flow over their bodies like water. Hoods obscure their identities. They're huddled close, clinging to one another, whispering, pointing, until finally, one speaks.

"Problem Solver, we have a problem that needs solving." I cannot tell which member of the Consortium is speaking, as they remain huddled and constantly in motion.

I say, "At your service."

"There is a Large Man."

"A Large Man?"

"Yes. He is murdering family members of the Consortium."

I don't know quite what to say. My pulse beats insistently against my collar. "Horrific. Tragic."

"Yes. Yes. We're all frightened and very angry, and of course, demand justice."

"At your service."

"Direct your attention to the video, please."

A white curtain falls in front of the members of the Consortium. From somewhere behind me a projector whirs to life, my own shadow darkens the curtain, and giant, grainy images flicker before me.

A plain bedroom chamber. An ornate bed, brass posts reaching toward a vaulted ceiling. A sleeping form under the bedcovers. The person in the bed is blurred out. Identity still to be protected. The bed covers are blue. A Large Man, presumably, *the* Large Man suddenly fills the curtain screen. If the dimensions of the projected room are to be trusted, he must stand over eight feet tall. His shoulders are as broad as the horizon. He wears a fedora and a trench coat. That there was a trench coat of that size produced at all strikes me as a horror. The Large Man turns momentarily toward the camera, his face is obscured by shadow, tufts of thick, dark hair curl around the hat's brim, perhaps a mustache, perhaps a beard. He shuffles slowly to the bed. The blurred-out victim—I already presume the person to be the victim—stirs, and then screams. The scream has been modified to protect the identity of the screamer. I am thankful for the blurring and modification, as I don't want to actually see what happens, but at the same time, I do. I do so very much. The Large Man pulls two large rats out of his pockets. Their tails are as thick as ropes. The nasty clicking of their teeth is audible despite the victim's (modulated) screams. The Large Man releases the rats and holds down the victim. The blur turns red. The terrible sounds continue.

The Consortium play me four more videos. Each bedchamber is similar. Each death by rats is similar. The only difference is the size of the blurred-out victim. The last one is distressingly small.

The projector goes quiet. I am breathing heavy, and I wipe my eyes with a handkerchief. My shadow no longer stains the white curtain. The curtain rises.

Some members of the Consortium pantomime weeping and grief, others console them. One member separates from the group and speaks. "We don't yet know who the Large Man is."

"May I?" I ask, and pull out a small notebook. The notebook is red. "Are the rats—"

"As far as we're concerned, our long-standing truce with all the City's creatures, including the rats, remains in good standing." The speaker's tone is annoyed.

Problem Solvers aren't supposed to ask questions of the Consortium. I know this, but I can't help myself. I feel feverish with questions, with the idea of daring to ask questions and where those questions might lead. I ask, "Have the birds—"

I am interrupted again. "The birds either know nothing or they wish to remain neutral observers."

"Do you fear that whomever this Large Man is, he is trying to start the war again?" This time, I am allowed to ask my presumptuous and potentially dangerous (to me) question.

"We fear nothing, Problem Solver. We want the truth, and we want to know who the Large Man is and his whereabouts. That is what we want from you."

"At your service. I know I've already overstepped my bounds, but in wanting to ensure that I fulfill my duties to their fullest, I'd like to ask if I will have permission to apply my skills in the field, if necessary. Do I have permission to confront and apprehend the Large Man myself, should the opportunity be presented?" Despite my longing to be out in the field and away from the Great Hall, the prospect of physical confrontation dizzies my head, but in a way that makes me smile. I know I shouldn't be smiling. I look down, and away, as though hiding my eyes will keep my yearnings a secret.

The speaker doesn't respond, so I continue. "While weapons and apprehension, if that is the correct word, are not my forte"—I pronounce *forte* properly, as "fort," as all Problem Solvers have been trained to do— "I'm quite confident, if properly equipped, in my ability to handle the entirety of the Large Man problem, as it were."

The speaker: "Once located, the Large Man will be confronted by members of the Army of Green."

"I understand, particularly given the potential diplomatic difficulties involved, I only would like to add—"

"That is most certainly enough! You will do as asked. We will supply you with all the information that you will need. We will ensure that you are well equipped for the task that is required of you."

"Of course. At your service."

Mr. C____ is dropped off at a curb in front of the Great Hall. He carries a plastic container of lukewarm broth and an umbrella even though it is no longer raining.

I am Mr. C____. I am dropped off at a curb in front the Great Hall. I carry a plastic container of lukewarm broth and an umbrella even though it is no longer raining. The umbrella is my weapon of choice, even if it isn't very much of a weapon at all. Ahead are the Great Stairs that lead to the Great Hall. Foot traffic is light. The surrounding buildings are brightly lit, but no one stands in their windows to look out at me. Still, I can't help but feel watched, as though I've been marked by my assignment. The only problems that I can never solve are my own.

I look down and there's a dead rat in the gutter. There are always dead rats in the gutter. Its body is flattened and desiccated. Flies and ants crawl in and out of empty eye sockets and its gaping mouth. An ant on its terrible yellow teeth. I nudge the rat with my foot. Insects scurry away but quickly regroup.

Problem Solvers are remade and trained to ignore our gut and remain coolly rational and devoted to data. I say out loud, as though speaking to the dead rat, "Without having consulted any further evidence than what the Consortium has already shown me, I think the rats are behind the Large Man attacks." Sudden and powerful nausea buckles my knees and I drop the container of broth and it spills, washing the rat into a sewer drain. My body quivers, rejecting my announced intention toward bias as toxic, but the nausea ebbs, if not disappearing completely. I breathe, then stand shakily, and I scurry up the stairs to the Great Hall. At the top of the stairs, I look back to the street and the discarded broth container, and I shudder with pleasure at the unpleasant memory of the bias-induced nausea.

The Great Hall's interior remains cleared. I sit at my desk, which buckles under the weight of a new computer. The screen is in the shape of a crescent moon and pulses with the blue light of its electronic heartbeat. I have been granted unprecedented access to the Grid; surveillance video; government files (including the most recent FFCS—Flora Fauna Census and Survey—along with the closely monitored migratory analysis, sentience quotients, and hive-mind constants of the numerous superorganisms within the City with which we have hard-earned peace pacts); consumer data including voting records and political affiliations; employee and banking records. I feel appropriate awe at the infinite gathering of information, and I imagine bytes of data parsed into quarks, and those data quarks are living organisms infesting every corner and crevice of my head. It's a glorious nightmare.

The problem that has been assigned to me is extraordinary, and I've rationally concluded that my methods will have to be extraordinary as well. Extraordinary means unorthodox and anti-policy. So I begin with bias, my delicious bias. I begin with the rats. I begin by assuming the rats are behind the murders of Consortium family members. I ask myself a question in a voice that crackles like a downed power line. "Why not simply murder the Consortium members themselves?" And I answer,

"Because the rats don't want the Consortium replaced, they want them to be afraid, and then be pliable, easily swayed, willing to compromise in the face of the terror of the Large Man's attacks. The rats know that Consortium members can be easily replaced with hardliners who don't have the albatross of loved ones." I smile at this induction, this simply calculated dream of mine. As a Problem Solver, I've been designed to ignore dreams. I am a human algorithm, a program trained to find glitches in the code, the diamond in the data, and intuition and imagination are words belonging to a dead tongue.

I close my eyes. I breathe. I imagine the rats meeting in their secret meeting places and planning their secret plans, twitching their whiskers, folding their little pink hands, and I am there, in a corner of the dark underbelly of the sewers with the rats crawling and planning and planning and planning.

I am light-headed, drunk with this imagining, and I know I should stop, but I can't. Only I can stop the rats. I am Mr. C____. Me, my newborn imagination, and my umbrella will find the Large Man they've coerced into their service and stop the rats and their attempted coup.

While in the throes of my reverie I maintain a modicum of procedure and build algorithms to begin sifting through the data, and I build algorithms for the algorithms until the computer is working by itself. On the computer monitor contoured to nearly wrap around my head this universe of information collapses down before my eyes into a singularity of a discovery, a singularity of a story.

Based in part on the shadowy stills culled from the videos of the attacks, the Large Man is Wenton Foles (a 95.45% probability match). He is thirty-seven years old, an unemployed union machinist who is described by coworkers as having a fierce temper but unwavering loyalty, twice divorced from the same woman, who has since left the City after changing her name, a cribbage enthusiast, an amateur anarchist who once received a citation for purposefully flipping a one-way street sign so that it pointed to the sewers below. In recent years he's taken to wearing a thick mustache and sideburns presumably to hide the facial features distorted by a form of acromegaly, a once-rare disease that results in unchecked growth of facial features. Four other union machinists have the same disease, although they each believe that they suffer alone. Wenton is two weeks behind in rent. He was last seen alive purchasing flounders from the Market nine days ago. He is not eight feet tall. The change in height is puzzling, though perhaps that can be attributed to something as simple as platform shoes. The Large Man does not move well, perhaps due to shoe-enhanced size.

I imagine that Wenton does not move well under the weight of his betrayal and guilt, and the weight of unhappiness. His trade, his training, his preordained station in life has yielded him divorce and disease, and what else? Perhaps he is thinking, *Why not help the rats? They couldn't do worse than the current tenants of Parliament.* No, there's more to our Wenton, and if I were *not* to follow protocol and *not* simply report my findings and his name to the Army of the Green I would then find out how much more there is to Wenton and his story. If I were to attempt to confront him myself, perhaps a few hours from now, when it'll still be raining . . . as he tries to sneak out of his apartment's back window, he had returned to his apartment for money or his fake ID or a picture of his ex-ex-wife, the one he still loves, but Mr. C____ is there sitting on the fire escape, the tip of his umbrella pointed at Wenton's barrel-sized chest, Mr. C____ cruelly makes light of the mountainous terrain of the man's morphing facial features to let Wenton know that Mr. C____ is not afraid of him, and that really, Mr. C____ only has to look at him a certain way and Wenton will then tell him everything he needs to know, Mr. C____ lies, telling Wenton that he paid a visit to his ex-ex-wife, the one who *already* told him everything he needed to know about Wenton, the one with a beauty mark that tickles her upper thigh, Wenton attempts to strike Mr. C____ but Mr. C____ swats it away nonchalantly, Mr. C____ then tells him that he knows of Wenton's work-life spent inhaling and absorbing factory chemical fumes, and Mr. C____ knows of the years spent flirting with the underground, as though his lifestyle was a child's dare, and Mr. C____ knows of the unpopular, unwelcomed, and *exciting* company he keeps, and Mr. C____ knows his bars and his alleys and what Wenton likes to drink and who he wants to fight and who he wants to fuck, and Mr. C ___ knows that Wenton yearns for something more than what's hidden in the sweet lies of a better life promised within the diaphanous whispers of the rats, Wenton listens and then promises to show Mr. C____ everything he's learned from the rats, including how feeling pain is better than feeling nothing—

The computer beeps harshly at me and I twitch in my chair, almost falling out of it. I understand the computer's language of beeps. My algorithms found Wenton. There is a 98.4% probability (which is a near statistical certainty) that he is holed up in one of the floating ships in Old Bay. All I have to do, all I'm supposed to do, is make a few keystrokes and inform the Army of the Green of my findings. It's all there. Another job well done. Another to be assigned shortly thereafter.

I grab two fistfuls of my own graying, curly hair and I let the computer beep at me.

Mr. C_____ guides his gondola between the abandoned ships of Old Bay. Mr. C_____ has never been on a gondola before.

I am Mr. C_____. I guide my gondola between the abandoned ships of Old Bay. I have never been on a gondola before. I am doing surprisingly well, I think, with the standing and pushing my boat along with the long oar. My legs feel like rubber, a headache bores greedily into the inner fathoms of my skull, and I've thrown up twice, but I am doing well.

The rusting ghost ships of the City's fabled merchant-marine past hulk above me, blotting out all but a thin strip of the night sky. The gently lapping water echoes off their bloated tin stomachs. Dowsing paths between the ships becomes increasingly treacherous until, finally, the mass of ships funnels my gondola into the blue ship's hull.

There are rats thrashing around in the dark water, swimming away from the ship, away from me, as though they are fleeing. But they are not fleeing, are they? No, they are not. They are amassing for an assault on the City. I don't have much time.

Climbing the ship's moored emergency ladder with its thin rungs and slicked handholds proves exceedingly difficult, a physical task that I fear is well beyond me. But I climb anyway, awkwardly clutching the umbrella. My mind desperately reaches for a memory, an experience or a relationship from which to draw strength, and finds only an empty space that perhaps was once filled with something other than regret. My will to fill that empty space with a new memory of my own making is enough for now.

I clang and clatter onto the ship's wide deck, and into light. Gusting wind pushes and prods at my unsteady body, but the sky has cleared and a deep, full moon shines patiently above me. My head buzzes with pain. I don't care. I am Mr. C_____ and I have left my desk in the Great Hall, and I have managed to transport myself onto the blue ship in the middle of Old Bay. I am here. I am.

The surrounding ships, those floating headstones, are swarmed by thousands of rats as they head to the City. There is a handheld device in my pocket. I cup my hand gently around it and feel its battery-powered warmth. I can signal in the Army of the Green at any time.

I stumble across the deck toward the main cabin. The doorway is a shadow. The cabin door is missing, gone. In the doorway there is a shadow inside the shadow. The shadow is the Large Man. It is Wenton. He is waiting for me.

"Hello, Wenton. I am Mr. C_____, and I insist that you come back to the City with me to face the consequences of your heinous crimes."

The Large Man steps out of the cabin, onto the deck, and into the moonlight. He towers over me. He is larger than the problems that can never be solved. He wears the familiar fedora and trench coat. His face, having been further ravaged by acromegaly, is almost unrecognizable; a jigsaw puzzle that hasn't been put together correctly. His chin juts further than the prow of the ship, cheekbones made of marble, and his eyes are black dots, and uneven. I mean to say his black-dot eyes are not level and they pock his face below a brow as thick as a park bench. Wenton walks like a mountain might. His legs are disjointed, unwieldy masses that are lifted under obvious and considerable strain then dropped and allowed to collide cacophonically with the deck.

I slowly back away and he follows. His hands are ominously in his pockets.

I point my umbrella tip at his face. "Don't come any further, Wenton!" I scream, louder than I intend, and my head nearly splits in two from the pain. "I know you've had a horrible go of it, believe me, I understand. I understand your suffering and your fears and your disappointments. The disappointments are worse than the fears, aren't they?" I stammer and pause, knowing that I'm speaking in vague platitudes and sentiments, but I believe in the sentiments, and I do believe I'm getting through to him, that he understands me, that someone understands me. "I am not so different from you, Wenton. I, too, yearn for something more. A new reality, yes? I want to be remade, but by my own hand, my own remaking. It's what this is all about, isn't it? For the first time, I've figured that much out on my own."

Wenton sways in the wind and doesn't say anything. I watch his hands. My free hand goes to my pocket as well, and the handheld.

"Come on, my good man, let's go back to the City. We can talk more if you'd like. Have a coffee. Perhaps some broth. We could do that. You could tell me about your life. I'd love to hear everything about that, actually. I won't judge you. I'll listen. Forget about the rats and what they want and just come with me."

At the word "rats," the Large Man reanimates and steps closer to me. He says, "You don't know anything." The voice is a whisper, but one made out of a thousand other whispers. It's not an emotional retort but a cold statement of fact. It's this coldness that coalesces with the disjointed legs and mismatched face that makes me realize what has happened to Wenton.

I strike the advancing Large Man in the head with my umbrella. The fedora tumbles off his head and pieces of his scalp and face slide off and fall to the deck in strips and chunks. Underneath the skein of what used to be Wenton is a writhing mass of rats. Exposed, the rats themselves begin to break rank and fall to the deck. The Large Man melts away, sloughing bit by bit and rat by rat.

I frantically pull out my handheld, open the emergency two-way line—although I don't know if anyone is listening to me—and shout, "This is Mr. C____. It's the rats! The Large Man is made out of rats!"

One rat runs across the deck and bumps against my foot, but it does not attack. It just drops to its side. It appears to be dead. A dead rat. Dead like the rat I'd encountered in the gutter in front of the Great Hall; that other dead rat that was the source of my biased assumption, the inspiration of my intuition, the fuel behind my adventure. *This* dead rat that was alive only moments ago is desiccated and its eye sockets are empty, but now I look more closely at it and its skin boils, its *dead* skin boils as though there are thousands of other rats contained within the dead rat, and those other rats are bursting and straining for final release.

Instead, black and madly twitching ants pour out of the dead rat, which deflates as quickly as the Large Man did. The deck quickly turns black as countless ants stream out of all the rats' bodies, forming a billowing storm cloud that converges on me. Ants inside of rats inside of Wenton . . .

I want to run away and jump off the deck and hopefully into the water and not crash into the gondola even though I do not know how to swim. Despite the approaching horror or maybe because of it, I do not seem capable of running. Particularly now with my legs more than ankle deep in an ever-growing ant swarm.

I never considered the ants. Who would ever consider an ant?

Mr. C____ stands in situ before the members of the Consortium, as is required by Parliamentary Procedure. He is dressed in black and waits to be addressed.

We are Mr. C____. We stand in situ before the members of the Consortium, as is required by Parliamentary Procedure. We are dressed in black and wait to be addressed.

Mr. C____ once stood before the Consortium many years ago, during his Initiation, when his memories of a previous life of intolerable suffering and sadness were wiped away, when he was first remade. We have remade him again. He will be our legend, forever remembered for his part in the beginning, the beginning of our greatest triumph.

The members of the ill-fated Consortium stand behind a marble-white desk that spans the cavernous length of Parliament. The decreased membership still clings to their black silk robes and hoods obscuring their identities, but we know who and what they are.

"Problem Solver, now that the war with the rats finally nears the end, we again have a problem that needs solving." We cannot tell which member of the Consortium is speaking. It does not matter.

We who are Mr. C____ do not say "At your service," as is required by Parliamentary Procedure. We begin with the Great Swarm that issues from Mr. C____'s mouth.

THE DEAD THING

It's Thursday, and instead of walking with Stacey to the skate park (it's next to the high school, so it isn't a good place for people [especially seventh-grade people (especially seventh-grade girl people)] who aren't in high school to go to unless you like the smell of weed, rape jokes, and getting cigarette filters and lit matches thrown at you), and instead of walking down the train tracks behind the driving school and to the combo gas station Honey Dew Donuts that this late in the day only has plain bagels and stale donut holes left, I decide to go straight home. I feel like I have to go even if I don't want to because I worry something bad (or worse [worse than the bad that is every day]) has happened or will happen to Owen, because the elementary school gets out fifteen minutes before the middle school and Owen is probably home and sitting on the couch and burning through another bag of sunflower seeds (eating seeds is how Owen deals with everything, and he deals with a lot because he's too young to know anything or understand like I do so he eats seeds because Dad figured out if Owen had a mouthful of seeds he couldn't ask about Mom or cry as much so, yeah, sunflower seeds, the ones baseball players eat and spit, and Owen eats so many seeds most days he's not hungry for dinner or breakfast or whatever food you try to put in front of him, and the kid is getting smaller instead of growing bigger, I swear), and what if Owen is watching TV and he accidentally swallows some of the seed shells (I've seen him swallow and scratch at his throat like he was dying and then be okay two seconds later and back with a mouth of seeds, my baby brother, the world's saddest gerbil) instead of spitting the shells into a cup or an empty (or half-empty) can of soda and he's choking for real, and Dad is passed out next to him on the couch or maybe he didn't even make it to the couch today, so I'm going home because that feeling of something *worse* is stuck down in me. Stacey wants to come with me, but I told her she can't and it's this joke between us how she never gets to go to my house when I go to hers all the time. She only jokes about it with me, which is why she's the only one I'm totally honest with. I've told her why she can't come. She says she gets it, but I don't think she totally gets it, and it's not her fault because she hasn't seen the house, and I mean the inside of the house because her parents have dropped me off so they've all seen the outside, which is bad (red paint is fine but the window frame's white paint is coming apart and the yard is all overgrown) but like a normal bad. Maybe I should let her come home with me once and I can give her a tour and I'd start with the kitchen and tell her, hey, yeah, that's the sink full of nasty dishes and flies as big as grapes and I keep two bowls (one for me and one for Owen) clean in my room, and don't open the fridge, you won't like it, but then I'd point at the walls, which is what she'd probably see first anyway, and using a fancy tour voice tell her that this is where Mom tore all the wallpaper off the walls because she was drunk or high or both, and Dad tried to stop her but she told him, don't worry, I'll put up new wallpaper and it'll be great, and she said that to him while standing on the stained and splintery plywood, which would be the same plywood we're standing on during the tour because a few months before she ripped down the wallpaper she jacked up all the linoleum tile because home improvement, right?, it was going to be a big project and make our kitchen look like the ones they show on those home-improvement shows, and while in tour mode I'd whisper so no one else could hear me that Mom was super drunk or high or both (and I could tell because her eyes would be red and big and she'd breathe only out of her mouth so it sounded like she was laughing and puking at the same time, and she looked like that when I saw her for the last time or the most recent last time because I don't know yet if it's a forever last time) so yeah it was makeover time for the kitchen, and Dad was drunk or high or both (and I can tell with him because his face and body sags like he's a human beanbag chair and he huffs more than speaks so the words come out of his nose) and Dad tried (not very hard, in fact, he sucked at trying) to stop Mom from buzzing through the floor tile but she told him to shut his assy mouth (that's a direct quote) and that she'd put in the new laminate flooring herself and without his worthless assy ass because he was too lazy to do it, and I wouldn't yell like they yelled while on the tour but I could do perfect impersonations of them fighting if I wanted to. I don't know if Stacey would make it past the kitchen on the tour so it's easier just to tell her that she can't come over today, that I have to help Owen with something and I say *something* like it's two different words (some thing), and we both laugh even though it's kind of stupid and she says okay and tells me to FaceTime her after dinner and I can do that when I'm in my room because my room is like a bomb shelter of regular clean in a nuked house. So I walk home by myself listening to music on my phone and I like to pretend that dressed all in black I'm a shadow or a blur or like a smudge of someone that when you drive by you don't really see them. I get home and I can hear the TV through the open front windows (no screens) and it sounds super loud, louder than normal, and I panic because it sounds too loud and that has to mean something's wrong, or some thing is wrong, so I run inside and drop my backpack and it bass-drums on the kitchen floor, and I obstacle-course past sagging garbage bags in the hallway to the TV room and Dad is on the couch asleep, passed out, whatever, and sports talking heads are shouting on the TV, but Owen isn't there, maybe he's already in his bedroom. I think about asking Dad where Owen is, and I think again. I try to turn down the volume without the remote (because when I got close to the couch Dad grumbled something and there were black dots of seeds and shells all over the cushions and I didn't want him to wake up and blame-yell at me about it) and I can't find the stupid volume buttons on the side of the TV. The back slider off the kitchen crashes open so Owen must've been in the backyard, and I somehow didn't see him out there when I got home. I run back down the hallway and I want to yell, *Where've you been?* and say things to make him cry but I also know that's not me so I swallow all that down to deal with later (I don't eat sunflower seeds, but I record messages on my phone and write things down and that's how I deal) and I find him (and I always think that I'm finding him, like he's lost) closing the slider real careful and slow with his foot, which is poked through the screen at the bottom and he shouldn't be doing that because he's making the rip in the screen bigger and we'll get bugs (more bugs) and mice (more mice) in the house, but then I zoom in on what he's carrying. Not that I can see it yet because his back is to me and he's curled around and over whatever it is he's carrying.

Owen, what do you have?

Nothing.

Seriously. Tell me.

Nothing.

Don't be a shit. I won't tell Dad.

(nothing)

Did you steal something? You can't be—

I found it.

Where?

Outside.

————What is it?

(nothing)

It better not be a mouse or a squirrel or something. Or like a shrew? Is it a shrew? You can't keep that in here.

It's not.

What is it? Tell me?

(nothing)

I could rip it out of his hands and look inside, but I won't. I could hit him and then take it away from him, but I won't. I don't hit him, not ever, but that awful, terrible, no-good thought flickers through my brain like someone waving a flashlight in my face (I see myself hitting him and what I see is more bright than what I normally see and then it goes dark in my head when I shake the thought away or say no no no, but then it flashes bright again when I see myself hitting him again and again), and maybe because I don't hit him I think about hitting him more (and I'm afraid I'm thinking about it more and more because I'm getting older and I'm afraid that's what goes on in all adults' heads, I'm afraid all they think about is doing violent, terrible, no-good things, and especially to the people they're supposed to take care of, I mean all the violence in the world has to start in our heads first, right, and I'm mostly afraid I'm thinking like Dad when he stabbed Owen's Nerf dart gun through the plaster in his bedroom and I'm thinking like Mom when she would tell me what an awful, stupid, fat-ass daughter I was, or like when she wouldn't say anything to me and just stare at me with her mouth closed so tight and I could hear her saying nothing to me). I won't ever hit Owen (I'd chew my own hand off first) but it's hard, it's all so hard, but I can't believe he won't tell me what it is, whatever it is inside the cardboard shoebox that is dark green and doesn't have a logo, which is weird, I mean, everything has a logo on it, so maybe it isn't a shoebox (or sneakerbox, I think they should call them sneakerboxes) and is just a rando box. It's smeared with dirt and mud and there are dark spots on the cover and on the sides, and those dark spots look like the grease spots on the inside cover of a pizza box, so now I'm thinking that whatever is inside the box is nasty and leaking through the cardboard, and I want to tell Owen to wash his hands, but then he's scurrying past me, or trying to, and I block him, tickle his stomach with my left hand (there really isn't any stomach to tickle, only his sticklike ribs) and grab for the box with my right, and it works, kind of, because he flinches and for a second I have the box balanced in my hand, only it isn't very balanced and whatever is inside of it shifts, and whatever is inside of it feels bloblike, oozy, and it's so gross I might throw up, actually it's so gross I'm past throwing up because my stomach turns to goo and sloshes down into my toes, and more gross, the bottom of the box, the underside, feels damp, and then oh my God the smell, worse than the smell that comes out of the laundry room on a hot day, worse than the septic tank being pumped, and even worse than opening that garbage bag I didn't realize was full of months-old garbage (because it was sitting in the hall coat closet we never use anymore and I only looked in it because Dad left the doors open and I thought it might be the dolls and toys that manic-phase Mom collected in a "Morgie" bag [and she never told me what Morgie meant or stood for but only that was where your old stuff went to give to the poor people (like us now)]), and then Owen whines like a puppy, swats my hand away, and his eyes are all red like he's been crying and they're sunken into his head too, and then he is past me and running down the hall, bouncing between all the bags and junk like a mini parkour pro. I yell after him and then Dad slur-shouts something from the TV room, so I stop running, frozen in place, and I don't want to talk to him now and I tell him to go back to sleep in my head, which I know never really works but it works this time, but it doesn't matter because Owen gets away and locks himself in his room. I wait until Dad is out again and I tiptoe past him down the hall to Owen's closed door and I smell the box's smell (and still feel the box's feel on the tips [and the insides, I swear] of my fingers).

Owen. Come on.

(nothing)

Can I see it?

No.

Why not?

(nothing)

This is stupid. Just let me in.

No. Go away. Please.

You can't stay in there forever. I'm gonna get in there and I'm gonna see it.

(nothing)

...

I go to my room and shut the door and instead of screaming or crying or trashing everything I neaten (old-Mom's old word) it some more (the room is already clean, so clean you could eat off it [something Mom, old-Mom used to say with a smile] so it's like straightening, or picking up stuff and putting it back where it was), and, I'm telling you, *neatening* is something I never did before Mom left, before things got worse-worse. When I was Owen's age, my room was a pit and I loved it, owned it, and it really was a beautiful pit, but now it isn't. Clothes are in my bureau and hanging up in my closet and books are in the bookshelf and everything has a place (the glass in my two windows are cracked and have pieces missing, but you can't really see it [but you can feel it on cold nights] unless you open the curtains, and I would fix if it I could, but I don't know how to unbreak broken glass), and none of it makes me feel better, and it makes me feel anxious because my room is the nexus of the universe (something me and Stacey came up with, or she came up with it because the word "nexus" was in a book she read, she loves to read [I have too much time to read so I don't and I can't stay in my head that long without other stuff creeping in, so I draw sometimes but most of the time I shut off my brain watching music videos on YouTube and videos that show ghosts are real even though I think most of them are faking even if I want them not to be]), or if I'm not that important to be the nexus of the universe, my room is the nexus of this house, which means I have to keep my room like this or the worse-worse will get even worse (it can always get worse) and everything will come crashing down. I try to FaceTime Stacey but she isn't answering and I hope she isn't mad at me and I think about making my own video to show her what the rest of the house looks like (besides my room, which she sees every night when we talk), but I hear Dad up and creeping around the house like a creep, and the wooden floors creak and groan and are so tired under him, and then it's already dinner time, or what is supposed to be dinner time, and I leave my room (with one of my clean bowls, and I hold it like shield), and Dad is back on the couch eating Pop-Tarts and drinking beer, and we still have these plastic one-serving cups of mac 'n' cheese and I make one for myself, three minutes thirty seconds in the microwave and add the radioactive yellow cheese dust, and I pour the stuff into my clean bowl (I won't eat out of the microwaved plastic cup because I don't trust it's not melted) and toss the plastic into the full sink because I don't care if the kitchen is clean or not because the kitchen isn't the nexus. I stand and eat quickly even though the mac 'n' cheese lava burns my tongue and the roof of my mouth and I think about making Owen a bowl and bringing it to him because a good big sister would do that, but I don't feel good right now, and I'm going to wait him out of his room, like waiting is some action, a thing that I can throw against his door and break it open, but I don't want to wait, I so don't want to wait I even go into the TV room to talk to Dad.

Owen won't come out of his room for dinner.

I'll take care of it.

He needs to eat.

Worry about yourself.

Dad—

He'll eat when he wants to.

(nothing)

This isn't going to go well because I know, I can feel it, that Owen shouldn't be in his room by himself with whatever it is he found in that box, that dead-smelling thing, and that's all I can imagine is in the box, some dead thing, and why would he save that?, and I picture him just staring into the box at some awful mess that used to be alive, and there's blood and ripped-up fur and pink guts and dark, empty eye sockets (and in my head the eye sockets look like how his do now and then I can't unsee Owen standing there looking into the cardboard box with no eyes, with nothing eyes) and I see him touching it and he's there in his room crying by himself and he's sad for the dead thing because he doesn't really understand what dead means, and I think he thinks it means you simply go away when you're dead because, like, a week after Mom left he asked if she was dead and Dad laughed and said, "Why not?" So I'm standing here with steam coming out of my mac 'n' cheese bowl and it feels like it's coming out of my ears, too, because I'm so mad and so don't-know-what-to-do and I stomp out of the TV room the way Dad hates, like, really hates, and I yell at Owen to come out and bring out the shoebox and I pound on his door, and then Dad comes thundering down the hallway yelling at me, at us, at everything, normally Dad being Dad would turn me quiet and small but I'm so mad I don't really hear him and it sounds like everything is underwater and I throw my bowl at Owen's bedroom door and it bounces off and shatters on the floor and Dad is too drunk-slow to grab me, but it doesn't stop him from wrecking-balling into a wall trying to block my escape, but I easily sidestep him and duck into my own room and lock the door and then he's banging on my door swearing at me and calling me names and saying I'm just like Mom but I don't care about any of that and I let his pounding and yelling be underwater sounds, but I'm crying because I broke the bowl and now there's only one clean one in the whole fucking stupid fucking house.

r u ok Hanna banana?

           no

☹

talk?

           can't hell hear me
           he'll
           no facetime tonight
           pretending I'm asleep

that bad?

           always
           I'm sorry Stacey

don't be

can u sneak out and stay over at my house?

Mom wouldn't mind

she says u can stay here whenev

> can't

why?

> I just can't
> Owen brought something weird bad
> home

???

> worried about him
> tell u tmorrw at school

k

what about tomorrow night?

> ???

sleepover my house tomorrow

> idk maybe idk
> I'll be ok

I wake up and it's the kind of dark that fills you through more than just your eyes (when I was little I used to ask my parents about how I slept at night because I didn't like thinking about me laying there with my mouth open so anything could go inside and I wouldn't know and I would get upset and ask them to check on me [this is what they used to tell me] and push my mouth closed if it was open before they went to bed and I'd ask them to double- and triple-check my mouth if they woke up in the middle of the night to use to the bathroom). The house feels quiet, but like a fake kind of quiet, like there are things crouched and waiting to jump out at me and then I realize there are noises in the hallway and they were there when I woke up and I heard them without hearing them, which means the sounds were probably there when I was asleep, too, and that makes it sound worse now, so I listen and I don't know what is making those wet sounds, not like something dripping, but more like a squish, a wet sponge in a fist, and then maybe that sponge is sliding and slurping across a door, not my door but Owen's. I sneak out of my bed, grab my phone (I fell asleep watching videos and I didn't plug in and charge, so there's only three percent battery left) and sneak across the room and stand with my ear only inches away from my door and I cover my mouth (not because I think something will go inside) to keep from breathing too loudly and keep myself from calling out, not because I think Dad is out there cleaning (yeah, like he'd ever be out there cleaning, ever, never mind the middle of the night when he's likely a case of beer deep into in his blackout) but because it must be Owen cleaning up the mac 'n' cheese mess, and that means he's out of his room, standing in front of his door and that means his door is not locked and if it's not locked, then I'll be able to get in his room and to the shoebox if I'm quick and I'm careful, and no, forget quick, I don't want to scare him, so I turn the knob slow and hope he doesn't hear the little click that sounds like a crash, and I'm about to open the door when I notice there's no light coming from the hallway, and I used to always go to bed with the hall light on and I'd stare at that glowing line under my door until I fell asleep, so, okay, that's really weird, right? I mean, why would Owen be out there cleaning up in the dark (he hates the dark more than I ever did, and he usually sleeps with a light on in his room)? He must really be trying to not wake me or Dad up, and if he doesn't want to wake me it's because he doesn't want me going into his room, and it's like he's making me and Dad out to be the same person, and we're so not, and I want to cry and instead I open the door and start to tell Owen that I'm sorry I was all over him earlier and that I grabbed the box away from him and that I won't make him do anything he doesn't want to do and maybe I can help him clean up the mess and then I'm worrying he's out in his bare feet and there are probably still big shards of broken cereal bowl on the floor (when I was seven I cut my wrist and had to get stitches after falling on a broken coffee mug and the scar is a fat, red worm or a slug curling down my wrist), and then my door is wide open and the hallway is so dark and empty, and it's hard to tell but there's no outline of Owen standing in front of his door at the end of the hallway, but I think the door is open, and yes, it is and it's open into more darkness. I'm standing there in the hallway and the wet sounds have stopped and I hear my ears trying to hear in the silence and there's a small, muffled clap from down the hall, near the collection of dark lumps that is the broken cereal bowl, at least I think it's the cereal bowl, and I turn on my phone's flashlight app, and the light it throws is a weird white, like bones on an X-ray, and on the floor is Owen's shoebox, all by itself, I mean there's no cereal bowl and the mac 'n' cheese mess is all gone, just the shoebox, and it looks bigger than I remember it, way bigger actually, like it almost stretches from wall to wall in the hallway, and is it a different box?, its color is hard to tell in the flashlight, but I can see some of those damp spots on the cover, and it's a few feet away from Owen's door and I can't smell it, but I know if I get closer I would, so do I get closer? This is my chance to see inside of it, yeah? Instead I stand there and listen and there's only the electric hum of the fridge coming from the kitchen, and I whisper Owen's name, and he must be in his room because I don't hear him in the bathroom or in the kitchen or anywhere, I mean he was just out here cleaning up the mess, right? That's what I heard, I swear, and I don't know why he'd leave the box on the floor and his door open, and my feet finally shuffle forward and then the phone flashlight dies and it's like the house and the world and everything went away and left me floating in darkness, and I blink my eyelids as fast as a hummingbird's wings trying to adjust, and I say Owen's name again, a little louder and a little less brave, and instead of the shoebox I look where his open door is and I can sorta make out the doorframe and then within that dark, I see something move, or I think I do, sliding around the corner, coming out from Owen's room, or more like the shape is expanding, like how a balloon fills up, and it's big, or tall, and it's not Owen, way too big for Owen, so it's Dad, but that's me putting the math of who's in the house together to come up with *it's Dad* because I swear it doesn't feel like it's Dad and I know middle-of-the-night-stuff is always weird and wrong and off but I'm totally awake and totally aware, like super aware, like an animal-instinct aware, right, and I can't see Dad, and he doesn't say anything to me, which is whatever because he's probably drunk, but again this doesn't seem like what's going on, and now his breathing sounds broken down and not in rhythm, and like real underwater sounds, and he must've knocked the box over (not that I hear it) because the dead-thing smell takes over the hallway and I cough and I back up and go into my room and shut the door and run to my bed and go under the covers and I leave the light off because I don't want him to know I'm awake, if he's drunk enough he'll forget or not bother, and I'm always dying and surviving because of his not-bother, and the hallway floor creaks with his weight then the creaking stops, and it didn't stop in front of my door, and there's a long nothing, the longest nothing, and my mouth is covered and I breathe through my nose just in case, and then I hear the cardboard box sliding on the hallway floor, slowly, sliding away down the hall, away from my door, and in my head I see Owen (not Dad) dragging the box across the floor and into his room because it's now too heavy for him to carry it.

The sun is bright in my room and I bolt upright in bed and I'm in a panic because I can't miss school, not because I love it (I hate it [and I hate almost everything and everyone there except for Stacey and a few other kids and Ms. Whiting is cool too, I guess] and my stomach turns into a stinging ball of pain when I'm there most days) but because I stupidly hope doing well in that awful school is my only chance, which isn't much of a chance at all, and I have no idea what time it is and how could I have slept through my alarm?, then I look at my phone and it's dead and I remember last night and the hallway and it seems far away and at the same time it's still there in the room with me because the rest of the house is still and quiet even if I'm running around my room slamming draw-ers and putting clothes on. Why didn't Owen wake me up?, he's usually awake before me and watching TV (the morning is pretty much his only chance to have the TV to himself) and then I make him and me break-fast with the two clean bowls and I walk him to the bus stop and it's all fine because Dad isn't there to yell at us or do nothing. I go out into the hallway hoping that Owen is out there waiting for me (maybe he didn't come in to wake me up because he was afraid I'd get mad he was coming into my room when he doesn't let me go into his), and the hallway and the house is quieter than it was last night, and I tiptoe (afraid to disturb something, and maybe I still should be asleep, like I woke up during some secret hour or time I shouldn't see, that no one should see) into the TV room and no one is there (just empty beer cans on the floor and chip bags and sunflower-seed bags on the couch) and then I dance around the big trash bags and into the kitchen and no one is there (just more trash and dish piles and open and empty cabinets), and then I go back to the hallway, our hallway and the floor near Owen's door is clear (no broken cereal bowl, no mac 'n' cheese, no shoebox) and his door is open halfway, so I walk toward it, and my stomach is in that ball of pain, and I don't want to go in his room now that it's open. I whisper-yell.

Owen? You still asleep?

(nothing)

It's time to get up. We don't want to miss school.

(nothing)

We'll get in trouble.

(nothing)

I'm coming in. Okay?

(nothing)

I stand there, listening, maybe I can hear Owen breathing or turning in the covers if I listen hard enough, and the weakest, saddest, scaredest, lostest, youngest part of me screams at me to go get Dad, go get Dad, but I will not, no matter what, and I shimmy through the open door, careful to not make contact with the wood (as my face passes by, I notice there's no evidence of last night's mac 'n' cheese explosion) and I can't remember the last time I've been in Owen's room and by the looks of it, maybe it has been since Mom left, maybe it's been for as long as he's been alive, and I start crying because as bad as the kitchen is and the rest of the house is, his room is worse, because it smells like an unchanged hamster cage and it smells like a dead thing and I can't see the floor through a sea of trash and toys and torn-up books and clothes and stained underwear and seeds and seeds and seeds, empty shells spit out everywhere and half-full plastic cups and overfull cups on the windowsill and seeds and smaller seed-shaped pellets that I'm afraid aren't seeds and are mouse poops (I've seen plenty of those throughout the house) and water stains on the wall-paper, and his elevated bed frame has no box spring and mattress (they must be on the floor under everything else) and there are cans of Coke on the platform where the mattress used to be and some cans are on their sides and caked in seeds and there's one can upside down stuck in the corner of the bed frame, and I can follow the syrupy stain leading down the frame and splashed black on the walls, and I turn away and I see his closet behind me and it has no door and it's full of trash and I see empty beer cans and maybe full ones (Does Dad hide them in here? Does Owen hide them from Dad?), and I can't possibly see it all, and now all I'm thinking is that I'm going to pull Owen out of here no matter what it takes and to not let him back in this place, and then the smell again, like in the kitchen when he brought in the shoebox and last night in the hallway, and I wade through the room whispering Owen's name, and to where I think the box spring and mattress must be underneath the pile of bedding and I pull away the blankets and it's the shoebox but now it's the size of the mattress and it's the same color with the same stains, but it can't be the same, it can't be, and without thinking I scream for Dad.

(nothing)

And there's rustling inside the giant box and so I open the cover, and the cover is heavy but I can handle it and it feels wet and damp and cold and that cold gets under the skin of my hands and I hate touching it but I don't let go and inside is darkness, is all the darkness collected and saved, and way down inside I can hear noises and they are faint but I can hear the slurping, sloshing, wet noises I heard when I held the box and in the hallway last night, the dead-thing noises, and I hold the cover open over my head and look down and down and down.

Owen? Are you in there?

(nothing)

Please, Owen?

(nothing)

We'll go away, okay? We'll run away to someplace better? We'll be okay there.

(nothing)

We won't get in trouble. I promise.

(nothing)

I'm coming in. Okay?

(nothing)

HOWARD STURGIS AND THE LETTERS AND THE VAN AND WHAT HE FOUND WHEN HE WENT BACK TO HIS HOUSE

Howard Sturgis received the first perplexing letter from CIRCE GROUP in early June. He was in the middle of final exams week. For the weary students, summer was no longer an impossible dream. For Howard, the end of another academic year was a clanging toll of a bell that would one day soon stop ringing. Howard taught mathematics at Bishop Fenwick, a Catholic High School in Danvers, Massachusetts. Having officially retired from public school teaching three years prior, Howard supplemented his modest retirement income by teaching part-time at the private school. Howard was sixty-eight years old and was a slight, birdlike fusspot, but a kind one. He couldn't have been more out of touch with youth culture and his students' world, and to their delight he used earnest phrases like "Isn't that wonderful?" after computing a derivative or integral. Howard arrived at school by 4:30 A.M. each day (thereby avoiding any traffic on his commute) and he spent the bulk of his before-school hours helping other teachers' students, and by help we mean he would do their homework problems for them. He lived alone in a small ranch-style house on a wooded lot. He wore wool suits that he dry cleaned three times year. Howard told his newest colleagues nothing of his family or of his past. Suffice it to say his joys and regrets were perhaps equal, but never felt equal.

Dear Howard,
    Parcel received, but no letter. Please advise.

Regards,
Terrance Norton
CIRCE GROUP

The second time Howard received a letter from the group was in early July. This letter was slid directly under his front door. He found it upon returning home from SAT tutoring. His student had aspirations of being a collegiate swimmer, but she needed to add at least fifty points to her math score, or so she was told by three coaches from three different schools in three different time zones. She wasn't sure if she wanted to swim in college but she couldn't tell her parents that, given the collective money and time spent and their emotional investment. And she couldn't tell her parents that she did not like working with Mr. Sturgis; frankly, he smelled of body odor that lingered in the room like an angry ghost, his pale skin was too dry, his thin black hair was too black, and his hands were too long, and she didn't like how after presenting a problem he turned his head and smiled in a way she interpreted to mean his intelligence was a gift he was sharing with her and she may not be worthy of it.

Dear Howard,
    My CFO would kill me for putting this in writing, however, the astounding contents within your parcel (the old commercial jingle, "a little dab will do you," comes to mind) changed everything for us. We're more than willing to discuss some form of remuneration or collaboration and/or many other-ations. Help us help you help us more. We want to work with you. We, to be plain, want more. Please advise.

With Deepest Regards and Respect,
Terrance Norton
CIRCE GROUP

A third letter arrived at the school on September 17. Part of him was convinced students were playing a prank, given the prurient ending of the letter. The previous winter a senior created a playful Wikipedia page outlining Howard's fabricated biography (Howard was the first television weatherman and creator of green-screen technology; Howard created a mathematical model of a rat upon which the government tested with mathematical viruses; Howard financially supported a children's hospital in Nicaragua; Howard holds the world record for amount of clementines consumed within twenty-four hours; Howard discovered an eleventh and twelfth dimension when he was thirteen) and enumerated some of his more outré political theories. Howard proselytized a conspiracy-laden brand of politics whenever the opportunity presented. The students humored him as long as it resulted in a truncated class or a completed homework assignment or a better quiz grade. The faculty, in general, did not humor him, save for one man who had been at the school for fifty years and was now only allowed in classrooms to proctor study halls.

Dear Howard,

While the time, I'm sure, is not ideal, given the start of another academic year, but in another more important sense, the time has never been more perfect. The time has never been more now. You'll be astounded at our uses and applications, the discoveries and advances and designs and implementations and successes and even our failures have been . . . interesting. To wit: The Libido Rub (poorly named, I agree) was a terrible, disastrous idea, not because it didn't work but because it worked too well and our test subjects, well, they tested themselves on all manner of objects, animate and inanimate. Live and learn. Given any new discovery, where do our lizard brains tend to go at some point, am I right?

Regards,
Terrance Norton
CIRCE GROUP

Howard thought of the letters as entities unto themselves, as existing without and beyond whomever their claimed author, Terrance Norton, might be, as being capable of forethought, decision, and deception. He knew it was silly to think that way, but he also knew that this peculiar paranoia might, somehow, be closer to the truth. Despite the letters' entreaties, none of them contained contact information, or even a return address. The postmark was within the same state but beyond that, he was unable to glean more information. Internet searches for CIRCE GROUP came up empty. He was surprised by the number of men named Terrance Norton who lived in the New England area, and he didn't find any usable or actionable information from afternoons spent gawking at social media posts and pictures of spouses, kids, and pets belonging to the collective of thoroughly average Nortons. On his monthly call to his younger-by-fifteen-years sister Gretchen (she lived in California and had seven children spaced two years apart and they all, unfortunately, looked like her husband, Gary; his facial features were the exaggerated and elongated balloons of a child's drawing made flesh), Howard deviated from his usual script of asking for an itemized update on the doings and goings-on with his nieces and nephews and then breathlessly sharing his latest and greatest political conspiracies, to which she was not a sympathetic ear (Gretchen once hung up on him when he told her she should discontinue any and all vaccines for her children). During this call, he asked his sister if she knew any Nortons, average or otherwise. He did not explain why he asked.

Dear Howard,

Words are failing me, aren't they? Failing us? I understand. I do. WE do. Yes, we—I do speak for a WE, for the GROUP. If corporations can be people too—to quote a contemporary American politician—then corporations can learn and dream and love and evolve, and we can evolve more quickly because we are a WE, we are evolving together, and it's a more focused evolution. What takes nature millions of years to achieve we've achieved in a blink. And we achieved this because of the miracle within the parcel you sent, Howard. You're to blame! (joking, of course)

I've searched for inspirational quotes to send you, but nothing fits. See the enclosed photo of our most recent and most astounding R&D project.

Evolutionarily Yours,
Terrance Norton
CIRCE GROUP

The photo (printed on card stock) featured, of all things, a large blue van in an otherwise empty, maroon-colored showroom. It was the blue that Howard fixated upon and the unnaturalness of its naturalness. Howard looked out his front bay window, through the glare of the sun and the dusty glass, at his own car, a small, tan electric hybrid of which he kept detailed mileage statistics. He looked back at the photo and the van's swooping and smooth lines, no corners or edges or angles, as though it was molded and shaped instead of being constructed, and he was lost again in the van's azure blue, which shined like a beetle's carapace. There was something unmistakably biological about the color.

Howard brought the photo with him to school, but he didn't show it to anyone else. Instead of eating lunch with faculty or helping students, he stayed in his classroom with the door shut and the pull-shade closed over the door's portal glass and stared at the photo. He swore that the blue color changed (ever so slightly, enough to keep him looking, staring, even running a fingertip across the photo) not only with the light of the room but with his mood changes. The photo, in his mind, was proof that he wasn't being pranked by his students.

The thing of it was Howard had no memory of mailing a package or "parcel" to CIRCE GROUP, although he could not be sure he didn't mail them a letter of some sort. Howard spent his waking hours at home (hours that he would describe as lonely, but not desperately so) scribbling and then mailing (both the postal and electronic variety) all manner of consumer complaint, I'm-on-to-you accusations, and promises of boycott with dizzying detailed financial forecasts of the effect of his purported boycott to a diversified group of businesses, corporations, investment firms, health-insurance providers, manufacturers, and even one chain of (purportedly) organic supermarkets, all according to the whims and rages of a political Reddit he followed and read religiously but to which he did not ever contribute. It was possible that one of his letters intended for Corporation X was bureaucratically forwarded to this CIRCE GROUP. But a package? When was the last time he mailed a *parcel*? He would've remembered that, wouldn't he? Howard was unable to imagine what might've been inside the parcel in question. His mind conjured only images of empty boxes, ranging in size from shoebox to large enough to hold a refrigerator.

Howard,

A peek at some of the current inner workings. The goal is to go to market (I love that quaint phrase, don't you?) ASAP. Branding our R&D projects is not our strong suit. I've argued (in vain) that we need help from focus groups and/or advertisement and PR firms despite our need for a certain level of, shall we call it, strategic secrecy. Alas . . .

This is confidential (and why we do not communicate via phone or computer) and I trust you'll keep it so.

Respectfully and Confidentially Yours,
Terrance Norton
CIRCE GROUP

Below are my comments on the early go at proposed catalog copy. We cannot send copy to design or the digital team until there is final copy approval first (and waiting on word of a possible letter from the president to include as well). And I'm afraid we're far away from the final. We can/have to do better.

Terrance

Still sounds too kid-like to me.
And too German.

Too on the nose. Don't want war association. Pioneering?

WUNDERKAR

The World's First Zero-Emissions Smart Car that Customizes Itself ✓

A MIRACLE OF 21ST-CENTURY RENEWABLE ENGINEERING, MEET THE ~~REVOLUTIONARY~~ WUNDERKAR.

WunderKar's smooth lines of endless innovation fulfill the promise of the future while delivering unparalleled function and performance.

What needs?

Tires that conform to the environment and even the weather, seats that adjust to your body's needs, colors that change to reflect who you are, there's no end to the customization possibilities. With almost unlimited MPG and mileage the only limitations to where you can drive WunderKar is your imagination.

too "millennial"

Clunky. The sentence before it isn't great either.

(text space reserved for specs and technical data)

With all the talk of innovation and discovery and evolution, Howard had to admit he was disappointed they were preparing to sell, essentially, a van. However, after careful and deliberate, well, deliberation, Howard wrote a letter to the group. More of a note really. He didn't use a full 8.5 x 11 piece of paper, as though using a full sheet were committing to something he wasn't prepared to commit to. He used one of his palm-sized reminder notes, a gift from his 1998 BC Calculus class. There were only maybe twenty sheets left from the stack that had originally been thicker than a dictionary. The gray sheets had yellowed at the edges. All manner of mathematical symbols and operations danced across the heading like a child's fabled dream of sugarplum fairies.

By responding, Howard feared he would be further entangling himself. As he composed the note he feared saying too much or too little. That said, he'd never seen anything like the photo of the van, or more specifically, the van's color (which, on this morning, had a metallic green twinkle within the blue, and he wasn't sure but it seemed like the shape of the van's front end was different, more sleek, more daring; it was a smile, or a knowing smirk, a curled lip on one of the matinee idols he secretly adored as a teenager), and coupled with the barrage of strange letters, he no longer thought of his current situation as being a random harassment, as being a mistake. He instead thought perhaps this (whatever this was) was an opportunity for—he wasn't sure what. If nothing else, his answering the group with a note of his own would prolong these out-of-the-ordinary days of intrigue, which would be more than welcome. The phrase *this might be your last opportunity* rang in his head until a quieter voice, one that had been appearing more frequently as of late, whispered, *this could be your last hurrah*. He decided to be to the point, professional, worldly of the ways of business and marketing and not a dusty, fearful academic, to be confident but not overly so, to sound like he was already *in the know.*

$$\sin \delta \ \infty \ \pi \ \beta \ \forall \ \iiint \ \Sigma \ \lim_{n \to \infty} \ \left(1 + \tfrac{1}{n}\right)^{n} \ \left(\begin{smallmatrix} 1 & 0 \\ 0 & 1 \end{smallmatrix}\right) \ e^{-ti\theta} \ \tfrac{dy}{dx} \ \int d\theta$$

Dear Terrance,

I agree that WunderKar as a vehicle name doesn't work. I suggest the GROUP search Greek mythology, as you did for the name of your company, or search other myths and folktales for inspiration.

Sincerely,
Howard Sturgis

Howard left his note on his own front stoop. He placed it inside a plain envelope and the envelope inside a sealed plastic sandwich bag, as he wasn't sure how long the letter would be outside and there was rain in the ten-day forecast. He considered calling in sick to school the next day (it would've been for the first time in over a decade) to wait and watch, but there was no guarantee his note would be retrieved while he was home. He considered purchasing some form of security surveillance for above his front door and allowed himself to indulge in that scenario before dismissing it with a tinge of misplaced regret.

Three days later, on a Thursday, upon returning home from school, his note was gone, and was replaced by a new letter, the longest one yet, which was nestled in a padded envelope.

Dear Howard,
    When the history of CIRCE GROUP is written, you will get a dedication—no, you will get your own chapter. New employees and trainees will forever be extolled to be like Howard Sturgis, though your genius and

generosity—your spirit—will never be duplicated. T-shirts and bobblehead dolls will be fashioned in your likeness. I don't think a statue in one of our courtyards would be out of the question. And a fountain; your statue within the fountain and the children of our employees will throw pennies and make wishes in your name. Nations will fall and nations will rise and as our group endures and grows our corporate songs will be forever sung in your name.

Your suggestion to consult (or re-consult) mythology and/or folklore is spot-on. It's smart and wonderful and imbued with foresight and wisdom. If only I could convince the rest of us to see our folly, and the importance of a <u>name</u>. A rose by another and all that . . . If it was up to me, I would have you named to our board of directors this instant.

Howard, let me run this by you:

Perhaps if you were to come to our complex and make a presentation, it would change hearts and minds and collectively course-correct our branding vision, maybe even our overall vision for the future of the group. We are not going to stop at simply producing smart vehicles—as I'm sure a man of your frankly historic intellect has already surmised. We are going to change all aspects of life and society with our products and improvements upon other products. Our products will become more than a lifestyle. Our products will be integrated within our consumers' very being— entertainment, communication, fashion, health, exercise, the sleep we sleep, the dreams we dream, the food we eat, the water we drink, the air we breathe, the people we people, and more and more and more.

In this, the dawn of our rise, you'll be our eyeglasses, Howard, so WE can see 20/20. Better than 20/20.

Your presence within our complex would be an event, sir. Standing room only. The cafeterias and break rooms would be empty; metaphorical tumbleweeds would roll through the empty halls and offices and cubicles. The applause with which you'd be greeted would deafen strong ears. We would cheer, cry, hug our fellow coworkers, and exclaim in the exuberance of ensured victory. It would take minutes for the ovation to stop and would stop only when you raised a hand. Then we would listen. We would be yours.

Of course, you could begin your presentation by telling (showing?) us how you came to be in possession of the substance (you already know we struggle with branding, so yes, we call it, simply, humbly, "the substance"). Where and how did you find it? Did you make it or discover it or something-else it? Did you realize what you'd discovered when you discovered it? Do you cultivate it on your land, or within your home, in the basement (we've found it grows best in a dark, dank environment)? Are you a closet mycologist or any-other-ologist? Have you used it yourself and discovered its limitless benefits? Have you tried consuming any of the substance (our results have been hit-or-miss—to be kind)? Can you tell us how handling the substance has changed/improved you? Why did you mail it to us? Have you sent it to anyone else? Should we be worrying about competitors or corporate espionage? Are you looking to enter our group in a bidding war (we are nothing if not prepared to battle)? Do you realize that you cannot and will not stop our progress should you decide to not give a literal or metaphorical blessing (we don't mean for that to sound like a threat)? Have you told any family or friends or neighborhood busybodies about the substance? Loose lips at a local bar (we are not implying you have a problem with alcohol or substance [not that substance] abuse) or within your faculty room?

Sharing some or all of that information would have us eating out of your hand(s). We would be your putty (no pun intended). Then you could present to us your idea(s) for naming the Super-Van (my suggestion), and we would all live happily ever after. And the group will grow and spread from there. I am not hyperbolizing.

May I ask this of you, Howard? Don't answer. Allow me: I may. I may ask this of you, and I must ask this of you, given all that has transpired.

We will pick you up in the van-that-has-yet-to-be-properly-named (and you could experience its wonder-ness for yourself), and you will come to our complex and you will have a tour and you will be the first non-group member to see the growing room, and you will then give the ultimate presentation, a presentation to end all presentations, the one that exists within Plato's cave and the world of forms, and you will be rewarded handsomely, of course. Consultants often can name their own price (I'll name one for you, so the GROUP's answer won't be no or to haggle. We do so love to haggle).

I've prattled on too long. Howard, we will be arriving tomorrow afternoon with tears of pride and anticipation in our shining eyes.

Yours, Always, Yours,
Terrance Norton
CIRCE GROUP

Howard fretted. He made the mistake of imagining their shining eyes.

There was so much to parse from this letter in addition to the quirk of the last line ("tears of pride and anticipation in our shining eyes" instead of "tears of pride and anticipation shining *in* our eyes": was this a hurried error or was it purposeful if not a literal representation of their eyes?). Howard reread the letter's first page and then he read it out loud twice. Terrance employed an appealing and nonthreatening speech pattern and rhythm, the syntax and syllable count optimized. It was a symphony of language working in concert with the environment, the temperature and dew point, and so on. The man hit the loftiest high points of flattery, all of which Howard greatly appreciated, as empty as it likely was (still, it was nice), while engendering an insidious curiosity about the group, of who they were and what they did and what they had been sent.

Howard was sitting in his computer nook, and he looked over his shoulder at his little empty house. He briefly took a mental tour of the interior; floating into and through the immaculate, spartanly decorated, lonely rooms. This vision suddenly had the terrible weight of premonition and futility, and a sadness swelled, similar to (but different in an ineffable way) the shade of sadness that overtook him whenever he considered the inevitable prospect of permanent retirement from education.

There, in the near constant quietude of his home, his twilight home, Howard wanted to be picked up, wanted to ride in the magically blue van, and wanted to go to the complex and stand before their crowd and accept their adulation, whether or not it was warranted.

What were Terrance and the group going to say or do once they inevitably figured out that Howard was not the source of their parcel and the substance? The "mycologist" reference and Terrance stating the substance grew best in dark, damp environs seemed to be tells or giveaways as to what the substance was. But how could organic, fungal matter have yielded the WunderKar? He shuddered—not entirely unpleasantly—at the thought of the Libido Rub.

Perhaps now he had enough information to make the presentation. He could research various fungi online and fumble his way through a speech, maybe even a PowerPoint slide show. Still, there was no way around there being unavoidable consequences once CIRCE GROUP figured out he had not sent them the substance.

Howard tried deciding he didn't care, and he would deal with whatever he would have to deal with the moment that the reveal happened and not a moment before, which was so out of character he laughed at himself. He imagined the WunderKar arriving to pick him up and Terrance greeting him with a smile and a hug (Howard was not a hugger, did not like contact, but he would make an exception), Terrance looking like his old high school friend Woody Piacenza (he of the red hair and surprising baritone and freckles and bowl haircut), whom he hadn't seen or heard from in decades but found himself thinking about at odd moments. He imagined the interior of the WunderKar would be white and clean and soft as it self-navigated through private woods and secret unpaved access roads until they reached a clearing and the complex, which was a geodesic dome full of sparkling windows and like the WunderKar, it was made of arcs and smoothed lines and its girder skeleton was visible and the same living blue as the WunderKar, and inside, the complex floors and walls were white and clean and the hallways were more like tubes, the passageways of a honeycomb, the secret paths within a living organism, and Terrance's coworkers were happy to meet Howard and everyone's eyes shined (Howard didn't like that, but once the image was in his head he couldn't be rid of it), and the tour went belowground, and the tunnels were tinted red, a healthy red, a blood red, and to the cavernous growing room where the substance was kept in the dark so he couldn't see it but he knew it was there, so he didn't linger there in the dark, the deepest of darks, and then he was led upstairs to a grand auditorium near the top of the complex and the roof above them was made out of glass so refined it was as though there were no roof at all, and the group's applause at his introduction was a warm river, and then the lights would dim, the windows self-tinting and going dark, and a spotlight, and his presentation.

Only, there would be no presentation. Howard would not go with Terrance or anyone else. He could not go.

He knew this all could be an elaborate prank, a ruse with no greater purpose than amusement for the perpetrator(s), or perhaps he was being set up and this group would be making a cash grab next, and, yes he was self-aware enough to realize he'd spent the better part of his later life researching and believing (or wanting to believe, which is the same thing) all manner of conspiracy. Howard considered all these things and more, but he decided what was in the letters was in fact the truth because it felt like the truth, a terrible one that should remain hidden.

Howard folded the two-page letter and placed it back inside the envelope and suppressed the urge to hide it or destroy it so that he might be able to feign ignorance as to its existence.

Howard then wrote his second and last note to the group.

$$\sin \delta \ \infty \ \pi \ \beta \ \forall \ \iiint \ \Sigma \ \lim_{n \to \infty} \ \left(1 + \tfrac{1}{n}\right)^n \begin{pmatrix} 1 & 0 \\ 0 & 1 \end{pmatrix} e^{-\pi i \theta} \ \frac{dy}{dx} \ \int d\theta$$

Dear Terrance,

It is with more than a little regret that I am writing to inform you that I did not mail the group a parcel, certainly not one with any sort of substance. I may have written a letter, which somehow found its way to your desk, but not a parcel or a package.

I apologize for not calling your attention to this mistake sooner. I cannot properly explain why I did not. It's, shall we say, complicated. For that, I also apologize. I wish you and the group all the best with your endeavors.

Sincerely,
Howard Sturgis

The next morning Howard called in sick to school. It didn't feel like a lie because he felt ill; his stomach churned and stung. Nausea kept him from eating anything more daring than a plain English muffin.

He split time pacing through his one-floor home and engaging in fruitless Internet searches for information on the group until the morning became the afternoon, until he heard the high-pitched whine of an engine that sounded like his hybrid car's when powered solely by the battery. As the sound got closer, there was a lower-frequency growl at the edge of the audible range, and it made his nausea worse.

The WunderKar parked in front of his house. Howard only glanced out of his front window at the blue blur, afraid he would be spotted by the driver and/or passenger(s). Howard had originally planned to hide in his bedroom and ignore the doorbell, their knocks, and their entreaties with the hope that once they read his note they would leave him alone.

Plan B. Howard crept through the kitchen and out the rear slider. It was the WunderKar's sound that sent him scurrying across his leaf-filled backyard and into the brush. He crouched and quietly skulked among the fir trees before ducking behind the partially collapsed remains of a stone wall (about thigh-high; he'd attempted to restore a missing section of the wall on his own a few years ago but one afternoon of lifting stones had been too much for his back) that snaked off deeper into the woods, delineating someone's long-forgotten property lines. Howard found a protected (he hoped) sightline to the WunderKar, with its glowing, spar- kling blue that gave the appearance of movement, of rippling flesh. The sound of its engine, or the echo of the sound, or the outline of a frequency he couldn't identify or properly hear, or the sensation of the sound on his skin, which permeated into his tissue, into his very being so that he was hearing without hearing, that un-sound was worse now than it was when he fled the house. It blurred his vision and took root painfully in his head.

As though sprung from a trap, Terrance (he never identified himself as such, but he didn't have to) shot out of the front passenger door and stood triumphantly on the front lawn. He was dressed in nonthreatening tan khakis and a white polo shirt that showed off his fit (but not too fit) and tan (but not too tan) arms. His brown, red, and silver beard was perhaps too full, but it gave his vulpine face character. His eyes did indeed shine.

Terrance tapped the WunderKar and the side panel swooped upward, unfurling like a wing. The van's interior shined an antiseptic white. There appeared to be an L-shaped, cream-colored bench seat that traced the driver's-side wall all the way to the rear of the vehicle. There were no other seats or chairs taking up the rear passenger space.

Terrance jogged to the house's front door, which wasn't visible from where Howard hid. After a moment or two of silence, the doorbell rang out. Then it rang out again. Terrance did not knock. Howard held his breath and crouched lower behind the stones.

Terrance eventually emerged, walking slowly away from the house and reading (or rereading) the note Howard had left taped to his front door. When Terrance was again standing beside the WunderKar he folded the note and slid it into a back pocket. He said something Howard couldn't hear and two people spilled out from the van, from out of the rear interior that was empty only moments ago. They were dressed the same as Terrance and their eyes shined too. They marched down the thin cement walkway to Howard's house and opened the locked front door, roughly by the sound of it.

Terrance and his groupmates spent a considerable amount of time inside the house. Howard didn't have his phone or a watch, so he could mark time only with the dimming afternoon light, dropping temperature, and the worsening body aches from his protracted crouched position. They did eventually leave, though Howard remained in the woods for hours after they left. He remained in the woods lying on the ground behind the stones until it was dark. He remained in the woods lying on the ground behind the stones and in the dark until the memory of the WunderKar engine's nauseating, nerve-stripping pulse could do him no more harm.

Howard shivered and staggered through his yard and slunk inside his home through the back slider. He walked through every room turning on the lights, although he was afraid of what he might find with each flick of each switch.

Nothing in the house looked amiss in the weak sepia glow of his energy-efficient lightbulbs (he kept only one bulb instead of the two required within most of his lamps and fixtures). If the group had taken or moved anything, he couldn't tell.

What had they been doing in his house for all that time? He checked his computer browser history and there was no evidence that anyone else had logged on or had tampered with his files. He figured people like that probably knew how to leave no digital trail or evidence behind and now he wondered if the group was a double-secret, deep-state government agency who were keeping tabs on him.

So it was that everything in the house began to look staged and too normal, as though Howard were outside and alone in the woods for an epoch before returning to a home he no longer recognized. There was something sinister in the sameness, or, more subtly, the something sinister was revealed by the sameness: the futility of his choosing to continue to play out the string while giving up the opportunity for not-sameness offered by Terrance and the group.

As dim as the light was inside his house, the darkness outside his windows was extra inky and thick. Howard imagined the group uprooted his home and then painstakingly relocated it somewhere else, perhaps in the basement of their complex, within their growing room.

Howard shuffled to the front door, careful to not breathe too loudly. He hesitated with his fingers wrapped around the cold doorknob, but he eventually opened the door. There was more of the sinister sameness: the quiet street and neighbors' homes cloaked in autumn's heavy, soporific darkness, his uneven walkway path through his dying grass—but at his feet, on the front stoop, was a letter and an unsealed, cube-shaped cardboard box, the top flaps folded over each other to keep them closed. The box was not large or heavy, and he cradled it in the crook of one arm. He brought it inside.

The letter was handwritten. The ink was black.

Howard, you don't understand. You most certainly sent us the package. Even if you don't remember doing so, even if you sending us the package was somehow as accidental and unintentional and nonsensical as primordial life's initial spark from nothingness into being.

No matter. We do not make mistakes. As I've already told you, we make improvements.

T.

Howard sat at his computer desk with the box in his lap. He read the note two more times. Then, unsure of what to do with it, he placed it within the nook of his computer desk in which he kept other forgotten scraps.

He opened the box, the interior of which was lined with what appeared to be wax paper. At the bottom was a layer of a flaky, crumbly substance that looked like dried manure but for its blue color. Howard didn't hesitate and filled the box with his hands. The substance didn't feel as dry as it looked. It was warm, moist, but not wet, and he luxuriated in passing the substance between his fingers and palms. He carefully lifted his hands out of the box. The blue substance was both granular and fibrous and it filled in the jagged, cracked lines of his aged skin. His hands shined and Howard felt as though he were falling away from himself and into something else, and it was what he wanted. Was that what he wanted?

Howard held his breath and flexed his fingers and listened to the quiet of his house, which suddenly didn't sound so quiet. There might've been footsteps coming up his basement stairs and the WunderKar might've been pulling up to his house again. Before he would again lose his nerve, he scooped more of the substance from the box and applied it to his forearms, his neck, his face, and his eyes.

His front door opened and closed, and so did the basement door, and people were excitedly discussing a WunderKar guerilla marketing campaign very close to where Howard was sitting now, but it was the un-sound from hours earlier that Howard concentrated upon. It vibrated through vessel, tissue, organ, and bone, starting at his fingertips. The un-sound wasn't unpleasant this time. It had been improved, just as he was improved, just as we'll all be improved.

THE PARTY

"I'm leaving my purse under the seat. Don't let me forget. Ugh, we're so late," Jacqui says. She proclaimed they were going to be late every five minutes during the drive down from their apartment near Central Square in Cambridge; *You're not driving fast enough* the unspoken accusation.

With the prophecy fulfilled, they exit the car. Frances says, "It's fine. No one is late to a party."

"Look at all the cars parked on the street and driveway. Everyone is here already."

Jacqui is a generally charming, socially anxious extrovert. When the anxiety builds toward a boil, Frances has found asking simple, borderline-annoying questions helps Jacqui to release some of the steam. "Who is everyone?" Frances asks.

Jacqui smirks and narrows her eyes. "I know what you're doing. Thank you, and you can stop." She clutches the bottle of Merlot Frances picked out. Neither of them is sure if it will be to her boss's liking.

"I'll answer for you: work people. People you see and talk to every day. People who like you and admire you and on occasion steal your lunch from the office fridge." Frances takes Jacqui's free hand (her fingers are shockingly cold) and leads her up the long, woods-flanked driveway clogged with SUVs and luxury sedans.

Jacqui wriggles her hand free, nervously adjusts the scarf hanging loosely around her neck, and says, "I didn't want us to be the last people here. Everyone staring at us as we go in. Maybe we should stay outside—you can have a smoke—until someone else shows up and we'll sneak in behind them."

Frances runs a hand through her shoulder-length, graying hair. "Oh, we're definitely the last ones here." She tries to say it with a smile, or to pluck one from Jacqui.

"We should go home," Jacqui says. "We have this bottle of wine."

"I don't like wine."

"I meant for me."

They have been living together for almost a year, dating for nearly two. They met when Jacqui tornadoed into Frances's House of Brews, a small café by day and specialty-beer bar by night. Jacqui ordered a large black coffee to go and accidentally left her phone and purse on the counter. When she returned twenty minutes later, Frances was sitting at a small table with the phone and purse along with pastries on two small plates. She had taken off her apron and put on a black blazer in an attempt to look more like the owner and less like she'd been behind the counter for the prior sixty hours the place had been open. Jacqui missed her conference call and they sat and talked as she finished her coffee. Jacqui returned later that night for a free beer at Frances's insistence. Frances is fifty-one years old, which is fifteen years older than Jacqui. There are times when that gap feels like an epoch. She knows Jacqui's anxieties are the root of how she is reacting to their lateness and it's not that she's embarrassed to be seen with an older woman at a work party. However, Frances is tired of the it-doesn't-matter-if-they-stare-at-us conversations and tired of her own teenlike insecurities that pick and nag and never seem to go away.

"Can't go home now. The Work People"—Frances pauses here, accentuating the playful, purposeful nickname—"have seen us already."

Jacqui surprises Frances by laughing. As though reading her mind and purposefully tweaking it, she says, "You're my old lady," and hauls up Frances's hand for a mock chivalrous kiss.

The '70s-style ranch sprawls atop the private, hilly lot like an inkblot. Twin floodlights illuminate the cobblestone walkway at the end of the drive and the home's dark-brown exterior, which shows if not its age, then its yearly battles with the extremes of New England weather. Rigorously landscaped shrubs flank the front entrance.

Frances says, "Cute, but smaller than I imagined."

"Wait until you see inside. She's shown me pictures."

"I bet she has."

"You're not funny." The front door is ajar, leaking conversation and laughter from the party. "I guess we just go in."

"This is your party. You can cry if you want to." Before following Jac-qui inside, Frances looks behind them. Beyond the floodlights and walk-way there is only the dark. She cannot see the street or the length of the drive. It's a silly thought, one reflecting her own unspoken anxieties of having to be "on," of having to—in her mind—justify who she is to a group of strangers, but it's as though nothing exists beyond the house and this point in time.

Frances says, "That's what I call an open floor plan." From what she can see from the foyer, the only walls in the house are the exterior walls. An expansive kitchen, dining room, and living room flow into each other and overlap, the boundaries ambiguous and arbitrary. The interior is brightly lit, almost garishly so. Yellows and golds mix with copper and other earthy tones. Elegant, modern light fixtures drop from the ceiling. The massive kitchen island is quartz-topped and has a deep farmer's sink. The wall to their left is all windows and glass, floor to ceiling, offering a view of the lantern-lit backyard. Bookshelves ivy the rear wall in the living-room area. Well-dressed revelers fill this space, everyone drinking and showing their teeth.

One of the guests rushes over, gives Jacqui a hug, waves hi at Frances, and within the same breath of the greeting offers to take their coats and wine. The rules of the party house always to be fumbled through and fig-ured out as one stumbles along, Frances is about to ask if they should take off their shoes, but the younger woman disappears with her arms full of their coats. Jacqui is stunning, as always, in her little black dress. Frances wears her threadbare blazer over an untucked, white button-down, and her best skinny jeans.

An older man in a gray suit appears next to them with a tray of red-tinged drinks in tumblers. He explains that it's a cocktail made especially for the party: Four Roses Bourbon, Campari, sweet vermouth, and orange zest. Frances asks if the drink has a name. "It's called simply 'The End.'"

"As in if you drink one it'll be the end of your night?" Jacqui accepts a glass with a little bow of thanks.

"Festive," Frances says. She declines, as she's driving. She asks if there's any beer, the hoppier the better. The man points her to a lonely table set up against the wall of windows.

Upon returning to Jacqui's side after the beer run, Jeanne Bishop, the owner of the house and the CFO of Jacqui's company, stands in the middle of the great room and taps her glass with a fork until the party quiets. She says, "Thank you all for coming. I'm generally not one for speeches." The party laughs at the irony or self-deprecation as they are supposed to. Frances is self-aware enough to know her predisposition to not like Jeanne Bishop isn't entirely fair, but thinks, not without some satisfaction, that she is made of sharpened, uncompromising angles, and that she sounds as dry-cleaned as she looks. "I'll keep it brief and to the point. Eat, drink"—Jeanne pauses to sip deeply from her half-empty glass—"and fuck, for tomorrow we die."

The party in the great groom roars and claps its approval.

"Is the head of HR here? I'd like to lodge a complaint," Frances whispers into Jacqui's ear.

"I don't think that line was in Corinthians," Jacqui says. She's clearly more relaxed having walked through the pre-party fire of anxiety, and she links arms with Frances.

At the physical contact, Frances smiles, she can't help herself. "She's using the New Living Translation."

"Why are we here again?"

"She's your boss."

"Right. You should've told me to say no. Really, you're supposed to protect me from things like this."

"I failed. That toast was kind of weird, right?"

"Rich white people are weird. She's not like that in the office."

"Do you mean she's not rich and white or she's not drunk in the office?"

"Shh. We should go say hi. Those are the rules, right?"

They wait politely in an informal greeting line that has gathered around Jeanne, who wears a red sequin gown. A man in a gray suit, carrying what looks to be a straw-woven picnic basket, comes by asking for cell phones. Most of the people around them hold up empty hands, signifying they'd already complied with the demands of the basket.

Jacqui looks at Frances expectantly, or is it questioningly? Frances cannot tell. Earlier, Jacqui made a show of leaving her purse and apparently her phone under the passenger seat. Did she know this phone request would be made? Frances says, "There's no way in hell I'm giving up my phone."

Jeanne steps between them and says, "Putting phones out of reach is one of my office rules when we have meetings. I'd rather people fully engage with one another without distraction. Hello, my dear." Jeanne hugs Jacqui quickly. "I'm so glad you made it." She holds Jacqui at arm's length and drinks her in. Jacqui apologizes for being late, muttering something about the drive being longer than they anticipated. Jeanne turns her attention to Frances and says, "I've heard so much about you, Frances, it's wonderful to finally meet."

They hug and Jacqui widens her eyes, clearly enjoying Frances's discomfort.

"It's very nice to meet you too, Jeanne," Frances says. "I'm sorry about the phone thing. But if something goes wrong at my café, like if it catches fire or something"—she laughs at her own joke that she knows isn't all that funny—"I need to know."

"Of course, of course. But even if it did go up in flames tonight, God forbid, we know it wouldn't matter since the world is ending tomorrow." Jeanne laughs.

"I guess that's one way of looking at it." Frances drinks from her beer bottle. She's either not in on the joke or is the butt of one.

"Oh, Jesus, Frances, I'm sorry." Jacqui nervously darts her eyes between the two women. "I don't know how I forgot, but I did. I didn't—" She pauses, gestures at Frances, and speaks directly to Jeanne: "I didn't tell her there's a theme to the party."

Jeanne's rigid posture momentarily curls. "You didn't tell her?"

"Yeah, you didn't tell me?" Frances's voice goes higher-pitched than she intended. She did not want to sound so obviously hurt.

"Surprise? I'm sorry. I feel awful. Jeanne, I don't think I've told you, and it's not a big deal, really, but I tend to stress out and my brain can shut down before—before gatherings like this—"

"Oh, Jacqui, I'm sorry, I had no idea."

"No, it's okay, please don't apologize. I'm fine. It just takes a little extra work to get me to the party. Once I'm there, I'm always fine, and I have a great time, and I'm usually the last one to leave, right, Frances?" Jacqui grabs Frances's hand and squeezes.

"Well, I'm glad you're here, Jacqui, and please let me know if you need anything. And, yes, Frances, the theme of the party is the end of the world. We're not celebrating apocalypse per se, and I don't mean it to be morbid, but think of this as more a celebration of living in the here and now. Now that I'm talking about it this way, it's a terrible theme, isn't it?"

Frances says, "No. Not at all. Maybe we'll try it out at my café some-time. Offer to serve everyone their last cup of coffee or pint of beer."

Jacqui says, "Ugh, I'm the worst. I'm sorry to you both."

Jeanne fusses and insists Jacqui stop apologizing. Frances does not.

After a silence of some length that wilts polite smiles and glows with the embers of confusion and resentment, Jeanne says, "I am disappointed no one dressed up like Mad Max or Imperator Furiosa."

Frances says, "If I'd only known. I'm big into cosplaying."

Jacqui rolls her eyes, and says, "Your home is absolutely gorgeous, Jeanne. I can't stop looking at that wall, all those beautiful windows."

"Thank you, Jacqui. You're too kind. It was a lot of work. Worth it in the end, I think. But"—she pauses to sip and while swallowing points a thin finger—"with all that glass, we'll be totally exposed tomorrow when the world ends. Maybe we'll be kept as pets, like fish in an aquarium, and they'll watch us as we either slowly starve or go mad. I'm just kidding, sorry. We're not planning on staying in this room. Too exposed. Okay, I'll stop joking. I do get into the spirit of my themes. Perhaps too much. Jacqui, I'm guessing you did not mention to Frances my offer to stay the night? I have plenty of room, and it's such a long drive back to the city. And for what?"

"Why didn't you tell me the theme?" Frances holds up quote fingers around "the theme." "Am I making too much of this? I don't think I am. You had weeks to tell me."

"I don't know. I'm sorry."

"What do you mean you don't know? There has to be a reason. Did you think I'd make fun of it or say I wouldn't want to go?"

"I really don't know."

"I don't get how you don't know."

"I'm not lying to you."

"You could've told me when we got here. You could've told me when that guy brought you 'The End' drink? Jesus, why not tell me then?"

"Look, I'm sorry. You know how I get before social gatherings, and my answer isn't going to change even if you keep asking."

"What about the collecting-phones thing? You left your phone in the car. I saw you do it. Why not warn me about that? I mean, it's like you brought me to a—to a secret cult party."

"Seriously? You're being ridiculous."

"Am I?"

"Yes. 'Secret cult party' was last year's theme."

"I knew it. Total cult. Work People Cult. You have your glass of Jim Jones juice. Plus that Caligula toast/speech she made. And the shit about being in the aquarium is more than kind of fucked up."

"Now you're being a jerk. I can't even deal with you right now." Jacqui's arms are crossed over her chest, and she smirks, likely trying to appear more bemused than she actually is.

"Fine. I'll stop. But there's no way we're culting here overnight."

"Yes, I know. Give me a little fucking credit."

Frances has pushed far enough, if not too far. Their brief but intense argument ran its course from stung feelings to resigned attempts at humor but is in danger of heading back out toward hurt again. She shakes her empty beer bottle regretfully. "If I go outside to smoke, will I be the first one sacrificed?"

"Only if we're lucky."

Past the kitchen and down a narrow hallway, Frances finds the bedroom currently serving as the coatroom.

The ceiling lamp has been left on, but the fog of decorative frosted glass dims the light. The walls above the wainscoting are creamy yellow. The darkly stained headboard, a pirate's flag for the king-sized bed, spreads out before the rear wall. Guest coats and jackets have been carefully if not obsessively arranged atop the white-duvet-covered mattress. The number of coats is overwhelming. Are there that many people here? And there's something about the way the coats are laid out, like trophied pelts. She makes a mental note to make a joke to Jacqui later that she would've been back to the party sooner, but finding her coat was like finding a needle at an archaeologist's dig site. She finds her overcoat right away, though, and retrieves her cigarettes and lighter.

Across from the bed, tucked into a corner of the room, and beneath a large window is a sitting area; plush chair, small bookcase, and a circular, one-post wooden table. Atop the table is, well, she's not sure what it is. The red, lumpen, smooth-surfaced thing is shaped like a strawberry yet is the size of a birthday cake. Bigger, actually. Frances decides it is a cake as she walks around the bed to the sitting area.

With the cake designation clear in her mind, she assumes the red exterior is fondant icing, but upon closer inspection, the surface isn't smooth. The longer she looks the more organic the thing appears, although there is no sign of stem or stalk. There are random patches with small, raised bumps and with black dotlike pits, or pores in its skin. She does think of the outer layer as a skin. Sitting briefly in the plush chair, she wonders if the skin would be as soft as the cushion beneath her, or crusted and hard. There's a sickly sweet compost smell, almost smoky, that stings her eyes with its unpleasantness initially. She quickly becomes used to it. Beneath the object is a porcelain platter or serving dish and pooled at the object's base is a dark-red, almost purple, glistening liquid. Frances leaves the chair but maintains a crouch, and maneuvers to the other side of the table, the side facing the window. The skin here is acned with pustules and weeping sores.

Frances stands and shimmies a few fleeing steps away from the sitting area, wringing her hands absently. She doesn't turn on a heel and leave the bedroom. She instead returns to the chair, bends, and reaches a finger toward a section that appears the smoothest, the most unblemished. The surface breaks at her touch as though it were made of rice paper. Liquid saps out from a fingertip-sized hole. It felt like touching a rotted tomato, only worse, because it is not a tomato.

Outside the bedroom and standing in the middle of the hallway is Jeanne. "Did you find everything you need?" she asks.

Frances says, "Yeah," and holds up her pack of cigarettes with one hand. She wipes her other hand on her jeans. Witty rejoinders die on the pad of her greased fingertip.

"You're welcome to go out back. I left a standing ashtray at the edge, where the brick meets the grass. It looks like a tall, skinny birdbath. Can't miss it. The glass doors to the patio are unlocked."

"Thank you. I will." Frances walks past Jeanne, almost pressing against the wall to avoid any glancing contact with her.

"I know it's a lot," Jeanne says, "but my offer stands for you and Jacqui to stay overnight. You can have my bedroom if you like. I don't mind."

It's a clear, cold night. Unlike being in the city, bubbled within its desert of light, there are stars visible in the sky. Some of the pinpricks of light are larger than others. Some flicker and waver, others are hard, steadfast, unblinking.

A breeze enables the grass and trees to speak. Standing at the edge of the bricked patio but not on the grass—she will not step onto the grass—her back to the house, Frances stares into the wooded lot. The ankle-high grass leads to a thick grove of trees. She does not look at their heights and tops and wonder how long the trees have lived, how long they have left to live. She instead strains to identify the mishappen mounds crowding around the bases of their trunks until she can't bear to stare at them any longer.

Can anyone from the party see her out here? Would she, undetected, be able to watch them revel while in—how did Jeanne put it?—their aquarium?

Frances mutters, "Shouldn't it be a terrarium, Jeanne?" She throws the cigarette butt onto the grass and not the ashtray. A small act of defiance, one that twitches a smile.

Frances turns around and looks inside the teeming, glowing house. Jeanne and Jacqui are standing together by the patio doors and looking out into the yard, presumably at Frances. They are far enough away that their faces are featureless blurs. Judging by the hand gestures and her bobbing head, Jeanne is doing all the talking.

The man with the drink tray comes by and offers Jacqui another red glass of The End. She takes it. She raises the tumbler in the air, tipping it out toward Frances, toasting her.

For Shirley Jackson

THE BEAST YOU ARE

By K. Bristle

BOOK ONE: THE FIRST AGE

I.

There were other
First Ages
before this one.

A Bevaur village Archivist named Spire
was a brown rabbit
self-conscious of her unevenly lengthed, cornstalk ears
carefully folded under a floppy gray baker's hat that had once been her mom's.
She kept meticulous records
shelved within the dusty stacks
of cavernous Ryde Hall.
The hall was named
after two of the many who had died
for Bevaur.
Spire often wondered what the old goats Kir and Tham Ryde
were really like,
more specifically, she wanted to know
what was inside their Ryde hearts
when they stopped.

The tireless rabbit had recently discovered
within a basement chamber

evidence of a twelfth
(counting backward)
First Age.
The triptych carved into a block of wood
was over one thousand years old.
The images
told a familiar story
in three ages.
The twelfth was the oldest known First Age.
Spire suspected
there were more.

II.

The morning of the Ceremony there were three children
who didn't know their names
would be called
later.

Magg was a dog,
an athletic spitz mix,
eight years old, bright-eyed, soft-mouthed,
with thick chestnut fur.
Magg ate her usual oatmeal breakfast at the kitchen table with her parents.
She attacked the bottom of an orange ceramic bowl with a serious spoon,
and bobbed her right leg up and down, tapping a code on the hardwood.
Mom pretended to read a dissected newspaper.
Dad leaned on the counter, interrogating a cup of coffee.
Mom and Dad were nervous.
Magg was too,
in theory.

Magg knew her classmates were already at the Commons,
planting family flags and claiming the best picnic spots.
She wanted to be there chasing a Frisbee with her friends.
She daydreamed about how she would outrun them all.

"Can we please go early? I'm done eating. See?"
Magg held up her empty bowl
like it was the winner's cup.

Dad tilted his head,
glasses slid down his whitened snout.
He said, "There's no need to be in a rush. Today is a solemn day.
Today is a dreadful day for some.
Today is a dreadful day for many."
He amended himself one more time. "For most."

Magg said, "But not for all."
She knew it was a horrible thing to say.
The truth of it was the horror.

Mom frowned, a look more sad than angry, and said, "Your ears are always
    up, Magg."
A saying normally uttered when Magg was being "cheeky" or a "pill";
when Magg was smaller
she would run her paws
over the points of those rigid ears
and curl a smile.

"I know," Magg said. "I'm sorry.
I didn't mean it like that."

Both parents raised brows and ears, silently questioning
how she meant it.
Mom said, "We'll leave in an hour. I know you want to be with your
    friends. But there's no need to be early."

Magg slumped shoulders,
a silent protest.
The kitchen smelled pleasantly of cinnamon, honey, and apple.
Dad shuffled to the table, wincing at his dysplastic hip.
He scratched the top of Magg's head and placed her empty bowl in the sink.
The kitchen also smelled

of more complex, animal smells,
ones that could not be described
in a thousand-hundred lines of poetry.
Magg still imagined she was at the Commons
outrunning everyone,
outrunning everything.

)

Tol was a toad,
ten years old,
with six siblings.
He was the youngest,
skinniest shortest quietest,
fond of small hats and red stockings pulled over his gentle webbed feet.
Tol blinked frequently
as though forever in disbelief.
He loved being with his family, especially when he didn't disappoint them,
but he preferred the company of books,
the thickest ones he could find,
even if he didn't understand
all the words.
This morning, Tol spent extra time
in the locked bathroom
tilting a blue beret over his forehead,
a slash of color in the mirror.
"Still getting ready," he said.

His impatient father, a river-dock foreman, a boisterous bullhorn of a toad,
    bellowed,
"You cannot live life afraid," and then laughed, an infectious laugh for most.
But not for all.

Tol did not think fear was a choice.
He blinked more rapidly, even though
he was the only one who could see him.

His sister Pen, twelve years old, was already outside, miming hopscotch on
   the grass,
shouting to the open bathroom window,
"Come on down, it'll be okay, my Tollie!"

When Tol didn't open the door, Dad left for the Commons
in accordance with the fevered will of his other children,
pulling a wagon overflowing with food and games Tol didn't want to play.

After a short time of grace,
Mom gently rapped on the bathroom door.
She was older than most moms
and had seen more, which was why, Tol assumed,
she was so kind.
He opened the door, the beret twisted in his hands.

She held out his favorite book, *Toliver's Travels*, and said, "We'll find a
   perfectly shady spot, so you can better read this."

"I don't want to go."

"Neither do I, to be honest. But we have to."

Tol said, "I am afraid."

"I am too," said Mom.
She always shared with
her youngest son.

)

Mereth was a cat,
fourteen years old, an unknown mix.
When asked, she made claims
to Ragdoll and Rex, Calico and Cymric,
among others.

Her father had often accused her of being a liar
and worse.
Orange splotches mottled Mereth's black-and-white fur.
When the younger children at school stared,
she stared back
until they looked away.
Sometimes she told them her fur-covered skin
was a map to a faraway, magical place.
Other times
when she needed a reaction
different from boring old wonder,
she told the children
their skins were maps too,
and one day
she would collect them,
every single one.

Early morning, prior to the Ceremony,
Mereth had one of her father's antique village maps
dating from the prior First Age
unrolled on the floor of the great room,
each cracked corner held down with a muddy shoe.
The yellowed parchment was as long as she was tall.
The funny and sad and disappointing part:
Dad wouldn't even know the map was missing.
Lately, many things in their large empty house
had gone missing,
including
an ice pick with a crow-skull handle
and an assassin's dagger,
the blade as long and sharp
as another lie.
Mereth kept most
but not all
trophies and secrets behind a loose baseboard in her room and a trick panel
    within her bedroom closet.

At night, she took the dagger out,
mimed parries and thrusts,
twisting turning slashing stabbing,
learning what it could teach
until the hungry blade grew tired
of her games
and tasted her blood.
The weapons were two of nearly one hundred collected and ignored by her
    father.

A quote-unquote esteemed Council member, who greased as many palms as
    he shook,
dear old Dad
slept off his pre-Ceremony debauch
alone in his locked bedroom.

Mereth delighted in the possibility
of Dad missing his ceremonial speech.
"You embarrassed the family name yet again."
She rehearsed saying exactly this,
using his peculiar and mocking intonation and tone
(she excelled at mimicking voices)
while perched on her elbows
atop the memorized map
that smelled like wet leaves in late autumn.
She held a crumbling corn muffin in one hand
and an eager red crayon in the other.

III.

The Commons was a sacred space,
a literal and public square.
If Bevaur was a compass,
the Commons stamped due north.
To the west, the impassable Kroning Mountains.
Their craggy snow-topped peaks

sourced the Syme River,
the village's carotid artery,
and according to the Farmers' Almanac
the mountains insulated Bevaur from the greediest storms.
To the east, the amenable and seemingly unending Limwood Forest,
Bevaur's source of lumber, passively accepting within its canopy
anyone carrying a saw and ax.
To the south, the Green,
a thick, lush network of marshes and swamps
into which the Syme River emptied.
Every schoolchild in Bevaur learned
the Green cleaned the water pumped through
the heart of the village,
and that water journeyed
until it fed the clouds and storms roiling in the distant southwest,
and those storms flowed north and blessed the crowns of the Kroning
   Mountains
with rains and snows
so the water may continue to run free through Bevaur
eternally.

What is to the north?
Well,
there was a proverb
with varied applications and meanings:
"Winds from the south
die in the Northwood."

IV.

The Ceremony officially began at noon.
Revelers arrived at first light.

Villagers dressed in their finest,
except for the Cult of Awn adherents,
who wore monochromatic robes,

the colors correlating to enlightenment level achieved,
and they carried white latex masks to wear later,
featureless but for two eyeholes
and a small mouth slit for breathing and whispered conspiracy.
Most villagers did not engage with Cultists during the Ceremony,
ignoring their longtime friends and neighbors
because the Cult used this day to aggressively recruit.
Their growing numbers
impossible to ignore.

With permission from the Mayor, the Council, the Rotary Club,
the pernicious Cult of Awn,
the academics, the writers' and actors' guilds, the farmers,
assorted labor groups including the loggers, smiths, carpenters, and
    electricians,
Spire the Archivist
opened the afternoon-long Ceremony
marking the beginning of the end
of this First Age.
Her speech,
neither flashy nor falsely modest,
detailed her momentous discovery of
the previously unknown
First Age.
The applause was neither reverent nor enthusiastic
and was somewhere
in the disinterested middle.
She thought, No one appreciates
the great and terrible yawn
of history.

Everyone gathered in the Commons
had only a mind
for the monster.

More speeches were made through crackling loudspeakers.
Councilman Ford Grahm arrived disheveled and late for his speech.
He insisted on making his
forgettable regrettable remarks.
The only laughter from the audience
came from between his daughter's snarled lips.

Throughout the afternoon villagers shared
food and drink and nervous well-wishes and aphorisms,
promises of brighter days.
In the bustling Common, a temporary market filled baskets and mugs
and emptied pockets.
Performers plied their arts on ramshackle stages.
The old complained about what entertained the young.
The plays, songs, and dances were earnest anxious expressions of joy,
and there were biting satires
and melancholic laments.
The hope we associate with art and expression faded with the daylight
    hours,
as though the shadow of death would lengthen to encompass everyone
on this day,
not some nebulous future day
that could not
be seen or believed.

Mayor Gib Grine, a gray squirrel who favored an obstinate monocle that
    refused to remain properly pinched between brow and cheek,
had earlier boasted about prosperity and a forthcoming technological golden
    age
("A television in every home and rhubarb in every pot.").
Mayor Gib Grine, his tail sprouting from the back of his tailored trousers,
had endured the traditional good-natured jeers and grumbles from political
    rivals
and the disruptive chants from Cultists.
Now, glowing in the fading sunlight,
he again stood before the hushed village.

By this time,
tents had been dismantled,
blankets folded,
picnic baskets packed up,
carts and booths and anything on wheels retreated
to the safer southern border of the Commons.
Mayor Gib Grine, sweat darkening the armpits of his pressed dress shirt,
lifted his right paw.
The bell above Ryde Hall chimed thirteen times,
once for every First Age.
With the last toll still ringing in heads,
Mayor Gib Grine, his stentorian voice gone reedy, said,
"The names I will read
have been determined by a lottery overseen by esteemed Council and union
    heads,
and with special thanks to Mrs. Clee Winster,
our primary school's fearless and most capable principal,
who has already coordinated a team of grief counselors for the students,
and their families.
As is decreed,
only residents under eighteen years of age are eligible to mark
this final day of the First Age
and by doing so,
their selfless sacrifice
preserves our future ages."
Mayor Gib Grine paused when he didn't intend to.
The duration of the pause grew
as though the gravity of silence
was self-sustaining.
Later that evening, he would weep, while his wife, Dit, held him,
and he would swear he didn't mean to drag it out
like a carnival barker.

After the pause,
one that spelled his political doom
in a recall election thirty-seven days after the Ceremony,

Mayor Gib Grine announced the three finalists
alphabetically
by last name.

Within the crowd
gasps of horror,
relieved sobs,
curses directed at their witless acquiescence to what was and would be,
a terrible secret joy that good fortune viciously continued to smile on the
    smiled-upon.
Some villagers collapsed to their knees in thanks,
some in shame.
Parents hugged their children.
Their children gone still as stone
under the gorgon gaze of truth,
the monster finally real to them
even though it had yet to arrive.

From two isolated families
tears and shrieks
and a repeated word,
a command, negation, desperate plea,
"No!"

The Cultists folded their heads
into their masks
through which eyes bulged
greedily, triumphantly.
They linked arms in
ecstatic hopeful fervent anticipation
of a prophesied end.

V.

At the northern edge of the Commons the three children were to stand on a
    brick dais and face the Northwoods.

Tol's wailing mom and siblings engulfed him in quivering limbs.
Dad shouted, threatened, and had to be restrained.
Tol blinked and he blinked and said he was sorry, but no one heard him.
He gave Mom a kiss,
then he gave his blue beret to his sister Pen, and whispered, "It'll be okay."
There was still a chance he wouldn't be chosen by the monster,
but it would never be okay.
He pulled his red socks up to his knees and wondered
if the red would attract the monster.
His walk across the Common
was long and lonely.
The first child to take their place on the dais,
Tol stepped onto the circle-shaped engraving on the left
and blinked some more.

Magg ran in circles, saying, "What did I do? Did I do something?
Did I do something? What did I do?"
Magg's mother slowed her down
and said through tears,
"Be brave. Keep your ears up."
Dad told her,
"You run if you can, if you get the chance.
Never mind any of us. We're not worth it."
Magg had to be pried away from her parents and carried by village police;
two brawny Rottweilers and one warthog with a missing tusk.
Magg was squirmy and strong,
impossible to hold still.
She stopped resisting when they allowed her to carry the Frisbee
she'd chased all afternoon.
The disk was as yellow as the sun once was
and maybe would never be again.
She stepped onto the triangle on the right side of the dais.
Her legs
twitching itching
to run.

Yes, Mereth was afraid,
terrified really.
At the announcement of her name, her legs went liquid,
a bowl of electricity pooled in her gut.
Mereth was also thrilled.
Something interesting was finally happening to her.
As the dimwitted and incompetent officers
muscled that bratty, mouthy dog from the lower elementary class
to the dais against her puny little will,
and as her father,
Councilman Ford Grahm,
pounded his narrow chest,
pulled at bent whiskers,
shouted the fix was in,
demanded a recount,
and oh, that hammiest hackneyed clodhopping actor
had the gall, the temerity, to say,
"No Grahm would be chaff!"
Mereth held her paws over her mouth
yet could not keep
giggles from spilling out.
Her father was an odious ridiculous creature,
one grafted together, equal parts
family money ignorance aimless lazy cruelty,
(he could never focus beyond his own wants; a fatal flaw)
born to cheat and win in a broken system,
but it didn't mean that dumbass doth protesting too much and too baldly
wasn't right about the fix.
Regardless,
Mereth sprinted nimbly
to the square in the center of the dais.
She bowed with a flourish of her arm and tail
and a wink for Daddy.
The promise of revenge
boiled in her heart.

Spire the Archivist
would record Mereth's bow
as protest, defiance, a political act,
and auspiciously
as the true beginning of the next age.

The Cultists shouted a name,
the secret origin of which
they claimed to keep
and honor.

"Awn!"

VI.

The sky shaded purple above
the hulking wall of the Northwood trees.
If the dazed and sleepy insects of early spring made any sounds,
they could not be heard.
The three children faced
the darkening wall of the Northwood trees.
They could not be heard.

The villagers cried and held each other and consoled and rationalized and
said there was nothing we could do and they covered their eyes and said
we can't watch and tell us when it's over and peeked through their covered
eyes and whispered, "Maybe this time, it won't come back," and a few
wondered, What would we do then?

❯

Mereth said, "Where's your hat, toad?"

Tol blinked and answered sincerely,
"I gave it to my sister Pen. She'll keep it nice."
He always answered sincerely,
even to questions that didn't need to be answered.

Mereth said, "You gonna ask it to play with you, dog? Oooh, maybe throw
    the disk like a decoy, hope it chases?"

Magg wanted to growl,
it came out a whine.
She looked at her clutched Frisbee
and for the last time in her life
felt like a child.

Mereth said, "If it chooses me, I'm going to fake like I passed out, 'oh dear!'
    as it puts me into its mouth then it'll be all
bite scratch and scratch bite and bite scratch
its tongue, gums, tonsils, I'll open a red line down the back of its throat
and it'll taste its own stupid blood."
She didn't say, but thought,
Maybe if I drink its blood I will live.
Her tail wavered like a cobra
ready to strike.

A rumbling rumor passed through the Northwood.
The villagers chorused a held breath.
Cultists inched forward
to be a little closer to eternity.
Rhythmic tremors shook the grounds
percolating screams
like kettle whistles.

"Fuck you, Awn!" Mereth shouted.

Magg snickered and thought,
Run, run, run, run.

Tol smiled, resigned
to not belonging here.

Spire wrote in her notebook,
the script hushed and thin,

"After thirty years
and thirty more before that thirty
and so on and so on and so on,
the impossible
happens again."

The rounded shadow of a rogue mountain
had lost its way
and fogged over the sentinel line of the Northwood.
Branches and limbs cracked,
infant leaves shuddered, loosened, and plumed,
clouding the infant night.
Trees swayed and bent
and reluctantly parted.

The monster,
amorphously bipedal
(some villagers would falsely remember it crawling on all fours),
a stygian protean mass adorned with the detritus of the living forest,
green, mossy long hair obscured its eyes and maw and stalagmitic teeth,
which existed in the long memory of middle-aged and older villagers
and in everyone's nightmares-to-be.
Swinging arms
birthing zephyrs,
it glaciered to the dais and the children,
grinding the earth under its bulk,
the scarring terrible and final.

Villagers staggered and fell to their knees.
Spire's mouth dropped along with her pen and notebook.
The monocle dripped from Mayor Gib Grine's cheek,
the world's largest tear.
Magg's parents held paws and watched their daughter's quivering legs and
    tail and lost hope for her and for everyone.
Tol's father wept and squeezed his children tightly to his chest.
Tol's mother whispered, "Please."

Councilman Ford Grahm chewed on his claws,
fretting over possible outcomes,
though unlike the other parents
he had a hunch
the monster would not choose his child
just to spite him.
Cultists mimicked the movement of the monster
and they opened silent mouths behind their masks
as wide as their faces would allow,
praying their god would do the same
and swallow everything.

VII.

The monster bent,
eclipsing the night,
falling over the children.

Its breath smelled of heat and decay.
Tol thought it might be ill, that it might not live much longer.
He was sad for it and sad for everyone
and the sadness momentarily filled his heart.
But fear drained it again,
as fear always had.

Its breath smelled of epochs and ruin.
Magg searched for its eyes
through the tangled matted nest of green fur.
It was important to see the monster seeing her.
She could outrun it
if she knew exactly where and at whom it was looking.
She could outrun it
if she could dodge the first low long swipe.

Its breath smelled of delirious bargainless gluttonous animal fear.
Maybe Mereth smelled Tol and Magg and the rest of the village.

Her father once told her, "Fear greased the world's gears,"
the first and last time in his life he wasn't full of shit.
Mereth extended her claws
and shouted,
"Fucking decide already!"

The monster bent lower
with speed, elasticity, and grace as fanciful as its size.
A previously camouflaged neck
telescoped the giant head.
It hovered two and a half elephant trunks away from the children.
The gravid mass fissured,
a jagged crack split
oystered open,
revealing its teeth.
Oh, its teeth.
Plague yellow,
of ludicrous size,
and chaotic formation,
sharpened cones spires needles
overlapped,
an eager crowd
shouldering for space
with thick foundational blocks blunted by
chewing gnashing gnawing.
Oh, its teeth,
puzzle pieces
that shouldn't fit together.

The Cultists
were blissfully horrified
by the privilege
of the toothsome night.

Magg could not run after
viewing an apocalypse.

Tol hyperventilated and swayed,
a wheat stalk waiting to be scythed.
Mereth hissed as she heard a voice in her head,
the same as her own voice
but not the same.
"I choose you."

The monster recoiled its neck,
stood at its previous height,
looming
over the dais.

Some villagers allowed themselves to hope
the thing would return to the Northwood without eating any of the
    children.
Others feared
and Cultists prayed
the monster would reject their blood offer
and would soon rampage through Bevaur.

The monster swung one mighty arm,
a blurring whooshing pendulum
that wiped Tol away
from his circled spot.

The village wailed,
briefly unified.

Magg fell backward
then slowly crawled toward the monster
making herself watch
until there was nothing to see.

Mereth slumped,
unable to understand why she was disappointed
in another broken promise.

The grieving moon rose
empty and staring blankly
as the monster receded
into the Northwood.

VIII.

The monster's plucking squeezing hand
battered Tol to near unconsciousness.

Perhaps
it's easier for us to believe
the fleeting moments of his remaining life
were mercifully confusing,
disjointed,
a dream in which he was both
flying and falling.
Jumbled kaleidoscopic images,
the sky dappled with star streaks,
the forest canopy rolling in waves,
distant desolate mountains,
and a dark yawing cave with teeth,
didn't fit together,
didn't make sense.

I am sorry to say
at the end
the shrinking shriveling essence of Tol
understood this was all real,
terribly real.

IX.

As was tradition,
Magg and Mereth walked paw in paw from the dais.
Having survived the Ceremony, they were now "Frera";

sisters not by their own blood
but by someone else's.

Two Cultists broke from their coordinated ranks,
rushing the new Frera.

A teenaged mallard duck named Acor offered his mask to Magg.
Wide-eyed and earnest, green feathers tousled on his forehead,
he breathlessly spoke of sharing honor, the memory of Tol's brave sacrifice,
and how she knew
more than anyone else
the awesome power of Awn.
Magg growled, broke her link with Mereth, and sprinted to her parents.

A fox named Civ, orange fur and ears slicked back, owner of the most
    beautiful tail in Bevaur—just ask him—
twirled his blank mask on a paw, offered it to Mereth, along with a
    smirking leer.
"I thought for sure you were a goner. Surprise, surprise, right?"
Civ was a Village Manager who hit the bars with Mereth's dad on
    weekends
and weekdays.
Mereth knocked the mask off his paw.
Civ shrugged and leaned in, a conspirator,
his bushy tail peacocking from beneath his forest-green robe.
"No hard feelings on my end, little kitty.
And if you join our merry band,
it'll piss off your dad."
Mereth's inner voice, the new one, the same one,
told her what to do, what she could do,
what she will do.
She listened even though the voice had lied about the monster
choosing her.
She listened because she liked what it said.
Mereth stepped on the mask
and flipped off Civ and the rest of the Cultists.

X.

No more speeches,
no more talk of prosperity
now that, for the moment, the cost was unimpeachably clear,
and once again
the future was untenable.

Parents carried their children home,
or pulled them in small red wagons,
even the ones too big to be carried or pulled.
Parents wished they could keep their children
hidden in their pockets
as the question
What kind of world was this?
was loudly followed by more questions
they couldn't and didn't want to answer.

The bars were closed for the rest of the evening
by order of Mayor Gib Grine.
Some voters grumbled they needed a drink
or twelve,
but what they meant was
they didn't want to be alone.

The Cultists shed their masks,
abandoned them,
more than a hundred blank faces and stares
on the trampled and torn grass.
Then they milled aimlessly about the Commons
until they were cleared out.
Some went to the Home for further reflection.
Most went home
doing their best to ignore
the heavy eyes
of their neighbors.

XI.

Magg's parents didn't know what to do when they returned to their quaint warm house
haunted by unsure steps.

They hugged Magg,
consoled her,
told her they loved her very much,
asked if she wanted anything to eat,
did she want to watch something on television,
should Mom get a fire going in the fireplace?
Magg said no to everything.
Mom built a fire anyway.

They sat on the hearth "as a family," which was Mom's favored phrase and
    idealized formation;
"We're eating dinner at the table as a family,"
"We're going to the market as a family,"
"We will get through this as a family."
Basking in the fire's warm glow,
no one dared say, "This is nice,"
because it was
and they felt guilty.
Magg wondered, had they always been guilty
as a family?

Dad said, "Maybe we should talk about tonight. Now.
Not let what happened fester."

Mom said, "In good time. When Magg is ready. No pressure, honey."
Magg could not imagine the *in good time*.

Dad struggled to stand, then limped to the kitchen.
"Are you okay, Dad?" Magg asked.

"Just a cranky hip on a cool night."

Magg couldn't believe how old and broken-down he looked,
another sadness that could only be observed from within the greater
    sadness.

"Where did he go?" Mom asked, raising the flag of her nose higher. "Did he
    open the back door?"

Dad returned with a plate and puffy white marshmallows
skewered atop three crooked sticks.

Mom said, "Really. Inside?"

"Why not? We're all marshmallow-roasting experts here."

Magg reached for the longest stick.
Mom and Dad kept their marshmallows a cautious distance from the
    flames,
rotating their stick slowly, dutifully.

Magg hugged her stick close to her chest and asked,
"How can I stop the monster from ever coming back?"
Magg meant her question sincerely, all the sincereness she could muster.
She wanted it not to sound like a question a kid might reflexively ask about
    the unanswerable,
like "Why am I me?" or "Why do I have to sleep?" or
"Why do we feel pain?" or "Why do we have to die?"

Mom said, "You can't stop it. None of us can."

Dad cleared his throat,
as though making room for something big.
Instead, he nodded and patted Magg's twitching knee.
The flames danced in the lenses of his glasses.

"I'm sorry," Mom added, as though scolded by the silence.
"That's the truth of it."
Her eyes were dark shimmering pools.

Magg said, "I am going to stop it.
I'll find a way, even if it takes all my years. I have to."
She speared her marshmallow-tipped stick directly into the fire.
The sugary skein blazed,
then charred black.

XII.

Mereth walked ahead of her lagging father.
He jogged half-assedly to keep pace.
They made their way south and over the Syme River.
Mereth reveled in the stares from the villagers she passed.
While she heard their whispers,
she only had ears for the inner voice.

Back at their boring old lump of a decaying house
that had been in the family for generations,
Mereth sprinted up the curled staircase to the second floor and her room.
She shouted, "Hold my calls," slammed the bedroom door closed, and
    locked it.
If there were tears—Mereth would contest this if given the chance—they
    were tears of anger, of consecrating rage.

Councilman Ford Grahm, pit-stopping first in the larder for a dram of
    wine, wandered to the second floor, rapped a jaunty knock with furred
    knuckles on Mereth's door, and cooed,
"I was so worried about you, my dear. Shocking really.
The whole thing shocking. To be at all associated with that ugly mess.
Heads will roll at the Council meeting this week.
Roll right off their dirty necks.
I will give you one of their heads as a present, if you'd like,
my little beastie."

Mereth stared daggers through the door and beyond.

He added, "Oh come now, you know as well as I do that you'll be over the
    drama after a good night's rest, if you're not over it already.
I'll be in my room should you need me,
dear."

Mereth sprawled on top of her covers, pressing the pads of one paw into the
    claw tips of another,
counting clock ticks.
At seven minutes past midnight,
not a second more,
Mereth crawled out of her window,
shimmied down the creaking, vine-riddled trellis.
Halfway down, she said, "Fuck this,"
and let go and fell to the professionally landscaped grass.

Mereth crept through quiet neighborhoods and empty streets
and over the cobblestoned Bilhurn Bridge.
The windows of every house and tenement building were dark.
Wooden shutters covered the bay windows of shops and restaurants.
Vandals had smashed glass up and down Devet Street on the same night
    thirty years prior,
a night that had ended the Third Age,
and had rebirthed the First.

What age were they in right now?
History decreed the next age, the Second Age, would begin at dawn.
Yet the last age ended with the monster.
So, she figured, this was the between time.
The voice spoke in Mereth's voice
even if it wasn't hers.
"This is your time."
Mereth agreed.
This was her time
—tonight and the days and nights of the Second Age to come.
She would take it all and make it hers.

She would be as inevitable
as the dead of night.

Mereth arrived at the Commons, stalked through its heart, on her way
to the Northwood line.
She ran her paws over trees rent and bent.
She lowered herself into the depth of a footprint, sinking to its bottom
    without a wish,
sinking into a coagulating mist,
and she suffered
the sole chill of the evening
—a feeling of déjà vu mixed with a goose walking over her grave plus a
    devil's and a doppelgänger's wink—
iced the length of her spine and into her curling tail.

Suddenly unable to breathe,
Mereth scrabbled out of the hole and retreated to the dais.
She stood on the square and faced the Commons.
Spread out before her, the Cultists' masks,
those blank disembodied heads.
The masks would not be gathered and thrown away until DPW arrived for
    cleanup in the morning.

Mereth crawled on all fours,
an act in public that if witnessed would've made her father furious.
"The better to see the masks with, dear Daddy."
She found the one that fox fuck Civ offered,
and she stepped on it again.
The thought of Civ's mask going over her head made her retch.

She was no Cultist, would be no Cultist,
found them as odious, if not more so, than the rest of the villagers,
including her father.
But a mask.
The voice said,
"Yes, a mask."

She took her time
prowling the Commons
in the between time, where
she was convinced
there was no time.
She gave each mask a look and a sniff and a paw swipe.
They all looked the same on the outside,
but they weren't the same.
She circled,
patient,
certain.
Finally.
The one.
The right one.
She must have somehow missed it before and before and before and before
because as soon as she laid eyes
and paws and whiskers and tongue on it . . .

"I choose you."

XIII.

The next morning
villagers left flowers, notes, and candles beneath Tol's bedroom window.
His mother, Lannik, collected the memorials in a wooden chest
kept in his sister Pen's room.

The next morning
Magg wrote a note to Tol's family,
and she wrote a note to her parents, which she sealed and hid inside her
    music box,
and she wrote a note to herself she would keep inside her pillowcase
so she would hear the paper crinkle at night.
Written on the notes:
"I promise to stop it from coming back."

The next morning
Mereth stayed in her room
and painted a lion's face
on her mask.

The next morning
was the first day
of the next thirty years.

BOOK TWO: THE SECOND AGE

I.

Year five.

How he could've better spent his evening,
let him count the ways:
planning his mayoral run in two years,
raising funds,
or his specialty,
making the rounds at the bars, including his home turf, the Watering Hole,
backroom deals to be had,
sealed with folded bills and clinked glasses.
Instead, Councilman Ford Grahm moldered in the mildewy Village Hall
    basement meeting space,
faking concern and empathy in the company of the popular jackass Mayor
(not an actual donkey, Wilp Mornd was an anteater of prominent profile, a
    former B-list star of stage and screen,
he of the folksy sayings as empty as his promises)
plus his legion of staffers
(so much for small government)
and volunteers,
think-of-the-children do-gooders, performative grievers the lot of them.
They planned Bevaur's fifth-year memorial service
for Tol Salientee, the little boy
the town insisted on remembering.
The number of villagers who would attend the service would be less than
    the year before,
and less than the year before that.

Ford was so tired, demoralized, exasperated,
he skipped the bars and hailed a cab,
arriving home nauseous from diesel fumes
with a rat-chewing-the-cheese-of-his-brain headache from the jarring ride
    over rutted, scarred, dug-up roads.

The construction mess was a political and fiscal boondoggle
to make way for the new pay-TV cable lines,
a luxury service few residents could afford
(It should be noted, the cable contract lined the streets and Ford's and Civ
    the fox's pockets).
As Mayor Wilp Mornd was fond of saying,
"The price of a little pain today,
for the windfall of wonder tomorrow."
Ah, progress.

The cabbie, a ferret in a porkpie hat who had spent the trip laughing at his
    own non sequiturs about political life, quipped,
"What, are you afraid of the dark? I thought cats could see at night,"
as he pulled into Ford's driveway.

Every light in his damn house was on.
Even the single pull-chain bulb in the attic, an attic you could only get to
    using a creaky ladder with a missing slat on step three.
The house glowed.
A beacon. A warning. A ghastly sight.
Ford said, "Maybe I should tip you less, wise guy,
so I can pay my electric bill."

Both men laughed,
though neither thought anything was particularly funny.

Ford padded across the slate-stone front walk.
The chorused humming of lightbulb filaments
replaced the rat in his head.

Inside.
His anger and annoyance morphed to unease.
He wandered through rooms as if entering them
for the first time.
Beyond the unusual sight and circumstance,
having never seen nor been in the house with every fucking light on
(overhead fixtures and table lamps and the library's corner floor lamp he

could've sworn didn't work and even the oven's interior yellow light),
the air in the house was wrong.

He resorted to authority.
It was all he knew.
"Mereth? Why are all the fucking lights on? What are you doing?"
He returned to the front foyer, then walked room to room, shutting lights
     off as he progressed and continued ranting.
"Is this supposed to be funny? I know funny.
I'm famous for knowing funny,
You know they save my speech for last at the Harvest Day Roasts"—
(note to the reader: not true)
—"and this, this bullshit isn't funny.
Get your own place and light it up if you want.
You're fucking nineteen years old.
I had a job and my own midtown apartment when I was your age."
(Purchased by Daddy,
he conveniently left out.)

When he finally stopped
flapping his gums in the vertiginously long dining room,
he noticed,
in the other rooms through which he'd walked and darkened,
the lights were on again.

"I've had a day. I don't need this."

In the electric air, the humming air,
his voice didn't carry.
No echo
despite vaulted ceilings and empty spaces.
He felt like a tree in the forest about to fall
with no one to hear him.

Ford pawed for the closest wall switch,
turned off the electric chandelier that hung like a swollen spider
above the dusty wooden banquet table.

He blinked in the new dark.
The cabbie had said
he should be able to see.

Click.

The chandelier lights splashed on.
A masked, robed figure stood
at the opposite end of the dining room,
next to the other wall switch.

Ford panicked,
animal instinct
flicked the light switch off again.
This dark lasted longer.
Ford convinced himself the figure was Mereth,
(wasn't it Mereth?
had to be Mereth?)
wearing a Cultist's robe, a white/beige color,
a color he could only compare to a shaved, mange-riddled hide,
and a garish, painted mask,
golden yellow but for the dark eyeholes, brown nose,
white fur and whiskers
around a toothy red mouth.

Did she join the goddamned Cult? Why the painted mask? Was it supposed
    to be a lion?
He shouted,
"What have you gotten into this time?"
He didn't pause to consider,
the more pressing, more appropriate question,
if it was indeed Mereth,
why would that bring him comfort,
especially as he felt her
grinning behind the mask
in the dark?

Click.

The masked figure was in front of Ford,
a whisker away.
She had flicked the switch
next to which
Ford stood
with the tip of an ice pick.
In her other hand
flashed a dagger.

He turned to run,
but was knocked by unseen paws,
spun around as though he were weightless, made of no matter,
and shoved,
his back against the wall,
a painting to be hung.

The painted mask stared but didn't change expression.
Ford said, "Stop," and, "Don't," and
the last word he said was one he hadn't earned.
"Please."

Her head tilted,
mild interest or slight surprise or bemused indifference,
and the dagger raised,
a cresting steel wave.

A cobwebbed part of Ford's brain recognized
the sinuous blade.
He felt every curve
as it slashed through the center of his chest and out his back
into the drywall,
pinning him like an exotically named butterfly.
He tried to speak
but had no air of his own.

The ice pick was eager
and next.
Placed point-up, a tent pole under his chin,
then she pushed
and pressed,
the metal sprouted into his mouth,
through his darting desperate tongue and the soft palate,
then bone,
and higher still,
until Councilman Ford Grahm's light
was turned off.

She waited for the blood to stop.

She took off her mask,
draped it over one bloody paw.
She imagined the lion head of death
floating,
speaking in her voice
that was not her voice.

The lion assured
she would not be caught,
not this time, or the next or the next or the next or the next or the next or
    the next.
She would not even be a suspect.
There would be no evidence of her involvement
or the police would be made blind to it.

Mereth thanked the lion
for choosing her.

The lion told her
how and where to cut
to make a new robe.

II.

Year eight.

Magg and Mereth continued the Frera tradition
sharing an annual meal.

They met at Sall Mandr's,
a restaurant that would always save a table for the Frera.
The special that night was balsamic large-mouthed bass, leafy greens, and
    roasted butternut squash.

Mereth strolled to their table, ten minutes late,
wearing a cocktail dress and tiger's eyes.
"Hey there, *sis*," she said. "Don't get up."

Magg stood up anyway, too quickly,
knocking into the table, rattling the forks and water glasses.
They hugged.
Magg felt the other diners watching,
she didn't break the clinch first.

Mereth said, "You look good enough to eat."

Magg's ears dropped, and she brushed breadcrumbs
(she had buzzed through the basket of dinner rolls)
off her dusty jeans and orange Stum University hoodie.
"Sorry, I lost track of time—couldn't change—
and I came straight from studying at the library."

"Oh, you're fine. And that's right, you started uni, a year early. You're so . . ."
She twirled a paw in the air, sifting the ether for a word.
"Ambitious. No, driven. Is there a word that means both? Either way,
there are big things in your future.
Big things."
Mereth laughed and loudly ordered a glass of wine from the turtle waiter.

Magg thought she could smell and see through
Mereth's shock act,
a cover for pain, grief, loneliness.
Magg was committed to her own act,
the public act of being Mereth's sister.
She didn't like her,
didn't trust her.

Mereth said, "I suppose, my brilliant sister, you've already chosen a major."

"Actually, two. Sociology and history, with a concentration on folktales."
Because Magg didn't want to talk about why she chose those subjects
she asked, "Are you still working at . . ."

"Oh, yes, tending bar part-time at the Watering Hole,
full-time living off my inheritance,
eagerly awaiting the fall of my house.
So gothic, right?"

They small-talked about Magg's parents, the bar, school, politics, the new
   music television cable channel, movies, dating or lack thereof.
After dinner, Mereth asked if Magg would be walking back to the dorm
   alone.

"I'm living at home to save money,
at least for this year,
but yes, walking back alone."

"I hate the thought of you by yourself
at night
and the Bevaur Butcher at large."

With Mereth's father being the first victim,
it was difficult for Magg to dismiss Mereth's interest
(a subject that had come up at each of their prior three meals)
as garish or ghoulish.

Perhaps more than anyone else, Magg understood obsession.
"It's terrifying, of course,
but I can take care of myself," Magg said.

"I'm sure my father,
the four other victims, including the two students living off-campus,
thought similarly."

"I didn't mean to be insensitive—"

"No need to apologize, I'm being a prat.
But let me ask you, the budding sociologist, this:
Isn't it strange the Butcher removed the hides from my father and
    Councilman Civ
—who, between you and me, was dreadful and a terrible influence on my
    father, and not for nothing, I'm surprised that more discoveries of his
    corrupt dealings haven't come to light—
Anyway, where was I?
Oh, why take their hides, but not the other more recent victims? Any
    thoughts?"

"I can't say I have any thoughts on that."
The waiter arrived with two plates of tiramisu, flutes of Champagne, and a
    wink for the underaged Magg,
on the house.
Magg drank a sip to be polite,
bubbles went up her nose.
She sneezed three times into her sleeve.

Mereth said, "I think the Butcher is a Cult member.
Hearing whispers he wears a robe and mask.
Oh, I love tiramisu."
Mereth rubbed paws together as though warming over a fire.

Magg couldn't help but feel like
Mereth was celebrating the gears of a byzantine long con
set in motion.

III.

Year ten.

In the northeast, an area
—we'd never deign to call it a neighborhood—
we named the Forge,
every year it grew and spread
like an oil spill.
The lumber and paper mills that had once marked the border of Limwood
    now had a barrier, a swelling plateau of landfill plus three stump-pocked
    miles between mills and retreating forest.
"New land to expand," was a slogan celebrated and derided,
depending upon your lot and political stripe.
A handful of blocks west of the mills, which had stood for a century, was
    Factory Row:
plastics, chemical, foundry, refineries, pharmaceuticals, textile, canners,
    automotive, printers, and many more,
stacks smoking and plots and fences chain-linked.
Between the mammoth manufacturers,
like bits of food caught between teeth,
subsidized employee housing;
concrete warrens and high-rise hives,
brutalist dreams and blackened lungs.
In this tenth year of the thirteenth recorded Second Age,
one-quarter of Bevaur's population lived in the Forge,
where life was brutish and short,
its residents suffered from cancer, asthma, stroke, heart disease, lead
    poisoning, rabies, alcoholism, overdoses, and suicide at the highest rates.

The Butcher's seventh victim, Nurl, was a penguin who worked
    maintenance at the toy factory.
The Bevaur Times spared a single personal quote about Nurl, from his
    foreman: "He kept the assembly lines rolling."
His aerated body was found in an alley between building forty-five and
    forty-six,
the press and assorted armchair sleuths insisted the numbers were code.

Bevaur lived in fear of the Butcher,
the kind of fear that sold newspapers and drove television ratings.
Nurl's missing eyes turned up, or looked up, a week after his murder, downtown,
in the overnight return box
of Hub Video Rental.

IV.

Year twelve.

The Archivist Spire ferried a stack of scrolls and documents no bare
   paw was allowed to touch for fear of damaging oils, to Ryde Hall's
   subbasement conference room, the one with the humming fluorescent
   bulbs within in the drop ceiling.
After depositing the ancient cargo on an already-cluttered table,
the winded old rabbit re-tucked her ears under her jostled hat,
straightened her cranky spine, and flittered a thought:
she could retire now, live off her pension,
but what would she do then?
"I'm sure one of us should have something better to do on a Friday night."
She didn't say it unkindly.

Magg said, "Not me.
But I can lock up if you have a hot date with Hoin.
Again."

Hoin, a widower stoat who lived three doors down,
had asked Spire to dinner and a movie once a week for nearly a year.
"Don't tease," Spire said. "If I said yes every time he asked, where would we
   be?"
The question was not rhetorical.
"You should be outside,
a crisp clear fall night like this, walking the cobblestones downtown,
or strolling along the river,
enjoying the dry scent of dead leaves and the soured mash of fallen apples
   and pears—"

"And after the bars let out, the tang of vomit splashing to the cobblestones."

"Such a brat."

"I know."

"The point being, my dear, you'll become an artifact yourself,
if you aren't careful."

If Magg heard more regret than reproach, she didn't let on.
Magg ceremoniously stretched and snapped latex gloves over her paws
and set to the bliss of spelunking through decades and centuries.
The documents were
more valuable than treasure maps and religious tomes,
written in the old languages, each letter and symbol scrutinized and
    compared,
their messages honored with her breath and blinks.
Magg took notes but didn't need to.
She memorized every folktale and legend
about the monster Awn, including:
Awn was made of the night sky and lived on the dark side of the moon;
Awn hibernated somewhere in the Kroning Range, atop a missing
    mountain, veiled by perpetual clouds and snow and sorrow;
Awn was a mountain turned monster and would grow and grow and grow
    and someday consume the world;
the first resident of Bevaur was a bear (or a bull or a panther depending
    upon the translation) who lived for thirty years within the pristine,
    forbidden Northwood, until cursed by the Creator;
deep in the Northwood was a hole in the ground that led to the underworld,
    and there, fattened on the bones of the dead, Awn slept, dreaming our
    nightmares;
the last of a forgotten breed of animal, one so desperate for longer life, Awn
    consumed brothers and sisters, hoarding their collective strength and
    spirit;
The Creator, ego bloated by arrogance, made a terrible mistake, fashioning
    a creature with hungers and desires too closely mirroring Its own, and
    instead of owning it—to use modern parlance—It turned Its back on

Awn, pretended Awn didn't exist, so Awn swore to exact revenge upon
     the Creator's cute little pets, Its furred and feathered chess pieces, as a
     price for Awn's existential loneliness;
Awn was a warning, an agent of the lion of death, an omen, a portent, a
     parable, a threat, a mystery, a disaster, a plague of one, an embodiment of
     the horror of history doomed to repeat every thirty years.

Magg also memorized each hero's journey
from primary to purported first-person accounts
to barroom boasts and rumors,
of brave, foolish citizens
who confronted the monster, including:
The first recorded sacrifice sparing the village from siege was a baby
     hedgehog and a mother who refused to let go, we have forgotten their
     names;
Driter, an adult swan, chosen to end the fourth Second Age, ran and hid
     under Fnog's Bridge, which Awn destroyed and then, like a finicky eater
     removing hated peas from Shepherd's pie, it carefully brushed aside debris
     for the feather, meat, and viscera;
in the fifth First Age, a week prior to the Ceremony, a small army baring
     fangs of blade and arrow, financed and led by the mercurial merchant
     goats Kir and Tham Ryde, traveled deep into the Northwood and never
     returned, and we still sing their songs;
the Fliner Rebellion of the twelfth First Age, spearheaded by anarchist
     Grygi Fliner, a charismatic owl, dressed in a self-ascribed peasant's
     uniform, rallied farmers and factory workers to take up arms instead of
     filling the sacrificial spots on the dais with their children, their blood, but
     rakes, spades, clubs, and too few shotguns were no match for Awn, and
     two hundred twenty-seven villagers died.

Magg worked deep into the night,
past the hour Spire locked the Ryde Hall doors,
past the bars closing and the choreographed halfhearted fights in the
     streets.
She walked home alone,
vigilant but not afraid.

and if anyone watched,
if anyone followed,
unseen,
they would've spied Magg shivering in a black denim vest,
unbuttoned and opened,
displaying a red T-shirt plastered with the iconic portrait of Fliner,
wide owl eyes turned upward, toward unseen heights,
revenge dreams, and better days.

V.

Year sixteen.

Despite having very little contact beyond their yearly meal,
the two Frera grew to consider themselves
real sisters.
They enjoyed their time together, and promised to meet more often,
knowing the promises were doomed to be broken.
They were wary, defensive, on alert,
the other was an adversary to be respected and feared,
their thrilling, pleasurable duels sharpened who they were
to fine points.
Oh yes, they were sisters.
After all, they joked,
they'd put in the time.

"Do I call you Dr. Maggs now?"

"I demand it be so. Plus, a slight bow of the head when you say it."

"Of course! Congratulations, again, on your PhD, my dear. All those years
    of hard work. You've made your older sister very proud."

Raised glasses.

"Thank you, Mereth. That means a lot."

"So now what do you do, right? The ink isn't even dry on the diploma and
   I'm already hectoring . . ."

"As a newly minted research professor I don't have to teach, thank
   goodness,
so I'll continue to haunt Ryde Hall
and my parents' house, apparently.
I've temporarily moved back home."

"How is your mom. Holding up?"

Their sisterhood had been sealed for Magg when Mereth had attended her
   father's funeral,
carrying one white rose for his grave.
"The easy answer is she's okay, she's managing.
But she's sad and broken. She openly talks
—like she's looking forward to it—
about the day when her heart will stop like Dad's did.
She eats like a bird now.
Sighs more than talks.
If Dad were here, he'd be so worried, but I can't get her
to do much of anything
beyond putter about the house.
Sorry, this time of year does it to me every time."

Mereth reached across the table, placed her paw over Magg's.
"It's okay. Your father was a lovely man
and he helped raise a lovelier daughter."

Magg pulled her paw away, hid it in her lap.
"That's only half right. I'm sad and broken too."

Mereth finished her glass of wine, ordered another.
"Aren't we a pair of sad and broken,
doomed to eternity within our ancestral homes."

"You say that with a little too much glee."

"It's the wine. Also, I say everything with glee,
otherwise I'd always be screaming."

"Fair enough. But your house,
weren't you thinking of selling it?"

"I was. I am. I do. It's a warm daydream
so easy to get lost in.
But then I think about all the cleaning and packing.
There's nothing worse than packing—"

"The worst."

"And I think where else would I go?
Where else should I be?"

"I get it. But, um, hey speaking of the past . . ."

"Were we talking about the past?"

"We were."

"I thought we were discussing real estate, though I suppose
we're always discussing the past in a way."

"Don't try mind tricks on the good doctor."

"Perish the thought."

"I've become friends with Pen, Tol's sister. Do you know her?"

"Only by name. Like you, I don't think she has ever set foot in the Watering
   Hole, shows she has good judgment."

"Yeah, well. She's very nice.
We connected, or reconnected, in Ryde Hall,
when she was putting up flyers for a charitable event,
to raise funds for the sick residents of the Forge
who can't afford rabies vaccines or pay their doctor's bills.
She plans to build and run a free clinic within the next five years."

"She sounds too good to be true.
Perhaps you should petition the Council
to have Pen replace me as your Frera."

"Stop it. No need to be jealous, sis."

"You know I'm teasing. I'm overjoyed to hear of you branching
beyond books and scrolls."

"How about you? What's new and exciting?"

"Aside from the charming regulars at the Watering Hole?
I did twist and accidentally break the forepaw of that pig Wendig,
when I caught him rooting through the till."

"Charming."

"Elsewhere, my Butcher newsletter has really taken off.
Over two thousand subscribers."

"Oh, I keep meaning to . . . you can add me."

"I know it's not your bailiwick."

"I cannot believe the Butcher hasn't been caught yet.
What are we up to, twenty victims?"

"Twenty-five."

"Fucking hell."

"I agree. Our police force is incompetent.
However, the Butcher's ability to evade being seen
by anyone who is still among the living,
to enter homes and buildings seemingly like a vapor,
to leave no physical evidence or clues,
purported feats of physical strength in manipulation
and staging of the bodies,
it's almost supernatural."

"You don't believe that, do you? Not you?
Maybe there's more than one perpetrator,
some sort of conspiracy,
but nothing supernatural."

"I don't know what I believe, Magg. That's the truth of it.
You're judging me, aren't you?"

"No, I'm not. Really I'm not."

"I will share with you that I certainly don't believe the Butcher is in service
for the Cultists. Have you heard that rumor?"

"I have.
That the Butcher might be a Cultist makes sense to me."

"It's more complicated than that, I think.
I have some moles within the Cult,
they tell me the Butcher's exploits
are being celebrated as a sign of the end to come.
But at the same time,
as their political aspirations rise with their numbers,
they are preparing to mount a PR campaign,
accusing the press of waging a disinformation war,

and they will target any columnist or newscaster who opines the Butcher is
    a Cultist."

"They can't be serious about their political aspirations, can they?
How can they be anything but fringe,
a loose screw or two within the Council?"

"It's not a matter of if,
but when we'll have a Cultist mayor."

"No. No way."

"I hope I'm wrong.
Aside from my small army of amateur sleuths gathering Butcher
    information
for the good of the community, of course,
my other agenda is to prevent the Cult from gaining more political clout,
more than they already have,
and they do have a considerable amount, I'm afraid,
given their considerable coffers."

"Dammit, well, that's almost as terrifying as the Butcher.
Sign me up.
How often do you send out newsletters?"

"Weekly. I just bought a computer
—so cutting-edge, right?—
and I plan to supplement
with short daily electronic updates and messages."

"I hope Ryde Hall won't go all-electronic, though I suppose it's inevitable.
Is everything inevitable?"

"Evolve or die, Dr. Magg."

VI.

Year eighteen.

Four bridges curled their aging spines
across the Syme River.
The Flind Bridge, farthest north and west,
abutted the hydroelectric and waterworks plants.
In recent years
the water level of the Syme had dropped
due to exponentially increased water demand
and the changing climate.
The electric plant relied less on hydro
and more on coal harvested from the Kroning Mountains
and more on oil sucked from the muck of the Green Swamps.

The Butcher's thirty-third victim was not that pig named Wendig;
he had been the twenty-sixth,
his trotters scattered to the four bridges.
As salaciously entertaining
(Is that the right word?)
as it all is,
sometimes it's difficult to keep track
of all the loss.
Anyway,
the thirty-third victim was the fifth Cult member to die.
There were enough victims
to have subsets of victims.
Clyff the pelican worked third-shift security at the electric plant, most
    nights he didn't leave the glass security booth,
keeping one rolling eye on video monitors, the other on his regimented
    game of solitaire.
(He prided himself for having never cheated.)
His title and role within the Cult was not known by the average villager.
Judging by the royal blue of his robe
he was high-ranking.

Clyff was the first victim to be found alive,
drawing crude lion faces on the marbled steps of the Cult of Awn's sacred
   meeting place,
The Home.
He'd suffered an ice-pick lobotomy via an orbital socket.
He couldn't speak
and he clicked his beak
and grinded glottal nonsense,
his throat pouch undulated,
a tattered flag in a storm.
Dipping a feather into the saplike blood
leaking from his right eye,
he made his art.
Many of us began to believe the Butcher
would never be caught,
would never be overcome,
like time.

)

The Syme River was a hard line
dividing Bevaur
separating Old Town, New Town, and the densely populated, industrial
   north
from the affluent homes, farms, wineries, and fisheries of the south.
We referred to the south as the Farms,
though independent/family farmers had long ago sold
(or lost)
their land to one of the two corporate agricultural conglomerates.
The family farmers could no longer afford to live in the Farms.

The water that ran clear and fast from the mountains
turned sluggish with sediment and pollution by the time it oozed into Old
   Town.
The gondolas and riverboats still paddled

and peddled romantic water dreams.
Depending on the time of day or night, upon the direction of the wind,
the smell was chemical, tanging and itching deep in the sinuses,
or the fecal smell of waste,
the sewerage of today,
the decay of tomorrow.
There was a fragile hope (for some), a sweeping
(too expensive and restrictive and un-Bevaurian, cried the congloms)
commitment to cleaning the river,
was to finally pass legislation, prior to the next Council elections.

Old Town had been decreed the "historically significant district,"
a thin rectangular strip along the river veined with cobblestoned streets,
huddled and crowded buildings over two hundred years old,
the sins of the past they'd witnessed, now charming secrets and lessons long
    forgotten.
Stum University and Ryde Hall marked the outer borders of Old Town.
Like the rings of a tree,
New Town and the fevered business hustle, concrete, steel, pavement, buses,
    trolleys, gridded streets and shrinking lotted green spaces and homes
swelled around Old Town
and threatened to consume it.

On walks to and from Ryde Hall, Spire imagined her tightening asthmatic
    chest
as the municipal squeeze.
Part of why she hadn't retired,
she could better ignore the expansion, the insatiable mandate of progress
from the insides of her beloved library.
Her last night closing Ryde Hall was caught on surveillance cameras,
the same cameras she'd described, to anyone who'd listen,
as ugly intrusionary eyesores pockmarking the sacred building.
Spire, the grayed old rabbit, still wearing the hat that hid her tired ears,
toured the rooms and their stacks,
time nor ultimate destination seemingly of concern.

Spire held a breezy conversation with herself
about the merits of her leftover squash and carrot stew
waiting at home.
Pinned under one arm, a slim volume on the Bahrd Apple Bob, a quaint
    (to some) historical footnote; a drunk mob had dumped bushels of apples,
    along with Mayor Bahrd, into the Syme to protest austerity measures.

A camera with a blinking-red, motion-detecting eye followed her progress
as she wraithed alongside blurring shelves of books,
the biography section, alphabetical by subject.
That there could be so many books, their voices stilled, mostly forgotten,
made some of us think of death and we were afraid,
made some of us think of death and we leaned closer to the viewing screen.

Then, from behind Spire, a book fell from a shelf about chest height,
a single, thudding clap, timed with her soft footfall.
The jarring noise spurred her forward.
Another book fell, and another,
and more books spit out, their crash landings
syncopated with each of her increasingly frantic steps.
None of us can outrun every disaster.

On the video, it appeared the books were pouring out of her back and
    bricking the floor,
plating a path behind her heels, a path of where she was.
One newscaster described the books as falling like leaves,
in an attempt to be poetic,
but leaves didn't plummet, their collision with the ground didn't echo a
    lament, and then lay permanently stilled.

Spire eventually stopped and straightened.
Resigned, perhaps.
Behind Spire, coiled within a shelf
she'd just moments ago walked past,
the Butcher.

This footage would be replayed and replayed
and replayed and replayed and replayed and
replayed and replayed.
In one frame the shelf was an empty space, the next,
it was filled with the Butcher,
unfolding from the bookshelf to the floor in a herky-jerky, stop-motion-
    animated manner that made us wonder if there were more frames missing
    from the video.

The Butcher held an ice pick in one hand, a dagger in the other,
wore what appeared to be a Cultist's robe,
its color indeterminable.
The video quality was grainy and a ghostly green.
Colors were not real colors on that night in Ryde Hall.
Upon closer inspection, the robe was not made from cloth,
and was stiff,
striated with scars,
and would later be identified,
by experts in such matters,
as being made of stitched animal hides.

Spire was rooted in place, and she held out the book, not as a weapon or a
    shield,
but in the desperate way she always held out books;
come and see what I have,
come and see what was,
and wonder with me, please.

The Butcher fell upon her,
a storm of arms and steel.
The networks blurred the images,
muted the sounds.
(We have the luxury of looking away
from the worst of it.
For now.)
In a way, the blurring of the image was another desecration,

the formless, then motionless pixelated blob sped up Spire's erasure from
    our plane.
In all the other ways, the uncensored video and soundtrack was worse,
couldn't be unseen, couldn't be unheard.

The website hosting Mereth's wildly popular Butcher NewsGroup
hosted the leaked uncensored video,
which then was quickly downloaded and circulated on the infant Internet,
along with conspiracy
after conspiracy after conspiracy.
Those paranoid and ignorant viruses
were our new folktales.

After Spire's death,
the Butcher, covered in blood, walked toward the camera,
filling the screen, showing off the lion painted onto the mask.
The video ended, blinking first.

This horrible night at Ryde Hall,
incredibly, improbably, but not impossibly,
marked an inflection point in the political ascendance
of the Cult of Awn.

VII.

Year twenty-one.

She was careful
to follow quietly,
to keep her distance,
keep it from her sister,
another secret hoarded,
one that itched to escape.
She didn't have
her mask
to protect her.

)

The sun stalled high
over the Limwood canopy.
A full day's walk from the outskirts of Bevaur,
the air was cleaner
than her memory of clean air.
Tol's older sister, Pen,
map and compass in hand,
obsession pumping through her heart,
navigated and drove their group of four east.
This was the second day of her first weeklong vacation
after eight months of working sixty-hour weeks
at the Wrilt Sons' Free Clinic and Palliative Care Co-op.

The Wrilts were voles who had lived in the Forge,
respected, if criminally underpaid, machinists,
parents of four sons,
all of whom died
before the age of nineteen
from rare nervous disorders
linked to mercury, lead, and a periodic-table-length list of other toxins.
The Wrilts won a landmark lawsuit
against the industrialist Lun Rundt the rooster, owner of a quadrangle of
    chemical factories;
their wastewater and smokestacks
choked the Wrilts' tenement building.
The Wrilts were terminally ill
when the gavel miraculously dropped in their favor.
With so many residents in the Forge without health insurance or the means
    for health, they founded and funded the clinic.

Pen's husband, Pawl,
a tall and willowy Fowlers Toad,
wilted under the weight of his pack,
asked, "Is it time for lunch yet?"

He was a mathematics teacher,
unusually exacting and stern
for someone of his appearance,
fiercely forgiving and loyal
outside of school
when he wasn't in charge of anything.

Pen said, "When we find a clearing,"
and dowsed a path
through the brown-and-green brush.

Magg paused her march,
stretched her neck,
turned up her snout.
Attuned to the forest's olfactory syntax
of long grass, wildflowers, leaves, pine needles, mildew, moss, lichen, bark,
    sap, and soil,
there was underlying
a hint,
a familiar waft of musk,
a breath of threat
she'd previously associated
with late, paranoid nights skulking home through Old Town.
She had assumed, then,
what she had smelled was the fermented vinegar
of her own fear
and excitement.
To be in the verdant now
with that scent memory
misting in the hollows
was disorienting.

Hunge was an Irish Setter and retriever mix,
Magg's partner of two years,
Professor of mycology at Stum University.
Equally reckless with enthusiasm for his own opinions

as well as his attention to and affection for others,
he asked, "What is it?"
then declared, "I don't smell anything."

Magg rolled her eyes at the question,
growled at his preemptive dismissal.

He bent, rooted under the grass,
resurfaced with a chanterelle,
bright orange and funnel-shaped,
and he held it out to her like a forgive-me rose.
"I apologize. I know your nose knows."

Magg ate the mushroom, said,
"It tastes like shit."
(She didn't like mushrooms,
which made Hunge that much more charming.)
He held a paw over his easy unwounded heart,
and they howled laughter.
Magg sprinted,
headlong,
as fast as she'd always been
in daydreams.
Hunge chased
but lacked the fearless reckless commitment to speed.
Magg overtook Pawl,
and smacked his bony butt
as she passed.

)

She didn't bring a pack or a tent or a sleeping bag or food,
yet was prepared to spend
a night in the woods
alone.
A vigil

and a fast,
watching,
listening,
dreaming.

)

Pen found a suitable clearing
a few sweeps of her watch's shorter arm past lunch.
The foursome erected two tents,
built a fire hemmed within a ring of stones.
After dinner and tea warmed by flame and whiskey,
they waited for the stars to show off eternity.
With a crooked stick,
Pawl traced mythic constellations,
and after a few more drinks,
he made some up.

Later,
Hunge and Pawl staggered to their tents,
singing a drunken song.
Magg stirred the coals, conjuring new flames from the glowing embers
and asked Pen, "Were you able to find
where we are on your map?"

"To within a square foot. My geomatics and cartography degrees
finally being put to use. Sorry, Mom and Dad."

"I suppose you don't get to use maps at the Co-op Clinic."

"Afraid not."

"How is it—"

"I don't want to talk about it, not out here."

"Yes, of course. I'm sorry."

"Don't be. I love my colleagues and the patients.
As sad and infuriating and awful as it all is, the work we're doing
is my life's work, at least for now,
but when I'm away, I need to be fully away."

Magg added another log to the fire.
Gray smoke billowed from the loose, damp bark.
"When we do this again, in the north,
it won't be as easy a holiday."

"I am well aware."

"I know. I'm reminding myself.
I too often fantasize about what it will be like in those woods
and to see the monster again, and—
and then I wonder what building a future generation
might name for us and our failed attempt."

Pen laughed.
"A new waste station, probably."

"Dare to dream."

"Have you found any usable northern maps?"

"I found one with the Northwood painted as a vast green sea
filled with serpents, and monsters."

"That probably won't do."

"I'll keep looking. If you can believe it,
there are stacks upon stacks of books and scrolls in Ryde Hall
that haven't been touched in hundreds of years."

After sitting in silence, basking in the fire's warm glow,
Pen pulled Tol's blue beret from her jacket.
"Now that we're here. I don't want to burn it.
But I don't want to bring it back. I've always brought it back with me.
I can't bring it back this time."
She kneaded the tattered, thinning fabric.
"Maybe it will disappear between my hands
like magic."

Magg didn't say anything
She wasn't supposed to.

Pen stood, approached the fire pit,
tested the temperature of the stones with the toe of a boot.
She lifted one of the larger rocks,
as though it were a trapdoor to the underworld,
dropped the beret into its shadow,
and closed the door.
She straightened and stretched and asked,
"Do either of those chuckleheads know this is our grand practice run?"

"I haven't told my chucklehead yet."

"What about Mereth? Have you talked to her about coming with us?
Your dinner with her is coming up again."

"I haven't.
And I don't know if I will.
I go back and forth."

"We need numbers."

"We do."

"You don't think she could handle it?

I love him to pieces, but if we bring Pawl,
we could bring anyone."

"Oh, she could definitely handle it."
Maybe too well, she thought.

)

Magg thought it loud enough that
fifty feet away, fifteen feet up, hidden within the bicycle spokes of a tree,
Mereth heard it.
Mereth was both alarmed and pleased,
and not for the first time,
nor the last,
wondered,
How well do you know me,
dear sister?

)

The next morning, the foursome moved their camp
another day east, toward the edge of Pen's map.
They spent two more nights in the accommodating Limwood,
then the group headed home,
and passed through the footprint and the memory of their first camp.

Pen stood at the outer ring of the ash-filled fire pit
and asked, "Should we break this up?"
She didn't want Tol's hat, but she also didn't want it marked,
where she could easily find it again.
In the light of a new day, she wasn't sure
which of the rocks of the past
covered it.

Pawl said, "Nah, let Magg tell one of her graduate students
about a recently uncovered ritual site to be studied."

Magg tugged Pen's elbow,
gently led her away.

If Pen had overturned
every stone
she wouldn't have found
the blue hat.

VII.

Year twenty-five.

Zant Lanre, a bear gone gray around the muzzle,
managing editor of the *Bevaur Gazette*'s prizewinning
investigative journalist unit, Moonlight,
exposed avarice, corruption, fraud, malfeasance
for more than two decades.
She published a five-part series
about the seven years since the murder of the Archivist in Ryde Hall,
how the event spiderwebbed into convoluted conspiracy
to the benefit of the Cult
and politicians ravenous for power,
and how much overlap there now was
between those two circles.
The final part of the scathing series
outlined sweetheart real estate deals in New Town,
land grabs in the west, south, and Limwood,
plus tax breaks
for the Cult.

Mayor Ize Flank (a warthog with only one tusk, former police chief, once
     charged but acquitted of racketeering) along with
a growing majority of the Council,
a cadre of industrialists,
the Cult-owned media empire *Tod News*,
and fearful villagers of a common political stripe,

condemned Moonlight,
combating their impeccable and vetted sources
with rumors and lies,
referring to the *Gazette* as "Fowl Paper."

Nine days after the finale of the series published,
Zant Lanre was last seen enjoying an afternoon cup of tea and honey
at Café Blu in Old Town.
Three days later
in the dark of pre-dawn,
a commuter gondola's oarsman,
an unpleasant, twitchy otter named Gnash, known around the Old Town
    dock for his pugilistic and reactionary leanings, rumored to be too ornery
    and unpleasant, even for the Cult,
made his initial morning run without noticing
Zant's body
slashed and lashed
to the prow of his gondola.
Most objective Bevaurians found his late discovery of the body
hard to swallow.
He returned to shore with a sardine smile
after hundreds of Old Town residents and commuters
witnessed the bear's riverboat humiliation.
Gnash was not charged with murder,
but was fined for negligence
and willfully disturbing a crime scene.
He boasted,
to anyone who would listen,
he wanted to give Butcher victim number forty-seven
(a number in dispute)
a proper send-off.

)

The Home was the oldest building
in New Town.

A modest two-story
clapboard and cedar-shingle dwelling, painted yellow,
an outcast of Old Town
at the time of its construction,
it initially hosted clandestine candlelit meetings,
the low ceilings and thick walls
hoarded survivors' tears
and whispers from the fearful and fatalistic.
The founding Cult members
driven and desperate to find meaning and solace
within the incomprehensible awe and terror
of acceptance and worship.
Situated so the dome of Ryde Hall
was visible from a second-floor hallway window,
perhaps an unconscious symbol,
(the most honest, telling kind)
that the true knowledge they claimed to seek
would remain beyond their reach
while sequestered inside
the Home.

During the prior Second Age,
the first floor was gutted
repurposed, reshaped
into a ceremonial hall.
The Home now
dotted the center of a campus
larger than Stum University.
The Cult's founding was a purposeful mystery,
with multiple conflicting origin stories involving
mysticism and supernatural acts defying interior logic,
never mind regular logic,
none of which are worth our time, frankly.
The Cult insulated information from nonmembers
(they called us *chaff*)

with insider jargon, wealth, court-backed legalese, peer intimidation,
tactics that have always been successful.

The Dawn Room,
a perched hollow on the Home's second floor,
once boasted a view
of the sun rising golden over a modest garden.
Now, morning light didn't leak
over the monolithic campus quad peaks
until midmorning.
The Dawn Room was reserved for Cult members
who had gained Wna status,
the highest level of enlightenment.
Four Wna sat at a round cottage oak table,
the wood fabled to have come from the north,
an avuncular fabrication,
the kind upon which
faiths and empires were built.

The Wna were so enlightened
they didn't wear their robes.
Served barrel-aged liquors,
they sipped moderately,
as their quarterly review was a working lunch.
They grazed from an Autumn Harvest–themed basket,
a "lousy veggie tray,"
according to the rooster, Lun Rundt Jr., the youngest Wna.
The others rolled their eyes and correctly interpreted his complaint as
    disappointment that there were no greasy fish sticks or fries.
Go-getting Cult members—wearing their stratified robes—cycled through
    the Dawn Room,
presenting reports on the newly installed, wall-sized Sharp Screen.
Colorful pie charts and Potency Point presentations displayed deep data
    analytics on recruitment numbers and trends, website and social media
    traffic, online search numbers, print and electronic media mentions,

financials and funds, real estate holdings and developments, strategic
planning of the capital campaign to fund a campus in the south to be
tent-poled by increased donations from lower-tiered Cult members, and
lastly, the latest polling numbers on Council members and an early (never
too early) forecast of future mayoral candidates.
The presentations ended, Sharp Screen logged off and powered down,
handlers and assistants dismissed,
food basket picked clean, tumblers empty.
The four Wna ceremoniously shut off their phones and placed them
facedown on the oak table.

A silver horse named Clomt adjusted his handsome, plaid vest
and said, "Any other business?"

"Zant Lanre was a mistake," said Melk, the eldest Wna,
a self-described oilman,
though his fortune had long since
sourced from the crude.
He was a rheumy-eyed, graying brown bear
and dyed his fur blond.

"Take it up with the Butcher."
Ranx, a racoon, owned three breweries and scores of bars,
and was the Mayor's Deputy of the Interior.
Bored by the old bear's physical and mental softness,
proud the journalist's murder was her idea,
she added, "The media has already turned in our favor.
We finally get to dismiss the other side
as being the batshit crazy
conspiracy theorists."

The murder
of the journalist
investigating the Cult of Awn
had been expertly spun,
like wheat into irony,

to somehow mean
the Butcher endeavored to frame and cast the Cult as the dastardly villain.
The Butcher did so in an attempt to foment fear into outrage directed at the
   Cult
and its myriad business partners and interests,
which would set off a chain reaction
to still the great grinding gears
of the Bevaurian economy.
One side of the political aisle clamored for
more protection from this bloodthirsty anarchist and his radical collectivist
   politics,
more protection for the Cult and its vested fiduciary concerns
for the good of all.

Lun Rundt Jr. said, "I want to discuss our terrible lunch.
I'm not a grazer, a forager, or a garbage eater."

Ranx said, "Someone get this child a bag of fish sticks.
If we're lucky, he'll choke."

Lun huffed and puffed.
"The gall! The temerenty! You're not nice!"

"Nice has nothing to do with anything.
Never has."
Ranx raised a flask that had been hiding in her handbag.
"To kill the brain cells that
logged you saying 'temerenty.'
It's temerity, by the way, you oaf."

"Go fuck yourself."

"Friends, that's enough."
Clomt didn't shout to be heard.
He didn't need to.
His timing, impeccable,

his low voice, placating,
the blasts of air expelled from wide nostrils, threatening.
"Our future Mayor will have fish sticks waiting for him
once we finish here.
It's not an unreasonable request."
Once an orphaned foal of unknown origin,
two kindly farming badgers adopted Clomt.
He inherited the soy farm upon their passing when he was eighteen.
In the years since, his rise has been impossible to map.
The breadth of his portfolio and influence,
associations with businesses large and small,
associations with, as whispered by those who foolishly dared to do so,
    various and varying criminal enterprises
were so clandestine
their cat's-cradle interconnections so convoluted,
a true accounting remains unknown even to your humble author.

"Thank you, Clomt. For your, um,
foresight."
Lun smoothed his comb
which was not as tall
as Daddy's.
"And with your support, I will mayor like no one's ever mayored
in the history of Bevaur."

Clomt and Ranx exchanged looks
dropping the temperature in the room.

Melk said, "If I may return us
to the concerns of the present."
He tried for dignity
but didn't achieve it.
"I know I'm the worrier of this group,
as its oldest member."

Ranx said, "Certainly our blondest member."

Melk was too old
to be baited.
"I think it's a mistake."

"Please elaborate," said Clomt.

"The truth seeks light and all that. The otter talks too much."

Lun grunted.
He did that well.

"We've been through this."
Ranx stood, then unsteadily paced the room.
"The river otter doesn't know anything.
Just like Lun."

"Which makes him
all the more dangerous," said Melk.

"Do we disappear him too?"
Lun smiled, satisfied that he'd contributed,
then daydreamed about everyone
he would disappear
when Mayor.
"Wait, did you mean
him him was dangerous
or *me* him?"

"Yes," Melk said.

Ranx showed
her small nicotine-stained teeth.
"How about the other pronoun.
By *we* do you mean the royal *we*?"

Clomt's eyes,
as large as apples,
opaque as stone,
unblinking,
remained pinned to Melk,
staring into someone's bleak future.
"In time," he said.

Melk couldn't parse the horse's carefully annunciated phrase.
Had Clomt meant to say
in due time,
all in good time,
or that the otter's disappearance would occur in the nick of time?
The two words by themselves
left too much unsaid.
Melk continued speaking,
as though rationalizing his anxiety.
"We're risking further antagonizing the real Butcher,
who has already killed eighteen of our brethren."

"That's an unofficial number," Ranx said.
"It's more like twenty-two."

Lun said, "The number is overblown. Even if it isn't,
he only kills losers.
Besides, it's not like the Butcher is going to tell on us.
Am I right?"
(The latter phrase would become his insipid campaign slogan
plastered on hats, T-shirts, buttons, and digital avatars.)

"No, never, not once have you ever been right," Ranx said.

Clomt stood to his full height,
eclipsing the room,
looming over Melk.
"Regardless of that number's accuracy or impending increase,

the Butcher is a tool
we will use to trim the fat,
remove warts,
or whatever metaphor you find
the most palatable.
Now,
dear Melk,
did you have any other concerns
I might assuage?"
The horse could intimidate and threaten,
and follow through.

Melk said,
"I wonder if the esteemed royal *we*
might consider trimming
Mereth Grahm.
Her most recent podcast episode
is causing quite the stir online.
She argues Zant is not one of the Butcher's victims."
Terrified as he was,
Melk would be damned if he rolled over
and completely exposed his belly.
"Correctly, I might add."

"No."

"Why not?"

"You're very astute, Melk.
But in a reverse kind of way.
Anti-astute, if there was such a word."
Clomt whinnied a laugh.
"I enjoy her podcast, for one.
It's irreverent, smart, and cruelly logical.
Whether or not she knows anything about the Butcher is immaterial,
though I suspect she knows quite a bit.

I view her as a potential asset.
If you three don't mind my having already taken the initiative"
—He paused and held out hooves to the room,
stared at each member until they looked away.
No one objected—
"I've deemed Ms. Grahm
—with her considerable net worth, familial political legacy, and formidable
   digital platform—
to be a recruit of interest."

Lun found his voice again.
"Shouldn't we vote on that?"

Ranx said, "Oh, look who wants votes to be actually counted now."

Lun laughed, pointed a wing at the racoon, and said, "Tushy."

"Don't point those stubby feathers at me.
And it's *touché*.
Dumbass."

Clomt said, "We've extended an invitation for Mereth to join our merry
   band,
at an accelerated tier.
She said yes."

VIII.

Year thirty.

Five Days to the Ceremony.

The Chamber of Commerce
in tandem with the construction company owned
by Mayor Lun Rundt Jr.'s oldest son, Bun
(his employees

called him Bunzo),
were late in completing their work
to prepare the Commons
for the biggest Ceremony yet.
Bun's company, having won the lucrative contracting bid,
cut all corners
erecting the Rundt Amphitheater.
The Mayor insisted it be large enough
to accommodate the fawning audience
for his address
and monthly rallies.

)

The abandoned, condemned Krult Bros. ceramic tile factory
sagged at the northeastern border of the Forge and Northwood
like a deflated toadstool.
Once a favored spot for teens and urban explorers,
the factory was purportedly haunted.
Ghosts of the Butcher's victims
collected in the darkest rooms, forgotten corners, under stairs and tables,
their eyes and wounds glowing.
If you locked eyes with one of the apparitions
you were to be the next victim.
Hundreds of stories had been written and shared
on online message boards and wiki pages
along with fake videos and video fakes
of a trotterless Wendig ghost.
Within Bevaur's considerable homeless population,
rumor had it
the Butcher used the factory as home base,
performed blood rituals,
palavered with the floating lion head of death.

The night before their morning rendezvous
Magg turned rumor into legend,

scaring away a group of squatters
with yellow bedding linen worn like a robe
and a well-timed growl.

Pre-dawn,
Magg, her onetime partner Hunge, and Pen
met inside the tile factory.
Others had quit the group two months ago.
Their expedition,
years in the planning,
once had featured as many as seven members,
was now, apparently,
down to three.

Pen's husband, Pawl, stayed home with their two young children.
The night before Pen left for the factory,
she read two bedtime books
to little Lotte and Ville.
Lotte, as skinny and wriggly as a tadpole, sometimes slept under his bed
    with a flashlight. He wanted to see everything even when he knew it
    would scare him.
Ville might spend an hour sticking balled-up clothes and stuffed toys under
    her blanket to transform her bed into a relief map of a mountain range on
    the moon or another planet so that she might have better dreams.
Born one year apart,
they weren't twins
but they had their own language
and a way to meld their two minds.
They knew without knowing
something big and scary was happening with Mom.
So they asked her to read a third book.
They asked for a story about Uncle Tol and his magic blue hat.
They asked again where Mom was going.
They wanted to go on an adventure too.
They insisted they were big enough, strong enough.
Pen agreed they were strong, brave, and smart,

which was why she needed them to look after Daddy,
because he didn't do well by himself.
They asked if Daddy was afraid of the dark.
Pen zipped her lips shut
then nodded.
They giggled.
They said they were not afraid of anything,
their eyes brimming tears.
Ville insisted Mom give her "sleep kisses."
Lotte said he wanted some of those too.
Pen asked what sleep kisses were.
Ville sighed, as if it were all so elementary.
She said, "Sleep kisses are kisses,
dry ones, no wet lips please,
on the top of the head.
You give them to someone when they are asleep
and dreaming
but you don't wake them up.
They stay on your head longer
if you don't wake up."
Pen promised she would give them sleep kisses,
lots of them.
The hardest part
was just one more sleep kiss
pressed to a warm forehead
before leaving.

Magg, Hunge, and Pen checked and rechecked their supply packs
which had been stored in the subflooring,
hidden by a leaf pile of loose boards and tiles.

Hunge said, "We're officially one-hour overdue.
The sun will be up soon.
Now can I ask where the fuck is Mereth?
I knew we couldn't rely on a Cultist."

Last week Magg and Mereth
had their annual Frera dinner.
The meal was dour, dampened
by the outlandish expedition
and their expectations of each other.
There wasn't the usual banter
as chaotic and choreographed as a fencing match.
Mereth said she wasn't superstitious,
but thought not meeting on the traditional day was bad luck.
In the hours and days that followed,
Mereth ignored Magg's calls, texts, and knocks on her door.
The two Frera did not have the shared mind of Pen's children,
but Magg was not surprised
Mereth didn't show at the factory.

Magg said, "Maybe she got cold feet.
Just like your fawning little grad students."
Magg knew that wasn't fair to Hunge, nor fair to Mereth,
but she said it anyway.
Then, to her dear friend, Pen,
"I'm sorry."

"No need to be sorry.
It's not your fault.
I'm still going in.
This is our only chance."
Pen opened Mereth's pack,
added ten more poison-tipped arrows to her quiver
and an automatic handgun.
She said, "Even with her no-show, Mereth did her job.
She got us weapons."

The group left the remains of Mereth's pack behind
including two long blades
tamed in scarred leather scabbards.

Light rain misted
as they exited the haunted factory,
weighed down
with the ghosts of the past, present, and future,
and slipped through a mouthy hole in the rusted chain-linked fence
and into the primeval Northwood.

From a third-floor window,
the glass fogged and cracked,
Mereth watched Magg trudge into the green canopy
through the eyeholes of her mask.

She wanted to go into the woods
to fight alongside them
or to kill them at Awn's feet.
Why not both?
Mereth did not believe in destiny,
not in the conventional sense.
She'd learned
blades and flesh
were fickle
perfect partners.

She was convinced dearest Magg
(who Mereth loved in a way
a child might love
a bug kept in a jar)
would find her end
awash in blood,
and she felt duty-bound
to witness.

It wasn't too late.
Mereth could gather her pack,
the two blades,
and maybe two more,

and hunt into the woods after them.
She could also haunt the woods,
go in her own direction,
one of her choosing,
one left to chance.
There was an undeniable appeal
to slipping away unseen
into the forest
with nary a ripple in the branches and leaves.

The lion mask reflected in the window.
The mouth moved
as though chewing.
It said,
"Remember.
I chose you."

Mereth pulled off the mask
and pirouetted away from the window,
holding the lion
at the highest height
above her head.
"Yeah yeah yeah.
Hey, Lion Face, have you ever thought,
maybe, just maybe,
that I chose you?"
Mereth was dizzy with fear and pleasure
and a limb-thrumming want
for the lion to speak more.

The lion was patient.
"We make and will continue to make a good team."

"Go team."

"What do you want, Mereth?

Do you want to go north?
Do you want to live alone with the trees and your memories for the rest of
    your long life?
Do you want me to make it a short life, instead?
Do you want to die between Awn's molars or toes?
Do you want to die now?
A ceiling collapse?
Or something in town,
something more splashy,
something with a bit more public spectacle?
Or
do you want to continue our work in Bevaur?
Tomorrow night is *your* night.
It's the night I promised you
almost thirty years ago,
if you still want it."

Mereth knew what it was she wanted.
And yet she wanted more.
She said, "Want. Want. Want.
Want is a tricky thing
when coupled
with the disappointment of getting."

"Oh, I promise
you won't be disappointed.
Not on this night.
Not on your night.
But you get to choose.
You always get to choose.
I only require
you say what it is
you want."

Mereth was not in a trap.
At least,

she didn't believe
she was.

She said to the mask,
"If I were to flay you open,
would you bleed too?
What if I were to roll you up,
leave you here,
tuck you into a hole in the wall
to never be found
unless you screamed for help
loudly?"

The lion mask was silent.

Mereth could not abide
silence.
She said, "I'm joking of course.
I would never disrespect you
like that.
Don't mind me.
I'm having a midlife crisis.
What does it all mean,
you know?"

She was being more honest
than she intended.
The years of youth and blood
suddenly seemed like
something that had happened
to someone else,
as though she couldn't remember how the blood
felt, smelled, tasted,
how sometimes it first appeared shy,
clinging tightly to fur, feather, and hide,
other times the eager blood was an explosion, a geyser,

always rushing,
always escaping,
from the present
into the past.

She put the mask on,
fitting her mouth into the lion's,
and listened to her own
exaggerated breathing.
There was no question,
she would stay in Bevaur.
A big night was coming.
The biggest night,
as that sack-of-shit Mayor might say.

Four Days to the Ceremony.

To mark the end of the Second Age,
there was to be another lottery
to select the three brave citizens,
who would stand on the dais
and face Awn
for the good of Bevaur.
By rule, the chosen three were to be adults
who were children at the time of the First Age's Ceremony.

Breaking with the tradition of holding the lottery
within Council chambers.
Mayor Lun Rundt Jr. and his lead advisor, Clomt,
invited handpicked Council members
and CEOs to his office.
This was the first lottery in modern memory
not to be overseen by union heads,
a now-dying breed.
Police dispersed protesters who had gathered outside
with the help of batons, shields, rubber bullets, and tear gas.

The Mayor said, "We're all busy, and to save us time
—my dad, a great man, a great great man,
taught me time is precious. And not to spend more than you have—
I have already pulled three names
from the lottery barrel.
I almost got a splinter from that old thing. I think it's time for a new one."
He waved a wing as though
the barrel was right there, in the room.
The Lottery Committee chortled.
One egregiously slimy sycophant thanked the Mayor
for risking grievous injury on everyone's behalf.
The Mayor pulled three balled-up scraps of paper
from his trouser pocket,
dropped them on the table
like he was tossing pennies at a beggar.
Each name had been written sloppily.
Two names were misspelled,
but there was no doubt
as to their identities.

Three Days to the Ceremony.

Magg woke with the sun.
Hunge and Pen asleep in their tents.
She started a fire, boiled water for tea,
and wrote in the blank pages of a new journal.
Back at her house, hidden between her mattress and box spring, were three
    filled journals each cover a different color.
The first journal, golden yellow,
a golem made from her words,
comprised solely of letters to her deceased parents,
addressed to one or the other,
rarely both.
Her journaling has evolved
to allow entries addressed to other animals
who have been in and out of her life,

practicing conversations she wanted to have,
initiating conversations she wasn't brave enough to start.

Dear Mom and Dad,
The air is different here.
Cleaner, obviously, yet thicker, somehow.
It's like breathing in the age of this place, which, isn't quite what I mean,
    because, like Dad would always say, every place is the same age.
Not sure how the archaeologist feels about that . . .
Okay, so it's more like, I'm breathing the air of the past,
the air from before us.
There's not a hint of Bevaur.
It's wonderfully disorienting.
The ground is thick with moss, roots, lichen.
The trees are greener, huddled closer,
and they keep the sunlight to themselves.
I miss home, the concept of home, of what it once was, of what it once
    meant, with a longing that is irrational.
Yet I want to stay,
although I know why I am here,
and I know it's a matter of time
before I am expelled.
Love,
Magg

Dear Spire,
You'd be pleased to know,
of all the Northwood maps you'd catalogued,
the most helpful is perhaps the most fanciful.
The *Map of the Northwood Seas* has been uncannily accurate
in marking glacial boulders and streams.
We are only five miles south of Awn's purported lair.
Alas, the map's monstrous menagerie, including the winged serpent Bix,
has been greatly exaggerated
much to our relief and disappointment.
If Awn's lair is where it says it is,

I'll be tempted to continue north,
to see the edge of the world,
and perhaps meet you there.
Yours,
Magg

Dear Mereth,
When I first proposed this expedition,
you'd quipped it was a suicide mission:
death by Awn,
or, more likely,
death by boredom.
Camping wasn't your thing.
Well, for the moment, I remain among the living,
barely, stubbornly.
I am beyond thankful for your supply help.
Pen is as well.
Never mind that cur Hunge.
You never cease to amaze, confound, and slightly terrify me.
I lean (perhaps almost falling over) toward gullibility, but I never thought
    you were going to join us in this fight.
You are engaged in a fight of your own.
I don't know what it is. I fear it is an ugly one.
Still, I had hoped against hope that you were going to come with us.
If nothing else, I would've paid good money to see your cosmopolitan cat's
    feral reaction to this forest.
I joke, but I've always admired how adaptable, how chameleonlike you are.
I tell others when they ask about you—and I'm asked frequently—that
    given the number of citizens you know and the social strata borders you
    cross without a self-conscious thought, you are the real Mayor of Bevaur.
If only, right?
If I return from this,
I wonder who we will be to each other
and who we will be to ourselves.
Yours,
Magg

)

At the Home,
Cultists buzzed in their hive,
making final preparations
for the biggest and most important meeting and sacred celebration
of the Second Age.

Qant, a squat, nervous ewe, head of the celebratory committee,
was responsible for overseeing
the decorations, the centerpieces,
the appetizers and aperitifs,
the candles and candelabras,
stage construction in the garden/quad for the two opening musical acts to
    be livestreamed on the Cult's website,
the seating chart,
the speaker order.
Qant asked everyone and anyone she passed by,
"Where is Mereth with the programs?"
The programs needed to be numbered, QR coded, and later scanned when
    they were to be collected at the end of the meeting.
"She had one job!"

Upstairs, in the Dawn Room,
Clomt alone
smoked a cigar
and stamped out small brush fires,
metaphorically speaking,
via speaker phone.
Assorted PACs and big-money contributors
were not pleased with the Mayor,
or more accurately,
were not pleased with their lack of mayoral-agenda input.
Clomt assured there was a solution to every problem
if they and their wallets were serious enough.

Pytr, a sweaty lemur, timed his entrance with the hang-up.
He carried an open laptop as though
it might explode.
"I'm sorry to interrupt, sir. I think you need to see this."

The latest episode of Mereth's Butcher podcast had just dropped.
Title: Five Years Later, What Really Happened to Zant Lanre?

Clomt said, "I am aware.
Mereth and I already had a long, fascinating discussion
about this episode not two days ago.
I even bought ad time.
Pricey, but it's sure to be
worth the investment."

"Respectfully, sir, have you listened yet?"

"You'd said I need to *see* it."

"Oh, my apologies."

"It has a run time of almost two hours, Pytr.
I'm a wee bit busy."
He exhaled a cloud of smoke,
as billowing, choking, and dangerous
as ego.
"Can you give me the gist?"

"Mereth speculates
—I really can't speak to the quality or, um, the identity of her sources at this
    time—that Zant was not a victim of the Butcher, which of course we all
    know to be true, but was instead murdered at the behest of the Cult."

"Is that so."

"I'm afraid this episode is trending.

We have already received press inquiries,
asking for a response.
She doesn't name names, per se,
but heavily implies, implicates . . ."
Pytr didn't finish the sentence.
He closed the laptop and scratched behind an ear.
He stared at a wall, not at the war horse leavening from his chair,
and he briefly indulged in a running-away fantasy.

"This is unexpected."
Clomt twirled a hoof,
a speak-now-
or-forever-hold-your-tongue-as-I-might-hold-it-for-you
gesture.

"Yes, sir. And, um, libelous.
Shall I alert Legal?"

"Is Mereth on campus? Is she in the building?
I assume she was to pitch in with the celebration committee.
Though it appears we probably should stop
making assumptions about her."

"She is not here. I have checked myself."

"Thank you, Pytr, that will be all.
Leave your laptop with me."

Pytr placed the laptop on the table,
wiped his hands on his thighs,
and backed out of the room.

Clomt pushed the computer to the floor
crushed it under a hoof.
He called an associate
who called three more,

requesting they look for Mereth at her place of employment
and her house,
requesting that they look hard.

With the room quiet,
the preparations in the hall below a thrumming murmur,
he mournfully snuffed out
the glowing embers
at the end of his cigar.

)

Mereth in her ancestral home,
with the lights out,
curtains closed,
the unfolded programs
fueled the flames
in the fireplace,
a communion,
a ritual
older than the Cult, older than Bevaur.
Fire could be controlled
until it couldn't.

One of her father's many daggers,
the blade provocatively curled,
pinned the sole remaining program
to the wall above the mantel.
In the dimming firelight,
the lion mask draped over one paw,
a red pencil in the other,
Mereth set to working out
where she would fit
within the program.

Her planning interrupted
by a heavy pounding on her front door

followed by broken glass
and other sounds associated
with brutish, amateurish entry.

Mereth put on the mask,
eager to participate
in pre-program
festivities.

)

Dusk.
Magg, Pen, and Hunge set up camp in a clearing,
the first they'd encountered since entering the Northwood.
The trees parted reluctantly,
exposing the base of a hill
furred in short shrubs and long grasses.

"More of a hillock," said Hunge,

Magg and Pen conspired with the map,
took turns saying,
"Well, this is the spot."
The map outlined nothing but more forest
to the north of Awn's crude silhouette.

Hunge loosened the rifle strapped to his pack,
wielded it like an ungainly extra limb.
"How are we supposed to track the fucking thing"
—he trudged up the hillock's incline—
"when there are no broken trees,
no sunken footprints anywhere?"

Magg was suddenly overwhelmed by the years spent in school,
The years spent in the Ryde Hall archives,
the years spent studying histories,

secret histories,
legends and lies,
overwhelmed at her smallness,
her finiteness.

Hunge at the hilltop,
twirled, weathervaned,
shouted.
"Shouldn't we be able to smell it or hear it?"

Pen smooshed the map
into Magg's chest.
"Are you saying the monster
is not out here somewhere?!"

Hunge jogged down the slope
to join the huddle.
Panting, he said, "No, I'm frustrated and scared.
And maybe relieved."

Pen and Hunge rehashed
an old argument
about ambushing Awn during the Ceremony,
which perhaps might inspire others to fight back.
With a waning commitment to Hunge
a waning commitment to her cause,
to causes and ideas in general,
Pen said they would not, under any circumstances,
reenact the failed Fliner Rebellion and its hundreds of innocent dead.

Hunge claimed no one was innocent,
the desperate canard of the intellectually and morally outmatched.
He lamented they were instead cosplaying Kir and Tham Ryde,
the famous disappearing goats,
the hero fools, or fool's heroes.

Magg didn't engage, tilted her head at the hill,
which struck her as odd-shaped, misplaced
unnatural,
cruelly obvious.
Magg asked, "Hey, Mr. Mycologist,
do you have a professional opinion
of the surrounding flora?"

Hunge said, "What? Oh. Well, given my lack of firsthand experience
with this region and its moist mid-latitude climate—"

Volleying to renew their battle,
Pen said, "I thought it felt more highland or highland-adjacent."

"No. Anyway, a small glade—"

"Glade?"

"A clearing, like this, could be the result of a long-ago fire,
or inconducive soil, or more likely laminated root rot
caused by fungus."

"It's always fungus with you."

Magg said, "I meant specifically the hill."

"Hillock."

"Whatever," Magg said, and groaned.
"Look at it again, please.
Tell us why there aren't any trees growing on it."

"It's probably a boulder or boulders, covered in only a few inches of soil.
  Or—"

"Exactly. Or."

Magg continued pointing at the hill.
Accusing it.

The rifle in Hunge's hands shook
as though he were preventing it
from flying away.
"No. No or. Right?"

Pen said, "Shit. We're idiots."

)

The evening began with a video reenactment of the Cult's fabled
   first meeting.
Candle-lit, somber, solemn.
Animals in clay masks spoke in hushed, delicate voices,
"Yet powerful enough to stir the dust of history," according to a full-
   throated narrator.
The camera soft-focused on the humbled and reverent gathering,
then the image blurred,
and the camera carried
our eye to the wooden pioneer walls,
"built by forgotten hands that continue to hold us and point the way,"
the Cultists' flickering shadows expanded, combined,
grew into the shape of mighty Awn
(thank you, DigiCiti Lights and Effects).
The narrator recited the opening line in the Book of Awn:
"We can only be we forever, within your embrace."

The lights turned up,
an insidious four-chord pop song kicked in,
the MC jogged onto the elevated stage, put on his mask,
adjusted his wireless mic
and barked, "Roll call!"

The members divided into regional chapters,
competed to be named *the* chapter of the Second Age,

applauded and chanted and held up signs.
"SouthPrime East will always bring it Awn!"

One chapter was not defined by region or neighborhood.
These stridently pious members remained unnamed.
Purposefully seated in the rear by the organizers,
they held their books and assorted sacred artifacts
or sat on their hands,
refusing to applaud throughout the bloated event
that, as it dragged on,
spent more time talking about the Cult's growing influence
and plans to remake Bevaur
than the promise and hope of Awn's final visit,
and their accompanying journey to the paradise beyond the north.

The headline speaker, Clomt, eventually strolled onto the stage in full
   regalia,
impossibly tall,
his robe black, magisterial,
his shoed hooves gaveled the stage floor,
echoes of the past, warnings from the future,
within the latex confines of his featureless white mask,
there was no mistaking his equine profile,
his piercing walnut eyes.

The overhead lights dimmed,
candles extinguished but for stalagmitic ones adorning the lectern,
a soft spotlight sunbeamed Clomt.
The hushed audience
donned their own masks.

Clomt thanked the organizers, the planners, the speakers,
including Bevaur's most famous film actor,
which triggered light applause.
Then he began his speech
at a volume greater than the previous speakers,
a volume amplified by the tech crew.

"Friends, new and old, I congratulate you,
at this precipice of a day thirty years in the making.
Hundreds of years in the making.
All the work, all the hope, all the worship and reverence and
   demonstration,
the vigilant daily defense of our ideals,
the defense of our identities, the defense of who we are, the defense of who
   we will be;
all of it, everything!
We don't do this for fleeting personal gain or individual wealth,
those pernicious lies that so many in the press cynically clutch
like swine pearls.
Our selflessness, our sacrifice is for the promise,
the promise guaranteed to be fulfilled.
Our reason, our way, our why
is about to return
to teach us another lesson,
and if we are blessed,
the apotheosized lesson."

The audience raised arms and held each other up,
they let tears flow,
they whispered please and yes and thank you.
Some had their exaltation pierced by melancholia, thoughts of their families
   and former friends and if only they could witness this, feel this, then they
   would understand.
Others dreamed of gory cosmic victory over enemies, real and imagined.

The unnamed in the back rows,
one by one,
quietly gasped or coughed,
and slumped,
and knocked into the seats and the backs of other members
as they bonelessly slid to the floor
pooled in their own collecting blood.

Within that section of seats
one animal remained standing,
wearing a painted mask
no one could yet see.

During a dramatic pause within Clomt's speech,
a pause he had practiced and timed,
confused murmurs brush-fired through the audience.
He couldn't see what the fuss was about.
It took his considerable collected self-control
to not diminish the heft of his speech
by admonishing the gathered,
who he thought of as needy, impulsive, impertinent children,
as much in need of his discipline as his vision.
However,
he wasn't so self-absorbed to not sense,
a new heaviness and panicked charge;
the atmosphere had changed,
perhaps irrevocably.
Clomt spat out his final lines,
prickling
with the first spines of fear.
"What grace, what glory,
that our awesome, terrible god is tangible,
that the earth trembles beneath its feet
and we move in accordance with it.
We, the blessed few, know this.
Our future ends tomorrow.
Our future begins tomorrow."

Standing atop the backs of the dead,
the Butcher shouted
what would be the only word
the gathered would hear from her
that evening.

"Lights!"

Then there were lights.

）

The moon was full and bright enough
to show them what they needed to see.
Their headlamps did little more
than identify the wearer.

They unpacked, gathered, and loaded their weapons.
Pen droned on with a familiar pep talk,
one they'd heard for years,
one in which they'd once believed,
about how Awn wasn't a god, wasn't a supernatural creature;
it was a beast,
no more no less,
and that meant it could be stopped,
it could be killed.

Crossbow drawn,
gloves insulated her hands from the concentrated fungal amatoxins coating
    the tips and shafts of the arrows,
Pen asked, "Did anyone bother poisoning my camper's shovel?"

Magg laughed at the absurdity of their plight;
their chaotic capricious lives
and the collected history of Bevaur
somehow
leading to if not culminating in
this nighttime attack,
which was to be as obviously feckless
as three mutinous fleas on her hide.

Hunge said, "None of our weapons will penetrate soil

and then Awn's hide.
And here I'd thought Mereth wanting to bring swords
was ridiculous."
Ridiculous
was a vicious word.

Magg imagined Mereth
standing on the hilltop,
arms and blades outstretched,
victoriously stabbing both swords
down to their hilts,
then the earth shuddering, screaming,
and Mereth laughing.

They made one last plan as a group.
Hunge would dig into the hill,
and if Awn was indeed hibernating
under soil and shale
they would fire their weapons
into its exposed flank
point-blank.

They walked together, in a line.
Pen said,
"We're attacking a mountain."

Hunge said, "Klut Mining Corp blows up tops of mountains,
literally decapitates mountains,
to hollow out the coal."

That horror seemed impossible, to Magg,
in the face of another horror.

"And this is just a hillock," Pen said.

"A fucking trifle."

Hunge skipped ahead.

"Nothing we can't handle
in late-stage Second Age."

"Should we be whispering?" Magg asked.

Nervous giggles percolated.
Hunge crept a few steps up the incline,
gently probed the surface with the shovel tip.
He looked over his shoulder
at Pen and Magg,
nodded,
exhaled,
slid the shovel into soil.
He peeled up a layer of sod and moss,
and after only a few more scrapes
he uncovered a thick mass of fur,
shockingly green in the glow of his headlamp.
He ungloved, reached down,
and pressed against it with a shaking paw.
"Impenetrable," he said to himself,
fell backward,
slid down the slope
into Pen's and Magg's legs.

They asked him a thousand unanswered questions
as they pulled him upright.
He unslung his shotgun
and scrambled back up the hill.
They told him to wait.
They should fire together, at the same time.

He shouted, "Impenetrable!"
pressed his gun muzzle
into what he'd uncovered,

and fired.
Because he was off balance,
the recoil sent him back down the hill.

The hill stood up.

Pen and Magg fled the flash avalanche of dirt and rock.
An instant dust storm
erased the clear night sky.
Magg coughed and choked,
wiped furiously at her eyes with forearms.
The crashing rubble settled into a light drizzle.
Underneath,
underworld,
a low, guttural grumble
thumped against and inside
her chest.

Magg was all turned around
but there was Pen,
her lamp piercing and accusatory,
ten paces to her left.
Pen sent arrows
hissing into the blotted-out night.

Magg pointed her handguns somewhere above her
and shouted for Hunge.

His headlamp flickered like a dying star
from an impassable distance
and depth.
Magg heard his wild gunshots;
they had to be his because she hadn't yet fired.
Then his light cut out with a detonative tremble and roar,
and another dust cloud billowed into Magg.
She fired into it

and she fired above her head
even though she couldn't see Awn,
couldn't see the forest,
couldn't see the trees.

)

This is the part.
You've been waiting
for this part.

The audience shouted, recoiled,
pressed toward the stage.
The only exits
—a fire hazard to be sure—
were behind the Butcher.

Some survivors would go on
to describe the mask
as its paint having faded, smeared, cracked,
as an uncanny abstract nightmare
and not a lion.
Some survivors would go on
to describe the mask
not as a mask,
but as a skein
as an actual lion's head.

The Butcher planted
dagger and sword
into the bodies at her foot.
The blades stood at rigid attention
by her side.
She waved and waggled open paws,
taunting the cowering crowd.

Come closer.
I don't bite.

Two burly Cultists
edged up aisles
and rushed her,
a sloppy and obvious pincer attack.
The Butcher bent,
retrieved both blades,
and in a blink
the Cultists lost their heads.
She deftly volleyed one,
arcing it into the crowd
with a rear-paw kick.

Clomt bellowed into the mic,
conjuring Cultists with earpieces and guns.
His expedient position atop the Cult's hierarchy notwithstanding,
Clomt was not beholden to faith, superstition, or powers greater than his
    own,
yet he felt the eyes of the Butcher's mask track him across the stage
as he was whisked away,
and feared he would feel them, helplessly,
until his own eyes closed for the final time.

Cultists, from the lowly tiers, in their clean and bright colors,
attempted to follow Clomt to safety.
The door stage left
remained closed to them,
and barred by security officers.

Countless Cultists
broke like water
around the Butcher.
She hacked and slashed through
the amorphous flagella of the crowd,

the mindless superorganism.
Short sword
long enough to skewer and sever two necks at once.
The dagger blurred and stung,
killing Cultists who didn't realize
they were dead.
The air misted red,
arteries fountained blood
from desperate hearts.
Dying paws and hooves
anointed her path.

The Butcher kept count.
That there never would be a number big enough,
was the first disappointment of the night.
She quivered with want
and promise,
and lamented the beating benighted hearts
that had somehow escaped through the exits.

Two security members remained onstage,
flanking the barricaded door
through which Clomt had fled.
Their unsure gunshots
echoed in the hall,
bullets probing the disintegrating crowd.

The Butcher killed a young badger
by folding him in half,
backward,
then used him as a step
to ascend onto the stage.
She spun on a heel,
faced the audience.
Their future was here
for all to see.

The Butcher danced briefly at the lectern;
slicing the wax,
twitching her wrists,
flicking the flaming candle heads into the back wall covered in flags and
      tapestries.
The flames were gluttonous
upon their release.

Burning strips of cloth fluttered to the stage like dying dragons
as the Butcher stalked toward the two security officers.
They pulled their triggers,
shooting without aiming,
waving their arms
as though they were drowning,
pleading to be saved.

Bullets puckered the Butcher's robe
as though it were made of clay.
She did not bleed, did not fall.
The security shook and fumbled and whimpered.
"Did you hit it?"
"It's not an animal."
"This isn't real."
"This isn't possible."

Before she pounced
and shared her savage embrace,
she cut the rope tied around her neck
with the clever tip of her dagger.
Rib cages and chest plates
—taken from the two who had foolishly entered her home earlier that
      evening, the two who had spent their adult lives trading in violence but
      had never learned anything about it—
weaved and reshaped and refashioned into unholy armor,
spilled out from under her robe,
clattered chitinously to the burning stage.

The security's stomachs fell to their shoes
as she zippered open their guts.
She used their slackened but still breathing bodies
to ram and batter through the stage door.

She killed her way
along the path upstairs,
not noticing the path dimmed, faded,
not once wondering if the otherworldly strength, skill, and fortune,
was hers or the lion's.
She assumed they'd always been one.

She threw another victim,
one who cowered, covered his eyes, and had said, simply, "Please,"
exploding into Dawn Room,
When she followed inside,
teeth bared, tongue quivering under her mask,
there was no Clomt.
The room was empty.
For the first time that night,
her breathing and her heart rate elevated.
She shook her head
and growled.
This was wrong.
How could he get away?
He was supposed to be here.
He was promised.
He was the promise.

The Butcher tore apart the room
as it filled with smoke from below.

She leapt through the bay window
two stories down to the quad,
landing on her feet, of course.
The night wasn't over yet.

She would not allow it to be over.
How could it be over so soon?
She brazenly stalked through the campus
not taking care to be unseen
by approaching sirens and flashing lights,
because no one would stop her,
no one could stop her.

There had to be more.
This wasn't it.
But the illuminated path she had followed was no more.
She took random, directionless turns
and cut through alleys and lots and yards,
trusting she would flow downstream to Clomt.

She washed up in a residential neighborhood,
stood at the base of a crooked set of wooden stairs
leading up to a modest bungalow.
Somewhere inside
three glowing lights that only she could see.
If she couldn't have Clomt,
she would have them.
She would not be denied.
She would have them all.

Pen's husband, Pawl, sat on the couch,
Lotte and Ville drowsing under each arm.
It was past their bedtime.
On the TV played
a movie populated with heroes and villains
they'd seen enough times
to memorize the lines.

The front door opened
a mournful creak,
a bloody, masked figure clouded into their space.

Pawl recognized
who had come for them.
He stood to his full reedy height,
filled his empty hands with a blunt, stubby poker from the fireplace.
His children,
fully awake,
clung to Pawl's legs.
One asked, "Who is it?"
The other said, "Go away."
Pawl told his kids to run,
run out the back door and keep running,
and he added a lie.
His children knew it was a lie, by the quaver in his voice.
"Mommy is outside waiting for you."

I will not detail,
will not give a blow-by-blow account,
however,
I'm not sure we deserve
to be spared the truth
of how languidly the family was killed by
Mereth the Butcher,
as we've been rooting for her
all along.

The Day of the Ceremony

The Ceremony was to officially begin at noon.
Protesters arrived at first light.
They sat, linked limbs, formed living chains to block the main villager and
    vendor entryways to the Common.
They wore bloodied newspapers and white placards with the names of
    missing dissidents or dressed as miners and factory workers and farmers
    with turned-out pockets and red tape X-ing out their mouths
or wore gas masks and lugged clouded buckets of Syme River water labeled
    toxic.

The protesters blocking the Commons
had only a mind
for the Mayor.

It was after 2 P.M. by the time the police and the Village Guard
violently cleared the protesters.
The Ceremony didn't begin for another hour.

Mayor Lun Rundt Jr. was furious when he made his speech.
A final, galling indignity: his brand-new amphitheater was only half-full.
Half-full if you were an optimist.
He would fire Clomt
for not filling those stands.

The Mayor halfheartedly read the brief speech Clomt,
or some fucking intern hack fresh out of Stum U
had written.

"We have suffered great, inexplicable losses in recent days.
My continuing thoughts and prayers to the victims and their families.
Take heart, my fellow Bevaurians, we have found the Butcher, and he is
   dead.
I won't say his name—"

Here, the Mayor paused, then ad-libbed.
"Not that his name was a shock to anyone paying attention,
I mean, I could've solved this myself. I practically did.
I told the police chief weeks ago, *weeks* ago,
'You know, you should keep an eye on that otter guy,
he's a bad guy.'"

The morning after the rash of Butcher murders,
the old riverboat otter Gnash was found dead
in the belly of his gondola,
forearms slashed open from paw pad to elbow.
He was dressed in the Butcher's regalia.

The blood spattered on his robe
reportedly matched his most recent victims.

"But I won't say that bum's name.
Not here, not today, not on this sacred day of celebration.
We must not look fearfully backward, or react in fear to our present,
but move forward, look to the future, to our bright Third Age.
It'll be the best Third Age anyone has ever seen."

He paused for applause,
saluted those cheering from his amphitheater.
What they lacked in numbers
they made up in zealotry.

"Let's get to it then," the Mayor said.
"The names I will read have been determined
by a lottery overseen
by esteemed Council,
our best business leaders,
only the best, I choose only the best,
and, of course, me.
The names are
—I feel like a game-show host here—"
His sons' braying laughter caught by his mic.
He read the names:
the raccoon and excommunicated Cultist Ranx Flimnit,
Council's Minority Whip, Gille Grine, the squirrel daughter of the former
    Mayor,
and a blue heron named Blune Sanp, a journalist who'd taken over Zant
    Lanre's post
(all three were vocal critics, the vocalest critics, of Mayor Rundt Jr.,
obviously).
The Mayor performed to the can-you-*still*-believe-his-appalling-behavior
    gasps
from pockets within the crowd,
holding his wings out wide, shrugging,

and said, "That's the way the cookie crumbles. Am I right?
We thank the chosen for their bravery and honor."

As the three citizens were forcibly escorted to the dais,
Ranx shouted obscenities,
the Whip and the journalist demanded transparency,
requested an emergency legal injunction that would not be forthcoming.

Drunk villagers booed and cheered and started halfhearted fights
they didn't see to the end.

Cultists, in their newly diminished numbers, wandered the Common.
Some walked in groups, flinching in fear that the Butcher would still find
    them,
Some took advantage of the newfound sympathetic public sentiment in
    their manic recruiting efforts.
One dressed in a sky-blue robe was irrevocably lost in a fog of grief and
    pain.

)

Waiting for the sun to sink into the Northwood,
Magg and Mereth stood next to each other,
their fellow villagers gave them a wide berth,
out of respect and superstition.
They wore red sashes, as was stipulated by tradition,
to represent the brave offer of sacrifice necessary for the well-being of
    Bevaur,
to represent all citizens having been granted a second chance, a Second
    Age.

"Were you successful?" Mereth asked,
her voice hoarse from the recent hours of constant
one-sided conversation
with her silent lion mask.

Magg said, "We found Awn."

"Oh? Wow. I mean,
I'm surprised but I'm not surprised.
If anyone could've found Awn,
it would've been the good Doctor Magg.
Where exactly, was—"

"Hunge was killed."

"I'm sorry.
And I'm sorry about Pen's family, of course,
which is the worst thing I've ever heard.
How is she?"

Magg couldn't tell if Mereth was chastened or bored.
"To answer your first question,
we'll find out shortly if we were successful.
But no, I don't think we were."
Awn had fled north after their attack.
When the dirt and debris had settled, and the night sky could again preen
    its cold infinity,
they had searched the crater for Hunge's remains.
Pen had found all but one of her arrows.
Magg had allowed herself to hope
maybe one arrow penetrated Awn's fur and hide, maybe one stuck,
maybe all that was needed was for one arrow to stick.
That hope had evaporated upon return to the village
and to the horror of what had befallen Pen's family.
"Are you going to apologize
for not coming with us?" Magg asked.
"We needed you.
I needed you."

Magg stared at Mereth.
Her stare softened as the normally lithe, kinetic figure Mereth cut
was diminished and wan,

fur matted, sleepless nights bagged under her eyes.
Magg believed Mereth was haunted by what she must've seen in the Cult's
    Home,
haunted by the news of what happened at Pen's house,
haunted by an unnameable loss.
Maybe her haggard look was longer than the recent days,
maybe it was thirty years in the making:
How were we here at the Ceremony again?
How were we still here?

Mereth patchworked her imperviousness,
crooking a familiar smile
vexed with a you're-better-than-that sneer.
"I think we should've tried killing
the Mayor instead.
Bad joke, I know,
but I have to joke.
It's all—it's all too much otherwise."

Around them bubbled
nervous and impatient giggles,
boastful shouts of "Am I right?"
whispers of a fixed lottery, of a hoax,
disapproving murmurs,
fearful sighs that seemed to say
How can we fix
any of this?

)

Vendors shuttered their carts, packed their tents and wares.
Blankets rolled under villager arms,
parents ready to cover their youngest ones' eyes
when the moment came.

Everyone waited for Awn.

They waited more.
Magg allowed herself to think,
"Maybe . . ."

Then a rumbling tremor in the shrinking distance
increased in volume at an unsustainable rate,
became rolling, cascading thunder,
the sound itself living, breathing, growing, consuming,
shaking leaves from the treetops
and screams from the villagers.

"Is it fucking sprinting here this time?" Mereth asked,
a paw on Magg's shoulder, her claws out, primping, digging in.
She pushed herself up to a greater height,
better to see,
better to whisper into an ear.
"I fear you pissed it off,
dear sister.
Big time."

Magg swiped Mereth's paw away
and bared her teeth.
She had never been so angry,
and in the moment, became another animal,
considered lunging, fitting Mereth's neck between her open jaws,
not to kill,
but to squeeze a different look
from Mereth's eyes.

The snarl was not enough
to earn that change.
Mereth stumbled, ragdolled onto her haunches,
and laughed.

Magg held her quaking ground.
Awn approached and the crowd retreated.

She would bear witness
to her calamitous failure.

On the other side of the Common,
a Cultist
who was not a Cultist,
broke from their huddled ranks,
shed her mask and blue robe,
the same blue as her little brother's hat.
Pen pulled a bolt cutter from her belt loop,
ran to the dais,
determined not to be a complicit celebrant
in yet another apocalypse.

Police were slow to react
to the Mayor shouting from his private box adjacent to the amphitheater,
"Who the fuck is that?"
He might've been the only asshole in the Commons
who didn't recognize Bevaur's most tragic figure.

Magg barked and howled,
tried to run through the crowd to stop Pen.
Mereth wrapped her arms around Magg's waist.
If she didn't quite hold Magg in place,
she slowed her down
enough.

Awn split the trees,
muscled through the Northwood line.
The recurring generational nightmare
swayed unsteadily,
legs lifted and feet jackhammered into to the earth, as though aiming to
    punch through to the other side,
thick arms flailed,
it twitched and revolved its planetary head,
moved too rashly for its bulk to remain balanced.

That the monster lacked the measured movement and grace
from cultural memory,
from myth and legend,
made it more terrifying.

Awn's fur was no longer the uniformly lush, mossy green
of thirty years ago,
marbled with wide swaths of off-brown patches, the color of dried, dying
    grasses, and the whitish gray of diseased, exhausted tree bark.
Magg paused in the struggle to be free of Mereth,
wondered if Awn's appearance was a form of epochal camouflage
—did it always look this way at the end of the Second Age?—
or was the result of having been woken early from underground slumber
or did a little lucky poison from Pen's arrow swim in its blood?

Pen snipped the chain at the journalist's ankle, pushed her off the dais, and
    yelled at her to run.
Pen tossed the bolt cutter to Minority Whip Grine and stood tall in the
    journalist's place, in Tol's old spot.
Would that everything that had happened
in the time between Tol and now
was a beautiful, horrible dream,
one in which she could live forever,
one she could instantly forget when it ceased.

Pen had planned to have her stand on the dais end
after diving hands into her deep, dark pockets
to retrieve the small T-shirts that belonged to her children
and hold them against her nose,
close her eyes,
inhale what little of their scent lingered.
But she wasn't granted the time.

Awn dropped to all fours,
its head an asteroid crashing to Earth
—an extinction event—

mouth opened,
teeth flashed, clicked, and scraped against the brick dais,
and Pen was gone.

Awn gathered the Whip and Ranx
into its maw,
then backhand-swiped the fleeing journalist
knocking the heron flying
into the amphitheater.
Her body punched a hole through the seats
and bent a load-bearing stanchion.
Villagers mobbed and climbed over one another.
The wounded amphitheater creaked and swayed.

Magg had fallen to her knees
and crawled toward the monster.
How are we here at the Ceremony again?
How are we still here?

Awn stood, exhaled,
slumped its shoulders,
as though it were tired of the never-ending dream
and was disappointed in everyone.

It gently batted at the trail of floating blue feathers
left by the journalist.
With each pass of the mighty paw
the feathers swirled,
floated higher
and away.

Unable to catch one,
Awn turned
and loped north
into the woods,
into the future.

BOOK THREE: THE THIRD AGE

I.

A brief guide to the village,
thirty years into the Third Age.

Syme River fishing and shelling licenses were reinstated despite
previously reported levels of nitrates, phosphates, cadmium.
"A temporary patch to boon the economy and the recalibrating
—but soon to be thriving—
village food web,"
according to a press release.
No mention of the rolling brownouts
planned to ease the strain
on the electrical grid.

Summer, autumn, and spring droughts
dried wells,
decimated the farms,
fueled Limwood wildfires.
In the south,
fisheries collapsed,
the Green's wetlands were drying up.
Older estates within the southern gated communities
remodeled in favor of open concept
and new quartz countertops.

North of the Syme,
New Town and the industrial Forge were distinguishable
only by lines on a map and postal codes.
Most of Old Town's historic buildings, cobblestone walkways, and Stum
    University's campus
had been washed away in winter floods,
eroding banks and the riverwalk

were replaced by storm walls and levees
that Mayor Rundt III touted as marvels of engineering,
but were always one storm behind.
At the construction site of Storm Wall IV, at the base of the Bilhurn
    Bridge,
a nineteenth Butcher-copycat victim, the deer Blin Xorn, a small-time
    bookie,
was found filling an excavator's bucket lift.
The copycat Butcher was a rat named Cob.
Ex-cop, ex-security, ex-ride-share driver,
he went to the local bar next to his high-rise tenement
carrying one of Blin's sawed-off antlers,
still wearing a store-bought lion-mask replica and blood-spattered robe.
He was easily apprehended
like the other copycats.

II.

The night before her first day on the job,
Kots the fox described Grahm Manor as
"the bougiest assisted living home across the river."
Her partner, Ante, was a fiercely loyal coyote and tightly wound sociology
    major.
Ante said, "How bougie are they if they hired you as an uncertified
    assistant?
You can't even take your own temperature with an ear thermometer."

The commute from graduate student housing
via bus, rail, then another bus
was more than ninety minutes.
Kots could not face having to do that twice a day,
could she?
Kots studied geoengineering and had recently switched to part-time to get
    a job and save money and extend the timeline before the ruinous student
    loan payments kicked in.
Her meager wages wouldn't be worth the hassle

if she lost a sizable chunk of it to bus and rail fees.
She wrote herself a phone memo
to investigate ride-share scooters and bikes,
though she'd never been steady on two wheels.
Today, after work, she could walk home,
and not tell Ante.

Kots arrived thirty minutes early
(she was always early to everything)
and walked the immaculate grounds that kept its green
despite the water ban.
Grahm Manor was a repurposed family estate,
two floors and five thousand square feet of living space
lounging on three manicured acres.

Once inside, Kots met the staff,
signed some papers,
put on a white overcoat, two sizes too big,
and assisted Nurse Mill, a cheerfully stern muskrat
who wasn't much younger than the patients,
on his rounds.

The largest private room was upstairs,
more than twice the size of other patient rooms,
with its own full bath
and a set of windows and padlocked French doors
overlooking the entrance and tree-lined circular drive.

As Mill and Kots entered,
a graying, elderly cat paced the hardwood,
wringing her paws and muttering to herself.
She wore an ankle-length white nightgown
dotted with blue wildflowers.

Upon seeing Kots, the cat stopped pacing, threw up her arms,
and asked, "Where is my sister?"

Kots said, "Your sister? I don't—"
and looked to the nurse for help.

Mill said, "She is coming tomorrow. We're all very excited."
He turned his back to the cat,
winked and mouthed at Kots, *There is no sister.*

The cat pulled at the kinks and wrinkles in her nightgown.
"Yes, well, someone better clean up then. Clean up good.
Tell everyone to stop sucking thumbs and puzzle pieces,
keep their paws out of their pantaloons.
Maybe hide Ralp, that fucking guy.
He smells like shit."

"That's not very nice, Mereth," Mill said, and could not hide
the amusement in his rebuke.
He shepherded Mereth to a small table in the corner,
and sat her in a padded chair.
Mill said, "It's time for your medicine
and I brought along a new friend. Meet my assistant, Kots.
She'll be helping us out now."

Kots didn't know
if she should extend a paw, or wave,
or excuse herself and run from the room.
"Hi, Mereth, it's lovely to meet you."
She bent over as she said it,
as though talking to a child.

Mereth twitched and bobbed her legs,
bared and retracted chipped, ragged claws.
Her whiskers were long and bent, extending her downturned mouth,
a lip curled over a snaggletooth.
One eye milked over with a cataract,
the other,
well, the other could see.

She said, "My dear, I could just eat you up.
Maybe after my sister visits.
Something to look forward to."

Mill said, "She talks a mean game but
she likes you, Kots. I can tell."
He rapped knuckles on the tabletop,
waggled a digit at Mereth.
"Behave, ma'am. Just because you own the house
doesn't mean we won't throw you out."

Mereth laughed. "I'd like to see you try."

Kots thought the elderly cat looked spry enough
to climb the walls.

Mereth counted the pills inside the paper cup three times,
swallowed them with one sip of water.
She said, "You both can help me then.
I want this place to be nice. Very nice.
My sister is an important person, you know.
A doctor. A smart one.
Not like any of the quacks that come here.
She's someone who really learned something."

III.

Magg spent the better part
of three decades continuing Pen's work
caring for the sick and uninsured
at the Wrilt Sons' Free Clinic and Palliative Care Co-op.
She spent the better part
of three decades
preparing for her last chance.

She knew that her sixty-eighth birthday
would be her last.

How odd it was now
to be confronted by accumulating numbers
ending.

She was to meet her longtime on-again/off-again partner Mlic
for a birthday dinner at Sall Mandr's.
After the floods of '23, the famous restaurant had relocated from Old Town
to the suburban south.
The new owners replicated the footprint, interior decorations, and menu
but not the prices that once welcomed lunchtime and happy-hour crowds
    of dockworkers, students, and retirees, as well as serving would-be robber
    barons and starry-eyed cognoscenti in the evenings.
Once the heart of the village
where its blood pumped and mixed,
the restaurant was a mirage, serving nostalgia,
the bill outrageous.

Mlic was early and ordered a bottle of wine,
two bulbous glasses one-third full and waiting.
Gray peppered his muzzle and black fur.
He wore a black fedora, black tweed blazer, slate-gray trousers, and a
    salmon-colored scarf.
He sat with his legs crossed, which Magg knew was less a well-dressed
    gentleman's affect than a position that eased the pressure on his dysplastic
    hip.
They had video-chatted a few times, but they hadn't seen each other in the
    flesh for more than six months.
Mlic was always such a handsome, warm, patient dog.
Magg loved him in an arm's-length way,
and while there wasn't regret, per se,
as she was content with their arrangement, for lack of a better term,
she was sorry on his behalf
that she was unable to be
who he had wanted her to be.
Maybe she wasn't being fair to either of them
with the always-insidious what-could've-been sentiment.

There was both joy and the glistening sting of sadness in his brown eyes
when she entered the dining room.

They hugged and shared a brief kiss.
Mlic took off his hat with a flourish
hoping it distracted and hid his shock
at Magg's wasted appearance.
A year ago, she had been strong enough to hold him up
while he'd rehabbed his balky hip.
Now he wondered how she managed to walk across the room
under her own power.
She was gaunt, hunched, and frail,
her thinning fur hadn't grayed, but the chestnut color had faded, washed
   out,
her eyes were heavy, weighing down her head.
It was all he could do to not ask, *Are you sick?*
He wanted to share more of their dwindling days together.
That she was a mysterious part of his life,
a comet that irregularly returned to flash through his sky,
would have to be enough.
She smiled,
which seemed an act of extraordinary effort and resolve,
and he sank into his chair knowing whatever this evening was or would be
was beyond celebrating her birthday.
This was goodbye.

"Why are you looking at me like that?" she asked.

"You're a vision, and I stare in wonder at the vista."

"Oh please. You're a terrible liar, but I appreciate it."

They clinked glasses,
a warm, silent toast
to all the unsaid things they never needed to say.

Magg said, "This place is dreadful, isn't it?
Sorry, I promise to not be a total wet blanket, for once."

"No, it's a mockery. But the wine is decent."

They placed their orders and caught up.
Mlic did most of the talking, giving her updates
about his two adult children from a previous marriage;
his son was an overwhelmed schoolteacher in the Forge, and was thinking
   of quitting, but had no plan B,
his daughter worked with a nonprofit that built sustainable rooftop
   vegetable gardens and composting.
When their entrees arrived, they joked about the minuscule fish portions
correlating to the restaurant's claim of having the lowest levels of mercury
   and plastics per serving.

Their plates bused and dessert ordered,
Mlic said, "I'm afraid to ask, but have you finally
decreased the number of days or hours at the clinic?"

"It was all paws on deck there for the past six months,
with the spike in H1N1 flu,
trying to get as many animals vaccinated as we could.
I was even going door-to-door at one point,
trying to convince folks
we weren't poisoning them."

"How'd that go?"

"Do you have to ask?"

"No, I don't suppose I do."

"However, as of two months ago,
I'm mostly retired."

"Mostly."

"I go to the clinic twice a week."

"That is great news. Cheers!
What have you been doing with your time off,
besides not visiting me?"

Magg stuck out her tongue. "I've been spending time
with my old partner. You've met him before, I'm sure.
His name is Ryde Hall."

Mlic fought to appear unflustered,
until he got the joke, and then laughed too hard.
He leaned forward, elbows on the table.
To get Magg to offer even a crumb of her prior life as the Archivist would
     be an achievement.
"Do tell. How has the old boy aged?
He can't look as good as I do.
I expend more resources in maintenance."

"Ha! He looks as creaky as I feel."
She would not admit how bittersweet
the morning trips to Ryde Hall were.
Magg mourned her old life as much
as she unwaveringly committed
to this other one
and to its end.

"Do you ever think about what your life would've been like
if you stayed there?
Is that too maudlin of me to ask
on your birthday?"

"Yes and no.
No and yes.
The truth is, I was different then,

and as I've discovered while wandering the stacks,
that old me is almost unknowable to the now-me.
How many different animals do we carry around inside?"

"One for every day we live."

"Do you really think so?"

"No, but it sounded good."

"You're obnoxiously charming."

"I try. Oh, I try."

They held on to a brief, warm silence
as small dishes of raspberry gelato arrived.

Mlic asked, "Any interesting research or discoveries?
A secret basement chamber, perhaps?"

"Like anyone else who goes to Ryde Hall,
I'm not allowed into the areas I was once allowed."

"And you let that stop you?"

"Of course not. The current Archivist is a glorified accountant,
too busy working to defund the place.
His clueless sycophants hunt and remove texts critical of the Rundt family
    and the Cult,
luckily, they're incapable of processing allegory or metaphor."
Magg paused for a shared, above-it-all laugh.
The truth was the stacks were being decimated.
So much history and literature lost, and likely lost forever
was itself a metaphor she could not bear to face
without using gallows humor and farce to declaw the pain and fear.
She added, "No one has time to stop and question an elderly dog
who knows where she's going and what she wants."

"And what do you want, Magg?"

Magg's tale of biblio-skullduggery was fiction,
one for Mlic's benefit,
and fine, for her own benefit as well.
She adored being the successful star of imagined adventures through his
  eyes.
In this manner,
she would tell Mlic everything
without telling him.

"Do you know the story of Mayor Mithrid from the fifth Third Age?"

"I do not," Mlic said, and settled in his chair,
raised a paw at the server, signaling for more wine.

"Not many do. He was an obscure, tragicomic figure
in the way history makes us all tragicomic figures, I suppose.
Anyway, Mithrid was the son of a marriage arranged
by two powerful families of landed-gentry geese.
As soon as he was of age, he was installed into the Mayor's Office
to ease the families' tax burden.
The frauded election was so ineptly bald-faced—"

"Sounds familiar."

"—his enemies were legion.
Mithrid became paranoid that different factions, from low and lay animal to
  nobility, including members within both sides of his family,
wanted to assassinate him.
He wasn't wrong.
Which was both the tragic and comic part.
During his seventeen-month stay in office, he never once appeared in
  public.
He wore a thick helmet and chainmail day and night, sleeping in it, when
  he did sleep.
He had a small kitchen built in his chambers to oversee meal preparation,

toward the end of his reign, he cooked for himself, or did not eat at all.
Not satisfied with these safeguards, he sent his most trusted charges,
a trio of nephews a few years younger than him,
into Limwood to gather all the poisonous fungi and plants they could find.
It was rumored Mithrid himself, on moonless nights, skulked into the
     Northwood for the same purpose.
He ingested small amounts of the mushrooms and leaves each day,
to build a tolerance."

Magg paused for dramatic effect.

"I can't believe I haven't heard this story before.
Did it work?"

"There was an attempt to poison Mithrid. He was gifted a bottle of wine
     from his family vineyard, with a forged note from his father-in-law.
It read, 'To a job well done.'
There is dispute as to whether the note was forged or not.
One of the nephews with whom Mithrid shared a glass died.
Mithrid, despite drinking a heroic amount, survived."

"Maybe I shouldn't have ordered another glass of wine."

"You'll be fine. I bet."

"What happened to Mithrid?"

"Mithrid did not survive the office.
His other two nephews blamed him for poisoning the third, as they'd been
     gathering the mushrooms and plants for him for months by that time.
In the madness of their grief, and with the help of a rival whispering in
     their ears, they thought their uncle had used their brother to test the
     efficacy of his poison tolerance.
His two nephews locked themselves within the Mayor's chamber, wrestled
     him out of the chainmail, and stabbed him thirty-two times."

"That seems excessive."

"Legend has it, Mithrid's blood was highly poisonous, collected in vials,
    and
subsequently used to great effect in the following year's Quiet Coup."

IV.

Mereth didn't know where she was
but knew she should know.
To keep from succumbing to incapacitating fear
she would be angry and remain angry,
and she would plan.
She insisted to herself that she had always been a planner, a schemer,
one step ahead of everyone else who were two steps behind.
She would escape this room
even though this was her house.
They'd said it was her house, anyway.
They'd hired a young fox to box her in.
There used to be another fox she didn't trust.
What was his name?
She searched under the bedcovers
for his name.

It was impossible to keep track of time.
Things changed so quickly, yet remained the same,
and all that was left
an inchoate animal sense that something was different,
something was irrevocable
and it had happened behind her back
without her input or permission.
It wasn't fair.
It wasn't fair to end like this.

Oh, they kept things nice for her.
They washed her clothes and sheets and body, they brought her food and
    drink, they played confusing card and dice games with her.
She was never a good sport.

They told her what she wanted to hear.
Their words were as anesthetizing as the pills they brought.
That was their greatest trick.
She would stop taking their pills and words.
She would tell her sister about everything, including the new fox,
and ask about the other fox
tomorrow.

Her sister was the only one she trusted.
Her sister's face was fixed in her mind from a time
when she looked over her shoulder, back at Mereth, while they were outside,
  penned in a crowd, the sky a toneless gray, her expression unreadable.
Mereth insisted to herself that her sister's expression was unreadable.
Mereth feared her sister saw something
she should not have.
Mereth would tell her sister she was sorry
tomorrow.

Mereth cried every night
because she couldn't remember.
How brutally frightening it was to not remember anything,
to realize you were nothing but a collection
of past events that changed and dissolved over time.
Fucking time time time.

She stopped looking for the old fox's name in her bedcovers,
because she remembered
there were hidey holes in the floor and in the baseboards.
This was her room after all.
It always has been.
That they had transformed it into her prison,
she would make them pay.
Mereth climbed out of bed, careful to not make any noise.
Her body did not forget how to be used.
She crawled on the floor,
tapped at the edges of the hardwood until she found a loose slat.

She pried it up.

Inside was a note written on a square of yellow paper.

'You must keep trying.'

She slunk and slithered, finding the other slats, her body moved through
   the circuit.

The other notes read:

'Talk to the lion.'

'The lion will come back.'

'The lion promised.'

'You won't always be alone.'

One slat revealed empty space with no note.

She could've sworn there was supposed to be one more note,

one that read, 'You are the lion.'

She walked the perimeter of her room,

one paw kept contact with a wall.

The closet was locked.

Had she been found trapped inside once?

She didn't want to remember.

She moved on and tapped a foot against the baseboards

finding a loose one, a wiggly tooth, under her bed's headboard.

Back on her belly,

she liked being close to the floor,

she slid the wooden piece away,

but could not see inside the space.

Greedy for another note,

she sent in a rough paw,

that recoiled

from the bite and cold shock of tapered, sharpened steel.

Mereth replaced the board and returned to bed.

She tried to summon the lion.

She whispered, "Hello?" and "Please?"

and tears came again

despite her anger,

because of her anger.

It was clear the lion wasn't here.
She would have to escape.
Her arms and legs spasmed at the prospect,
promised they were ready, still willing to be used, and used well.
She would be as violent as necessary,
as violent and cruel as her enemy, time.
She would make the attempt after her sister visited
tomorrow.

V.

Years ago, Magg had been forced to sell her parents' house
to Bevaur for pennies on the dollar.
She had moved into a small third-floor apartment
of a sagging triple-decker in central New Town.
When she had first moved in,
the overwhelmed landlord
was a kind if not distant red-breasted robin who had lived on the first floor
    and always had an unlit cigarette dangling from his beak.
He had warned
to boil the tap water
before drinking or bathing.
There were no such warnings
from the current landlords,
a real estate consortium,
impossible to reach by phone, email, or app.

Magg had not left her apartment
in the week since returning
from the dinner with Mlic.

It was the day before the Ceremony
to mark the end of the Third Age.
She was not feeling well.
And that was the plan.

Her round kitchen tabletop was cluttered;
journals filled with observations, measurements, trials and errors,
letters to family and friends that populated her past,
plastic baggies of her blend,
an analog scale and its village of brass weights,
her tablet computer, which she used less and less
(a paranoia that was a function of reality, dwindling time, and the side
    effect of induced chemical changes within her brain),
and books, including Hunge's pun-filled guide to fungi titled *From Bloom to*
    Shroom, the spine broken, pages yellowed, brittle, loosened, highlighted.

Magg cupped her paws around a steaming mug of breakfast tea,
closed her eyes to steady herself,
to not be swept away by nausea and dizziness.

She made marks on the calendar and a few lines of shaky script in an
    observation journal.
She drank tea while it was too hot to drink,
sifted through the pile of journals until she found the one with the red
    cover.
It was almost full.

Dear Mereth,

This morning I ate two times the amount of my blend,
than I had one week ago,
which is probably pushing it too far.
I need to push it, past the edge.

I'm still upright. Or, at least, sitting upright.
That I call my mushroom-and-leaf mix "my blend" is a joke for you.
Your straightlaced, responsible Magg using drug slang,
slang that's probably as old as we are.
I think I'd get a smirk out of you.

It has taken me over an hour and two cups of tea
to write the above two paragraphs.

Does anyone know what to write or say at the end
without sounding like a self-important, melodramatic fool?

How about this:

Here is what I know.

Whether or not Pen's poisoned arrow pierced Awn's hide
—I believe it did—
Bevaur could stop Awn tomorrow if there was a collective will to do so.
Bevaur could've stopped Awn many ages ago.
But for a few individuals here and there, Bevaur has always chosen
to do the easy thing,
to do nothing.

I don't write this to sound like a martyr.
I don't want to be remembered for what I'm going to do.
I don't want to be debated and discussed.
Have I wasted my years, my decades?
The hours and hours of study and experiments, the weekends of solo trips
   into Limwood and the Northwood . . .
For what?
Even if I am successful in killing Awn,
I'm swapping one apocalypse for the next.
The thought of starting over, beginning again, with another First Age
   seems a horror.
Bevaur is dying,
if not already dead.
How many ages does it have left before the death rattle?
By killing Awn now, who am I helping?
Who would I be saving?
A handful of animals at most?

I also know
it's lazy and cowardly and cynically pithy
to say nothing can be done,

to say we don't deserve to survive.
You might describe the sentiment
as the quitter's lament.

My years at clinic were certainly a worthy endeavor.
I'm not patting my own back.
Or maybe I am.
Did I counteract the *worthiness* because of intent, because of my endgame,
having unfettered access
to rabies and flu patients,
so that I could infect myself in the days before the Ceremony?

In addition to my becoming a poison pill,
I got my *viral plan B*—let's call it—idea from you, Mereth.
When we had stood on the dais together as children,
(it seems impossible we were once children
and I was a child yesterday)
you'd said, if chosen, you'd bite and scratch Awn's tongue, gums, throat.
Do you remember?

We were never sisters,
but I was you and you were me
when we were younger.

I don't know what my point is, or if I'm making sense,
or why I'm downplaying or negating what I'm going to do,
because I'm still going to do it.
Noble or futile or selfish gesture
be damned.
My reasons are my own,
reasons that have always been who I was and who I am.
My lifetime of choices and actions and loves and losses explain better
than a few lines on paper.

Now that we have that out of the way, dear.

I wonder
if someone from Grahm Manor
will bring you to the Ceremony tomorrow.
If so, I hope they remember your red sash.

I know I've ended every note for thirty years with
I should go see you.
I could apologize.
I could write that I've been meaning to visit,
but I haven't.
It has been better
for both of us this way.
That is not lazy, cowardly, or cynically pithy.
That is not a quitter's lament.

Time for a lie-down.
Fever, chills, and joints made of glass insist.

Sincerely,
Magg

VI.

The Common, Bevaur's public square,
was walled off from the rest of the village.
To the west, the humbled Kroning Mountains
and their strip-mined innards, nude peaks bereft of snow.
To the east, the deforested Limwood,
a cemetery of tombstone stumps and lumpen landfills.
To the south, the degraded Green
no longer possessed the color of its name,
To the north was the only promise
the village ever kept.

The Ceremony officially began at noon.
Revelers arrived early to be processed

at Gates A through D
(the committed and enterprising
could sneak in from behind the Rundt amphitheater).
None were allowed to bring their own food and drink,
each attendee granted one digital coin for a twelve-ounce beverage.
Ten bucks a pop after that.

Cult of Awn adherents and Mayor Rundt III supporters,
one in the same,
were the village majority.
Within the Cult were factions;
traditionalists patiently, wearily waiting for the end to come,
pragmatists of the enlightened upper tiers, scheming to legislate power and
    influence into the next First Age,
neo-Cultists (*neos* for short) believed Awn would arrive to smite their
    enemies, a not-so-secret weapon in the coming Civil War, and when the
    blood stilled, they would follow Awn and Rundt III north to paradise.

Dissenting non-Cultists, despairing villagers
herded into the muddy Commons.
Most could not afford the steep fines levied to non-attendees.
Cult recruitment teams quickly spotted and surrounded any animal not
    wearing a robe.
The ensnared were released back into the wild
after enduring the strong-armed recruitment pitch, holo-vid, and a QR
    code tag.

Cultists, in turn,
despite heavy police and Village Guard presence,
were harassed, sucker punched, and had fake blood smeared on their regalia
by villagers wearing replica Butcher lion masks.
A vendor managed to sell over one hundred masks and blood packets before
    she was arrested.
Whether or not the mask wearers believed the popular conspiracy theory,
they'd co-opted "AWN ISN'T REAL" as their slogan,
printed on flyers, graffitied on walls.

a single sentence
castigation and hope.

With a nod to tradition,
a cruel one, given Ryde Hall would soon be defunded and shuttered,
the Archivist
opened the afternoon-long ceremony,
marking the beginning of the end
of the Third Age.
His speech
a forgettable hagiography of Mayor Rundt III.

Throughout the dreary and damp afternoon
the spring sun did not burn through the layer of soot and smog.
Villagers boxed out space in the Common,
resettled into a hazy acceptance of their roles and lots,
shared nervous well-wishes and whispered dreads of the diminishing days
    to come.
Food and drink consumed despite the exorbitant cost.

An elderly dog wearing baggy jeans, galoshes, a waxed barn coat
shuffled through the crowd.
Few noticed.
Animals of her age knew what it was to be invisible.
Magg used it to her advantage.
She approached the dais and its coterie of armed Village Guard.

Their shared look of amusement changed
when she slung a tattered red sash over her shoulder.
One ram with a crow's voice said, "Watch out for the crossing guard."
The oldest of the group stepped forward to intercept; a balding middle-aged
    weasel who hated his job, himself, and everyone else.
His laughter died at the edge of his whiskers.
The old dog's eyes wept thick black discharge that stained her muzzle.
Mucus leaked from her nostrils.
Jaundiced drool and dried white spittle clung to her sagging lips.

She was clearly ill.

The weasel said, "Excuse me, ma'am. Are you lost?
Do you need help finding your family?
How about Rin takes you to the medical tent, okay?"

The ram Rin hid his snout inside his field jacket
and said, "You fucking take her."

Magg said, "No one is bringing me anywhere.
I'm volunteering for a spot on the dais."
She coughed.
Wet and loose.
The guards hopped back a step.

The weasel said, "Listen, lady, thanks for the offer and all.
You're, what, the tenth—"

Rin interrupted.
"Eleventh."

"Fine, eleventh."
He turned and spoke to Rin.
"I wasn't asking."

"Bad luck to lie to an old dog.
Or is it let old dogs lie?"
The guard pack howled
laughter and pile-on jokes.

The weasel said to Magg, "You're the eleventh villager
who has volunteered today."
The weasel failed to keep impatience from crouching within his voice.
He was tired of hearing himself talk.
"Bevaur appreciates it, but you can't volunteer. It's not allowed.
The names have to be chosen."

Rin added,
"Village-sanctioned suicide isn't a thing yet.
Give it a couple more weeks."

Magg pushed out her sash,
it identified her as a Ceremony legacy,
of having survived being chosen in the First Age.
She explained she was also a former Archivist
specializing in village law
(an exaggeration).
Magg exhumed a scrolled parchment from inside her jacket,
brandished it like a cudgel.
An expert forgery,
if she didn't say so herself.
"I am volunteering,
and as you will see,
it is my sole legal right to do so."
Her gambit worked.

The guards quieted, grew uneasy.
They were so used to heeling
in any shadow of authority.

VII.

At Grahm Manor
the old cat
hunched at her small table,
worried over a puzzle of a famous painting;
A Meadow Dying at the Golden Hour.
The long yellow grass pieces,
forming crescent-shaped islands,
in a scattered archipelago,
refused her
tectonic pleas.

Kots the fox stared out the second-floor window.
A weeping willow slumped adjacent to the circular drive.
Indifferent,
it had yet to grow spring leaves.

Mereth asked, "Kots the fox, are you there?
Fox the Kots?"

Kots was physically there, in Mereth's room, an essential healthcare worker
    designee.
Kots was also in the Common inside her head, frantically searching for
    family and friends.
She worried most about Ante, her wonderful and fearless and careless Ante,
    who had planned to smuggle masks and blood packs.
Ante had not answered her texts.
Had she been arrested? Or worse?
Kots could too easily imagine worse.
She felt guilty for the preceding days of honest relief
at having to be at Grahm Manor on Ceremony Day.

Kots said, "Yes, I'm sorry. Do you need something?"

Mereth's commitment to escape was the whetstone
that left her freshly sharpened.
No soft rounded corners, no slurry blurry thoughts.
Her sister wasn't coming.
The lion wasn't coming.
Beautiful as they were, neither were real.
Clarity. Lucidity.
She could even finish the blasted puzzle if she wanted to.
Mereth asked, "Is there something happening outside the window
that I should know about?"
Her voice had long since settled into an older animal's register and she
    delighted at the effect it had on the young fox.
On this afternoon, the fox's delicious fear
was not polluted with pity and disgust.

Kots answered before she could censor herself.
She wasn't supposed to talk about
what happened outside the Manor,
as the world moving on without them
upset the patients.
"Well, it's Ceremony Day, and I'm worried about my loved ones,
and Nurse Mill, too. I probably shouldn't even say it,
speak it into existence,
but I don't want
their names to be chosen."

"Being chosen is a lie. Maybe the biggest."

Kots assumed
Mereth made a pointed political statement.
"Yes, that's what I'm afraid of."

"I was chosen once."
Mereth squashed a puzzle piece
into a space it did not fit.
"And then I wasn't."

Kots wouldn't admit she already knew about Mereth's turn on the dais,
nor admit she'd plunged into an online Mereth Grahm deep-dive after her
    first day on the job.
"I'm sorry," she said.
"That must've been a terrifying, scarring experience."

"It was the most exhilarating time of my life."

Mereth and Kots shared a look.
A dare.
Mereth swept loose puzzle pieces off the table,
they swarmed to the floor,
then pinwheeled toward
the darkened spaces under the table and bed.

"Oh dear, I'm such a klutz," Mereth said
with a singsong voice.

"Okay, I think puzzle time is over," Kots said.

"Don't worry your pretty little head.
I'll clean this up."

Mereth turned liquid,
poured out of the chair
onto her belly.
She flowed halfway under her bed
before Kots could say,
"Please, no. It's okay, Mereth.
Leave the pieces.
I can get them later."

"No, now. I will get it now."

Kots crouched behind Mereth, unsure of what to do.
What if the old cat got stuck?
Should she forcibly pull her out?
Should she call for help?
There was only one nurse and one attendant on the day's skeleton staff.

Mereth muttered to herself,
an unsettling drone simultaneously muffled and amplified,
the kind of words meant to stay trapped under a bed
with all manner of lost and forgotten things.
Kots jumped, her ears folding against her skull,
when the incantation suddenly produced a hollow knock
at the base of the wall behind the headboard,
then a clatter of wood against wood.

Has the old cat knocked loose a bed slat?
All Kots needed

was for the mattress to collapse
on her charge.

Kots said, "Please, Mereth, you must come out.
Are you stuck? Let me help."

Mereth slid herself out from under the bed,
muttering, "Back up, back up.
Backing up, backing up."

Kots maneuvered to the cat's flank
and hauled Mereth up by the waist.

Once upright, Mereth pirouetted,
struck Kots in the jaw with an elbow,
clicking teeth and tongue together,
drawing blood.
Kots staggered back, but remained standing,
her ears ringing.

Mereth had overspun
fell backward onto the bed
landed in a childlike pose,
legs dangled over mattress's edge.
Her blue sweatshirt
and the fur around her eyes and mouth
mossed in dust clumps and cobwebs,
as though she'd been stored under the bed for years.
She smiled.
She wasn't missing any teeth.
With her right paw,
she clutched a dagger,
the blade as long
as the dying meadow's grass.

VII.

The Minister of Data and Information was Fyn Unter,
a fastidious, ageless skunk
fond of hats, cardigan sweaters,
the slow, Rube Goldbergian psychological torture of enemies.
Whether or not Magg's document was a forgery
(he suspected it was),
he advised the Mayor this straw could be spun into gold.
That Magg, a well-known leftist, volunteered for the good of Bevaur
demonstrated a political change of heart,
a near-divine conversion
—she so believed in the administration and the future of Bevaur
she was willing to face the monster again.
"After her sacrifice,
we'll find a treasure trove of diaries, emails, and videos
detailing her support of our greatest Mayor.
She will be our hero.
There will be songs and digital shrines and children's books written and
    assigned.
It'll be perfect."

The Mayor waved a wing and said,
"Sure, why not.
What happens if Awn doesn't take her?"

"Do you have to ask?"

＞

The bell above Ryde Hall chimed thirteen times,
once for every Third Age.
Mayor Rundt III, his sickle feathers bright and his comb lengthened,
said, "The names I will read
have been determined by a lottery overseen by esteemed Council,
and other important animals,

with special thanks to Mr. Fyn Unter,
who works almost as hard as I do.
By decree,
only villagers over the age of sixty, proud members of our greatest
    generation,
are eligible to mark
this last day of the Third Age.
Their final, selfless sacrifice
preserves our future ages.
Let's get right to it."
He read two names.
One belonged to a Stum University professor, a onetime vocal critic of
    Rundt III's father and grandfather.
The other name belonged to a writer who had been incarcerated for crimes
    against Bevaur.
Mayor Rundt III said, "Our third brave soul will be making history,
great history, by volunteering to again
stand tallest when the hour is the darkest."
He paused before he read Magg's name.
The duration of the pause grew
along with the crowd's silence and weariness.
Even the Mayor's supporters and Cultists
knew the source of their unyielding faith was fickle,
yet they resigned themselves to the bit parts
they'd been assigned.

Magg's name echoed across the Common,
causing a stir, a shift, a newly hungry growl,
reminding the most hopeless within the crowd
of their numbers.

Magg was the first to approach the dais.
She stood on the square in the middle.
Mereth's old spot.
Magg did not personally know the professor or writer
beyond having attended lectures and readings as a student.

The writer was an ancient mole named Karin Bristle.

Her most recent published work appeared a decade prior,

a collection of free-verse poetry and polemic essays titled *One Fight to Life*.

The mole stared at Magg through thick, cloudy glasses.

Perhaps Magg was projecting,

but she feared the writer measured her for fit in a work that would likely
never be written, and found her lacking morally and symbolically.

Magg suddenly wanted others to know why she was back on the dais and
the years of preparation and sacrifice and loss.

If she were to say to the writer, *I'm doing this for all of us*, it would sound like
the same villageist drivel dripping from the propaganda bastard's mouth.

She channeled her inner Mereth and said in a rush,

"This is all part of my plan."

Then paused.

Her inner Mereth lacked the soaring ego and accompanying linguistic
acrobatics that always, somehow, hinted at a brutal glory.

Back to herself, always herself, flawed and beautiful and earnest in all
matters,

Magg added, "I'm going to kill Awn."

The mole nodded,

asked, "With your bare paws?"

Magg could so clearly hear what Mereth's response would've been

—*Bear paws and bear claws*—

it reverberated like a cherished, formative memory.

Magg said, "Paws, teeth, and the rest of my mithridactic body."

She tried to smile,

her quivering curled lip

stuck on a canine.

The writer gawped, adjusted her glasses, and said, "Well, then."

She shuffled a few steps across the dais,

reached out, and squeezed Magg's right forearm.

The Village Guard swooped in,

shouting, whooping,
celebrating the chance to brandish their weapons,
and separated the two animals.

In time,
somewhere behind the gray sky
the sun fell.
The earth tremored
as though the leaden world-weary sun
had crashed into it.

Magg shivered
in the throes of a spiking fever
stoked by twin viruses.
Her morning-blend dose
had been twice what it was the day prior.
Her gummy eyelids wanted to close.
The window of her perception
blurred and shrank at the edges.
She struggled to remain upright
on the bones of brittle scaffolding.
How much longer could she continue standing
under the weight
that eventually collapses every animal?

Awn appeared,
the reality within our collective fever dream.
Had it always been this big?
Had it always filled our world?
Branches and earthen clods dripped from its height.
The folly of Magg's ludicrous plan crashed around her
like the falling sky.

Awn bent
to better inspect the offerings,
the funny little creatures who made and make such a fuss.

(To be fair, kind reader,
we are now supposing Awn thinks like we do.)
Its tendons creaked,
joints popped,
an echo of biological time.

As its head crested over the dais,
Magg searched for its eyes,
prospecting the matted nest of green-and-brown fur.
It was important
to see the monster seeing her.
She was eight years old again,
and she was eight hundred years old.
A long time ago,
she had thought she could outrun it,
and continue running forever.
How silly, how wonderfully silly, that thought was.
She couldn't outrun it,
and she had stopped running.
Could she kill it?
Was she being equally silly now?

Magg barked,
spraying saliva onto her jacket
and the brick dais.

Perhaps Awn recognized her.
Perhaps Awn was in possession of a shared, tethered will.
Perhaps Awn's choice was what it always had been,
whim and dumb chance.
(We will never know.
You will have to learn to live with it.)

Witnesses, unreliable as they were,
suffered from the converse of the observer effect,
having been irrevocably changed by what they saw and what was to come.

They described Awn as carefully, lovingly
lifting Magg away,
then turning its back on the village,
slipping into the stilled forest waters with nary a ripple,
as all hell broke loose in the Common.

A band of lion-masked villagers formed protective circles around the writer
    and professor, and whisked them away.
Other lions threw rocks, batteries, and empty spray-paint cans at the
    Mayor's box,
hitting Village Guard and Wna-level Cultists.
Rin the ram was the first guard, but not the last, to fire into the crowd.
Gunshots punctuated the Third Age's end,
the bullets indiscriminate, non-discerning,
rapacious.
The Common's gated exits blocked and bottlenecked,
villagers penned inside the walls
screamed, brayed, shot, prayed, shouted, climbed, fought, grappled,
    huddled, cried, laughed, hated, collapsed, trampled, helped, held, fled,
    hoped, despaired, lived, died.

)

The monster carried Magg farther north than she'd ever been.
She drifted, her consciousness a branch floating downstream,
sinking under then breaching the surface,
left to wonder
if the monster had been walking
for hours, days, weeks, eons.

The monster stopped at the edge of a clearing
marking the end of the Northwood.
The crisp air nipped at Magg's nose and panting tongue.
The sky was no longer compact and gray, hovering close to the ground.
Here, the sky was expanse,
a vast, star-spotted deep black and blue.

Hemmed in by the night, flatland spread as far as she could see.

Magg imagined that if they continued north or east or west,
trudging beyond the rolling prairie of grasses and shrubs,
there would be mountains and rivers and wetlands and trees,
the land a turning wheel.
Maybe this is what Bevaur looked like before, she thought.
She wished she could change
the old maps she'd saved from Ryde Hall's purge.
She had to settle with
changing what was in her head.

She wished to see her parents puttering about their kitchen, lost in their
    content and wordless dance, and she wished to see Spire tending to the
    books and stacks, and she wished to see Pen in the forest alight with
    possibility, and she wished to see Mereth's arch, checkmate glare and
    Mlic's patient adoration, and she wished to see everyone and everything
    she'd ever loved, even if fleetingly, including Bevaur itself,
one last time.
Maybe that burden would be too great to bear,
even greater
than the loneliness
she felt now.

The monster lifted her up, toward the night ocean.
Magg growled,
and worked up foaming saliva,
smeared it onto her palsying paws,
hoping the viruses and poisons she'd ingested
were crouched inside her, eager for release.

She tumbled off the monster's paw and dropped into its mouth.
Magg bit and scratched its hot, sandpaper tongue and slicked gumline.
She barked and whined and was very afraid
that it would hurt terribly
when Awn closed its mouth.

And it did hurt
until it didn't.

VIII.

Mereth breathed heavily and her heart galloped.
She blinked and shuddered,
stirring the dust clods tickling her nose and whiskers.
She was aware enough to know
there had been a break in the chain,
of something happening, of something supposed to have happened.
Where was her sister?
Had she missed her?
Why had her sister stopped speaking to her?
Had she done something wrong to make her angry, to frighten her away?
Maybe her sister had been here, moments ago,
had backed out of the room,
had closed the door softly, a final latch click,
and then her footfalls
hesitant to leave, to tread the dangerous path away
(Mereth should warn her the path away was always dangerous),
and Mereth had listened, holding on,
even after the footfalls could no longer cross
the expanding distance.

A fox held up her paws,
approached Mereth slowly,
spoke in a low, soothing voice
that wasn't soothing.
It was terrifying.

The dagger in Mereth's paw
meant something.
The dagger in her paw
meant she had done this before.
There was creeping horror in the thought,
as well as longing.

She said, "Please go away, leave me alone,
Whoever you are. I want my sister."

The fox said her name,
an awful syllable Mereth chose not to remember.
The urge to flee was sudden and all-consuming,
her dangling legs flippered up and down,
battering the mattress and box spring.

Mereth could,
if she so desired,
thrust the blade forward,
but do it slowly,
so the advancing fox could choose retreat.
That would be fair.
Or, she could wait
like a loaded trap,
wait for the fox to come closer,
swing her arm, swing the blade,
a mighty arc
blurring image and sound.

The fox jab-stepped,
reached,
choked Mereth's right arm at the wrist,
pried at the dagger's hilt,
speaking all the while,
using please as her weapon.

Mereth watched the struggle
as through from a remove.
And it was a struggle.
The fox grunted
cried out for help.
Mereth held the dagger tightly,
clawed and scratched the fox,

and she used her teeth
to conjure blood
from beneath the fox's orange fur.
Nothing was real
until there was blood.

Despite the injuries,
the damnable fox wouldn't let go.
Then the door to her room exploded open.

Mereth laughed.
She would no longer be alone.
This was her sister
—Finally!—
come to save the day.
After they'd saved the day together
they would burn it down to the bones.

Two large animals charged into the room, to the bed.
They wrapped themselves around Mereth's
flailing limbs.
They were strong,
too strong,
pulled her down,
weighed her down,
down down down
sinking her into the mattress,
then a pinch and a needle's sting in her shoulder.

Mereth could've kept fighting.
She too was strong enough
and she had the dagger,
she was still the trap,
yet she surrendered
because another promise
had been broken.

Mereth's speech slurred
as she asked,
if they wouldn't mind,
to hold the fox still,
so that she could show them
how to make proper use
of the dagger.

IX.

This is how
the story goes.

The next morning
the sun rose over the flatlands.
From the horizon line
there approached a great cat
as large as Awn.

Tawny brown and yellow-gold fur, white in the chest.
Broad, muscular shoulders
framed the thick skull and wide snout.
Golden eyes hovered at the peak of symmetry
above the triangular nose and patient mouth.
The eyes did not judge
nor did they proclaim,
they commanded
compliance.

Awn was afraid.
but it followed the great cat
as it turned
swishing its tail.

The grass under the great cat's paws
wavered gently

as though in thrall to a light breeze.
Awn stumbled, plodded,
gouging troughs, ruts, directionless paths
with its leaden, numbed feet.

Awn's chest was tight,
breathing was a struggle,
everything was struggle.
It needed to rest, to sleep.
If only there were another forest,
the next forest,
in which it could hide
from open spaces.
Awn hoped the cat was pointed that way,
but it knew better.

Time passed,
as it must.
The sun was high
but cold crept deeper
into Awn's bones.
Adrift in the flatland,
Awn fell,
collapsed onto its stomach.

If there was knowledge as to what and why this was happening,
it was secondary to the fear
that had always been inside
waiting wanting,
buried under days and dreams.
Deeper still,
a trickle of groundwater under thick layers of strata,
impossible memories from before, from what once was
linked to an equally impossible emotion
akin to relief.

Awn twisted a side of its face out of the soil,
stole another breath
and maybe a second.
It had turned its head
toward the right or wrong side,
depending on your point of view.

Awn did not see the great cat pounce,
claws extended,
jaws opened,
canines long, sharp, and clean.

X.

Mereth awoke
to the sound of her own voice,
but not exactly her voice.
Same timbre and intonation
with the subtle aural imprint
of another mind.
A voice she hadn't heard
in a very long time.

"Mereth."

The name wasn't a question
nor mere statement of fact.
Her name spoken like
a comma.

"Yeah, what?"
She couldn't hide her love, grief, and desperation
with anger and annoyance.

"Did you forget?"

"No. You forgot me."
Mereth lifted her head.
That was all she could lift.
Leather straps wrapped her wrists and ankles.

"I chose you."

"Did you, now?
Can't say I feel very chosen."

A lion's head
floated in the middle of her dark room,
glowed in moonlight.
Mereth thought
the moon must've been in the room with them too.

Mereth continued talking to keep from screaming.
"You forgot me until the end, is that it?
I'm an afterthought, like everyone else, aren't I?
I—I could've done
so much more."

The lion's face did not change expression.
Her eyes were golden
and older than stone.
She said, "I choose you."
The lion opened its mouth.
Teeth stretched
to fill the entropic space.

Mereth thrashed against her restraints
shouted, "No, no, no, no,"
and closed her eyes.

The lion lifted Mereth from her bed
by the scruff
like a mother carrying a kitten.

When Mereth next opened her eyes,
she stood in a clearing,
and in the dark
she couldn't tell
if it was a blasted land.

She asked the lion,
"Will I get my mask back?
And my other things?
I miss them."

"No. You won't need them."

They faced each other,
unblinking,
silent,
until Mereth understood.

She said, "Whoa, wait a second.
What's the point?
Bevaur is poisoning and tearing itself apart,
at the fucking seams.
It has always been tearing itself apart,
but now, fuck, it's full-on dying.
Really dying. If not dead already.
Will it even last another thirty years?
I doubt it.
Never mind sixty
and ninety and on and on."

"Oh, there will be an end
and soon.
But then,
they'll begin again.
You'll be needed."

"Why?
Again, what's the fucking point?"

The lion did not answer.

Mereth tried to goad the lion
into giving one.
"You don't even know, do you?
But, sure, I'll be there."

"Yes. You will."

"How long will I have to wait?
How long will that take?"

Again, the lion did not respond.

While waiting impatiently
for an answer that would never come,
Mereth paced and muttered and flexed her claws
working out her next move,
and she did not notice
the physical transformation
had already begun,
and at some time during
that eternal evening,
Mereth stretched,
swelled,
crossed over,
and ceased being
who she had been,
and became
something else
that someone else
had already named.

STORY NOTES

ICE COLD LEMONADE 25¢
HAUNTED HOUSE TOUR: 1 PER PERSON

I don't recall selling sidewalk lemonade as a wee Paul, but my daughter did. Well, she was never a "wee Paul," but you get the idea. (This "Story Notes" section is off to a smashing start . . .)

The following is likely an exaggerated memory, but there was one summer it seemed like Emma was at the end of our driveway at least once a week, flanked by assorted friends and neighborhood hangers-on, hawking lemonade and other ade drinks. Not wanting to squash her entrepreneurial spirit nor make her afraid of the weirdo public, we let her sell roadside beverages. What an odd kid-tradition thing that is to want to do. Along with my paranoid fears of the weirdo public, I imagined scenarios in which she sold other things, strange things (like marshmallow Peeps. I hate Peeps). Or, what if she offered to take people into our house and give tours as though it was haunted?

The "haunted-house tour meets lemonade stand" idea barnacled in my inner brain for a bit until Ellen Datlow asked me to write a ghost story for her epic 800-page ghost story anthology *Echoes*. I fleshed out the story by making myself the main character, partially inspired by one of my favorite writers and people Jeffrey Ford, who in recent years has penned a handful of tales in which he's essentially the main character (see his collections *A Natural History of Hell* and *Big Dark Hole and Other Stories*).

I also borrowed Emma's nightmare ghost/creature for the story. Her illustration (drawn when she was twelve) graces these pages. For a story about ghosts, real or imagined, personal or borrowed or self-inflicted, I thought the inclusion was apt.

For the record, Mrs. Boutin, I'm still salty about that C+ on my Ronnie Reagan project.

MEAN TIME

For a limited hardcover edition run of my now-out-of-print 2010 collection *In the Mean Time*, I wrote this odd little story for the cover. As in, the story was printed/presented in its entirety on the cover. I started with an image of an old man chalk-lining his way home or around town. Definitely a trust-and-follow-your-subconscious kind of story (which will be a recurring theme of these story notes) and follow until those chalk lines go missing.

I KNOW YOU'RE THERE

This was a pandemic story. Which is probably obvious.

I wanted it to be about the pandemic without it being about the pandemic. How'd I do? Don't answer that. Also, it's a ghost story about grief. Aren't all ghost stories about grief? Maybe, maybe not. Yeah, I'm being noncommittal in what I say about this story, partly because it makes me terribly sad in an almost superstitious way, which also, oddly, made me want to write it.

After surviving what we've survived in recent years, we're all dealing with a communal grief as well as personal grief. Grief changes you as an individual and as a society. Is that change for the better? Fuck if I know. But you can't fight change. Change is constant and so is grief. Grief is the ghost of who we were and who we loved.

THE POSTAL ZONE: *THE POSSESSION* EDITION

My younger brother, Dan, is a big horror fan. He has been his whole life. When we were kids, despite his being five years younger than me, he watched the goriest '80s movies that I was too chicken to watch. Not that it's a gorefest, but when *Poltergeist* ran on a near constant loop on HBO and the face-tearing-apart scene was about to come on, I would make a show of leading Dan out of the TV room like the responsible older brother I was, announcing that he was too young to see such an icky part and it would give him nightmares. The truth was, I wanted to leave the room but couldn't admit it, so I used the younger-brother cover. Won't somebody think of the children?

Fast-forward to our twenties, and Dan had a subscription to *Fangoria* magazine. It was almost like I had a subscription, because I'd read them when I went over his place. Thanks, Dan!

With the recent reboot/relaunch of the magazine, editor and good egg Meredith Borders asked if I would write a short story for the pages of *Fangoria*. I said yes without hesitating, despite not knowing what I would write. Shortly after responding to Meredith's email, I took my dog, Holly, for a walk. By the time I made it home, I knew I wanted to bring back my fictional *Fangoria* employee, Karen Brissette (the blogger from my novel *A Head Full of Ghosts*), and have her answering letters within *Fango*'s famous "Postal Zone" section.

So meta, right? All the meta. Meta in your face. Anyway, I hope it was fun visiting with Karen again. (And hello, real Karen, I hope you enjoyed this story too!)

RED EYES

I wonder if you are reading a story's note after completing the story, or if you're saving all the story notes until after the collection. I'm not judging either way. Regardless, and if it wasn't obvious already, I love giant monsters. This is the first of four stories in this collection featuring giant beasties. This was also another story featuring the sisters (Marjorie and Merry) from my novel *A Head Full of Ghosts*. If you haven't read that novel, don't worry, no spoilers here, and reading that novel wasn't necessary for this flash-fiction piece. (But go on, read that novel if you'd like. I won't stop you.)

Er, the above doesn't say much about "Red Eyes," does it? It struck me as a story an older sibling would tell the younger one. I think Marjorie is admitting she loves and admires her younger sister, Merry, but is afraid of her too.

THE BLOG AT THE END OF THE WORLD

I wrote this story in 2008, and while it centered on one of my fears (pandemics), the story was more about online existence and the proliferation of misinformation (sorry for the rhyme). The 2008-me never dreamed we'd be in the post-truth hellscape in which we find ourselves now, but I was fascinated by information, how it was and would come to be consumed and verified; themes and concerns I returned to in my later novels, including the novel that borrowed a big chunk of this story's title.

In the pre-social-media days of the Internet, I spent the bulk of my online time on horror message boards and on the LiveJournal blogosphere. LJ was the evolutionary (or devolutionary?) web step before social media. You'd have a feed of other LJ users you'd follow, and you could comment on their blog posts. I spent a fair amount of time blogging and reading blogs while learning to be a writer (I'm still learning, of course). I got into my fair share of useless online arguments in which everyone was immovably correct. So why not write a story in which we argued about the end of the world as it was happening?

As far as the pandemic aspect of the tale goes, it's more than a bit strange for me to revisit this story now (particularly the bit about masks), as its world feels like an oddly out-of-time/out-of-place dream I once had.

I'm still inordinately proud of the gambling-bot comment in the story.

THEM: A PITCH

I held on to the idea for this short giant ant story (and yeah, *Them!* and *Phase IV* are two of my favorite films; to wit, I wrote an essay about *Phase IV* for the book *Lost Transmissions*), thinking that, maybe it could be a short comic, one without any dialogue. But I didn't and don't know anything about writing comic scripts. Gabino Iglesias happened to be guest editing the *Southwest Review*'s October 2020 horror issue and he asked me for a story. I couldn't say no. I took a small break from working on the early chapters of *The Pallbearers Club* and I wrote this story in a few feverish sittings.

I don't want to bore you/explain (or fail to explain) why I wrote it with the comic pitch frame, but in the terrifying and rage-inducing June of 2020, the approach felt appropriate.

HOUSE OF WINDOWS

I spent the first fifteen years of this century almost exclusively writing short stories and publishing with small/independent presses, the blip of *The Little Sleep* and *No Sleep Till Wonderland* in 2009–2010 notwithstanding (given how little Large Publisher X put behind the latter of the two novels, it's *really* notwithstanding). Somewhere within those fifteen years I found my voice as a writer. I was also fortunate to meet incredible writers and make lifelong friends along the way. Two of those friends are tied up in this story. But before I get to them, the sad state of my bookshelves and lack of organization.

I'm embarrassed to admit, as of the writing of this note, I can't find the physical copy of the zine in which this story first appeared. I know it's somewhere in the house, which only narrows things down a little. I have a tall but thin bookshelf that's dedicated to my books and the books of my closest friends. Yes, I have a partially obnoxious *friends shelf.* That bookshelf now overflows. Books and zines hidden behind other books and zines. I need more bookshelves. And I need to clean up and find a better organizational system. I think a dog walker commented on that once.

Anyway, the magazine in which this story appeared was edited by my dear friend Laird Barron (stop reading this and go read his books if you haven't). I named the story after another dear friend's novel (John Langan's *House of Windows*), even though my breezy story has nothing in common with John's brooding, weighty, Peter Straub–esque ghost story. My "house" began with a trip into NYC and the NYPL to meet my cousin Jennifer. My memory here is vague, but at the time of this visit in 2011-ish, there was a small building next to the library that I didn't recognize or remember being there during my prior visits. The building looked so off, despite me knowing it was me who was (and always is) off.

A side note to this story note: I still owe John a Tuckerization/fictionalization. In Ellen Datlow's *Final Cuts* anthology, John has a novella called "Altered Beast, Altered Me," in which he and I are the main characters, and the name he gives my character is fighting words. He so nails my voice in the story it's impressive and cringe-inducing (for me). For now, borrowing his title is all I can offer. But I'll get him eventually, I'll get him good. Also, Laird put me in his story "Near Dark," so I owe them both a fictional comeuppance.

THE LAST CONVERSATION

Yet another story I wrote upon an anthology invite. This time Blake Crouch was the editor. There were six of us, and we were to write a science-fiction story on the broad theme of "discovery." I'm self-aware enough to know that I'm ~~somewhat~~ obsessed with self-discovery as it relates to memory and identity and the effect of environmental/exterior forces. The mystery of the self! So that's where I went with the theme and story. I used second-person point of view and tried to write it in a way that the reader might more easily imagine themselves as the narrator.

The opening occurred to me while walking in Borderland State Park. It struck me as a Brian Evenson–esque opening. Having previously tried and failed (see story note for "The Dead Thing") at writing a story inspired by Brian's work, this was another kick at the Evenson can. He likes to be kicked, when in can form. Big thanks to Blake and to editor Jason Heller, both of whom helped to mold this story into its weird shape.

MOSTLY SIZE

I wrote this story as a part of a charity ebook anthology in the U.K. to help raise money for Macmillan Cancer Support. The writers had a four-hour window to write a draft of a story. We were allowed to spend some time editing after that time period, but the bulk/bones of the story had to be written in that one sitting.

If I were to psychoanalyze the story, I'd say the kid is me and the monster is the horror genre. Or maybe, as an educator, I fear being the monster to the student who needs help/support.

But also, I remain genuinely curious how a giant monster might sharpen a pencil.

THE LARGE MAN

Another strange story written after my two crime novels but before *A Head Full of Ghosts* was published; a period in which I was licking my wounds from the butt kicking I'd received with my first go-round with a Big 5 publisher. During that four-year period I didn't write as much, partly because I was upset and bitter at how things went down with the Mark Genevich novels. At times I wallowed in self-pity, and worse, jealousy at other writers' successes. Indulging too much in those very natural feelings/emotions are mind and page killers. It's okay to feel that way, but it's not okay to let it take over your writing or mental life. I had to find a way to acknowledge those emotions but also to dismiss them. Easier said than done, of course. I don't think it's a coincidence that once I learned how to move on from failure (real or perceived, doesn't matter), the idea for *A Head Full of Ghosts* fell into my lap. The stories I did write during the bitter period (let's call it) were often me trying on other hats (including co-writing a now-out-of-print YA novel with Stephen Graham Jones) and/or letting my imagination run amok. This story falls under both categories, so let's call it a *hat amok* story.

Mr. C____ may or may not be named after another friend (and a genius writer) Michael Cisco, and I thank him for letting me borrow his large hat. Big thanks also to editors Maurice Broaddus and Jerry Gordon for inviting me to write a story and including it in *Streets of Shadows*, an anthology of supernatural noir.

THE DEAD THING

I'm not going to write about from where this story, as presented here, came from. Sorry. Instead, I'll tell you about the failed first attempt at a story with this title.

I often have nightmares, but I rarely if ever use them or write about them, although I did use a recurring floating nightmare in my novel *The Pallbearers Club*. I usually can't recount my dreams in detail; however my wife, Lisa, remembers her dreams vividly and often describes them to me. One morning she told me her dream about a shoebox with a dead thing in it and how it would be left around the house, almost innocuously, but it was there, always there. Man, it was creepy. Magpie writer that I am, I thought, Oh, I have to use that.

My first go at it was a failed attempt to write a Brian Evenson–esque story. Like I've said in a previous note, I like trying on other writerly hats. I wrote a story about the box being purchased at a yard sale (I can't remember if that was a bit from Lisa's dream), and then the story shifted to a kid building a weird diorama in his basement, and yeah, that story is nothing like the one included in this book. That other story is weirder but makes no sense and had too much stuffed into it. I knew this when I was finished. I sent it to Stephen Graham Jones, asking if he'd give it a read. He asked if I wanted him to read it breezily or read with the same critical eye he focused on the work from his graduate students. Wincing, anticipating the blows to come, I asked for the critical eye. Stephen sent me a long, thoughtful email that said, essentially, everything other than the opening paragraph sucked. He was right. I canned the story but not the dead thing in the shoebox. I came back to it and found a way into the story by focusing more on who the story was about and less about the weirdness. Now it feels like one of my stories. I think. If I'm allowed to say so, I'm quite pleased with the result, as dour as it all is.

HOWARD STURGIS AND THE LETTERS AND THE VAN AND WHAT HE FOUND WHEN HE WENT BACK TO HIS HOUSE

Christopher Golden and Tim Lebbon asked me to write a story for their *Ten Word Tragedies* anthology, which was inspired by the musician Frank

Turner. I am not familiar with Frank's work (sorry, Frank), but the anthology sounded like fun. After agreeing, they sent me some postcards and I had to write a story inspired by one of them. The one I chose had a blue van on it and some strange, out-of-context writing on the back of it. The rest of the story was a go-where-it-takes-you exercise. I got to work some math into the story, and I was happy to have the longest title in the anthology. Sometimes, I'm a competitive bastard.

THE PARTY

Ellen Datlow asked me to write a story for the Shirley Jackson–inspired *When Things Get Dark* anthology. I jumped at the chance to do so. (What a great saying. Yes, imagine me jumping. Not too high, though; I have cranky knees now thanks to my connective-tissue issues that run on one side of the family. In fact, just last night, my sister, Erin, cousin Michael, daughter, Emma, and I were standing in the kitchen, moving one another's kneecaps around. Don't all families do that when they get together?)

I'd had the general idea of an end-of-the-world-eve party set in a house as described in the story. That house was one Lisa and I toured while house hunting in the spring of 2012. It was a modest brown ranch set back a bit from the main road, backyard abutting a forest, and it had a beautiful, updated kitchen and open space. The rest of the place was rundown/hadn't been touched since the '70s. A cool house to write about, but we (mostly Lisa) didn't want to live there. So, I had a party and a house, but I didn't have any characters or a story arc to go with it.

With the Jackson-anthology invite, I immediately returned to that vague idea and spliced it together with Jackson's short story "The Intoxicated" (one of my favorites) and her brilliant novel *The Sundial*. Plus, my fear of accidentally stumbling upon a weird tomato/strawberry thingy in a friend's house. Sure, that's an oddly specific fear, but what would you do if you found something like that in their bedroom? Never thought about that before, did you? You're welcome.

THE BEAST YOU ARE

That was a thing, wasn't it? Named after an excellent record by Big Business.

I was an impressionable youth at a time when anthropomorphic or talking animals starred in serious/disturbing movies that were still, kind of, marketed for children, because, cartoon! I'm talking specifically of *Watership Down* (1978) and *The Secret of NIMH* (1982). My father took me to Beverly's venerable Cabot Cinema for a double feature of *Watership Down* and the animated *The Lord of the Rings* (1978). We didn't see those movies when they first hit the screens, but it this was probably only two or three years after they were released. I was young. Nine or ten. I went excited to see LotR because I'd already seen the animated *The Hobbit* and we had the audio record of the film in the house too. My father was a card-carrying Tolkien fan, or button-carrying, anyway. He had a button that read FRODO LIVES. He also liked to smoke a pipe like Tolkien. I wouldn't find out until decades later what he was really smoking in his pipe.

Despite my Tolkien leanings and how much I loved Smaug in *The Hobbit*, *Watership Down* stole the show. The realistic and yet trippy animation style, the story, the voice actors, the tonal gravity, all of it blew my little mind and did much to inform my nascent understanding of politics for the decade to come. Yeah, there was rabbit gore, and the massacre of the warren by the farmers and General Wormwort was scary, but the movie surprisingly didn't scar me or give me nightmares. (I should apologize to my son, Cole, here, as I showed him *Watership Down* when he was way too young. He broke down crying when Bigwig had the snare around his neck. Oops. But Bigwig lived! See, it's all okay.) That movie and those rabbits took root in my head, and many years before I'd read the novel. Later my brother and I watched that movie repeatedly, and we still randomly quote, "There's a dog loose in the wood" to each other. *The Secret of NIMH* was not as dark or violent as *WD*, but it was close (the scene with Mrs. Brisby going to see the Great Owl remains tense and electrifying), and *NIMH* played in the heaviest of HBO's heavy rotation in the '80s.

All of this is to say I've long had the itch and the want to write an anthropomorphic animal story. Furthering that itch (can an itch further?)

was Chris Irvin's excellent anthropomorphic animal novel *Ragged*. This collection allowed me to scratch that, um, furthering itch. The other itch I scratched was naming the dog Magg after Marjorie from *A Head Full of Ghosts* and naming the cat Mereth after Merry/Meredith from the same book, and the story's author Karin Bristle . . . well, you get the idea. As I mentioned previously, I've done a handful of Marjorie/Merry stories, and I thought it only fair to give Marjorie a shot at being the protagonist in a longer-form story.

Why free verse? Aside from my adoration for Toby Barlow's novel *Sharp Teeth* (packs of werewolves in Los Angeles) and *Beowulf* (do check out Maria Dahvana Headley's recent translation), I really can't explain why, beyond a little voice saying, *What the hell. Go ahead, try it.* Nothing gets written without that voice. I've learned to trust it. So many of the stories in this book started with that voice. I typically listen because if I don't, I worry the voice will stop advocating for the story ideas.

The hey-try-this voice was obstinately persistent in this novella's case, even with me telling it, "Not now, later, I promise. When I finish this novel. When I think I can convince someone to publish an anthropomorphic animal novella." (Wait, now there are two voices. One is me, the other is also me but that me is the subconscious story-advocate voice. Never mind.) I let those animals roll around in my inner ether for a few years. I never forgot them though. Luckily the story kept insisting on coming back and usually with more detail. By the time I was ready to commit to writing it, the village, the two main characters, the giant monster, the slasher, and the cult were all there waiting for me. I only had to figure out how it all fit, how to build that monster.

All stories are monsters, and how loudly and lovingly they smash through your town, your heart, and your head, is up to you, the reader.

March 29, 2022

ACKNOWLEDGMENTS

Thank you, Lisa, Cole, and Emma, for your patience and support. Thank you, Mom, Dad, Erin, and Dan, and to all my friends and family for their enthusiasm and for their lives from which I get to borrow details for stories. What good sports they all are.

Thank you, Stephen "Not Art" Barbara. Thanks doesn't really cut it for all you've done, particularly in the wild wacky dystopia of 2022, but it'll have to do for now.

Thank you, Jennifer Brehl, Camille Collins, Nate Lanman, Kayleigh George, Brian Moore, Rachelle Mandik, Rachel Weinick, and everyone at William Morrow. Thank you also to George Sandison, Lydia Gittins, and everyone at Titan Books. Again, I promise the next book won't be difficult (well, maybe a little difficult) to design.

Thank you, editors, who had previously commissioned and worked on many of the stories in this book. You've all helped me become a better writer. Or at least a writer who would write a free verse anthropomorphic animal novella. Thank you, Chris Irvin and Eric LaRocca, for being beta readers for the novella.

Thank you, writing friends, many of whom I mentioned in the Story Notes. I adore and admire you all more than you know. I like to imagine us as a large pack, roaming the streets at night, not being creepy at all. Extra thanks to Laird Barron, Nadia Bulkin, Brett Cox, JoAnn Cox, Ellen Datlow, Brian Evenson, Gabino Iglesias, Chris Irvin, Stephen Graham Jones, John Langan, Sarah Langan, and Bracken MacLeod. They know what they did.

And thank you, reader! May your ears always be up.

PUBLICATION HISTORY

"~~Ice Cold Lemonade 25¢~~ Haunted House Tour: 1 Per Person," *Echoes*, editor Ellen Datlow, Saga Press, 2019; *The Best Horror of the Year*, vol. 12, editor Ellen Datlow, Nightshade Books, 2020.

"Mean Time," *In the Mean Time*, limited hardcover edition, Paul Tremblay, Chizine Press, 2010; *Revelations: Horror Writers for Climate Action*, editor Sean O'Connor, Stygian Sky Media, 2021.

"I Know You're There," *Air/Light, no. 5*, 2022.

"The Postal Zone: *The Possession* Edition," *Fangoria* vol. 2, no.3, 2019.

"Red Eyes," *Growing Things and Other Stories* limited edition, SST Publications, 2018.

"The Blog at the End of the World," *Chizine*, October 2008; *In the Mean Time*, Paul Tremblay, Chizine Press, 2010; *Cyberpunk: Stories of Hardware, Software, Wetware, Revolution and Evolution*, editor Victoria Blake, Underland Press, 2013.

"Them: A Pitch," *Southwest Review* vol. 105, no. 3, 2020.

"House of Windows," *Phantasmagorium* vol. 2, 2012. *Horror for RAICES*, editors Jennifer Wilson and Robert S. Wilson, Nightscape Press, 2019.

"The Last Conversation," *Forward* collection, Amazon Original Short Stories, 2019.

"Mostly Size," *Green Ink Sponsored Write*, Macmillan Cancer Support, 2021.

"The Large Man," *Streets of Shadows*, editors Maurice Broaddus and Jerry Gordon, Alliteration Ink, 2014.

"The Dead Thing," *New Fears 2*, editor Mark Morris, Titan Books, 2018.

"Howard Sturgis and the Letters and the Van and What He Found When He Went Back to His House," *Ten Word Tragedies*, editors Christopher Golden and Tim Lebbon, PS Publishing, 2019.

"The Party," *When Things Get Dark: Stories Inspired by Shirley Jackson*, editor Ellen Datlow, Titan Books, 2021.

"The Beast You Are," original to this collection.

DISCOVER MORE BY
PAUL TREMBLAY

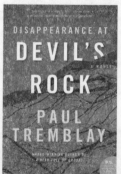

THE MARK GENEVICH SERIES